MW00462808

TAKEN

The Dark Necessities Trilogy

Book One

Felicity Brandon

The Dark Necessities Trilogy

Taken

Tamed

Entwined

This book is dedicated to all the misfits of the world; to the ones who think they don't belong. I am with you. You are not alone.

"Some women fear the fire, some women simply become it." ~R.H. Sin.

Chapter One

Do you have time for one more?"

The question came from a deep, masculine voice. It startled Molly, who was rummaging in a box under the desk. She glanced up wearily, braced for whoever had caused the interruption, but she hadn't counted on what greeted her. The face which met her blinking expression was lean and handsome. It was adorned with the most striking green eyes she'd ever seen, and cheekbones that would make any model jealous.

"Oh, of course," she mumbled, reaching for the pen lying on the desk between them. For some reason she couldn't fathom, she felt flustered as she gazed up at the man towering over her.

He thrust the paperback toward her. "I'm sorry," he replied, the tone of his voice vibrating through her. She'd been hearing British accents all day, but none of them resonated like this one. "I know you're just packing away, but I had hoped that you'd sign this for me."

She smiled, taking the book from him and scanning his choice. *Amelie's Abduction* was one of her bestsellers, arguably the book which had made writing for a living a realistic option. "Sure," she beamed at him. "Who should I make the book out to?"

The stranger paused, shifting his weight as those mesmerizing eyes drilled into her. "The name is Connor Reilly," he told her. "And thank you." He edged closer to the desk as she opened the first page of the book, smoothing the cover back. "I'm a little bit of a super fan, Miss Clary." He smiled coyly. "I really appreciate you taking the time to do this."

Her pen hesitated on the paper, and she raised her head to look at him as she answered. "It's my pleasure," she explained, trying not to let her tiredness show. "My fans are everything. I love meeting them."

She sounded like a commercial on cable television, but her words made his lips break into a broader smile.

"That's so good to know," he replied, watching her as she scrawled her name across the page for what felt like the thousandth time today.

She'd been here since seven this morning, setting up her stand for the book signing. It wasn't her first, but she was such an introvert that these events always made her nervous and uncomfortable. She'd be more than happy to get out of here, go back to the hotel and sink into a relaxing, hot bath.

"Here we are," she said, closing the front cover, and running her hand over its glossy surface. She gave the image a cursory glance, recalling briefly the many hours she had spent deciding upon the amaryllis which adorned it.

Connor's large hand appeared in her line of sight, his digits closing over the edge of the book. "Thank you, Miss Clary," he replied. "I absolutely loved this book."

Dropping the pen onto the desk, she rose from her seat to shake the hand Connor offered her. "I'm glad you did," she answered him. "It's one of my favorites, too."

Their eyes locked for a moment, her gaze grazing over the look of the dark stubble on his strong jaw. He really was pleasing on the eye, and she was happy he'd taken the time to stop by her stand. She had the idea that the expression on his face might spark the genesis of her next story. He seemed so dark and brooding as he loomed over her.

"Well, it's lovely to meet you." His voice broke the silence between them, as he dropped her small palm. "Thanks again."

She watched him saunter away from her stand, his ass looking unnecessarily provocative as he turned the corner and disappeared from her view. Sighing, she dropped back to her seat, turning her attention to the box once more. What she wouldn't give for a night with an ass like that. It had been a long time since she'd last had a decent sexual encounter. Her current relationship wasn't exactly blowing her off the page sexually, but the image of Mr. Reilly was one she thought would stay with her for quite some time. Why hadn't she asked him out? Things weren't really that serious with Steve, after all, but what would have been the point? She'd be leaving London for home in less than two days, they'd barely even have a chance to get to know each other.

Packing up her final few things, she paused to look around. Nearly all of her author friends had left, and foolishly, she'd already let her fabulous assistant, Hannah, go for the day. It was no use, she'd have to carry the box herself, and flinging her handbag over her shoulder, she picked it up with another long sigh. Her heels clicked on the hard floor as she struggled out of the conference center. It was three streets over to the place she'd left her rental car, and then quite a drive back to where she was staying. For the time being, the hot bath would have to wait.

Chapter Two

S he had no idea what time it was as she stalked up the street in the rain. Her dark hair, which she'd spent so much time perfecting this morning, clung to her face, and her heart sank. She was lost, or at least, she thought she was, but all the freaking streets in this city looked identical, and the wet summer evening wasn't exactly helping to clarify her location.

Molly glanced around. She'd parked her rental car on a road which looked just like this, but now it was nowhere to be found. The British authors she'd chatted to earlier had explained how these were classic suburban British streets, but to Molly it was all just foreign, so different from the ones back home in Pennsylvania. The roads here ran between endless lines of gray terrace houses, and the path she walked was broken by ancient trees with heavy, wet branches. She stared harder at the rows of parked vehicles, but there was still no sign of the rental car. Evidently, this was not the same street that she'd left it on. Frustration coursed through her at her own stupidity. Only she could be foolish enough to lose her way after such a long and exhausting day…

"Lost, are we?"

The unexpected voice was alarming, and she spun on her heel to see three men smirking at her. The one who'd spoken took a step closer, his face distorting into a sneer as she eyed them all. They were young, probably late teens, but clearly, they were up to no good. Who hangs around on the street in this weather?

"No, I'm fine," she retorted, throwing them a glare before she turned and trotted away, stumbling over the ridiculously uneven paving stones.

"Are you sure?" Another face flashed to her left, its youthful owner cutting her off as he leapt in front of her. "Is that an American accent? You look a little out of place here, love."

She gulped at the look of him. He was taller than the first, and looked much stronger. "I am fine, *thank you*," she answered him, clutching the wet cardboard to her chest.

The young man's face drew into a sneer. "Yes, you are fine. A little older than my usual type perhaps, but still…" His dark gaze seemed to be devouring her as he eyed her up and down.

"You'll certainly do," said another voice from behind her.

She gasped, twisting to see the other two closing in around her.

Fuck, she thought, panic bursting in her brain and sending adrenaline whipping around her body. "Leave me alone!"

Her voice was louder than she'd intended it to be, and somehow it bolstered her. She'd taken basic self-defense classes a couple of years ago. If she could just keep her head, she knew she'd be able to get away from them.

"I don't think so, love," said the one in front of her. "You look like you need some help. Someone to look out for you." He laughed as he took a step closer, reaching for her left breast, a wicked grin stretched across his face.

She yelped, jumping back to avoid his grasping hand, and dropped the box to the wet path below. "Fuck you!"

She was shouting as he closed the space between them. Molly glared up at his cocky expression, and did the one thing she'd been taught to do. She brought her right knee up as hard and as fast as she could, slamming it into his groin before he could even respond.

The look on his face was priceless as tears sprung to his eyes, and he doubled up in front of her, but the moment was short-lived. "Grab her," he snarled to the others. "We're going to teach this one a fucking lesson."

Two strong pairs of hands grabbed at her shoulders before she could even think about bolting. She twisted and shouted, trying to shrug the aggressors away, but they easily overpowered her.

"Get your hands off me!" Molly screeched, scratching and clawing at her assailants.

"Shut the fuck up."

The angry voice boomed at her from over her shoulder.

"Get her in the car," ordered the one on his knees in front of her. "The bitch is making too much noise."

At this point, things seemed to speed up around her. It's as though someone had pressed fast-forward on her life, and she had no control over the proceedings whatsoever. The sound of her heart hammering in her chest seemed to overpower everything else, and she watched in shock, as a fourth man appeared from behind an old oak tree. This one was dressed entirely in black, his face covered in a dark ski mask as his long legs closed the distance to the man on his knees in seconds. He grabbed the youngster by his short dark hair, and pushed him forward, slamming his face into the concrete beside her feet.

Molly gasped, eyeing the blood which stained the wet paving stones.

"What the fuck?" The voice of one of the men behind her shot past her ear, and instinctively one of them let her go as he ran to protect his friend.

The new aggressor turned to him, moving with surprising agility. She wasn't sure who threw the first punch, but soon, fists were flying everywhere, the low, wet thud of knuckles smacking skin echoing around her. She tried to make a break for it, but the remaining one had a tight grip on her, his arm shifting to her neck to keep her in place.

She strained against the limb as her airflow became restricted. "Please!" she gasped, trying to elbow him away. "I can't breathe!"

"One more fucking word, and you won't breathe again."

Molly began to panic. "Just leave me al…"

She never finished her sentence. The sound of a heavy weight hitting the path distracted them both, and her eyes flew to the two other men. She found the one in black looming over her, the other in a heap on the ground.

"Do you wanna play, too?" He shouted the question in her direction, moving toward where she stood while she fought against the arm at her throat.

"Fuck you, man!" The cry of the man holding her in place raced past her right ear. "I've got a knife in my pocket. You don't want to fuck with me."

"Get away from her, you prick," growled the aggressor in black. "Leave now with your little friends, and we'll say no more about it."

There was a moment of tension when nothing happened. Anxiety rushed through her body. Hadn't he said he had a knife? She didn't want to die. Not like this. Not in a wet, gray city like London! The rain, now a torrent, fell around them, as the one in black edged closer to her. Caught in the crook of the other man's arm, she continued to struggle, clawing at his jacket.

"Last chance," snarled the man in black. Beside him, the first guy moaned, trying to pull himself to his feet, but one swift kick to the head appeared to resolve that little problem.

Molly momentarily squeezed her eyes closed, a part of her sickened by the violence, while a larger part cheered for the man in black in her head.

"Hey, no way," cried the man still holding her in place. "This bitch is mine – go and find your own!"

The fist was so fast that she barely saw it move, but she heard the moment it connected with the face to her right. In a heartbeat, the man fell, releasing her from his hold as he stumbled backwards. She gasped, thrown off balance, and began to fall in the same direction, until a long arm reached forward to grab her left wrist. Suspended there in the rain, Molly's eyes took in the look of her rescuer. His face was covered, and he was so damn tall. The hand at her arm pulled her toward him, and she didn't resist as her body lurched in his direction. She landed uncomfortably against his frame, his arm encircling her waist to keep her upright.

He gazed down at her like a black ghost, only his green eyes visible. Wordlessly, he shifted her around the side of his right hip, putting his body between her and the three assailants, sprawled awkwardly on the path.

"Any of you boys hungry for more?" he asked, his tone foreboding.

The three of them blinked up at him, their expressions ones of absolute shock.

"Take her, man," cried the first one he'd taken down. Molly turned to glance at him, his face covered in blood where he'd bounced off the unforgiving concrete. His previously arrogant expression looked broken. "Just fucking take her!"

Chapter Three

She was shaking as he led her away from the scene, her mind unraveling as he splashed through puddles. She had tried to be brave, but where had it gotten her? The three of them could have done anything to her, and they would have too – if this stranger hadn't interrupted.

"Get in the car." His voice sliced through her thoughts, and she blinked up at him.

"What?" Her reply sounded small, swallowed up in the noise of the torrential downpour.

"You're in shock." His voice was hard, but the words seemed to make sense. "Get in the car, out of the rain, and take a moment."

He guided her down the street, his hand insistent at her lower back, until they came to a large black sedan at the end of the road. The rain was teeming at this point, the summer shower turning into something of a monsoon. As she glanced up at him, she could barely even make out his eyes in the endless gray water. The car opened with one click of the fob in his hand, and he held the door open for her. She took one last look around the dank London street before she climbed into the large back seat, joined moments later by her unknown rescuer.

The sound of the door slamming drew her attention back to him. "Thank you," she murmured, clutching the handbag still slung over her right shoulder. There was a moment when she remembered the box she'd been carrying, but it didn't seem to matter after everything she'd just witnessed. She shivered as the waves of shock rolled over her small frame, the freezing British rain adding to her misery.

His body was still, appraising her in silence, and she gulped at the way he seemed. It was all suddenly so malevolent. One moment he'd been the hero, and now? Now, who was he? This was stupid – she'd been stupid. She'd allowed his actions to cloud her judgment, and she'd climbed willingly into a stranger's car.

What had she been thinking?

"Thanks for your help back there," she said, forcing a feigned cheeriness into her voice. "I have to be going though, I…"

She never concluded that sentence. His right arm moved faster than she'd imagined possible, and one of his large fingers pressed against her open lips.

"Shhh." It was an order, his deep British timbre vibrating through the air around her.

"What?" She blinked at him, her lips stretching around the digit at her face.

"I told you to be quiet." His voice was stern, and something about the sound of it made her breath catch.

She had that sinking feeling in the pit of her stomach, a sense of dread which filled up the air around her like a stench. Her eyes scanned the darkness, looking for a door handle. There had to be a way out.

"I wouldn't do that if I were you." The sound of his voice made her body freeze, apart from her heart which was pounding out of control. "The doors are locked from the fob in my pocket." He sounded amused at the revelation, and a flicker of indignation stirred in her, fighting for air amongst the expanse of fear. "Things are going to go a lot better for you if you behave, Molly."

That drew her attention in an instant. *Molly?* How did this son of a bitch know her name?

"Who are you?" She sounded hoarse as she asked him; the fear rising into her throat was impossible to swallow back.

His lips curled beneath the black balaclava covering his face as he replied. "You don't recognize me then?" He lowered his hand from her face, resting it lightly against his right knee.

Molly tensed. Even amongst the panic furling inside her, that seemed an odd response. "Do I know you?" she asked, tilting her head to try and look at the man. He was tall yes, and strong, but the problem was the inside of the car was black, and all of his clothes were black. It was damn near impossible to see him at all.

In one full swoop, the hand at his knee rose to his face, pulling the ski mask up and over his head. It took a few seconds for the face smiling back at her to register, and then – when the realization hit her – she was even more confused.

"It's you!" she gasped. "From the signing? Connor wasn't it?"

His handsome face beamed back at her. "She remembers me," he mused. "I'm touched."

Molly stared at him, trying to read his expression, now that she had the benefit of it. "So, what is this, Connor?"

She heard the tremble in her voice as she asked, and she flinched at it. She despised how vulnerable she felt, and she deeply resented that this stranger had the ability to make her feel this way.

He glowered at her, the intensity in his gaze making her restless. Connor Reilly was either the hottest guy she'd ever met, or he was the scariest. Worst still was the possibility that he might just be both.

"This, Molly," he began, moving toward her a fraction. "Is the beginning of your new story."

She gulped, blinking at him. She barely wanted to ask, and yet she had to know. "A new story?" she replied. "What do you mean? What do you want from me?"

Connor shifted slightly in his seat, his gaze never leaving her. "Just relax," he soothed. "I only want you to do what you already love."

Molly swallowed. "What do you know about that?" The words flew from her mouth as little more than a hiss, her tone scathing.

Connor's eyes narrowed. "Watch your tone, young lady," he warned her. "I won't have any disrespect."

Molly balked at that. "What?" she cried. "Who the fuck do you think you are? I mean, I'm grateful that you saved me from those thugs back there, and all, but you can't keep me in here, and you can't tell me what to do."

He moved like a serpent, his actions so quick that Molly barely had time to catch her breath. Connor slid wordlessly against the black leather, catching her body and pinning her back against the side of the car. She gasped, raising her hands to push back against him, but he caught her wrists with ease, holding her in place as he leaned in toward her face.

"Ouch!" she wailed, trying to wriggle free of his insistent grip on her wrists. "You're hurting me. Please, let me go."

Her body trembled as he pressed himself against her wet clothes. "Let's get a few things straight, Molly," he growled. "*I* am in charge here – not you. I warned you just then not to be disrespectful, and then immediately, you run your mouth to me... Not very smart, I'd say."

He was so close to her now that she could feel the warmth of his breath against her face. The most peculiar aroma of spearmint washed over her. Molly gulped at him, literally terrified.

"Okay, I'm s-sorry," she stammered.

His eyes flickered over her petrified face. "You will be, Molly. You absolutely will be."

"Please," she whimpered. "Don't hurt me."

Connor's lips smirked at her. "This is how things are going to go." His voice was calm, although there was an edge of excitement in his tone, as though he'd been planning this moment out in his head for a long time. "I am going to take you, Molly. The only question is, how you want to be taken."

Her throat tightened at his words, and all of a sudden, it was a real effort to push the air in and out of her body. "T-take me?" she repeated, her body still pinned awkwardly to the side of the car. "Where are you going to take me?"

Connor's gaze scanned over her again. "It doesn't matter where I am taking you," he replied. "All you need to worry about is how this is going to go. Are you going to behave, or are you going to resist?"

Chapter Four

Resist? The guy had to be fucking kidding. No one was going to take her anywhere. She hadn't just escaped the clutches of those young assholes, only to be abducted by another one. And that's what this was — that's what he meant when he talked about taking her. *He wants to capture me,* she thought, her mind reeling. *He wants to keep me.*

"Well?" he demanded, eyeing her intently. "What's it to be?"

She hesitated, trying to think over the deafening sound of her heartbeat. "What do you want me to say?" she said eventually. "Do you think I'm just going to *let* you take me?"

Connor chuckled, moving away from her slightly. It was only a few inches, but it was all she had, and in that moment, Molly seized the chance and lurched forward toward him. Their heads connected, and she butted him as hard as she could muster. The impact hurt like hell, the contact ringing through her head as he drew away, wincing.

"Fucking bitch," he grumbled, his hands shifting to the place her forehead cracked against his.

Molly moved, sliding from the seat and landing on the floorboard. Her hands were at the car door at once, fumbling around in the darkness for the lock. Connor had said there was no way, but surely, he must be wrong? All cars have a door release, so why should this be an exception? Waves of nausea and panic crashed over her as her fingers scratched over the expensive interior. Where was the damn release mechanism? There had to be a way out.

She glanced around, painfully aware that the window of time she had bought herself was slipping away. Connor was shifting on the leather seat, still rubbing his head. Their eyes locked momentarily, his expression darkening at the sight of her wide-eyed panic.

"Looks like you made your choice, Molly," he snarled. "Another stupid move on your part, but hey – it was all yours…"

Terrified, Molly turned back to the glass, her fists rising and banging on the blacked-out window. "Help me!" she screeched, scrabbling around against the door. "Someone, please help me!"

She heard him moving, but it was too late. In the blink of an eye, a strap was passed over her head, and she blinked as the gag descended toward her mouth.

"No way," she cried, turning her face away to avoid it making contact with her.

Her hands smashed against the glass again. Surely someone would be passing by the car outside and hear her?

"That's enough of that," he purred. He was right behind her again, his body trapping her against the failed exit route. "Open up, Molly. Do things the easy way this time, and I won't have to hurt you."

She tensed at his veiled warning, twisting her body to see his face. "Don't do this!" she pleaded. "Please, just let me go. I swear I won't tell anyone, I swear I…"

Moving like lightning, his hands shoved the large plastic ball straight into her open mouth, pulling the straps hard behind her. She squealed against the ball, her lips forced apart in an instant. Connor secured the straps, buckling it tight at the back of her head, and instinctively, Molly's hands rose to rip the thing from her face.

"Uh-uh, naughty girl." He laughed, grabbing her hands and pulling them down to her sides. "That gag is staying in place until you can learn to be quiet."

She screeched against the plastic, terror spreading over her as she realized just how much trouble she was in. *Fuck!* she thought, straining against his strong hands. *Fuck no!*

"I was hoping I wouldn't have to be so aggressive with you," he growled, yanking her arms backwards and drawing her body helplessly against him. "But it seems, Molly, that you have a few lessons to learn about obedience."

His mouth grazed over her neck suddenly, and her body stilled. She was petrified, gagged and held in place by this complete lunatic, and yet – for all that – the feel of his lips at her nape captured her. It was sensual, unsettling and different. It felt almost tender. The act made her stop fighting for the first time since she had head-butted him.

"It's okay though," he murmured, planting more hot kisses toward her strapped cheek. "I am just the man to teach you those lessons, Molly…"

He moved behind her, one of his hands holding both her wrists in place at the small of her back, while the other fumbled for something under the front seat. Molly squirmed with frustration. It was beyond irritating that he could hold her so easily in place with only one hand, and the vexation mingled with the growing fear inside her. All at once, his attention was back on her, and she twisted to see a cloth of some sort in his right hand. Molly eyed it with trepidation, her heart pounding out of control as he addressed her.

"This isn't going to hurt you," he explained, bringing the cloth up and around to the front of her face. "You're just going to sleep while I take you where you need to be."

Noooo! It was her mind screaming, although Molly echoed its anxiety with the groan which came through the plastic ball in her mouth. She had to resist whatever was on that cloth at all costs. If she lost consciousness, that would be it. He would have her, and she'd be utterly powerless to stop him. The cloth approached her even as the thoughts shot through her head, showing her what she should have already known, she was too late. Connor pressed it over her gagged mouth, allowing her nose room to breathe in whatever he had covered the fabric with. In a panic, Molly drew in a large breath, inhaling whatever noxious chemical he was going to use to abduct her. The effect hit her like a wall of pain, her head pounding as her fate hit her. She spluttered around the plastic, trying to twist her face away from the cloth, but Connor was stronger and in control, his determination apparently honed.

"Stop fighting, Molly," he coaxed, his body flush against her.

His words riled her all the more. Fighting with all her might, the fingers of her captured hands clawed at his body behind her. But it was too late, and already she could feel the world around her getting foggy. Molly blinked into the darkness, her reactions giddy as though she had consumed one too many glasses of wine. Her head fell forward, the weight of it carrying it south despite Connor's hand, which was still at her mouth. He released the cloth slowly, and instinctively she tried to cough from behind the gag. She was vaguely aware of him flinging the cloth onto the floor, and his fingers gently dipping her head back against his chest. Her eyes were fluttering shut, but her breathing was calmer now, and she no longer strained against the plastic in her mouth.

Before slipping into a chemical-induced stupor, the last thing she heard was the sound of his low, seductive tone as it vibrated over her. "You're fucking perfect."

Chapter Five

The first thing was the noise. She was aware of sounds around her, small noises like people moving, the resonance of shuffling feet against the floor. She was calm because she couldn't remember why she would need to be otherwise. And then, all at once, she did remember. The horror of the memory hit her like a heavy weight, and the force of the injury made her eyes flicker open. Or, at least, it should have done. Her brain was definitely commanding her eyelids to open, but for the longest time, those lids would simply not obey.

A new panic sprung from her. Was she blind? Maybe this was it, and she'd never be able to see anything again. Maybe she had died and the darkness was all that was left. She opened her mouth and pulled in a painful breath. That's when she realized that the awful gag had been removed, and the fact made her absurdly grateful. Her mouth, though, felt terrible. It was dry, and there was the oddest taste whenever she swallowed, a side effect perhaps, of whatever she had inhaled.

"Molly."

Her body tensed at the sound of her name, her head shifting slightly to where his voice came from. Even the smallest movement made her feel queasy, and she groaned at the recognition.

"It's okay," he said, his voice sounding distant. "You're fine. It's just the effects of the chloroform wearing off."

Chloroform? She moaned again as the word registered somewhere deep in her mind. *Is that what he had made her breathe? Oh shit…*

"It requires a certain level of expertise to ensure you stay unconscious for the right period of time," he went on. "Plus, a number of top-up doses. But don't worry. I have smart friends who know this stuff. You didn't have too much."

Too much? The panic surged, his words doing nothing to reassure her. It was then that she realized her hands were bound behind her, and the terror became suffocating, shooting up until she coughed and gagged, trying to expel it. Her heart was pounding, faster and faster, the sound of it banging inside her mind.

"Open your eyes." The words were said in a soft, goading tone, yet the command was not lost on her, and this time she concentrated, forcing her eyes to open.

Molly blinked into the shadows of the room, her gaze taking in as much of the scene as her shocked brain would permit. She was lying on her left side on what appeared to be a bed. There was a window just beyond her head, and weak, silver light flooded into the room, illuminating the presence of Connor, who was towering over her.

She shifted her gaze, gasping as she met his intense, green stare. "Wh…" She hesitated, her parched throat felt like sandpaper as she tried to speak. "Where am I?"

He watched her, hooking his thumbs into the front pockets of his black jeans, motionless for a moment. "It doesn't matter where you are."

She blinked at him, taking in the air around her. It did matter. It mattered a lot, but she didn't have the energy to press him on the matter for the time being.

Connor edged forward, crouching in front of her face. "I removed your gag. I wanted to make sure you had enough room to breathe, but, Molly"—his face darkened as he spoke to her—"I won't hesitate to put it back on if you cannot control your mouth. Do you understand?"

His gaze was cold, and Molly shivered reflexively. "Yes," she whispered.

Her head hurt, and she was freezing and thirsty. So thirsty.

"How's your head?" he asked her, as though he actually gave a shit.

"It hurts," she croaked. "And I'm thirsty." She paused, unsure if she should ask for a drink or not.

"You'd like a glass of water?" His stare was dark, despite the striking color of his eyes. The intensity of that look was consuming. It was as though she was a meal he was about to eat. The thought made her shudder.

"Yes, please," she replied, nodding as though the point needed reinforcement.

"I will get you one in a moment," he promised, his gaze falling down the line of her bound body again. "But first, we're going to start with the ground rules."

Molly blinked up at him, flexing the fingers of her bound hands. "Rules?" she repeated. "What do you want with me?"

There was silence as the question filled the near empty room. The words resonated around her body, taunting her long after they'd left her lips. She was truly terrified. It was an overwhelming sensation which crushed her chest, making it hard to breathe. Molly had a good idea what a man might want with a woman when he abducted and bound her, and the thought made her want to heave. Yet, still, she had to know his intentions. He had, after all, been the same man who'd saved her from the gang of other predators.

Connor's face broke into a smile, the same suave one which had captured her attention at the book signing. "Don't worry about that now," he told her. "I'm not going to make you do anything you can't do, or won't want to do."

He shifted at her side, his fingers rising to her face. Molly flinched out of instinct, drawing her eyes closed as his hand approached.

"Open them," he commanded, and despite the banging in her head and the pounding of her heart, she complied.

Their gazes met briefly. His seemed calm and in control, although she thought she saw lust etched into the dilated irises. His hand met her face, but the touch was gentle, and wordlessly, he stroked the loose strands of hair there.

"That's better," he cooed. "Rule one, Molly. You are going to obey my every command."

Her breath hitched at that. He sounded like one of the heroes in her latest series of books. "Obey you," she replied, although it wasn't really a query, more of an echo.

Her tone was light and dreamy, as if her brain hadn't fully caught up with the status quo. She'd been kidnapped, for fuck's sake, but despite her terror at the idea, she couldn't bring herself to argue with him. Perhaps it was the chloroform, or just shock, but her head felt heavy, with no sense of urgency.

He chuckled at her, resting on his knees as he leaned a little closer. "Yes," he said. "Obey me. I know you may not find this easy at first, but with time, it will become second nature."

"Wh – why should I obey you?" she stammered, her tone breathy as she forced the words out.

"Because I am the one in charge here, Molly," he told her, "and you're the one bound on the bed."

She squirmed at his accurate depiction, riled and anxious energy coursing through her. Molly loved bondage usually. She loved the feeling of its grip against her skin, and relished the restriction it offered, but this was different. Unsettling. This was not a consensual game of kink. This was a stranger who had taken her to God knows where, to do who knew what. Her throat dried further as the explanation washed over her.

"Have you got it, Molly?" His expression was little more than a wry smirk as his tone caught her attention again.

She nodded, fighting the tears which suddenly threatened to well in her eyes. "Y-yes," she stammered. "I understand."

"Smart girl," came the reply. "Now, you're probably wondering why you've been brought here, and that brings me to rule two."

She twisted against whatever it was that held her wrists together behind her back. She'd never had great circulation, and she could sense the loss of feeling on her left side already.

"You're going to write for me, Molly." He presented the words as a statement of fact, but they nearly made Molly laugh out loud.

"Write for you?" she cried, trying to stifle her laughter. "Why would I do that?"

His expression hardened at once. "We're back to rule one," he said sternly. "Now I know you're an intelligent woman, so I'm not going to need to go over it again so soon, am I?" He paused, clearly waiting for Molly to answer.

She stared at him wildly, her heart threatening to burst from her chest. "No," she gasped at length.

"Good girl," he replied with a laugh. "So, tell me. Show me that you were paying attention. What was rule one?"

Molly writhed further, feeling the heat rising to her face as the admission sprung from her lips. "I am going to obey you," she mumbled, as though she couldn't believe she'd actually said it.

Connor's smile widened. "What was that?" he asked. "I could barely hear you, Molly. What are you going to do?"

She swallowed down the humiliation of having to repeat herself. Whoever this Connor was, he held all of the cards for the time being. "Obey you," she said, trying to make her voice louder.

There was a long moment of silence, as though he wanted her words to hang in the air around them.

"Exactly," he answered her at last. "And because you are going to obey me, you're not going to need to query every instruction you're given. Is that clear?"

Something about his tone made her pant, and in that moment, Molly understood something. It wasn't just the coercion of the situation – the terror and the uncertainty – which produced the response. It wasn't just fear. There was something else happening inside of her. There was arousal. She felt the color at her face deepen as the realization settled in her mind. This was the most intense and petrifying experience of her life. How on earth could any part of her find this exciting?

She gazed into his hard expression, realizing all of a sudden, that he was still waiting for an answer. "Yes," she murmured, trying to quell the feelings rising inside of her. "Yes, it's clear."

"Excellent," he said, rising to a standing position again. "So, Molly, you are going to write. It's something you do anyhow, most days I presume, so it really shouldn't be a problem." He stared down at her bound and vulnerable form, his eyes flickering with some unspoken emotion.

Molly wanted to argue. She wanted to question his logic. Yes, she did write every day, but why the hell should she be writing for him? Who the hell did he think he was? One look at his dark gaze told her this was not the right time to press the point. His expression was powerful, and almost taunting, as though he was daring her to defy him. The look of it made her

FELICITY BRANDON

stomach shrink with fear, no matter how much the bondage excited her. If she wanted to get free, then she'd have to play along with his little game. For now, at least.

"What do you want me to write?" she asked, her tone raspy.

He smiled, the look of it predatory. "We'll get to that," he answered. "For now, that's all you need to remember, just two rules. Obey me without question, and when you're told, write for me. Do you think you can do that, Molly?"

She blinked up at him aware of her eyes widening at the weight of his expectations. "Yes," she whispered.

Connor nodded his head, shifting his weight slightly to look down the length of her. She drew in a shaky breath at his quiet appraisal.

"Okay then," he said, after the longest time. "You stay put, and I'll get you that water."

Chapter Six

She drank the first glass of water greedily, but only after he helped her sit, and fixed the ropes at her wrists. Connor knew she'd need to move to ease her circulation, so, after a strict reminder of the rules, he unfastened the binds. She eyed her skin for abrasions. The ropes had cut into her pale flesh, leaving their tell-tale signatures, but Connor was pleased to see there was no real damage. He watched her like a hawk as her gaze rose to meet his again.

"Must you bind me again?" She sighed, her voice throaty, as though a well of emotion was on the verge of drowning her.

"Yes, Molly," he asserted, wrapping fresh rope around her wrists again. This time he bound them in front of her, and he left some slack in the bondage, so her hands could be separated by a few inches. "The ropes are necessary for now. We'll need time to build trust together, but right now, you don't trust me, and I don't trust you either. Plus, anyway, I know you like them…"

Her breath hitched, her eyes darting to him reflexively. Her gaze was questioning, *did you really just say that?*

Connor grinned at her response. "Yes, Molly," he answered, even though no words had actually left her lips. "I've read your books, remember? I have a pretty good idea of how you get your kicks, young lady."

Her expression altered, a visage of disgust settling over her which he didn't like one iota. He imagined what she was thinking as the final knots were secured at her wrists. That he had no right to do this, no right to take her, to keep her, no right to bind her. But she was wrong on all counts, she just didn't know it yet. Connor had every right. He was her biggest fan, and had been following her career for years, but it was more than that. He'd studied her, watched her, researched her. He *knew* her. Knew her habits, her routines, her nature. Perhaps he knew her better than she knew herself.

By the time he caught her eye again, her expression had softened, and the anger which had risen in him began to evaporate.

"Here," he said softly, "drink this." He shifted to the second glass on the dresser beside the bed, placing it into her right hand.

She took it gladly at first, evidently her thirst had become a big driver, but then, as she raised the glass to her lips, he saw the flicker of doubt. She hesitated, drawing the vessel away again. "What is it?"

He wanted to smile, but somehow, he suppressed the urge. Molly was smart. "Just water, like before," he replied, his tone deliberately reassuring. "Now, remember rule one? Drink please."

She drew in a large breath, eyeing the contents of the glass warily. Ultimately, he wasn't sure if it was her dry throat, or the fear of ramifications which forced her on, but she pressed it to her full lips and took a sip. He watched, almost proud, as she drained the entire contents in just a few seconds, raising her eyes to look at him once she was done.

The swell of arousal which washed over him at that moment took him by surprise. He had planned every moment of this adventure, and had fully anticipated being horny around her, but this was something else. If just the look of her drinking was going to make him hard, then this was going to be more difficult – and enjoyable - than he'd first imagined.

Connor swooped, taking the glass from her as he continued to watch her responses. "Another glass?" he asked, pleasantly.

He'd only brought two with him, but apparently his new guest really was thirsty.

She nodded her head slowly. "Yes, please."

"No problem," he replied, "but first, you'll have to do something for me, Molly."

That got her attention. "Wh-what?" she stuttered, her nerves about the situation more than clear from her voice alone.

"It's okay," he chuckled. She was so small, so fragile and so bound. Like a frightened animal. *She was his.* "It's nothing terrible. I just want you to show me a little more respect."

Her body tensed at the suggestion. "How?"

He placed the glass back on the dresser, approaching her again. Damn, he was so hard that he'd need to resolve his own tensions before he'd be able to concentrate this afternoon. Connor was a good-looking guy, and he knew it. He'd never had a problem attracting women, and there had been plenty. Only one had ever meant anything, and even she had nothing on Molly. None of them were as good as her.

"I just need you to call me Sir when you answer me." He paused, allowing the words to reverberate. The look on her pretty face was priceless. "Do you think you can do that, Molly?"

She blinked up at him, a look of fear and indignation etched into her beautiful features. "I…" She hesitated, uncertain. "I don't do that stuff in real life," she conceded after a moment.

He laughed, the sound deep and dark as it echoed around the small room he'd chosen for her. Slowly, he lifted his right hand to her face, stroking her pale skin before his digits dipped to her chin. "Well, Molly," he began. "It looks as though you do now, doesn't it?" He applied just enough pressure to the underside of her chin, so that her eyes were forced to meet his. He watched, mesmerized as she answered him.

"Y-yes," she stammered. "Yes, Sir."

Chapter Seven

It was a matter of survival. This guy had her bound and captured, and she didn't even know where the hell she was. Either she'd have to do as he asked, or she'd anger him, and she didn't want to think about what he might do then.

Molly answered him in little more than a whisper, but the finger at her chin ensured she didn't miss his expression. He was pleased as she submitted to his will. He *enjoyed* it. She resisted the urge to shudder, pushing down the small voice in her head which reminded her that she might actually have enjoyed it, too.

The grip at her chin softened, his digits caressing the underside of her face.

"Very good," he purred in a gleeful tone.

Molly couldn't decide how she felt about that. She knew she should be riled, irritated, disgusted even, and yet she was so tense she could barely process those emotions.

"I'll fetch you the water now," he went on. "Be a good girl and stay here."

Connor was gone before she could think to reply, having swiped the glasses from their place on the dresser and stalked from the room. He closed the door behind him, and for a while she just stared after him, her mind blank. And then the whole thing hit her like a ton of bricks. The son of a bitch had taken her, and now he *had* her. She had to escape, yet her mind was still cloudy and her limbs so heavy, perhaps the lasting effects of the chloroform he'd kindly made her inhale.

She twisted to look out of the small window. There were old shabby net curtains in place, obscuring most of her view to the outside world, yet shards of silvery light washed into the room. *Where the hell was she?* She strained her mind trying to think. Had he given her any clues about where he'd taken her? She couldn't recall, but all at once his full name came back to her – he was Connor, Connor Reilly. She'd met him at the end of the signing, just before she'd been ambushed by the gang of youths, when she'd been looking for her rental. *Had he planned all that, she wondered? Had the whole thing been a set up?*

Wrists bound, she wriggled across the bed, gaining traction with her tied ankles. She made it to the grubby looking window sill, resting on her elbows as she knelt up to try and access the view. It was harder work than she'd imagined it to be, moving without the assistance of all of her limbs, but by the time she'd made it, she was squirming for a different reason. Being bound made her horny, just like always. Even in this, the most dangerous situation of her life, her body was betraying her. The shoots of arousal made her head swim, almost as much as the chloroform.

Sighing, she tried to shift the bottom of the net curtain out of her view. She could only manage to hold it a few inches over the sill, before her arms began to tremble with the exertion, and she wondered just how much of the drug she'd inhaled. Her eyes squinted as they acclimatised to the new perspective. The glass, it seemed, was as filthy as the curtains, and it was difficult to make out much of anything. Molly pushed her raised fists against it, scrubbing a small patch to *clean* it. Straining to look through the small area, she was perturbed to realize that all she could see was miles and miles of countryside.

"Not planning on jumping, are you?"

The sound of his voice startled her. Molly hadn't heard him coming back to the room, and she spun to face him, losing her balance and landing awkwardly against her left shoulder. Connor laughed at the display, his arrogance evident as he placed the water back down on the dresser. The amused look on his face made the old indignation within her rise to the surface, and she knew she was scowling as she struggled to get herself upright again.

"Molly?" he asked, drawing his hands to his hips.

Her eyes assessed him, and she wondered what he saw in them? Fear, perhaps? Anger? Maybe something else?

"I asked you a question," he continued, his tone lowering.

Molly swallowed hard, her emotions threatening to spiral out of control completely. "I…" She closed her mouth, unsure what to actually say. She hadn't been thinking of jumping, but now that he mentioned it, she couldn't remember why she hadn't thought of it herself.

Connor took one long stride and pointed to the bed. "Sit," he commanded, as though she was some sort of dog.

She inhaled quickly, fighting both the urge to tell him to go and fuck himself, and the one which made her pussy wet, in equal measure. She eyed him fearfully, deciding that for the time being at least, there really was little choice but to obey as he'd asked. Moving on unsteady legs, she fell back to her bottom.

He stared down at her, and as she lifted her chin, she couldn't believe how tall he seemed, towering over her like some mythical man. "I'm waiting for your answer," he reminded her in a curt, unamused tone.

She straightened up as the weight of his intense gaze fell over her. "I wasn't going to jump," she answered. "I swear, I wasn't even thinking about it."

This was the truth at least.

"Really?" he inquired, apparently unimpressed by her response. "And how did I ask you to address me, Molly?" His dark brow arched as he questioned her, and the sight of it made her pussy clench reflexively.

"Sir." The word flew from her lips as though it was the most natural thing to say in the whole world. "You asked me to call you Sir."

He smiled, evidently proud, but the expression hardened almost at once. "So, why did you not use my title?"

She squirmed in her place. "I'm sorry," she replied, feeling absurdly flustered by the admission. The logical part of her brain, apparently still subdued by the toxins coursing through her system, knew she had no reason to be ashamed. Connor was the asshole here. He was the one who had taken her. He was the perpetrator.

But then, what did that make her? Her squirming stilled as the answer came to her.

It made her the victim.

Connor crouched down in front of her, so that their eyes were virtually on the same level. "Okay, little girl," he said in an annoyingly condescending tone. "How about this? I'll forgive you this time, but the next time you forget to address me the correct way, there will be consequences."

Molly drew in a shaky breath. "Co-consequences?" she stammered, overawed by his authoritative approach.

"Yes." He smiled, apparently all too aware of how he made her feel. *Bastard.* "Nothing too severe to begin. Just enough to make you *remember…*"

She stared at him, wide-eyed. She hated the way she was behaving. Why couldn't she get her act together and come up with a plan to get away from this sick fuck?

"So, let's put it this way," he continued. "Address me properly, or you'll find yourself stripped and over my knee for a bare-arse spanking. And believe me, pretty, I can be heavy-handed when I'm irritated."

She gulped at that. It was a physical response, and she guessed he saw it. Spanking. Had he just threatened her with a spanking? For fuck's sake, this was getting out of hand. This complete stranger was now intimidating her with the notion of violence. Her head spun at the idea, and yet even now, at this most terrifying juncture, her clit throbbed impatiently inside her pants. He'd threatened her with a spanking! How long had it been since she'd been taken in hand?

Too long, the tiny voice in her head reminded her.

"Am I making myself clear, Molly?"

The sound of his voice snapped her back to reality. *Not arousing,* she reminded herself. *This is not arousing. This is abduction...*

"Yes, Sir," she answered, forcing the words out before her brain could make her falter.

He rose to stand over her, moving back to the dresser and collecting the glass once again. Turning, he walked back to her, presenting her with the water. "Here's your reward," he said, smugly.

Molly bit her lip, ignoring his tone as she took the glass from him. She drained the contents in less than a minute. "Thank you... Sir," she replied, hating the gratitude in her voice. Yet there was no doubt about it. The water was clearing her head, and for that at least, she was grateful.

Chapter Eight

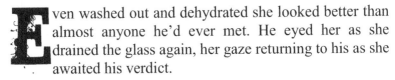ven washed out and dehydrated she looked better than almost anyone he'd ever met. He eyed her as she drained the glass again, her gaze returning to his as she awaited his verdict.

"Thank you, Sir..." She murmured, her voice full of uncertainty as she forced the final word out.

Connor smiled, inhaling deeply as his cock strained beneath his pants. "You're welcome," he replied, moving toward her and taking the glass from her small palms.

He returned it to the dresser, before coming back in her direction. "When you're a good girl, and obey my rules, then you will be rewarded," he told her.

Molly's eyes widened into saucers, and he noticed how she intentionally rested her bound wrists against her legs to stop her hands from trembling.

"I'm sure you can work it out, Molly," he continued. "You've been writing these plots longer than me."

His tone was sardonic, and he knew his right brow was arching as she raised her head to meet his eye.

"I..." She hesitated, as though the words were stuck in her throat. Connor suppressed the urge to smile as he imagined what else he could use her sweet little mouth for. "I never thought I'd be living in one of them... Sir."

Her gaze fell to her knees as though the embarrassment of telling him out loud had made it impossible to meet his eye.

Connor stared at her for a long moment, allowing her time to adjust to the reality. This was just like one of her bestsellers, and Molly was right – she was now the heroine.

"I think," he began, edging his large shoes closer to where she sat. "If you give it some time, you might find you enjoy the plot."

She sighed, the sound stilted by her obvious apprehension. She was scared, he knew that, but he sensed she was also aroused by her predicament. He'd need her fear until she was better trained. Being afraid made her more compliant – more likely to do what he asked of her – and he was more than prepared to use her fear to his advantage. Beyond that though, with some time, he hoped that the fear would dissolve into more of that sexual tension, the type he'd seen in her eyes when he'd threatened her with the spanking. He could use the arousal too, and he knew they'd both enjoy that better.

"Molly." His tone was deliberately abrupt, and he liked the way it captured her attention.

She raised her head to look at him, her eyes full of nervous energy. "Yes, S-Sir," she mumbled, still falling over that final word.

"Do you think you'll enjoy it?" His question was intentionally direct. He wanted to see her squirm, and her response did not disappoint.

She fidgeted against the bed covers, her face flushing as she paused to consider his words. "I don't know, Sir" she conceded, her gaze fixed to the bondage at her wrists instead of his face.

"Look at me," he commanded, and something about his tone made her obey without complaint.

He watched her gulp at the order, her gaze genuinely frightened. Some part of his brain realized that he should have empathy for her. She'd been drugged, taken without consent, and was now bound in a strange place with a guy she'd never met before. As he took in her large puppy eyes, and her pale expression, though, all he could think about was his raging erection, and what he was going to do to her. Yes, he was going to use that fear, he was going to make her obey him, but he was going to love every moment of the experience.

Christ, he was one sick fuck.

"How do the ropes at your wrists make you feel?" he probed, wanting to push the point, and get her to talk about how she was doing. It would make him seem more caring than he really was, and perhaps it would lure Molly into some sort of false trust. Either way, he knew that listening to her relating her feelings about the subject was going to make him even harder – if such a thing were possible.

"They make me scared," she admitted in barely a whisper.

Connor crouched down in front of her, resting one knee on the threadbare carpet below. "Scared?" he repeated, ignoring the fact that she'd overlooked his title for the time being. He was having too much fun with the line of questioning to correct her right now, but he would – the next time she messed up. "Why does it frighten you? I've already told you I'm not going to do anything that you don't want me to."

Molly swallowed deeply, her breath coming out in short pants as she answered him. "But, I don't know you," she replied. "You might be lying to me. You might want to do *anything* to me... Sir." She added the final word just in time to save herself, and this time he couldn't help but smile at her.

"That's true," he told her, keeping his tone intentionally hard. "You don't know me, so you're just going to have to take my words at face value, aren't you?"

She nodded, her gaze still wide with obvious trepidation at the verdict.

"Do you normally like to be bound?" he asked her directly. "When you're not being taken against your will, I mean?"

Connor snorted at the sound of his own joke, but she didn't return his smile.

"Sometimes," she mumbled, her cheeks blushing ever so slightly at the admission. "In the bedroom, but not like this!" Her voice crescendoed as she spoke, but then fell away into a protracted silence. "Please," she implored him, raising her blue eyes to meet his own intense stare. "Please, Sir, don't hurt me."

Connor watched her with aroused fascination. Molly Clary was just too damn perfect. And she was all his for the taking.

Chapter Nine

"**D**o you need more water, or do you feel well enough to make a start?" He fired the question at her matter-of-factly, as though he always took women from the streets and squirreled them off for his own personal amusement.

Maybe he did.

The thought made the bile in Molly's belly bubble, threatening to rise north. She was panting so hard she could barely catch her breath. In the panic of the abduction, she'd forgotten all about her asthma, but right now the condition hit her in the face. Molly had no clue how long she'd been here, but she knew she'd need medication, and soon. She blinked up at him for a moment, trying to get a handle on her breathing.

"Make a start on what, Sir?" she murmured, her tone no doubt expressing her desperation.

Connor smirked in her direction. "Make a start on your new story," he answered her with a wry smile. "Rule two, Molly. I assume you remember?"

She lifted her bound wrists a few inches from her lap as his words registered in her aching brain. "Yes," she whispered, her expression crumbling slightly. "Yes, I remember... Sir."

She added the final word just in time, noting how his face relaxed as soon as he heard it. Evidently, this guy got off on hearing her call him Sir. The thought resonated, sickening and exciting her in equal measure. She swallowed at the insight. *Who's the sick one now,* she taunted herself at her own twisted response to the situation.

"Good," he replied, rising from his place by her, and marching toward the wooden dresser. He pulled the middle drawer open and reached inside. Molly jolted at the sound of metal, her heart thumping even faster at what Connor's large palm produced from the dresser drawer.

"What is that?" she inquired as he brought the long metal chain into full view.

Connor's eyes narrowed at her question. "What was that, Molly?"

She gulped, acknowledging her error in an instant. "What is that, *Sir*?" She corrected herself, emphasizing the title as best she could as fear began to close up her throat.

Connor shook his head as he moved toward her. "Better," he told her, "but not good enough. You were warned what would happen if you forgot to address me correctly."

Molly was actually shaking by the time his body reached her. "I'm sorry, Sir," she pleaded, hearing the tremble in her voice.

She knew he heard it too, the thought making her wretched. How had she become such a quivering mess? She had always considered herself to be such a strong, independent woman, yet all it took to reduce her to this state was one man with a plan and his malevolent ingenuity.

Connor ducked down at her feet again, his agility taking her by surprise. For such a big man, he moved with shocking speed. She eyed the metal in his hands with renewed agitation. The implement was indeed a long chain, but it had a cuff at either end. Molly's stomach sank at the look of the thing, and she watched miserably as Connor clicked first one, and then the second cuff open in front of her.

"These are to contain you," he told her, his tone low and steely.

Molly's eyes flittered higher for a moment, locking gazes with him for the briefest interlude. What she saw there made her catch her breath. Connor's gaze was dark and intense. She found neither warmth, nor cold there, just an odd detachment as he lunged for her left ankle.

Acting out of instinct, Molly tried to kick him away, adrenaline rising in her as the panic registered. "Please!" She was screeching, trying to get to her feet.

Connor yanked her feet from under her, sending her crashing back to the bed behind her. Molly's body, still full of whatever toxins he had exposed her to, toppled with ease, and for a long moment she couldn't regain her composure. Her head spun, all of her senses screaming at her to move, to run, to get away even as she felt the metal encircling her sock.

"That's enough!" he barked, snapping the metal bracelet shut around her left ankle. "You will behave, Molly, or you will find yourself gagged and bound to this bed for the rest of today. If you're not ready to start writing yet, then I am prepared to accept the delay."

Her eyes widened like saucers, her heart pounding relentlessly inside her chest. "No," she gasped. "No, Sir, please. I'll be good, I promise."

Connor paused, greeting her frightened expression with a hard stare. "Oh, you better had, young lady," he warned her as his attention turned to her right foot. "You're mine now, Molly Clary, and the sooner you get used to your new arrangement, the easier you will find it."

As the second cuff clicked shut, her heart sank. She watched as he untied the rope that had bound her ankles before. Tossing it aside, he played with the length of metal chain now uniting her feet, drawing the length together. Though he'd allowed her a bit more freedom of movement, there was still only about twelve inches remaining between her feet. He was right, he really did have her now. Not only was she drugged and bound, but she was now in chains, literally unable to run from him. Tears pricked in her eyes, but she fought for some freaking composure. She couldn't let him see what this was doing to her. She wouldn't let him win.

"Right," he told her, his voice stern. "That will help to keep you in your place once we begin this new story, but first..." He rose, once again towering over her. "First, we deal with your insubordination, Molly."

She lifted her head to look at him, and for the first time she really looked. She had caught glimpses of the man before. The fan who met her at the end of the signing, the man who she thought had come to rescue her on the street, but she realized she had never really seen him until this moment. Connor was undeniably handsome. Tall, dark and smoldering with an unusual intensity, he was the kind of guy who'd have caught a girl's eye, but there was more than that. Much more than that, and it was only now that Molly registered what she'd instinctively already garnered.

Connor was dangerous.

Smart, organized, articulate and charming, Connor was a well-oiled predator, and it was her misfortune to have landed right in his trap.

He lunged for her bound wrists, tugging them north. "Up," he commanded, unceremoniously.

On shaky legs she obeyed, willing her thighs to carry her weight, and her belly to keep the rising nausea at bay as she stood next to him.

"How have you been asked to address me, Molly?" he asked, his tone clipped as he glared down at her.

She gulped, the look in his eyes threatening to overwhelm her. "Sir," she replied, though her voice was barely audible. "You asked me to call you Sir."

Connor nodded. "Correct," he continued. "And yet twice already you have failed in this endeavour. Is it really such a difficult task for you?"

She blinked at him, the sound of her heart hammering, drowning out everything except Connor's voice. She wanted to argue. Twice – had it really been twice that she'd forgotten? But the instinct to save herself kept her mouth sealed. Now was not the time for some sarcastic reply. Now was not the time to anger the beast.

"No, Sir," she mumbled, aware that her face flamed as she gave her answer. "It is not so difficult."

He pursed his lips. "I'm glad you agree," he told her. "Now tell me, can you recall what I promised you if you failed me again?"

Molly's throat dried in an instant. She could very well remember his words, they were burned forever into her psyche. He had threatened to spank her bare ass.

"Yes, Sir," she squeaked by means of reply.

Connor jerked on the ropes at her wrists, drawing her forward toward him. The metal at her legs clinked as she stumbled against his hard body, the sound and his sudden proximity drawing a gasp from her mouth as she eyed him. He was now right next to her, tall, imposing, and totally in control. Fighting to catch her breath, she tried to take stock, to see through the cloud of fear in her mind. But as she drew in a deep breath, the only other emotion she was aware of was her own stark arousal at his treatment. She hated the fact, but it was true. Every time he took away her liberty, she got a little hotter, and her pussy got a little wetter. She clenched the muscles between her legs at the idea, ashamed of her own reckless response to his dominance.

"And?" His curt reply shook her from her internal monologue with frightening ease. "What did I tell you would be the consequence if you failed to address me in the correct manner?"

Molly stilled, her breath coming out in short, frantic bursts. "You told me that you would spank me, Sir," she whispered, her face burning a deeper crimson at the admission.

Connor tightened his grip on her bondage, leaning even closer to her reddening face. "That's right, little lady," he replied, coolly. "I did promise you a spanking, and now I get to deliver one."

Chapter Ten

The look on Molly's face was priceless. She was blushing so deeply that he could practically feel her embarrassment as he leant over her. Connor inhaled, taking a moment to capture that look. Everything she did and said, each and all of her natural reactions were doing nothing to quell his rising arousal, but he knew he needed to get a handle on it. Now was not the time for that. There would be a time, and he knew it was coming soon, but it wasn't now.

"Time to deliver, Molly," he said again, ensuring his cool eyes penetrated her for just long enough. Just until she flinched, and he saw her physically try to withdraw from him. Just until he was sure he had all of her attention... Connor released her wrists. "Undo your trousers," he commanded, the timbre of his voice softer than before.

Her blush deepened as she blinked up at him with wide eyes. He could see the questions in them, the flat refusal to comply, the abject fury, but wisely the protests did not reach her sweet lips.

"Molly..." His tone had taken on a rather taunting quality, and he smiled as she jumped, understanding the meaning reflexively. "Don't keep me waiting, little girl," he told her. "Waiting makes me angry, and you won't like me when I'm angry."

Her hands reached for the button at her waistband, fiddling with it as best she could in the bondage. He stood watching her expression, and he could see the internal fight. Her natural temperament wanted to punch him in the nuts, but her self-preservation instincts had kicked in, and were overriding everything else. Molly wanted to stay alive, and right now she knew that meant playing his little game. His eyes darted south to find the button now undone, and slowly she edged the zipper downwards.

"Good girl, Molly," he murmured over her. "Now, hold still and let me help you with those."

In an instant, his two large hands were at her hips, and roughly he tugged the fabric down, exposing her pert behind to the cool air of the room. He was smiling as he jerked them a little further, so that the material collected at the middle of her shapely thighs.

"Better," he breathed from beside her, "but not good enough."

In one smooth action, he swooped again, collecting the silky material of her panties at the side of her hips and pulling them down her body. Molly gasped as the fabric moved, her face flaming as he left them intentionally pooling with her pants. He knew the act would humiliate her further. He was counting on it...

Connor reached for her bound wrists once again, noting her shaky intake of breath as he took physical control of her body. There was a lengthy pause when all he could do was hold her in place, taking in the scent of her hair and the look of her creamy, flawless skin. Christ, she was too much, so fucking beautiful. His eyes flitted down the length of her body, over the swell of her breasts and landed on the material bunched up at the top of her legs. The flesh there was pale and stunning, and he wondered how much effort it would take to turn the color into a warmer shade of pink, or maybe red. It was time to find out...

"I'm going to spank you, Molly."

There was really no need for the repetition. They both knew why he had yanked her trousers down, and what was going to happen next, and Connor knew it. The truth was that saying it out loud again gave him a thrill which connected directly to his throbbing cock, and frankly, he just couldn't help himself.

Molly responded with those large, fearful eyes, which were practically brimming with tears as she finally raised her head to meet his insistent gaze.

"Please, don't hurt me," she pleaded, her voice faltering as he pulled the ropes at her wrists even tighter.

He smiled. She begged so beautifully that there was really no need to make her practice the art, and yet somehow, he knew that he would.

"I'm not going to cause you any real harm, Molly," he replied, aiming to reassure her on this one point at least. "But I am going to punish you for your transgression, and it *is* going to hurt. There's no point of a spanking which doesn't inflict some pain is there?" He chuckled at his own question. "How is that going to help you to correct your behavior?"

She bit her lip in response, shaking her head as though she had no reply for those questions. Connor narrowed his eyes. He knew she was afraid, but that was no excuse for not answering him.

"Molly," he snapped. "I asked you a question. Two, in fact."

The sound of his stern tone made her jolt. "I'm sorry, Sir," she whispered, her voice hoarse. "I didn't hear the questions."

Poor little girl, he thought wryly. *She's so stressed that she's really not listening. Now, that was going to have to change.*

"You must pay attention to me, Molly," he admonished her. "Whatever else happens, you will listen to my voice and take heed of my words. Do you understand?"

Now she was nodding. Apparently, she'd been paying attention on that occasion. "Yes, Sir," she answered, breathlessly.

"Good," Connor replied. "I asked how a spanking which did not hurt was going to help correct your behavior?" He paused, watching as his words rung through her pretty little head.

Her lips parted and her eyes darted to his nervously. "I suppose it won't, Sir?" she said at length. Her voice came out in a long sigh, and Connor wondered if there was an air of resignation in the sound. Had Molly finally accepted this spanking, or, as was more likely, was she still going to put up a fight?

"That's right," he replied, "it won't."

As he spoke, his free hand rose slowly to her face. Molly saw its approach in her peripheral vision, her eyes moving to acknowledge it, and as his large fingers came to rest under her chin, he heard a small gasp escape her lips. Handling her with care, he used his thumb and forefinger to prop her chin up, forcing her face toward his gaze.

"Have you ever actually been spanked before, Molly?" he asked her. "Or is everything you pen just complete fiction?"

His voice had an edge to it, and he knew she heard it by the look in her eyes. He sounded almost betrayed by the notion that Molly's stories could be only works of utter fiction, although, of course, he had known this could be the case.

"I have been spanked," she told him in a shaky voice. "But only for fun, not as a real punishment, Sir."

Connor nodded in acknowledgement, ignoring the desperate plea of his erection tucked inside his pants. "Okay," he told her. "Then there's a good chance that this is going to come as quite a shock to you, Molly. Are you ready?"

Before she even had time to respond, he spun them both around. Taking a seat on the bed where she had previously been sitting, he sent her bound body crashing down over his lap. Sprawled over him, Molly's bound arms were now stretched forward over the bedding, and her exposed little behind rested perfectly over his right thigh. Connor's eyes surveyed the sight of her restrained and helpless body, and he drew in a sharp breath.

Fuck, he thought, fighting to clear the heady fog of arousal which threatened to cloud his judgement. *This is it. Time to spank Molly.*

Chapter Eleven

Molly was down over his lap before she could even catch her breath, her ribs splayed over his left leg and her ass hopelessly vulnerable behind her. He was going to spank her. He had made no bones about it, telling her directly what her fate would be, and now it was actually going to happen. She gasped, flexing the fingers of her bound hands as the realization dawned on her. He was going to spank her, and worse, she had no idea which emotion was stronger on the subject, her fear or her arousal.

She was frightened, that was for sure, and she knew that she had good reason to be. This guy was a complete stranger – some sort of uber fan who'd turned stalker and planned this – her capture and containment. She shuddered reflexively as the reality washed over her like freezing water, panting again as she fought to stay in control of her erratic breathing. But being bound this way, and thrown unceremoniously over his lap, there was no doubt it was thrilling, and despite her terror, she could feel the moisture pooling between her thighs. The fact that he'd had the audacity to yank her panties down made the whole thing even more scintillating, but then, she suspected this man had the audacity to do rather a lot more than just that. She pushed that thought away, needing to concentrate on what lay ahead right now. The threat of the spanking had made her seriously hot, but how would she cope with the reality of one?

"You need this spanking, Molly." The sound of his voice echoed around her, shaking her from her private monologue. "Why is that? Why do you deserve it?"

Molly eyed the pale bedding around her face. What did he expect her to say for God's sake? That she was sorry for not using his self-appointed title? That was crazy, and yet she knew it was true. That was exactly what he expected.

She drew in a breath, trying to decide how to force the words out.

SMACK!

The weight of his palm crashed down against her exposed bottom, the act catching her off-guard, despite her position. "Ouch!" she shrieked, flailing over his lap as her body adjusted to the pain. "I'm sorry! I didn't address you correctly, Sir, and I'm sorry!"

She'd barely concluded the admission when he spanked her again, but this time the strike was harder.

"That's right, Molly," his voice boomed from over her head, managing to cut through the sound of the strike which still seemed to be resonating through her head. "You didn't address me correctly, and you took far too long to respond to my question. An error which will cost you an extra five swats in this punishment."

Her mind reeled at that. Five more swats? He can't be serious, surely?

Her silent questions were answered by his hand which landed against her bared behind again before she could fully process his last comments. He spanked her five times in fast succession, each swat landing in almost exactly the same spot as the one before, causing her ass to sting unbearably. Molly flinched at the pain, her head becoming heavier with each strike. This wasn't the way she'd imagined punishment spankings when she'd written them. In her books, the heroine was always punished with a loving hand, knowing that her pleasure would be imminent if she only endured the penance. But Connor's hands were not loving, and there were no guarantees of anything for her now. She didn't even know when she'd be free again, let alone able to enjoy pleasure. A low sob caught in her throat as his hand moved against her punished ass again and again, and she buried her head into the bedding, grateful at least that she didn't have to see his face during the ordeal.

The spanking continued over Connor's lap, Molly's behind now surely on fire as his palm connected with her ass again. Her bottom felt several times larger than it had before, and she wondered if and how she'd be able to sit once he'd finally finished. He spanked her again and this one felt hard, even in spite of all of the previous swats. The next strike was harder still, and she gasped, fighting to resist the urge to try and move from her place.

"Please," she mumbled in desperation. "I'm sorry, Sir, but please. It hurts so damn much!"

It was a humiliating thing to admit, particularly in light of the position in which she found herself – upturned over a stranger's lap for a bare-bottomed spanking – but she was past caring about that now. It did hurt, a lot, and she wasn't sure how much more of it she could take.

"Hush," came Connor's reply. "I don't need your opinion, Molly. You'll be punished until I am satisfied, and if you can't keep quiet then I'll be forced to gag that pretty little mouth of yours again. Got it?"

His voice was as hard and unrelenting as his palm, and she knew in that moment that there was little point in further protest. Connor had all the power, and she really didn't want to end up gagged during the ordeal as well as bound and humbled.

"Yes, Sir," she whispered into the bedding, uncertain if her voice would even carry to where he sat. "I've got it."

"Good," he replied, landing another hard smack to her no doubt reddening bottom. "And that's the last time I want to hear you speak unless I ask you a question."

She nodded as he spanked her again, his palm landing over and over. As the onslaught went on, she began to lose hope that she could survive this – whatever *this* was. Not the spanking. However consuming the immediate pain, she sensed she could get through it. She could draw on some sort of reserve within her and survive, but the whole ordeal of being held by this guy. If this spanking was the price for her first ridiculously minor transgression, then what would be next? Would he chain and whip her for not sitting correctly, or not answering correctly? And what would he do if he didn't like what she wrote for him? Molly shuddered at the prospect as the strikes continued to rain over her. There was no doubt. She had to escape, just as soon as she could get away from him, but that wasn't likely while she was bound, chained and exposed.

"You look so good like this, Molly," he purred from over her.

His words stirred her, snapping her from the thoughts of escape, and filling her with fresh anxiety.

"You should see how gorgeous this arse is now it's reddening under my palm. Fucking beautiful…"

Molly gulped at that, startled by his irritating British lilt, and unsure how she felt about his admission. Of course, she was disgusted. Appalled by the way he was treating her. He had no right to take her, to bind her, or to spank her, and they both knew it. But as the swats continued to land against her, that most curious thing began to happen. Instead of registering the pain of each new strike, something else was transpiring inside her head. Now there was pleasure, too. Her mind acknowledged the motion of his palm, and perhaps even conveyed the impact, but it didn't really hurt any more. Or maybe it did, she wasn't sure, but *if* it did, then she welcomed the pain. She sought it. Yes, that was it. It *did* hurt, but now she liked it – she wanted it. It was the most bizarre realization.

Now when she pulled at the ropes at her wrists, and felt them cut into her flesh, she didn't want to run from the sensation, she wanted more of it. She realized she was reveling in the ignominy of being bared to Connor. Yes, it was still humiliating, but now the humiliation was making her wetter than before. Wet, and hot, and ready.

As though he was somehow akin to her thought process, his palm paused, and she felt the foreign fingers as they grazed over her hot flesh. She tensed instinctively, knowing just how close those digits were to her very real arousal. What on earth would Connor think if he noticed? Would he assume that she wanted this treatment somehow, that she was giving some type of consent? The idea filled her with a new horror.

"Do you now understand what happens when you disobey me, Molly?" he asked in little more than a growl. She couldn't tell if it was anger or lust laced in his tone, and equally she didn't know how the prospect of either made her feel anymore. "What will happen when you disappoint me?"

Molly pulled in a long breath as best as she could still draped over his thighs. "Yes, Sir," she mumbled. "I understand."

"What will happen?" he questioned her. "Tell me."

"You'll spank me, Sir." She exhaled in a rush as the reality hit her as hard as any one of his prior strikes.

The hand at her ass shifted, massaging the hot orbs of flesh roughly in a way it had no right to do so. Molly's breath caught in her throat again as she struggled to process the myriad of sensation. Just as the ordeal had begun to become pleasurable, it had stopped, and now this? What was this? Did she like the feeling of Connor touching her in this most intimate way; did she welcome it?

"At the very least I'll spank you," he corrected her as his left hand moved down her back to join the right palm at her bottom. "But rest assured, I will punish you, and you won't enjoy the experience. You belong to me now, Miss Clary. You'll obey me, and you will write for me."

There was a small whimper in response, a sound which escaped her lips without her permission. Molly hung her head. The shame which clouded her mind was as much a product of the way her body had reacted to his barbaric treatment of her, as it was his words. A thick mist of sensation loomed, threatening to numb her until all she could do was *feel* for him – feel pain, embarrassment, frustration and anger – but each as a result of Connor Reilly. She screwed her hands into small fists. Whatever transpired, whatever he did, she couldn't let that happen. She had to continue to exist as more than just his thing.

Chapter Twelve

The spanking had gone well, better than he'd dared to hope. Connor had expected her to fight, resist and cry, but in reality, she'd been reasonably stoic, as though the thought of showing him how much he was hurting her made the indignation even worse. He narrowed his eyes at that, pondering the point. Was he disappointed that she hadn't protested more? Had he hoped for a big show? He didn't like the fact that she could be holding back, but as he pulled in a deep breath, he reminded himself of the facts – this was day one. There would be plenty of time to break down Molly Clary. What he needed to do was stay focused on the task at hand, oh and enjoy every facet of the experience.

"Get up now," he commanded her, missing the warmth of her body as she shifted over him and slowly rose to stand.

Her hair hung in dank strands at her face, her eyes a little red and watery. The skin stretched over those high cheekbones was flushed with obvious embarrassment at having to stand in front of him with her clothes pooling at her thighs. The effect was satisfying. He wasn't as satisfied as he hoped to become in the coming days, but for now, the look of the woman before him was pleasing enough.

"After you're punished, you will apologise, young lady," he told her with a deliberately clipped tone.

Molly shifted her weight awkwardly, her face flickering with emotion. Evidently, she was both enraged and embarrassed at the decision. "I'm sorry, Sir," she whispered, seemingly pushing the words out in one long breath.

Connor eyed her for a moment, allowing his gaze time to run the length of her body and really explore her. It stopped at the collection of fabric caught around her thighs, and he knew he was smirking as his eyes drew up slowly to the neatly shaved little pussy on display. He paused, lifting his left arm and drawing her ropes away so they wouldn't obscure his view. The sight of her was utterly tantalizing, sending electricity straight to his already excited cock. He loved the look of her, and wondered just how good she was going to taste when he finally got to claim her. Then, just as his gaze was about to continue up to her toned midriff, Connor spotted something else. It wasn't obvious, and for the longest time he wasn't sure, but as he shifted his weight forward on the bed he could see it was true. Molly Clary was wet with arousal. The shaved flesh at her seam was glistening with what he could only imagine was desire. His eyes shot to her face, and he noticed how an even deeper blush engulfed her cheeks. So, she knew she was aroused then, and now she also knew that he had found her out...

For the longest moment, their eyes locked. Molly's were filled with a peculiar mixture of what he assumed was fear, shame and arousal. He didn't know what she saw in his, but the expression on her face told him it was probably lust.

"Did someone enjoy their punishment, Molly?" His tone was sardonic.

Her face fell, her humiliation seemingly complete – or so she thought.

"Molly?" He probed again, his tone still playful as she eyed him fearfully. "It looks as though that sweet pussy is rather wet, little lady, and I, for one, have not had the pleasure of touching it, so... I can only assume you enjoyed being over my knee. Tell me, is it true?"

She gulped, her face an absolute picture. She wanted to lie, that much was clear. Molly wanted to protest and tell him what a filthy pig he was for doing this, for spanking her, for claiming such foul untruths, yet how could she? Molly's body betrayed her, and they both knew it.

"A little, Sir," she admitted at length.

Connor rose before her, his height sending her backwards as far as the ropes at her wrists and the suit trousers at her thighs would allow. "That is unexpectedly good news, Molly," he told her with a dark chuckle. "We are going to get on well, you and I…"

He allowed his voice to trail away on purpose, although his stare never left the bound woman before him. "Since you enjoyed your punishment, you may also thank me for delivering it, Molly."

Her eyes found him again in a heartbeat, the look of indignation etched back into her pretty features. "Th-thank you?" she repeated, as though she hadn't heard him the first time.

"Yes," he replied, his tone lowering. "And don't forget what you were punished for, young lady. I'm not sure that beautiful behind could handle another round right at this moment, however much your pussy might want it."

Molly balked at that, her cheeks now a deep crimson. "I'm sorry, Sir," she said at once. "And thank you."

There was no feeling in the words, but she had said them. It was a start.

"Thank me for what, Molly?" he asked as his dark eyes penetrated her face.

She paused as she considered what he now required of her. "Thank you for spanking me, Sir."

Connor smiled as his right hand rose to her chin, once more propping it up so she couldn't avoid his eyes. "You are welcome, Molly," he told her with a devastating smile. "Now you can conclude your punishment with some corner time, and then – when you've had time to think about your error – we can finally begin our story."

Molly blinked at him as his words began to reverberate through her, the color draining from her cheeks almost as fast as it had risen. "Corner time, Sir?"

His smile grew. "Yes," he told her. "Shuffle over to that corner and stand there with that beautiful arse on display, and your hands on your head. That's all you need to do…"

She looked close to tears, her eyes following his hand toward the corner of the room. "But…" she began as she turned back to face him.

"Now, Molly!" he barked, taking her bound wrists in his hands and directing her in the direction of the corner. "Go now, and do not even think about answering me back!"

She flinched at his tone, shrinking visibly at his last comment. Without another word she turned and he watched with smug satisfaction, and an aching groin, as she literally shuffled toward the place he had instructed. Her movement, hampered by the clothing caught at her thighs, made any greater movement impossible, and the chains at her ankles clinked wonderfully as she made her way there. Once in place she lifted her bound hands as ordered, facing the wall on shaky legs.

"Good girl." He smirked as he watched her. "Now, don't you move a muscle. I'm going to get your new laptop, but I'll be back in a few moments."

"Yes, Sir," she breathed, her voice hoarse with her embarrassment.

Connor strode toward the door next to the corner where Molly was standing. As he approached it, he paused, turning once again to look at her trembling body. "Oh, and, Molly," he said, his voice cooler. "Don't even think about disobeying me, little lady. I will be watching you whilst I'm gone."

Chapter Thirteen

Watching? She pulled in a shaky breath as he left the doorway, that irritating smirk still etched into his otherwise handsome features, and all the while his words haunted her.

I will be watching you…

Molly leaned forward pressing her head against the wall for support as she tried to take stock. How the fuck had this happened? One moment she'd been finishing up from a successful day meeting and greeting her readers, the next she'd been attacked by a group of thugs wanting to do God knows what, and now this. She was captured, caught up in the whims of this Connor, and subject to whatever dark fetishes he may desire. A shudder ran through her body as she considered her plight. Here she was, standing horribly exposed in this God forsaken place, her bottom having just been reddened by this complete stranger, and her hands and feet both bound in denigrating ways.

She was in serious trouble here, and she knew it. Molly's eyes closed as she recalled how her own body had responded to the spanking. It had betrayed her, making her wetter than she'd been for the longest time, and now Connor had noticed. She wanted to cry, she wanted to scream, yet she did neither. Instead, she absorbed the fresh frustration which whipped around her body, swallowing back the ridiculous humiliation of her current predicament. Her arms were beginning to ache, and she lowered them a little to relieve the pressure. He'd said that he'd be watching, but how can that be true? Connor wasn't even here, was he?

Slowly, she turned from her place in the corner, her eyes darting around the empty room. He definitely wasn't here, that was for sure, so how was he watching her? The answer came to her then in a flash, the conclusion hitting her hard. There was only one logical way he could still be watching her, and that was with a camera. The son of a bitch had a camera in here – maybe more than one? Molly's gaze flew to the corners of the room, looking for clues that her deduction was correct. There were no cameras apparent, and it was difficult to tell without investigating the corners of the ceiling properly. As her eyes scanned the opposite corner, she could just make out a tiny black spot attached to the ceiling. That must be it.

Gasping, she spun back around, conscious that Connor could very well be watching her right now, and that she'd moved from her place facing the wall. *He had a fucking camera!* Tears welled in her eyes as the reality bit. He could be watching her now, and he could watch her any time he wanted to, jerking off to her every bound struggle. The realization made her nauseated, the power this man had over her now drowning her like a tsunami. Power play was one thing, and, yes, she'd enjoyed it many times in the past with consensual boyfriends, but this was different. This was not consensual and right now it wasn't fun or pleasurable. It was unsettling. Molly recalled what he had told her while she'd still been flung over his hard lap.

You belong to me now, Miss Clary...

And at this moment she believed him. Not in the romantic sense of course, but in the very literal sense that as things stood, Connor held all of the cards in this dynamic. Already he had taken her and punished her. He had her bound and on display, for what? Nothing more than his sick, perverted enjoyment, she presumed. The guy had even made her apologize for not calling him Sir, and thank him for spanking her. She shook her head as she remembered. She'd actually thanked him, God dammit! The nerve of him! No other man had ever achieved that in her thirty-seven years on the planet. Yet she swallowed as she realized the effect his authoritative show had had on her pussy. He'd aroused her; against all reason he'd managed to make her wet and horny. Molly pressed her thighs together as if to clarify the point, and there was the proof: her folds were hot, slick and wet, and flagrantly exposed for him to see whenever he wanted to. Her head fell forward slightly, her fingers catching in her hair behind her head. What was wrong with her? How could she find anything about this situation even vaguely arousing? Maybe she was as fucked up as Connor...

"Enjoying your corner time, Molly?"

Yet again, the abrupt sound of his voice made her jump, sending her heart racing as she twisted to see him in the doorway. He leaned against the wooden frame casually as he appraised her, one of his dark brows arching at his own question. Under his right arm she noticed a slim looking silver laptop.

"No, *Sir,*" she replied, her tone defiant for the first time since he'd spanked her.

Connor smiled at the response, pushing himself away from the door frame as he approached her slowly. Something about the advance seemed predatory and the knot of anxiety in her belly twisted as she assessed his cold stare. Perhaps the curt reply hadn't been so smart after all.

"That's pleasing to hear," he sneered as he neared her vulnerable body.

Molly tensed as he got closer, until she could feel his hot breath against the back of her neck.

"Because this is still part of your punishment, little lady," he went on. "It's not supposed to be enjoyable."

"Yes, Sir," she gasped in a low whisper, wishing more than anything that he'd just step back and give her some personal space. His proximity was more than uncomfortable, it was foreboding.

"Would you like to tell me why you moved out of your place whilst I was gone?" he asked, practically hissing into her left ear. "I thought you were going to be my good girl?"

Molly shuddered at the question, not just because she knew she was in trouble, but because the act was so disconcerting. Soft words whispered were usually associated with sensual, loving moments, not dark, intimidating ones like this. She pulled in another shaky breath as she replied, "I'm sorry, Sir." The words spilled from her now, with no real forethought or agenda. "I just wanted to look around the room. I never moved from my corner, I just looked around!"

Her voice was imploring and she hated the way it sounded, admonishing herself internally for such a pitiful display. Where was her wilfulness now? Where was her educated defiance? She knew the sorrowful truth well enough, and was well aware where they were hiding. She was scared, terrified really, of what this man would do to her, and she needed him on her side to survive this. Connor might be strong, but she was smart. She needed him to play nice, and that meant doing his bidding – being his *good girl*.

"Yes," he conceded, pressing his body right up against hers so that his trousers grazed her sore ass still on display between them. "That's true, but you were told not to move. My instructions were clear, weren't they, Molly?"

She could barely take a breath. He was so close now, his body almost flush with her own. The sound of her heartbeat was so loud inside her chest that she felt sure Connor must be able to hear it from such close proximity. "Yes, Sir," she replied, hearing the tremble in her voice. "They were clear."

"So, you disobeyed me intentionally?" he continued, and as he spoke, his hand appeared at her right hip, grazing a line past her suit jacket, up to her waist, and under her blouse.

Fuck, she thought, her body stilling like it was made of marble. Connor's touch was soft and gentle, and bizarrely it felt pretty good against her skin, but she knew she was in trouble. He was making that much obvious.

"No, Sir," she answered him, trying to compose herself enough to force a reply. "Not on purpose. I just..." She hesitated, uncertain how best to defend herself. "I just wanted to know..."

Her voice trailed away.

What was the point? There was no defense for this situation. Connor could do whatever he liked with her. Why even bother?

"You wanted to know where the camera was," he said, finishing her sentence for her.

She jolted at that, not expecting him to be so... logical.

"Yes," she replied, swallowing hard. "I'm sorry."

A dark chuckle was his only response, and it vibrated around her body as Connor's finger continued its path north until it reached the side of her bra. "I want this off," he told her, softly. "I want you naked from now on."

Panic rose in her chest like a heart attack, threatening to cut off her breath altogether. It seemed to take forever for her to force a reply, although in reality it was only a few seconds. "But—" she began, wanting to protest in the strongest terms.

"But, nothing," he snapped, cutting her off completely. "I told you already, you belong to me now. *All* of you." As he spoke, Connor's free hand delved south, brushing over the warmth of her punished behind. "Don't forget I know just how horny that spanking made you, little one. Whether you like to admit it or not, you love being manhandled this way, Molly, and we both know it."

Molly gulped, overwrought with her emotions. He was right. The sick bastard was right. She *had* enjoyed it, but what he proposed now was more than just a spanking. It was too much. She wasn't *his*... she wasn't anybody's.

"Please," she begged him, although no more words came to her lips.

The hand at her ass squeezed gently, massaging the firm flesh of her bottom. She panted at the way it ignited the sting of her spanking just as his right hand moved to cup the soft silky fabric cradling her breast.

"These are mine now, Molly," he repeated, squeezing both her ass and her breast to confirm the point. "Mine to punish and mine to view. You will be naked, so you may as well get used to the idea. Oh, and don't think I've forgotten your most recent transgression either."

She fidgeted in front of him, all too aware of his fingers at her soft, intimate flesh.

"You will be punished for moving from your corner without my permission," he concluded as his hands drew away. "But first, you will strip."

Chapter Fourteen

onnor drew away from the trembling woman, watching with a satisfied smile as she twisted to see his retreat.

"St-strip?" she mumbled, with large, shocked eyes. "You want me to strip... Sir?"

Molly looked so vulnerable that he wanted to rub his hands together with glee. This was exactly how he wanted her, defenseless and exposed. The fact that the punishment had also made her horny was an unexpected bonus, and one which caused his already engorged cock to swell larger. But that wasn't his primary objective. First, he had to break little Molly down, and then he wanted her to write for him.

"You heard me," he retorted with a smirk. "Corner time is over. Put your hands down and get those clothes off."

She obeyed at once lowering her arms, her fingers trembling at the front of her blouse.

His cock twitched as he watched her, and he blew out a large breath. "Turn around," he murmured from behind her. "I want to see you."

Molly spun to face him with surprising speed, a spark of defiance burning in her eyes once more. The expression stunned him, and for a moment they just stood motionless, staring at one another.

"Keep stripping, little lady," he commanded, lowering his voice in a deliberate attempt to make her jump.

Molly noted the change, that much was certain, her eyes flickering with a wave of uncertainty as her fingers resumed their work at the top button of her blouse, but there was still a bubble of rebellion in her expression, simmering there below the surface. Connor took a step toward the small woman in the corner of the room. He only moved a couple of inches, but the resonance of that movement was felt keenly. Molly flinched, her digits stumbling around the second button as she lifted her head to see him towering over her again.

"How long does it take to remove that smart little blouse, Molly?" he barked at her. "Do you need me to help you?"

"No, Sir!" she cried, shaking her head. "I can do it. I *am* doing it."

He could tell she was forcing the words out, making herself comply, despite her better judgment. Connor couldn't decide if the thought pleased him or not. He would mold this little lady into an obedient pet, one who would submit to him, write for him, and do whatever she was told, but he loved that little spark of fire in the woman. It would be a shame to lose her heat and fury altogether. Those were what gave her heart, that was part of what had drawn him to her in the first place.

"Good," he replied wryly. "Then let's speed it up."

Molly exhaled loudly, but she did as he asked, releasing the final three buttons as he stood over her. "I can't pull this off, Sir," she mumbled in a low voice. "Not with my arms bound this way."

Connor's lips stretched into a wide smile. "Of course," he agreed, closing the distance between them in one giant stride. "Let me help you with those ropes."

His large hands descended at once, making short work of the bondage which had contained her wrists during the humiliating spanking. "Don't forget your ankles are still chained, little one," he growled as he towered beside her. "I don't think you'd be stupid enough to make a run for it, but if you did, you wouldn't get too far."

His brow arched as he pulled the final rope from her flesh, and Molly's face blanched at the mention of her chains. "I'm not running," she whispered. "Sir."

He nodded at the answer, grinning at the way she corrected herself. "That's right, Molly," he told her. "You're not running, but just remember what I've told you. If you try to run, I will catch you, and when I do, I will punish you in the most unimaginable ways…" He paused, allowing his words to sink in as she flexed her wrists before him. "And I know you can imagine a hell of a lot, little one," he concluded with a sneer. "Now get that top off."

She peered up at his looming frame, eyeing him through her dark lashes. Her gaze brimmed with insubordination, and her fingers shook as she shrugged the smart jacket and silky blouse from her slim shoulders.

Connor scrutinized her thoroughly, watching the fabric fall away until it pooled on the ground next to them both. His eyes shifted back to her body, eyeing her pert breasts in their pale satin prison. He had imagined this moment so many times in his head, but nothing had prepared him for the reality. Christ, the woman was hot. He already knew what a great little ass she had, and now he could fully appreciate just how gorgeous her other assets were as well.

"Keep going," he goaded her. "I want you naked, remember?"

Molly blinked up at him, her face resigned. Evidently, she knew that she'd have to do as he told her, but it was also clear that she wasn't thrilled about the idea. *Well, tough shit*, Connor brooded. He wasn't here to babysit little Molly. He was here to dominate her, in any way he wanted.

Slowly, she slipped her toned arms from the small straps of her bra and reached around her back to unclip the hook. There was a moment when she stood there motionless, as though she could barely believe what was happening, and then she released the fabric, allowing the bra to fall away completely. Her tits were beautiful, and damn near perfect. Not too big and not too small, they were full and round, with wonderful nipples which seemed to bead under the weight of his stare.

"Very nice, Molly," he purred, allowing his voice to vibrate over the topless woman next to him. "I am going to enjoy having you naked around the place!"

Her eyes darted to his face, indignation rising in her expression. "Fuck you!" she hissed. "I am not yours to chain or display…"

She gasped as the words left her lips, her hands rising to cover her mouth as though she wanted to push them back inside. But they were out, and they had both heard them. "I'm sorry, Sir," she breathed as her fingers fell from her face. "I didn't mean it, I just…"

Her voice trailed away as she presumably clocked the look on Connor's face.

"Fuck me?" he repeated, that dark brow arching as he intentionally loomed over her. "Is that what you'd like, Molly? You want to fuck me?"

Connor pressed his body against hers, catching the length of her hair in his right fist so that he could hold her in place. Molly's eyes widened as the pain and restraint registered in her brain.

"No, I mean…" She blushed beautifully, her face coloring as Connor drew her neck backwards. "I mean, I'm sorry."

He held Molly in place, exposing her neck and pulling her to her tiptoes. "You will be little one," he told her in a menacing growl. "I promise that you will be…"

The intensity in his eyes made her flinch, and acting on some type of instinct, she tried to pull away, but his fist held her hair firm. "When I release you, you will strip out of the rest of those clothes and kneel before me. Have you got it, Molly? Do you understand my instructions?"

She nodded as best as she could, her eyes filling with water. "I understand, Sir," she replied, but her voice was barely audible over the sound of his racing heartbeat.

He glowered at her, before releasing his grip on the length of her hair. "Impress me with your obedience then," he ordered her wryly, taking a small stride backwards and folding his strong arms across his chest.

Molly pulled in a shaky breath, and for half a moment she just stood there before him. He watched as her nipples beaded into tight buds. Was she aroused? Did his show of strength actually turn her on? The thought was utterly tantalizing.

Slowly, she began to move, lowering herself to the ground as she removed the small socks at her feet. He'd taken her expensive looking shoes from her while she'd been unconscious. The heels on those things were so long, they looked fierce, and he hadn't wanted to leave her any obvious weapons which she could use against him. Molly rose on shaky legs. She offered him one final frightened glance, before easing the suit pants down the rest of her legs until they pooled at her ankles, held in place by the metal cuffs fastened there. Her small lacy panties landed on top of them as she paused, seemingly summating her position. Finally, she stood before him, gloriously naked apart from the clothes caught at her feet.

"I can't remove these, Sir," she explained in a small voice, gesturing to the jumble of clothes at her ankles.

Connor's eyes narrowed as he assessed her. Dammit, she was right. The chains were stopping the wad of fabric from sliding off her body. He pulled the ropes through his hands as he considered the conundrum. He'd have to remove those chains to get her completely bare, and bare, he decided, she definitely had to be. "Turn around," he ordered her.

She blinked at him, pulling her lower lip between her teeth, but she did at least comply. Shuffling awkwardly around the clothing caught at her ankles, she twisted right, spinning until she faced the corner again.

"Hands behind your back." He gave the next order in a deliberately low tone, watching her body shudder as the words registered.

"Please, no!" she whimpered, her face turning to meet his eye. "Sir, no!"

The scowl which met her made her visibly wince.

"I told you to turn around." Connor spoke slowly, keeping his tone soft and menacing. She obeyed at once, trembling as she forced her hands into the small of her back.

Connor grabbed them with his left hand, allowing the rope to drop to the floor as he dragged her wrists up her back in a split second. Molly yelped, but he held her tightly as he brought his right palm down hard against her nude bottom. The sound of the smack echoed around the room.

"Enough!" he barked at her. "You will do as you're told, and I will have silence, or you will be gagged. Consider this your final warning, Molly."

She mewled like a small animal, and the sound made his cock ache, but there were no protests. Her head fell forward after that, her will beaten – for the time being at least. He took a moment to compose himself after his outburst, closing the space between them again as he continued to hold her wrists behind her back. Molly was quiet, and seemed reasonably compliant, so he took the opportunity to enjoy this moment. Inhaling the scent of her hair, Connor bit back his smile. Molly Clary was here in his place, virtually naked and quivering at his touch. He must be fucking dreaming!

He bent slowly, ensuring her wrists were still contained as he reached for the rope which had landed on her trousers. Connor's face passed her reddened backside, and this time he couldn't suppress the grin which spread over his expression. He straightened up, passing the rope over her wrists, before he secured them behind her back again. She let out a low groan as the ropes pressed back into her delicate wrists.

"Sit on the bed."

He watched her responses carefully as the command resonated around her. Molly may be bound, but she'd already proven that binds did not guarantee obedience. He would have to keep a close eye on her. She ogled him in return, her gaze nervous, but she said nothing as she shuffled back toward the bed. As her slim calves met the bedding, she lowered her bottom tentatively to the covers.

Connor was smiling as he approached her again. He lowered himself into a crouch at her feet but made sure he was well on top of her so that she couldn't give him a swift kick in the process. Reaching into the small pocket at his hip he withdrew the tiny key which fitted her ankle cuffs. She stared at the thing wildly. It was probably the first time she'd even realized the metal at her feet needed a key to be unlocked. Connor moved fast. He unlocked her right ankle, ordering her to lift her leg so he could remove the clothing which pooled there. Once that leg was nude he refastened the metal cuff, admiring the length of her shins as he glanced up at her.

Molly's face was expressionless. She looked shocked, as though she simply could not believe this was happening to her. Good. The shock would buy him a few moments to get her naked and re-chained. Only then would he have her exactly how he wanted her. Connor shifted, turning his attention to her left leg. In just a few moments, this ankle was also free of clothing, and the metal cuff had been replaced around her flesh. All the while, she remained motionless, her breathing fast and ragged.

"Good girl, Molly," he told her. "Now, what else did I ask you do?"

Her gaze flitted to his face. "Kneel, Sir," she replied. Her voice was croaky, and Connor wondered if she was thirsty again.

He rose from his crouch, taking a step backwards to allow her room. "Do it then," he commanded. "Let's see you kneel."

Chapter Fifteen

er brain felt numb. There were sensations waiting to be acknowledged. She felt the sting in her ass and the burn in her cheeks, but more than that, she was absolutely aware of the humiliation of this moment. She was actually naked and chained in front of this guy – this sick stranger who had drugged and taken her against her will. Now he was demanding her to lower herself by kneeling at his feet. Molly shuddered reflexively. What the fuck was she going to do?

She raised her head to look at him. Connor's expression was dark and expectant, and the look of him made her belly knot in trepidation. She was going to have to do it. She'd have to kneel and do whatever he wanted, but God only knew what would happen next.

"Why are you making me wait, Molly?" he asked her in an impatient, curt tone. "Do you feel like you need yet more punishment?"

She shook her head fiercely, shifting from the soft covers to the threadbare carpet before she even answered. "N-no, Sir."

"I want you here," he ordered, pointing to the floor in front of his feet.

Molly drew in a shaky breath and shuffled over on her knees. She felt absurdly vulnerable like this. She was naked, and with her hands tied behind her back she was exposed. The journey was slow and excruciating, and she could feel the weight of his stare on her as she moved. Although she couldn't meet his eye, she was aware of the grin spreading across his face as she dragged herself forward. She felt his gaze devour her breasts each time they bobbed at the motion of her awkward movement. By the time she'd made the short distance to where Connor waited, her pride was hurting a lot more than her knees.

His hand rose to her face at once, and instinctively she squeezed her eyes shut. She felt the warmth of his palm at her neck, trembling as the hand shifted to her chin.

"Open your eyes," he instructed.

Molly obeyed reluctantly. She could see the lower arm which held her chin in place and beyond it the dark pants of her captor. She pushed her mind away from the thought of what may be waiting in there for her.

"I want you to listen to me now, Molly, but I do not want you to speak unless I tell you to do so. Do you understand?"

His voice vibrated over her head and she nodded slowly. "Yes, Sir."

"I know this is new to you. I know you didn't expect any of this, and you probably think you don't want it either, but your opinion is not relevant." Connor paused, and she could sense him eyeing her severely, but still she didn't meet his eye. "All that said, let me be clear. I will not tolerate your disobedience or your disrespect, and that outburst from you just now will absolutely not be accepted."

She gulped at his words, trepidation knotting in her belly.

"However frightened you are, you will never again speak to me that way. Do you understand?" Connor's voice was unrelenting.

She shook as she answered him. She hated it, but it was true. Her body trembled in an involuntary show of her terror as she knelt before him. "Yes, Sir," she replied breathlessly. "I'm sorry for the way I spoke to you."

She wasn't sorry. She wasn't even vaguely sorry, but he didn't have to know that right now. Molly knew she would have to do better at controlling her emotional responses if she was going to survive this ordeal.

Connor's gaze bore down at her. "I'm not sure that I believe you," he told her. "I'm going to need a show of obedience from you, Molly, to help me to believe." He paused, and the weight of his stare penetrated her face as his hand fell away.

She flushed beneath it, panting at how utterly helpless she was at this moment. This was exactly the sort of scene she'd penned in the past; a young heroine bound and powerless on her knees before her brooding captor. In those tales the scenario had always turned her on, and she imagined herself squirming in her seat as her fingers hit the black keys of her laptop. She *had* been aroused by the spanking, too. She hadn't wanted to be, but she knew she had been. But this wasn't fiction. She wasn't young, well not *that* young at any rate, and Connor wasn't brooding. He was freaking dangerous, a complete stranger who seemed to have studied just about every detail of Molly in excruciating detail. Had long had he been watching her, waiting for the opportunity to pounce? She swallowed again, wondering if she would ever get away from this lunatic.

"Are you going to do as you're told, Molly?"

"Yes, Sir," she whispered. "I'll try."

She didn't know if this was a lie or not. She didn't want to please him, but she needed to stay alive.

"That's good to hear," he replied, although his tone remained skeptical. "I want to believe you, Molly..." There was a hesitation, and Connor's hand rose to her hot face once more. Molly trembled as he cleared the limp strands of hair from her face. "I want this thing between us to work."

She gasped, only a small sound, but in the heavy silence of the room, it was more than obvious. *This thing*, is that what he'd said? What *thing* did he think was going on here?

"But first there's the matter of your punishment."

That made her glance up to meet his eye. She found his expression looming over her, a torrid mixture of lust and glee.

"P-punishment... Sir?" she stammered as the shock of his words radiated through her. Hadn't he just punished her with the spanking?

"Oh yes," Connor assured her, allowing his hand to fall from her face to her left breast. Molly watched in silent horror as her nipple beaded under his touch like an obedient little pet which had been trained to respond. A dark salacious smile spread over his face as he acknowledged her own body's betrayal. "You must be punished for the way you spoke to me, Molly. I need to reinforce the lesson."

Something about that expression made her want to run, made her want to hide, but in reality, she knew she could do neither. For the time being at least she really was his, bound and vulnerable at his feet.

"Please," she breathed. "Please don't."

She hadn't intended to beg, but the words were out before she could stop them. If she thought she'd been scared before, then she'd been wrong. This was fear. The knot of crippling tension in her stomach which made her want to double over in agony, that was terror, and with its arrival she found it impossible to be proud anymore. She was simply too terrified.

The hand at her breast shifted, initially cupping her flesh before pinching her bud cruelly. Molly yelped at the pain, her eyes darting to Connor's face for a response to her plea.

He glowered down at her. "I do like to hear you beg, Molly, but that's enough. You're mine, and I will punish you any way I see fit."

Chapter Sixteen

onnor took in the image of the trembling woman on her knees in front of him. He wanted to capture the look of her, and hold it in his memory for all time. She was clearly petrified of what he would do next, and she had good reason to be. Even he hadn't decided what fate awaited her.

And then – just like that – the idea came to him. He smiled menacingly as the plan began to formulate in his mind. He was one dark, twisted fuck.

"Since you were unable to control that pretty little mouth of yours," he started, "I'm going to make it my mission to do so."

He watched Molly's responses carefully, noticing the flickering fear in her wide eyes as his words registered. Her lips parted and Connor knew what she wanted to ask. She was going to inquire about how he intended to control her mouth, but wisely she thought better of it. *Don't fret,* he thought, grinning to himself. *You'll find out soon enough.*

Connor stepped around the bound woman before him, striding back toward the bed. Once he reached it, he grabbed the edge of the duvet and pulled it forcefully from its place over the bed. The fabric came away with ease, and he turned to see Molly's concerned expression as she watched him carry it into the middle of the room.

"Eyes ahead," he commanded her. She didn't need to know what he had in mind until her fate was sealed. Molly lowered her eyes, her expression sullen as though she wanted to protest, but slowly she twisted her head back toward the doorway.

Satisfied for the time being, Connor laid the single duvet out in the space beside Molly. The cover was old and faded, but it was perfect for what he needed today. He had the impression Molly wasn't going to complain about the soft furnishings. In fact, he'd make damn sure that she couldn't.

"Okay, little lady," he called out to her. "Shuffle that pretty little body over here onto the cover."

She shifted her weight as her glance fell over the duvet to her right. Her questioning eyes met his face.

"Now, Molly," he instructed in a brusquer tone.

She let out a long sigh before her knees began to move, and inch by inch she twisted and edged her way over to the waiting duvet. Watching her trying to move in his ropes and chains nearly took Connor's breath away. She could only manage small movements without the use of her hands, and the strain on her knees was written all over her pained expression.

Poor little Molly, he thought gleefully. *If she thinks crawling for me is tough going, she's going to love what's coming next.*

It took some minutes for her to make it to the centre of the duvet. Molly struggled on to the boundary of the cover, her knees fighting its corners as she edged herself on. By the time she had completed the journey, Connor was almost proud of her effort. Almost.

He took a step toward her. "Much as I love these breasts," he began, stooping to cup one and then both of them. "I'm going to lay you on your stomach for now."

Molly turned her head to meet his eye, and once again he thought she was about to speak. Those lush lips parted and she exhaled, but no words came out.

Clever girl, he thought, offering her what he hoped was a reassuring smile.

"Are you ready, Molly?" he asked, shifting his position to her rear. It pained him to leave her gorgeous tits, but they would have to wait. Right now, he had a lesson to teach. Gripping the back of her upper arms he pushed her body forward. Molly yelped as her bodyweight shifted, and in a flash, she landed on her belly. It was only Connor holding some of her weight which prevented her smacking her face against the covers, and her body shuddered as she settled onto the duvet.

"Now let's get this pretty hair out of the way," he mused aloud as he dug in his pocket for the small cloth-covered elastic band he'd put there especially for a moment like his.

Connor extracted it as he looked down over the bound and naked form of Molly before him. He shifted his body lower, squatting over her as he pulled her dark locks back into a scruffy ponytail in his hands. She mewled beneath him, squirming against her ropes as she twisted her head, trying to shake him off.

"Settle down," he warned her, intentionally lowering his tone.

She stilled at once, pulling in a shaky breath as he wrapped the band around the length of hair in his fist. With the ponytail complete he rose again, towering over her vulnerable figure as he assessed his handiwork. Well, it wasn't perfect, but it would have to do for now. Plus, he mused, he'd have plenty of time to work on his hairstyling techniques now that he had Molly for company.

"Now, that's better," he said playfully as he stepped over her thigh and came to stand by her head again.

She raised her eyes to try and see him, but from her position on the floor, it was virtually impossible. Connor smiled to himself, suppressing the waves of carnality seeing her there produced in him. He turned, his attention falling over the wooden dresser which waited at the wall behind him. Connor pulled out the second drawer slowly, his eyes devouring the look of all the wonderful toys and contraptions laid out before him. He'd been collecting items for Molly for months now, his old network of friends had been extremely useful in that regard. Connor was enormously proud as he surveyed the vast array of options available to him. Each drawer of the tall piece contained a different type of implement, but the one he selected now was home to his selection of gags.

"Time for your first lesson in mouth control," he told her as his right hand dipped inside the drawer and made its choice.

As he spun back to face Molly, he held out his chosen option, dangling the black leather in front of her. He watched excitedly as her eyes widened with recognition.

"No!" she gasped as he crouched down in front of her face. "I'll be quiet from now on," she promised. "I swear it."

Connor's cock swelled with enthusiasm. Christ, how he loved hearing the desperation in her voice. Was it possible that this was going to be even more fun than he'd imagined?

"I can tell you one thing, Molly," he cooed from over her head. "You will definitely be quiet now, for as long as I decide you should be, and this"—he dangled the gag just in front of her nose — "is going to remind you of what happens to you when you disobey or disappoint me."

He saw her gulp as the black plastic approached. "Open wide now," he called out, his tone taking on a sing-song quality. "It's time to take what's coming to you."

Chapter Seventeen

Molly was close to tears as she peered at the gag he held in front of her. She hated gags. Well, actually that wasn't true. What was nearer the truth was that she loved to hate them. There had always been a dark, depraved part of her that yearned to wear them – to be forced to wear them – just like this, but she'd kept that desire well buried. It surfaced sometimes in her books, her characters afflicted with the very worst of her taboo longings, but she never talked about them in real life. And she certainly never *let* anyone actually gag her.

But now here she was. Bound and naked, and Christ knows where, and this deranged lunatic was going to gag her. He was going to use one without her consent, and there wasn't a damn thing she could do about it. She eyed the black plastic as he dangled it over her face. It looked normal in most respects, if the word can be used to describe a device whose sole purpose was to forcibly silence a human being. The straps were black, and one end had a buckle which would seal it closed behind her head. Her gaze fell over the middle – the part which Connor intended to force into her mouth. Rather than a ball, or even a hole, there was a long black piece of plastic attached, which looked suspiciously like a dildo. Her mind reeled at the sight of it, her years of kinky research already telling her how this awful contraption worked. The plastic was to go into her mouth – down her throat – and it would stay there while the gag was attached. Forcing her mouth to be not only silent, but full.

"Open wide now," he called out, his tone equally annoying and patronizing. "It's time to take what's coming to you."

She watched fearfully as he shifted to his knees beyond her face. "Please," she panted again, barely able to pull the air in and out as cold panic took hold of her.

Unimpressed with her effort so far, Connor lurched forward, grabbing her ponytail with one fist and yanking her head back hard. "I told you to open."

Pain ricocheted through her at the sudden hurt, tears springing to her eyes as her face and chest were lifted from the duvet.

"But, I..." she began, but her words were cut short as the plastic descended.

Her words had given him the opportunity he was looking for, and he shoved the length of plastic rather unceremoniously into her open cavity as she started her defense. Molly squealed, writhing like a serpent as he pushed the intruder deeper into her mouth. Before she could comprehend the full enormity of her plight, the gag was already in place. Connor moved with lightning reflexes, the hand at her hair vanishing to capture the dangling strap, while his free hand darted from her mouth to grab the other side of the gag. He pulled them tight at once, preventing her from pushing the gag out of her mouth, and before she knew what had happened, she felt him securing the buckle at the back of her head.

She shook her head, furious at her predicament. Now she wasn't only naked and bound, but she was gagged, and in the most humiliating way. The plastic invaded her whole orifice, pushing her tongue flat and forcing her mouth wide, all at the same time. And worst still, there was nothing she could do to stop or prevent it. She was utterly powerless, a fact that made her pussy throb despite her horrid situation.

Her mind boggled. How could she find this exciting? How can any of this be arousing? Any yet, despite her anxiety, she knew she did, and if Connor chose to, he could ascertain as much for himself.

"Look at you," he purred as he stood over her writhing form. "You're fucking glorious, Molly, and finally I can keep that mouth of yours under control for a while."

She moaned around the plastic invasion, angry and disgusted at her treatment. Hot tears burned in her eyes as she imagined how she looked from his perspective. She was completely caught in his web now, and fuck only knew how she could ever get out of it, but somehow, she had to.

Connor laughed darkly in response to the guttural sounds emulating from her. He stood there motionless for a long moment, just watching her frustrated struggles. Molly was aware of him in her peripheral vision, and she knew he was watching her. She couldn't see his face, but she envisioned that smug smile plastered all over it, and somehow, she knew he was enjoying the sight of her powerlessness. *This* is what he wanted. This is what got him off. In fact, her show was probably making him hard even as she fought against the ropes.

Fuck.

The realization made her still for the first time since Connor had forced the gag into her mouth, and a low sob caught at the back of her throat.

"Stopped fighting already, have you?"

The sound of his voice interrupted her internal wretchedness, and she tilted her head toward it. Connor's intonation suggested he was surprised at the observation, if not disappointed. She lowered her face into the soft cover before her. It was the first time she'd relaxed her neck since the irritating plastic conquered her mouth. She had no intention of trying to respond to his query, and at any rate, she knew she couldn't. She dreaded to think how humiliating her voice would sound with this awful gag in place, and there was no way she was going to give him the satisfaction of finding out.

"Fine," he said, and this time she definitely heard his displeasure. "Then you can stay there for a while and think about controlling your tongue, because as this lesson will teach you, if you don't control it, then I will..."

There was a pause, and then the sound of his heavy footsteps moving in the direction of the door. Molly turned her head toward the exit, able to see him approach the doorway.

"Don't forget I'll be watching," he told her without looking back.

She stared as he walked out of view, leaving her miserable and alone.

Chapter Eighteen

ime. There never used to be enough of it. She had always been late, running from one appointment to the next, aware of each new deadline as it loomed over her. As Molly lay there, she remembered those deadlines. She remembered Hannah, and the long 'to-do' list they had for the next month. They were all still out there. Her next two books were due back to the publisher within weeks, and as the ropes dug into her wrists, she realized for the first time, she wasn't going to meet those targets anymore. Not unless something changed. Not unless she could get out of here.

Time here, in this small room, was quite the opposite of time in the real world. Here time was protracted. Seconds could fill whole hours and minutes felt like days. That's how it was as she lay stomach down on the old duvet, her wrists bound tightly behind her back and her mouth stuffed with the revolting gag.

Which makes you really wet.

She ignored the small taunting voice in her head which goaded her with its half-truths. Yes, she realized miserably, she may be wet, but that was irrelevant. This was not some pretty fairy tale. This was real life, and Molly had been taken, drugged and stripped. God only knew what else this Connor wanted to do to her, but the thought made her insides clench for all the wrong reasons.

What is it he had told her? He wanted her to write for him. Molly snorted, shaking her head at the idea. Write for him? She had about ten manuscripts at home which required her attention right now, and this crazy guy wanted her to write for him?

She lifted her neck again, peering around the room as best she could. She tried not to think about the bedding she was lying on or how dirty it looked. She tried not to think about the slight wheeze in her chest, or how long her lungs would hold up without her asthma drugs. She tried not to think about how ridiculous she must look as she squirmed. Or how the sick fuck was probably watching her right now through the camera in the corner right above her head, jerking off as she struggled. Instead she applied her focus to something more productive. Getting up from this absurd position. She may not be able to remove the gag with her hands bound, but her feet were still broadly free. If she rolled herself onto her back, then it was just possible she could at least sit up. Her abs were reasonably strong from years of pilates, and she reasoned it must be worth a shot. Sitting would be significantly less humiliating then rolling around the floor like some sort of stuffed pig at a medieval banquet.

Molly didn't waste any more time thinking about it. Instead, she acted. It felt good to actually move after goodness knew how long lying on the floor, and with one concerted effort she rolled herself left. She landed on her back against the thin carpet, but her bound wrists made the transition much harder than she'd imagined. As she moved, the chains at her ankles rattled. The sound reverberated deeply within her, reminding Molly that she was a prisoner here. She closed her eyes at the indignation of the whole thing, willing herself the strength to keep going. Panting against the large plastic in her mouth was all the more overwhelming now that she was on her back. *Get up,* she told herself. *Get. Up!* Engaging her toned stomach muscles, she did just that, rising slowly until she was sat upright at the far end of the duvet.

Relief coursed through her, and she wriggled her fingers behind her back. Even a few moments like that – with her whole bodyweight pressed into her bound wrists – had sent the sensation fleeing from her digits, and it was good to get some of the feeling back in them. She wanted to whoop at the small victory, but the gag made that practically impossible. Instead, Molly edged herself backwards, inch by inch, until her back rested against the side of the bed. Her chest heaved at the effort, and at how uncomfortable she still was, bound and naked in this strange place. Instinctively she glanced down at her naked breasts, watching the rise and fall of her chest. As she did, she felt drool collecting at the front of her gag. Molly jerked her head back up immediately, but it was already too late. Unable to swallow, she felt the saliva as it slipped from her open mouth, beginning its descent down her chin.

She sobbed unhappily, imagining just how she looked. She was a writer for fuck's sake, it was her job to imagine every excruciating detail, and she didn't need a mirror to see herself. Molly knew all too well just how humiliating this scene was. She rolled her right side against the edge of the mattress, eyeing the camera in the far corner. Was Connor watching her now? Had he seen her agonizing progress from the floor to the bed? The knot of tension tightened cruelly as she considered for the first time just what he might think. Would he be angry that she moved without his permission? Would he punish her even more? She glanced down her nudity miserably. She was already gagged, bound and naked, and had been soundly spanked. What more could he do to her?

The sound of footsteps outside drew her attention, and her heart began to race out of control. Eyeing the room around her she considered her options. Maybe she could make it to her feet, but even then, where could she go? In her panic, another pool of saliva made its way south, hitting her chest, and already she knew it was too late. She could hear his heavy footfall as it approached, and she knew what they meant. All too soon, she would have the answer to her questions. She would know what he thought about her little escapades, and exactly what he intended to do about them.

Chapter Nineteen

Connor entered the room, his towering presence in the doorway casting a long shadow which hung over the trembling woman. Of course, she was trying not to tremble, he could see that. Her face was impassive, her eyes ready to meet him, but beneath the steely exterior, he could see the tension in her body, the rapid intakes of breath and the flicker of fear beneath those long lashes.

"What's been happening here, Molly?" His tone low and foreboding.

Naturally he already knew the answer to his own question, since he'd been watching her antics with interest from his laptop in the kitchen. The question was rhetorical in many ways, and yet he did expect an answer. Locking eyes with Molly for a long moment he smiled. She was still nicely gagged, and as such, quite unable to respond regardless. His answer would have to wait.

She gulped in front of him, her eyes darting around his face as she presumably tried to decide how much danger she was in. Connor shifted from his place in the doorway, approaching Molly slowly.

"Naughty little Molly," he cooed from over her head. "You can't even behave yourself when you're being punished, can you?" By now he was towering over her body and acting on some type of reflex, Molly drew her knees up in front of her body.

"Look at me," he commanded, his voice less playful than it had been a moment ago.

Duly she obeyed, her widening eyes telling him that she was more than aware of the imminent threat. He held her gaze as he slowly lowered himself into a crouch by her right side. As his large hand neared her face, Molly recoiled, but still his palm continued its path, until it landed gently at her cheek.

"You are so perfect like this," he whispered to her, as though he was her tender lover instead of her captor. His fingers traced a line around the outside of the gag, his gaze burning into her face as he began the circle for the second time. "After all, Molly, you don't need your mouth to write for me. I can keep you gagged a lot if it pleases me…"

The evidence of her panic was clear as Connor's voice trailed away, and her expression made him hard again. She shook her head from side to side, forcing his fingers from her open lips as she moaned around the plastic.

Oh, fuck. That noise. The sound she made through the gag was almost enough to make him come on the spot. Connor drew in a deep breath before he responded in his usual wry tone. "You like the sound of that?"

Molly shook her head again, even fiercer this time, and he saw the tears burning in her eyes.

"How do you like your gag?" he continued, ignoring her pleas. "I chose it for you especially, Molly." He paused, eyeing the black plastic which was held tight in her mouth. "*Restrained* was actually the inspiration for this purchase, so in a way, you chose the gag."

He laughed at the trepidation in her eyes. Evidently, she had not been expecting one of her own bestsellers to be the muse for this moment. "I remembered how much Claire enjoyed the gag in that book," he went on, "and also how it helped her gag reflex to have the dildo in her mouth all the time."

Connor paused, throwing her a salacious wink and from beside him the woman began to pant. He surveyed her for a moment, before the hand at her chin fell to her exposed tits. They pebbled immediately at his touch, and with her wrists still bound and out of the way, there was literally nothing she could do to prevent him from exploring her wonderful curves.

"I was going to release the gag so that you could begin our story," he told her. "But in light of your recent actions, I think not."

He recalled the look of Molly as she'd struggled against the bondage. When she'd forced her body onto her back, revealing her pert breasts, he'd completely lost it. As he fisted his cock to satisfaction, it had been the image of those tits that he'd imagined coming over. They were perfect. He pinched the nipple in his hand as if to prove the point, the stimulus eliciting a groan from little Molly as she shook her head again. Apparently, she wanted the gag out.

"What's that, Molly?" he asked her, playing with her tightening bud a little more – just because he could. "You want to keep the gag in whilst you work?"

Molly shook her head harder, crying openly now. "Noooo," she tried to call, but the sound was hopelessly muffled around the plastic dominating her mouth.

"I agree wholeheartedly," he said, smiling at her wretched response. "Naughty girls who cannot stay where they are put can enjoy their penance a while longer."

With those words he rose, leaving her sobbing as he crossed the duvet to his favorite dresser. This time he opened the third drawer down, eyeing the extensive collection of restraints purposefully. Selecting another set of long chains, which matched the ones at Molly's feet, he turned and wandered back to her.

"Eyes on me now." His tone was suddenly curt, and it seemed to catch her by surprise. Her tearful gaze fell over him, her eyes catching sight of the new chains in his right hand.

"It's time for you to do some work now," he told her in no uncertain terms. "I was going to let you work from your lap, but since I apparently cannot trust you, I have had to rethink." He paused, watching as her chest rose and fell frantically at his words. "Instead I am going to offer you a chair, but since you're so keen to move, I'll be keeping you chained. And the gag stays in…" Connor took a stride in her direction, dropping once again so that he was eye to eye with his captive. "Do you understand?"

Molly's eyes were full with tears as she began to nod. He watched as the tear drops fell, meeting the pool of saliva now collecting at her chin. She looked amazing, and he hoped the cameras would be getting a decent shot of all the action. Just in case, he slid his mobile phone from his trouser pocket, activating the camera with one swipe and holding it out in front of her. She watched, wide-eyed as he took a sequence of images, starting at her gagged face, and lowering down the length of her naked body to the chains at her feet.

Damn it, she was so hot like this. Too fucking hot.

Chapter Twenty

Molly sobbed as he set about organizing the room. Her head throbbed in pain as he rushed from one place to the next, panic gripping her chest as he produced what looked like a dining room chair. There was nothing particularly disconcerting about the seat, but she hated what it represented; that was her next source of indignation – her next prison.

Connor arrived then with a small table. It seemed like it belonged to a nest, but it was just big enough for the laptop he'd brought earlier to rest upon. He turned to her, seemingly satisfied with his arrangements for the time being.

"On your feet," he ordered.

Trying to ignore the pounding in her head, she shifted her legs beneath her and steadied herself against the mattress as she found her feet. Standing it seemed, was not such an easy pursuit without the use of your hands, and she felt shaky and uncertain as she finally stood before him.

Connor eyed her suspiciously. Evidently what little trust he had in his captive had waned considerably after her recent performances. Slowly he approached, rounding her left side and spinning her body toward the waiting table and chair.

"I'm going to untie these ropes now," he told her in a low tone. "Don't worry, little Molly, there'll already be new chains in place before the ropes disappear, but you will have more freedom."

She pulled in another breath as a new barrage of drool cascaded down her chest. Shuddering with mortification, she listened hard, hearing the sounds of the chains she'd seen him with earlier, and then acknowledging a cold metal cuff as it slid around her right wrist. There was a hard tug against both arms. Hard enough to jerk her body backwards a little, and she gasped as best she could around the horrid plastic intruder still lodged between her lips.

"Now the ropes can come off," he announced dryly, "but just you remember what happens to little girls who piss me off."

She squeezed her eyes shut at his warning, holding her breath as the tight binds at her wrists finally fell away. The relief in her arms was immediate, and as her left wrist fell to her side, Connor slid the metal cuff over it, locking it into place. Even though she was still in bondage, she felt an unlikely gratitude for the chains, and the movement they permitted.

"Sit now," he told her, and his arm appeared at her shoulder, insisting upon her obedience as it guided her to the hard, wooden seat.

Molly sat down gingerly. As she assessed her place in the room, the table appeared in front of her. Connor tucked it neatly into position, switching on the laptop. Blinking around her Molly realized something. The table may be small, but it fitted over her legs perfectly, and the chair, while clearly unrelated to the table in anyway, was just narrow enough to slot within its confines. It was obvious her captor had been planning all of this for a very long time. Every last detail had been thought-through, every moment of her captivity was of his choosing. The realization made a new low panic reverberate through her. It began in the pit of her belly and resonated outwards until she acknowledged the sensation in the tips of her fingertips. Her abduction wasn't *bad luck*. Connor was no opportunistic kidnapper. He was a calculated one, and a man who'd spent God knows how long planning this crime.

"Let's get you set up."

His low tone vibrated over her right shoulder, and in a flash, two strong arms appeared on either side of her body as Connor leaned over her. He logged on quickly, producing a new word processing document for her in a matter of seconds. "There you are," he crooned, tilting his head to gaze down at Molly.

She could see him clearly in her peripheral vision, although she didn't turn to meet his gaze. She had no desire to do so.

"Lift your hands, Molly," he ordered softly. "You should be able to use the keyboard with no issues."

She obeyed miserably, already knowing that she'd find he was right. She imagined him sitting in this chair before her, experimenting with lengths of chain as he ascertained exactly how to contain her. Predictably she found he was correct. Her wrists were exactly the right distance apart and she was able to type freely.

"Now write."

He pronounced the command like an edict, and for the first time she twisted her head to glance up at him.

What should I freaking well write? She thought as she glared at his strangely handsome face.

Connor smiled at her expression, as though he had always expected it. "Isn't it obvious?" he answered her, although she had not asked any question out loud. "You write our story. Write the story of our time together, how we met, how I took you, and everything that has happened to you since. You can conclude at this moment – the moment where you first begin to write."

His tone was triumphant as he concluded and Molly's face fell back to the blank screen causing another pool of spit to fall.

"Oh, and Molly," he added.

His tone made her heart pound even faster and she tilted her head slightly to acknowledge him.

"Don't even think about not writing what I've asked for. This is your role – this is why you're here – and I have a special punishment in mind for naughty girls who don't do their job properly."

She gawked at him, trying to process his words. *A special punishment.* Something worse than this?

"Now, write," he prompted her again. "You have one hour, and then I'll be reading the start of our masterpiece."

Chapter Twenty-One

He watched her work in silence, taking in everything about the spectacle. Connor had dreamed of this – this exact moment – for longer than he cared to recall. Since the first time he'd picked up one of her books, he'd known. He knew this woman was meant for him, perfectly aligned to his needs and preferences, and he knew he had to have her. More than that though, he knew he had to have her write for him – for both of them.

Now, as his eyes fell over her heaving chest, the curve of her delicious breasts and the plastic still forcing her mouth wide open, he felt euphoric. *He'd done it!* The first stage of his plan was in effect. Molly was here, and despite a few minor infractions, she seemed reasonably compliant. And she was writing – that was the important part – he actually had her writing the beginning of their story!

He checked his watch again, noticing how she flinched at the sight of it. A smile spread across his face as he realized just how much she was hanging on his every deed. She'd been at it for a little over forty minutes, and that meant she had about twenty more to go. Time to spring the next part of his plan into action. Connor rose from his place in the corner, his eyes never once leaving Molly. Her chains knocked against the wood at his movement, her breathing accelerating as he approached. He wandered to the back of the chair, reading a few lines over her shoulder.

...forcing the plastic gag into her unwilling mouth...

His cock hardened as he read, and simultaneously his memory was drawn back to the exact moment she described.

"Good work, Molly," he cooed, leaning over her chained form. His body made contact with hers, and the pitter-patter of plastic keys went quiet as her fingers stilled. "No, don't stop," he told her urgently. "You have twenty more minutes, and I want you to use each and every one of them.

She nodded, and he inched right to watch the line of saliva which collected under her gagged mouth, falling to her chest. His eyes swept over the area, which was now awash with trails of her own drool, all running down to slip over her wonderful breasts.

Fuck.

She was too much. He'd have to take a moment to enjoy himself, he simply had no choice. His arms slid around her shoulders and both hands roamed her chest. She tensed as they made contact with her breasts, but her digits began to type again. Connor inched forward, cupping her weighty breasts in his palms for a moment before massaging them both roughly. Molly moaned into the gag, but it wasn't clear if the noise was a sign of complaint or appreciation. It didn't matter either way of course; she was his now, and she would have to get used to the fact.

The scene continued in weighted silence. Connor's large digits worked over her nipples, crunching the swollen buds in slow rhythmic torture as her fingers fell over the keys. His arousal swelled painfully inside his pants, and if he wasn't mistaken, it seemed as though Molly's breathing had become even more labored as his caresses turned to pinches. His little captive was turned on.

Connor's gaze fell over her nape and down the soft flesh of her chest to where his hands worked at the swell of her breasts. Molly was beautiful and he already knew how talented she was. This tale – their tale – was going to be perfection.

At some point, her fingers stopped, and the sudden hush drew his attention back to the screen. His eyes devoured the final paragraph, widening as he concluded. She had apparently indeed written everything he'd subjected her to so far, finishing with a graphic description of how his fingers felt against her tits.

"All done, Molly?" His tone sounded husky with his own arousal, and the timbre surprised him.

She nodded, sending yet another rush of saliva falling south.

"Good girl," he murmured, trailing an invisible line over her right cheek. Both of them had turned a satisfying crimson color. "Of course, I'll be reading it soon to check just how good your writing is, but I don't have any concerns on that front. We both know how great you are, little one."

Molly's eyes blinked at his words, her breathing coming out hard and fast as she processed them.

"But first, let's attend to your needs, Molly," he paused, considering her intently. "You've had that gag in a while now, and I bet that jaw is starting to ache?" His finger dropped to her chin as he spoke, rubbing the aforementioned jaw tenderly. "Would you like me to remove it, Molly?"

Molly stared up at him, her happiness at the possibility evident from her pretty eyes alone. She nodded slowly, as though she didn't want there to be any doubt on the subject.

Connor smiled, and chuckled lightly. "Try some words," he told her. "I'd like to hear you reply. Do you want me to remove the gag?"

Her gaze narrowed at his answer, but a muffled string of mumbles followed, each consonant sounding much like the next with her tongue forced flat under the plastic of the gag. Connor's smirk turned into a wide grin at the noise, his cock throbbing impatiently as though it had independent plans to follow the gag's dildo into her throat. Her inability to respond properly was so bloody satisfying, he wanted to call out in celebration. But he didn't. Instead, he watched her with a broad smile plastered all over his face.

"I'm going to assume that was a 'yes please, Sir?'" he asked wryly.

She nodded furiously, her face burning an even brighter shade of scarlet, if that were possible.

Poor little Molly, she so utterly belonged to him at this moment. She was so helpless and fucking adorable. He couldn't wait to get inside her.

"Okay then," he replied at last. "Since I know you've worked hard, I'm going to assume you've done a decent job, and remove this for you." He sauntered around to the back of her again as he spoke, his fingers already playing with the tight buckle which held the plastic gag in place. Seeing a few strands of her hair had caught within the leather, he first removed the band, releasing her ponytail. Within a few more seconds, the black leather was unfastened and he guided the strap forward, tugging the gag out of her mouth.

There was a guttural moan as the length of black plastic left her throat and a rush of remaining drool followed it. He caught the leather in his left hand and threw the gag toward the duvet beside them. There would be time for cleaning up later. First, he had a little captive to attend to.

"How's that?" he asked her in an almost patronizing tone.

Connor watched as she opened and closed her mouth a few times before answering. "Better, thank you, Sir," she replied in a hoarse whisper.

"Good," he replied, pleased that she had recalled the correct way to address him. "And can you remember why you were gagged in the first place?"

Her gaze returned to him fleetingly before she looked away to the chains at her wrists. "I..." She hesitated, apparently unsure how to continue.

"You, what?" he prompted her, trying to control his own ragged breath at the excitement of this moment.

"I was rude to you," she said at length.

Not quite what he was looking for, he mused, but still it was good enough. For now.

"Right," he replied immediately, his finger hooking under her chin and pulling her face up to meet his eye again. "And now you know what will happen to you each and every time you are."

Chapter Twenty-Two

The relief at having that thing out of her mouth was indescribable. Molly wanted to cry with joy, but she didn't. She dared not give him the satisfaction. Instead, she sat still, stretching her aching jaw as he continued to lecture her about what would happen the next time she was rude to him.

When he stopped talking, his large hands brushed her smaller digits away from the keyboard, and she watched mute as he saved the story to the hard drive. Molly swallowed, thrilled beyond belief to be able to do so again without the humiliating drool landing all over her. As he drew back, he turned to look directly at her. They were now only a couple of inches apart, and the proximity made her heart race.

"It's time to feed you," he announced, his tone softer than she'd expected.

Molly gaped at him, unthinkingly. *Feed her.* What was that? It made her sound like an animal. She pressed her thighs together reflexively as the analogy crossed her mind, and not missing a trick, his eyes flitted to the small action.

There was a pause as he presumably considered the deed. Molly held her breath, uncertain if it was fear or arousal which was leading her actions now.

"Are you hungry, Molly?" he asked eventually, although the question seemed loaded with double meaning.

She was practically panting as she replied, his face was so close that she could feel the warmth of his breath against her skin. She got a waft of the scent, the smell of spearmint washing over her as his face broke into a new smile. Clearly, he knew what effect all of this was having on her. The guy was playing with her, and to make it worse, it seemed she was actually excited about the prospect.

"I haven't eaten for a long time, Sir," she admitted.

Connor's smile widened. "Then let's do something about that," he replied, his gaze soft yet determined. "And while you eat, I'll be reading our story so far."

He vanished from her view in an instant, snapping the laptop closed, before wandering to the dresser behind her. Molly gulped out of instinct. Whenever he went to that piece of furniture, he returned with something ominous, and she trembled at the thought of what might be next. Connor might seem gentle for the time being, but he had already proven he had the means and the inclination to inflict fear, pain and humiliation on her.

She heard the sound of the metal before he returned, and her mind began to run away with all of the possibilities. More chains perhaps, like those which were already fixtures at her wrists and ankles, or some other type of restraint? Connor didn't make her wait long. He paced toward her soon enough, presenting her with the latest *gift* from his drawers.

Molly's eyes fell over the thing, and she shuddered. It was another chain after all, similar to the ones she already wore, but not the same. It was different for one reason. This chain was attached to a leather collar, like the sort you'd put on a small pet, only larger. It even had a small, shiny metal tag where the pet's name could be engraved. She swallowed, aware that her eyes were widening as she glanced up to see Connor's grinning face.

"You like?" he asked her, merrily. "I hope so. I had it made especially for you."

A wave of nausea rolled over her body as his words resonated. He'd had this made for her?

"Look," he commanded, and as he spoke, he twisted the metal name tag, bringing it up to meet her eyes. Engraved onto the fine-looking silver plate, she realized there was already a name. A name which made her heart stop beating for one long moment, before it raced completely out of control. The engraved letters spelled out the name, *Molly*.

Connor ran his fingers over the metal proudly as his gaze darted from his captive to the collar in his hands. "What do you think?"

Molly was almost shaking as she lifted her chin to reply. "Y-you made this for me, Sir?"

Every instinct in her body was in free-fall as panic spread throughout her limbs. The guy had made a collar for her, and he'd already shown his willingness to keep her bound and restrained. The knot in the pit of her belly tightened until it became unbearable, making tears spring to her eyes. She knew exactly what this meant. It meant he wanted to collar her and keep her chained up in this place, like a fucking animal. It meant Connor hadn't just taken her to write his damn story, Connor wanted to *keep her*.

"Yes," he answered her, his tone excited as he presented the leather and chain to her like it was a bunch of flowers. "I know how much you fantasize about being leashed and chained, Molly. It's a recurring theme of your last five novels, and I have to agree, I rather like the idea too."

Her eyes fluttered shut at that, as though blocking out the sight would somehow alter the reality. Of course, this guy was like some sort of deranged super fan. He had read seemingly each and every title she'd ever penned, and he was right – the last few had concentrated on the subject of pet-play. It was also true that the idea turned her on, but much like the spanking, it was something she'd never even considered outside the realms of her stories, let alone in some completely non-consensual forum like this.

"Molly!" Connor's terse tone snapped her from her thoughts, and she opened her eyes to find him staring down at her severely. "You will keep your eyes open unless I tell you otherwise," he commanded, lowering his voice as he gave the instruction.

She nodded, sniffing a little as the weight of her fate landed upon her. This guy, who'd already stripped her of any dignity, was now going to collar her and leash her like an animal. Molly pulled in a long breath as the notion invaded her mind, willing herself to stay calm. He was right, she was hungry and she did need to eat. Food was part of survival, and she had to survive this ordeal.

"Good," he brooded, his gaze narrowing as he admonished her. "And now for the part I've been dreaming about. Now I get to put this collar on you."

If someone had asked her what she thought she would have done in a sick scenario like this, Molly would have told them all sorts of things. She'd have certainly purported some resistance, a protest or complaint as the leather slid around her neck. Maybe she'd even expected a fight. Her arms may be chained, but she had free reign to lift them after all, and she could use her hands, and possibly even the metal to her advantage. In reality, none of those things occurred. Real life, unlike fantasies, happened in an instant, and before she could barely pull in another breath, Connor had looped the collar round her small neck and had buckled it closed. He yanked at the metal chain attached to the D-ring now against her throat, and instinctively she lurched forward, yelping as the loss of control hit her.

Connor smiled at the sound, watching as she panted miserably, using her hands to steady her against the small table.

"Very nice," he crooned at her performance. "Now the feeding room is on this floor, but it wouldn't do to have you walk, Molly. In fact, I don't think you'll be walking for some time." He paused, laughing at his own dark joke for a moment, and all the while, she shook beside him, shock reverberating around her body at the things he implied.

"Down now." The order came at her like a slap, forcing her head up to meet his eye.

"D-down?" she stammered, as though she didn't understand the request.

"Yes," he said evenly. "Get down. And remember how you address me, young lady, or do you want to feel the sting of my palm again so soon?"

Molly shivered, fidgeting her tender ass against the hard wood beneath it. She most certainly did not want to experience anything like that spanking again. "No, Sir," she replied in a rush, yet still she didn't move as he wanted.

"I'm not a particularly patient man, Molly," he told her in what sounded like a low growl. "Is there a good reason you're making me wait?"

She gazed up at him, her eyes like saucers. "You want me on the floor, Sir?" she whispered, as though she couldn't wrap her head around the concept.

He smiled, a sentiment which did not reach his eyes. "Exactly," he replied, pointing to the spot he intended.

Molly swallowed hard as the ugly truth hit her. This was really happening. This man really wanted her by his feet. A sudden wave of emotion rushed through her body. She couldn't decide if it was blind panic or lust which overtook her, but something made her move. She slid from the chair, all too aware of the leather at her neck, and the rattling of the chains at her limbs as she fell to her hands and knees before him.

"Better," he said sternly. "But don't make me wait next time."

Molly's hair fell forward in a dark brown curtain around her face as she nodded. "Yes, Sir," she answered the towering giant beside her.

Connor gripped her leash, tugging at it to get her moving. "Now crawl," he told her matter-of-factly. "I want to see how my little pet looks in motion."

Chapter Twenty-Three

Despite the veil of hair which was swept over her attractive face, he saw the look of disdain in Molly's eyes at his suggestion. There was a moment when he considered pulling her back to the bed, hoisting her over his lap again and spanking that expression away, but he decided against it. If her behavior didn't improve, then he was sure he'd have that chance, but right now was not the time. Now, he finally had her leashed and chained, and he got to delight in the look and sound of Molly as she crawled gingerly into the narrow hall.

He noticed her eyes darting around the place as he led her onwards, but this wasn't a tour, and he gave her no time to acclimatize to her new surroundings. Instead, he commanded her to keep crawling as he stood on the worn cream carpet, eyeing the long limbs and reddened arse that slunk past his shoes.

Fuck, she was divine.

The look of her at his feet made him want to chain her to the landing bannister and come all over that disdainful expression. He squeezed his eyes closed momentarily, urging himself to be patient as he led her into the larger room at the end of the hallway, the one he'd converted into an upstairs kitchen. Standing by the entrance to the door, Connor drew her into the room by her leash.

"In you go," he ordered as she paused, her flushed face looking up to meet his eye.

She bit her lip, pulling it between her teeth as she obeyed, crawling onto the tiles of the kitchen. Connor moved in behind her, closing the door and using the top bolt to secure it. He had installed strong bolts onto all of the doors. This meant he could either bolt her in – or out – of any room he chose.

He drew her body inside, directing her to the far wall, where he'd assembled an array of large clothes hooks, designed for hanging coats or bags on. But there would be no clothing on these pegs, in fact, they'd be no clothing for Molly at all. She had no use for that now. He intended to keep the house warm and his captive naked – at all times. Connor approached the first hook, a large metal peg which had been secured into the wall and lifted the handle of her leash. He wrapped it around the hook twice, tugging it hard to ensure it couldn't slip from its place. The act shortened Molly's leash, forcing her in the direction of the counter, next to the radiator. He watched excitedly as her eyes fell over the other contents of her little corner, his cock bursting to life at her expression.

"Yes," he told her, as though he was able to read her mind. "That will be your bed when we spend time in here and you're not required for any other *tasks*." He emphasized the final word deliberately, enjoying the look of terror which swept across her face before her eyes darted back to the object in question. It was a large pet bed, perfectly soft and round. He'd chosen it carefully, knowing it would be as comfortable as it was denigrating.

"Get in," he commanded her. "Try it for size whilst I prepare food."

She froze at his words. He actually saw the tension creeping through her limbs. "You…" She hesitated, as though she couldn't even begin to process his order. "Sir, you can't be serious," she snapped, her head tilting up to meet his amused expression. The chain at her neck tightened as she moved, forcing her closer to the animal bed. It was obvious from Molly's eyes that she could see how much he was enjoying her predicament, and she was right. He loved every second of it.

"I am absolutely fucking serious," he retorted, and quick as a flash he swooped, walloping her bottom with his large right hand.

Molly yelped, darting away too late and ending up exactly where Connor had intended her to be – in the pet bed. Her face flamed as she collapsed into the thing, apparently mortified and beaten, all at the same time. As she settled into its soft confines, Connor steadied himself. He squatted close to her chained body, his eyes devouring the haunted expression on her face.

"Do you need another lesson in respect so soon, Molly?"

She swallowed hard, looking close to tears again. "No, Sir," she whispered, shaking her head for effect.

"And what about that mouth?" he continued, watching the way her nipples beaded into tight peaks as he spoke. "Do you need to be gagged again, because I'm sure we only just concluded a lesson about how to speak to me?"

His tone was light, but you wouldn't know it from Molly's face. She looked fearful, and distressed, but as he stared at her, he had to wonder if it wasn't her own response to his treatment which had disgusted her the most.

"Please no," she mumbled, raising her eyes to look at him. "I'm sorry, Sir, it's just this…" She paused, her eyes darting around the animal bed. "All of this. It's just too much." Her voice died in the back of her throat and was replaced with a low sob.

Connor shook his head at her, half amused and half aroused at her show of self-pity. "This isn't too much, little one," he cooed. "We're only just beginning you and me. But don't you worry, you'll soon get used to your new routines." He smiled at her, wanting her to know how happy having her here made him. "In the meantime, I suggest you learn to control that pretty mouth of yours, unless you want it gagged permanently."

She sniffed, nodding her head contritely. "Yes, Sir."

He straightened, satisfied for the time being that they had reached a level of understanding. It was time to feed his little pet, and he couldn't wait to see her response to what he had in store for her next.

Chapter Twenty-Four

Molly watched as he rose and sauntered away from her. Her eyes flitted around the room, but she could barely take any of it in. This, the chains, the gag, the pet bed, it had temporarily stunned her. Shifting in her spot as best as she could with the leash holding her in place, she took a better look at her so-called *bed*. Another sob caught in her throat as she surveyed it miserably. It was literally a fucking mattress made for a dog, and now she was supposed to use it. She shuddered involuntarily at the thought. It was like all of her most depraved fantasies and worst nightmares had collided, and Connor was the orchestrator of them all.

The sound of running water drew her attention from her pitiful place on the floor, and she looked up to see him standing by a kitchen sink. A sink? Why was there a kitchen sink here? This was the second floor. She knew that because she'd eyed the stairs as she was led in here just now. How many houses have fully-integrated kitchens on their second floor? She looked around the place, taking in the small dining table and chairs immediately to her left, and the line of kitchen counters running along the right wall. At the end of the units was a large, free-standing fridge and next to that, the small counter which her *bed* was positioned against.

"Here you are," he announced, and Molly's head snapped up to find him striding toward her again.

The old knot of tension furled inside of her in response. He was so big and so in control, while she was literally naked at his feet. As she inhaled a raspy breath, her eyes fell to the two bowls he held in his hands. They were large, round and metallic, and she gasped audibly as she acknowledged what they reminded her of; dog feeding bowls.

He came to within a foot of where she cowered, a wide grin plastered all over his smug face. Molly could make it out in her peripheral vision, and she wished with all her might that she could find a way to wipe that conceit from his expression, but right now there was an even bigger problem at hand. The bowls. Those bowls – animal feeding bowls – which Connor lowered on the floor in front of her.

"Here's your food," he told her gleefully. "And look what a kind Master I am. I've even included a drink to wash it down with."

Her eyes scanned the bowls just beyond her. The first looked like it contained water, while the second had what resembled scraps of chicken inside it. Her pulse pounded as she absorbed what this meant, and she could feel the blood leaving her face. He wanted her to eat from these things – actually eat from them – like a fucking animal. Anger rose in her like a powerful old friend, sending her eyes narrowing in Connor's direction.

What the fuck? Who does this? Who treats a person like this?

Fury grew in Molly's head, clouding her vision until she drew back against the radiator. She knew she had to contain this emotion. One more outburst and God only knows what this psycho would do to her as recompense.

"Something you'd like to say, Molly?" His tone was knowing.

She swallowed back the vast number of retorts which presented themselves to her at this moment. There were a great many things she would like to say, but she didn't think any of them would help her now.

"You want me to eat from these, *Sir?*" she answered at last, forcing herself to say the final word.

Molly glanced up to him, watching as he smiled down at her. "Oh yes," he told her. "I bought these especially for you. You'll have all of your meals from them, unless I decide to feed you by hand of course."

She wanted to balk at the mere idea that she'd take anything from his hand, but somehow, she resisted. Instead, she bit down hard on her lower lip until she tasted her own blood.

"Come on now," he commanded her as his towering frame loomed overhead. "Eat up. There might be more for you later if you're a good girl."

With those words he turned, sauntering away to the far counter where he flicked a switch on the shiny kettle which sat waiting on the surface. As he waited for the water to boil, his expectant gaze fell back over Molly and her face burned with indignation. How had this happened? How had she allowed this to happen? And now that it *was* happening, how could she ever survive this humiliation? Hot tears pooled in the corners of her eyes and she wanted to wipe them away, but the clanking chains at her wrists mortified her even more as she raised her hands.

Connor turned, busying himself with making a hot drink and with his attention elsewhere, Molly considered the bowls before her. What was she going to do? She was famished, her growling belly was evidence alone of this, but could she really lower herself to do this – to eat from these animal bowls? The worst of it was his attitude. Evidently, Connor actually expected her to be okay with this, to just let him chain her up and make her eat on her hands and knees from now on. A spike of rage rose within her again and for one dangerous moment she considered throwing the bowls over the floor. That would show him what she made of his food. Yet she was ashamed to admit that she was too scared to really do it. Molly had experienced a small taste of what Connor would do when he was pissed off with her, and in spite of his dehumanizing expectations, she had no desire to see that side of him again.

By the time she looked up, Molly was shocked to find Connor right there, towering over her. She jumped at his sudden proximity, disconcerted that she'd been so caught up in her private musings that she hadn't even heard his approach.

"Is there a problem?" he asked her wryly.

She glanced up to the smiling giant beside her. "I... I don't know if I can."

Molly gestured in the direction of the two, metal bowls, as though there could be any confusion regarding her meaning. Connor snorted at her performance, placing his mug down on the table beside him before turning his attention back to Molly.

"Don't then," he laughed, his British accent thick with offense. "If you think you're so special that you can't eat from the items I've provided, then you're in for a rude awakening. Know this, Molly, there won't be any crockery or cutlery coming any time soon. So, when you eat, it will be from your bowl. You're mine now. My little writer and my pet, and you'll be treated as such."

He paused, leaving his words to be absorbed. Molly's eyes blinked in shock as his tirade flew around her head.

You're mine now. My little writer and my pet...

Oh fuck, she thought miserably as her eyes crawled over the chicken once again. *He really means it. He's going to keep me here, like this, for as long as he likes.* A shiver passed through her at the realization, despite the close proximity of the warm radiator. *I have to escape* she decided, her gaze darting to the large bolt he'd slid into place when he'd shut the door. *I have to get out of here.*

Chapter Twenty-Five

I'm going to get the laptop," he told her casually, as though speaking to a grown naked woman in a pet bed by your feet was the most normal thing in the world. "And you seem a little flighty." He paused, eyeing her as he took a sip of his drink. Placing the mug back on the table top he continued, "Just to make sure you don't have any silly ideas about getting away, I'll help you stay put."

Connor closed the distance between them in one large stride, stepping over the food bowls before swooping down to Molly's level. She leapt back at his sudden approach, forcing her body back against the radiator, but he ignored her response.

"Get down here on all fours," he instructed, pointing to a spot by his shoes.

Molly watched him nervously, but he smiled as she complied, shifting her bodyweight slowly until her chained wrists appeared close to where he crouched.

"Very good," he murmured, his tone as patronizing as ever as he reached down in front of her body.

Molly recoiled from his roaming hand, but it made no difference. His palm grasped both of her tits on its route south, stopping to pinch both nipples until they hardened under his touch. Her buds weren't the only things which reacted that way, and Connor shifted his hips to accommodate the growing length stashed away in his pants. She mewled next to him, lowering her face at this latest indignity.

There was a weighty silence as his palm left her body and fell down, lifting the edge of the dog bed to reveal a metal D ring embedded between the tiles.

"I created this for just such a moment," he told the wide eyes which rose to meet his knowing expression. "I knew you'd be a little jumpy at first, and I wanted to help you out."

Holding the dog bed back with his right hand, Connor's left arm rose to the neighboring unit, opening a small drawer at the top. He fished about inside for a moment, before pulling a new length of chain from inside, all the while his gaze never leaving Molly. Her eyes flitted away, and she caught sight of the latest addition, watching as Connor brought it down to their level. He dropped the metal, his hand rising instead to the leather at her neck. Molly flinched as he slid a digit between the collar and her flesh, jerking her head forward.

"Hold still now," he ordered.

He raised his hand to the small D ring at her collar, unlinking the leash which held her in place, before quickly connecting the end of the new chain. All of this took place in a matter of seconds, and before Molly knew what had happened, she was attached to the chain in his hands.

It was at that moment she seemed to notice how much shorter this chain was than the first. At only about nine inches, she was helpless as Connor tugged hard, commanding her body down with it. Once she was in his desired position, he connected the other end of the chain to the D ring in the floor, effectively pinioning her body there by the neck. He stood, surveying his little pet, chained to his kitchen floor.

"Don't leave me like this, Sir," she pleaded, her voice heavy with obvious panic.

He grinned, stroking his aching erection through the outside of his trousers. "Don't worry, little one," he replied as he unbolted the kitchen door. "I won't be long. Now be a good girl and stay put. There will be severe consequences if I get back here and find you've tried to escape."

He heard her whimpers as he closed the door behind him, re-bolting it from the outside for good measure. Back on the landing Connor drew in a deep breath, adjusting his aching cock again. Damn it, he was so hard. He didn't know if he could take much more, but he knew he had to. It wouldn't do to frighten his new little pet too soon. He was smiling as he wandered to her room, collecting the laptop from the small table and returning to the kitchen door. The smile broadened when he put his head to the door and heard the small noises coming from beyond it. Molly was even starting to sound like a pet, and the thought did nothing to calm the throbbing need tucked away inside his pants.

By the time he'd unlocked the bolt and slipped back inside the room, she was practically hyperventilating. He pushed the metal back into place again, turning to watch her. Clearly, she was having difficulty with the idea that she was now something Connor could chain to the floor whenever it pleased him, but to her credit she hadn't tried to unclick the chain. It seems his threat had been sufficient to tame her this time.

"Well done," he crooned, approaching her slowly. He loved the look of her like this, physically cowering to him with her delicious behind forced into the air. "You finally did as you were told."

Molly blew out short pants of air as he ducked down beside her. He dodged the dog bowls still untouched where he'd left them, and brushed back her mane of dark hair to find her face flushed with effort. "Why are you doing this?" she gasped, her eyes imploring. "Why me, *Sir*?"

Connor chuckled darkly, noting the emphasis placed on the final word, but choosing to overlook it. For now. "Isn't it obvious?"

He stroked the side of her face as he spoke. Molly shuddered lightly at his touch, but the chain at her neck meant she couldn't retreat from him.

"No," she panted. "It isn't obvious to me. Please, just let me go. I don't know who you are or where we are, and I swear I won't go to the police."

The hand at her face slipped down as he took his time, intentionally torturing her further as he inched his fingers to her chin, before dipping them to the collar at her neck. Slowly, deliberately, his digits tightened at the leather and he heard the satisfying gasp which escaped her lips. "There's no going back now, Molly," he told her ominously. "I've been waiting for this moment for months."

He released the chain at her D-ring with his free hand while the other held Molly's collar in place. She raised her eyes nervously at the action, trembling as he reattached her to the leash still hanging from the coat peg above her.

"B-but, please," she stammered again, her eyes filling with fresh tears.

He took a moment to gaze into them, seeing a host of emotions flashing back at him. It was obvious that she was scared, terrified even, and she had good reason to be. Molly didn't have a clue how long he'd been planning this, or any of the depraved acts he intended for her, but the last few hours had probably given her a taste of what was to come. Her eyes also offered confusion and exhaustion. The drugs he'd given her were probably just leaving her system and she must be seriously dehydrated by now. He'd have to make her drink something, even if the food would take some more *persuasion*. And then below all of those other emotions there was her lingering arousal. It might not be the dominant sensation at this moment, but it was certainly there. Connor had seen the moisture pooling between her legs after her spanking and how Molly had responded to his gags and bondage. Whatever she told him, her body was enjoying the way he denigrated it. Of that he was certain.

"It's alright, Molly," he purred, intentionally softening his tone as he propped her chin up with the hand which had just leashed her. "I know you're scared right now, but all you have to do is obey me. Remember the rules?"

She nodded, her tits bobbing beautifully beneath her at the ferociousness of the motion. "Yes, Sir," she whispered in a barely audible tone.

Fuck. It's as though he was temporarily mesmerized by the look of his tear-stricken captive. How many times had he fantasized about this? About having her here, chained and compliant? And now that things were finally coming to fruition, he couldn't quite believe his luck. Except this wasn't luck, this was careful planning and precision.

"All you need to do is remember the rules." Connor's voice was harder now, more insistent. He stared at her frightened little face as he spoke, wanting her to understand. "Obey me, and write for me, and you will be fine."

He released her chin, watching her responses carefully as she drew back an inch or two. "Okay," she sobbed. "I'll write for you. I'll do what you say, but, I don't understand. Why me? Why have you chosen me, Sir?"

He could tell she was still forcing the word from her delicious lips, but it didn't matter. She was addressing him correctly, and she was obeying. And that made him happier than he'd maybe ever been before.

"I chose you because I love your work," he replied. "Because this is our story, and I need someone to write it for me. And there is no one better than you, Molly."

As she blinked up at him, he hoped his words were beginning to register.

Chapter Twenty-Six

That was the moment Molly began to understand. Up until then she had known she was in trouble – big trouble – and she had an idea that Connor had been conjuring this plan for a while, but this was the instance which crystallised it in her mind. This guy was like her super-stalker. He had apparently read and devoured every one of her words, convincing himself that since Molly was the author, she must *want* this, she must desire to be treated this way.

Time stood still as she processed the realization. He thought she'd relish this treatment, and so he'd concocted the whole damn thing. This house, with the upstairs kitchen, the cameras, the equipment, it was all part of his plan. And those guys who'd attacked her after the signing, had they been part of his plan too? She doubted it. Most likely their attack had forced his hand, compelling him to take her. She shuddered at the idea, a deed which made the face in front of her soften.

"Are you cold?" Connor asked, his voice offering genuine concern.

Molly blinked at him again, her head fit to burst with all the competing concepts and emotional responses. "A little, Sir," she whispered, watching his face as she answered.

It was a partial untruth. She had felt quite snug being this close to the radiator, but ever since he'd chained her to the damn floor her limbs had become cold again, as though the shock had resonated to her extremities. Either way, she much preferred this more caring side of Connor, and knew she had to exploit it if she wanted to survive until she could escape.

"I'll turn up the heat," he told her, rising from his crouch and striding purposefully away in the direction of the door again. On the wall by the exit was a small thermostat, which he nudged upwards. "That should help," he continued as he paced back to the table beside her.

"Thank you, Sir," she replied, feeling utterly ridiculous for thanking the man who had captured her against her will.

Connor sat at the chair nearest the door, smiling as he started up the laptop. "You're welcome, little one," he cooed. "Now, I need you to get that water into you, and eat something while you do. You'll feel better."

Molly's eyes flitted to him. Feel better? Was he serious? He expected her to degrade herself further by eating from a bowl on the floor, like a fucking dog, and somehow, that was supposed to make her *feel better*? She wondered how much of her fury shone in her eyes as she caught the small smirk which lit his face. *Fucking bastard,* she mused, watching him as he turned his attention to the story she'd been forced to pen. He must realize how she felt about this. How could anyone *want* to be treated this way? But even as she thought it, she remembered the plotline from her 2017 release, *Captured.* In the book, her heroine, Sandra, had been abducted by aliens and forced to live as a human pet, and she recalled the exact point in the book where they'd compelled her to eat from dishes on the floor. Molly also remembered how shamefully wet writing that chapter had made her. She felt the color drain from her face as the awareness dawned on her. Connor was emulating a scene from one of her own books, and now she was going to have to live it – *she* was Sandra.

A long sigh interrupted her internal monologue and she turned to see Connor watching her, a sardonic smile decorating his face.

"Are you thinking about Sandra?" he asked, his right eyebrow arching over those dazzling green eyes as he posed the question.

Molly heard the gasp leave her lips, although she had not commanded it. His query left her dumfounded. How the fuck could he have known that? "Ye-yes, I was," she responded, the shock evident from her tone.

"I thought so," he quipped, taking a slug of his drink. "The analogy wasn't lost on me, and fuck, I loved those scenes, didn't you?"

He looked at her intently this time, his eyes penetrating her nudity.

"I..." Molly hesitated, uncertain how to reply. What could she say? She *had* been turned on when she'd written those words, an awful lot as she recalled, but that didn't mean she wanted to be chained here and forced to re-enact them. Connor had no right to do this. Gazing into his unwavering stare, she knew she'd have to be honest. He'd sense she was lying about this, which would no doubt initiate some terrible punishment as a consequence.

"I enjoyed writing it, yes, Sir," she conceded with her own small sigh.

"I guessed you did," he replied, his eyes sparkling as he watched her conflict on the subject. "Your writing oozes arousal, Molly."

She lowered her gaze, aware that her face was flaming with embarrassment at his words. It was hard enough to receive a compliment usually, but naked and chained like this, it was practically impossible.

"Don't be ashamed," he ordered her. "I love that you enjoyed those things." Connor put down the mug as he spoke, and the sound of it hitting the wood captured her attention. "Before I read your work, I'd assumed I was the only one who'd be into this kind of thing, but talking to you helped me to realize otherwise."

Molly gulped at that. "Talking to me?" she repeated. "When did we talk, Sir?"

He grinned at her again, his expression faltering just slightly as though he hadn't intended to divulge so much information. "Online," he told her. "I've been following your social media for some time, and I've been a part of your reader group for months now."

She was panting again before he'd concluded. Part of her readers group? Holy fuck! That meant she'd already let this guy into her life in some way. She'd answered his questions in her pyjamas before she went to bed at night. The thought made a wave of nausea rush over her.

"You hadn't realized," he went on, posing the words as a statement, more than a question.

She shook her head, forcing herself to exhale. "No," she replied, her eyes darting from his surprised expression to the two bowls still waiting in front of her.

"Oh well," he mused. "It doesn't matter now either way." There was a pause as he considered his own declaration. "I need to read this and you, Molly, you need to obey me. Now tell me, what were your orders?"

Molly drew in a shaky breath. He wanted her to say the words out loud and somehow the thought was even more mortifying than the actual deed. "To eat, Sir," she mumbled eventually, praying inwardly that her answer would suffice.

"Yes," he replied. "But how should you eat, and from what?"

She forced her eyes away from his smug visage, focusing instead on the shredded chicken in the bowl ahead of her. It felt like these bowls had become her nemesis. "Eat the food from the dog bowl, Sir," she mumbled, noting how breathy her own voice sounded at the thought, despite her mortification.

"Precisely," he answered. "And we both know you want to, Molly, so let's not pretend. You're going to do as you're told, aren't you? You're going to crawl over to that bowl and lower your face into it. The movement will tighten your leash, reminding you that you're naked and collared on my floor, and all the while you're going to eat that chicken."

She was shaking by the time he'd finished. She could actually see her hands trembling before her. But the worst of it was this, it wasn't fear which made her body move, but arousal. Just listening to his order had made her wet. Molly had felt the moisture gathering between her legs, and right now she could feel the need thrumming within her core. She glanced up to him, and for the longest moment their eyes locked.

"Go on, Molly," he coaxed her. "Make me proud. I know you want this."

Her eyes fell away from his expression, but already her body shifted at his words. As though she was functioning on some subliminal level, she felt her body moving, first onto all fours, and then forward as she crawled the short distance to the waiting bowls. Molly heard the creak of Connor's chair as he slid it back against the tiles, and in her peripheral vision, she was aware of him moving to get a better view, but even that humiliation didn't make her stop. Her only hesitation came as she hovered over the two bowls, her breasts swinging freely as she contemplated her fate.

"Good girl, Molly," he cooed, and she twisted her head in the direction of Connor's voice, surprised to see his chair now almost immediately to her left. Her face flamed at the realization, and for an awful moment, the shame paralyzed her as fresh heat engulfed her cheeks.

"That's right," he continued, his words coaxing her. "Spread those legs and lower yourself. You should have just enough leash to reach."

She took a deep breath, casting her eyes down to the right of the two bowls. Shifting a little in its direction, she complied wordlessly, feeling the tug at her neck as she pressed her body down toward the floor. It was the strangest thing, as though she was hypnotized, and like a moth to a flame she went, reveling in how unbelievably turned on she was as she degraded herself for him. There was a moment as the meat grew nearer to her mouth that she almost faltered. It was like a shot of reality when Molly pictured herself as Connor could see her, and the embarrassment nearly toppled her altogether. As though he sensed the panic rising in her chest, Connor lurched forward, kneeling beside her as she lingered over the bowl.

"Go on," he told her, his voice a little sterner than it had been previously. "Get that face right in there."

Molly panted at his words, her body jerking in response to the cruel pinch Connor gifted her left nipple. The pain was real enough, but in her current state of arousal, all it did was to catapult her forward into the bowl. She captured the first piece of chicken in her teeth. Gasping she sucked the meat into her mouth, chewing it slowly as she felt her face flame further. *Oh my God...* This was really happening. She was really eating chicken from a dog bowl on the floor, while she was naked and leashed.

"Oh fuck, yes," purred Connor lustfully, the sound of his voice drawing her head up again. "No!" he snapped, making her flinch. "Stay right down there over the bowl until you're finished. Do you understand me?"

She nodded, shamefully aroused as she swallowed down the first mouthful. "Yes, Sir," she replied, as she pushed her face back down for the next bite. Somehow the second piece was easier. She ignored the sound of the metal at her wrists and went for it, grazing the bowl of meat with her lips as she seized the mouthful. As she chewed, she felt one of his hands at her ass. It trailed a line over the tender place he'd spanked earlier, before dipping down toward her wet folds.

Molly's mouth stilled for a moment. She knew that she should halt the progress of his fingers. She shouldn't want this, after all. She hadn't asked to come here and be treated this way, and she hadn't consented to his touch, but there was something else. Something *more,* and the thought was unsettling. She did want this, and she wanted it more badly than she wanted to admit. She was so turned on right now, so tightly wound that she reasoned any touch could topple her into some depraved hedonism, and rather than make her shameful, the thought drove her on.

"Keep eating, little pet," he said, his voice almost a low growl.

Her jaws resumed at once, as did his fingers which found her glistening lips as she swallowed the food in her mouth. Molly moaned as his digits skimmed the edge of her pussy, and she heard the wry chuckle which followed.

"You do like this, Molly, don't you?" he asked just as one of those long fingers probed between her lips.

She groaned at the intrusion, her hips rocking out of instinct at the newest, heady sensation. He shifted his hand in an instant, and brought it crashing down upon her upturned and vulnerable bottom.

"Ouch!" she yelped, despite her mouthful of food.

"Keep those hips still," he warned her. "You do not take, Molly. You receive, got it?"

She nodded, mumbling her agreement as she chewed on her food, and in some act of reward, she felt the hand at her nipple reappear at exactly the same time as the one at her sex. Connor massaged the weight of her left breast gently, as he worked one finger in and out of her wet channel. And boy, was she wet. Molly mewled at the overwhelming sensations, hanging her head by the bowl as he pleasured her.

"Fuck yes," he said again. "You are so wet for me. Do you know that?"

She leaned forward, capturing the next piece of chicken as a new reflexive groan left her lips. How could she argue, even if she wanted to? The man was right. She was obviously wrong in the head, but something about this fucked up situation was driving her crazy, and she was sure she'd never been so horny in her life.

His digits were gone again in an instant, and three fresh smacks rained down on her behind. Her body jerked at the spanks, but the sting only made her more aroused and she moaned as he landed a fourth. "I asked you a question, little pet," his voice vibrated over her skin. "Answer me!"

"Y-yes, Sir," she whimpered, swallowing down the ignominy with the remaining chicken.

"I knew you'd make the perfect pet, and I was right," he cooed. "Get your face in that bowl and eat your food. Press those tits against the floor, demean yourself for me."

Molly gasped at his words, but one hard smack from his right palm sent her rushing to obey, and she did exactly what he'd asked, feeling a new surge of arousal coursing through her as she yielded.

"Look at you, denigrating yourself not just for me – not just for my pleasure – but for your own as well. You're mind-blowing, Molly," he whispered as he fingered her. "Fucking mind-blowing."

She moaned in response, despising herself for enjoying this, yet completely powerless to prevent it. The truth was she was more than just enjoying it. She was utterly enraptured by the experience, and as she devoured more of the meat in the bowl – her bowl – she wondered if there was any coming back from it. Could she ever just be the Molly who'd sat and typed erotic fantasies all day after this? Even if she could escape Connor's clutches, what resemblance of normal life could be waiting for her?

He pressed another finger inside her and slowly, rhythmically, both began to fuck her while she finished her food. The act should have been humbling, humiliating, soul-destroying even, and in so many ways it was. But it was also more than that. Exponentially more than that, and it became everything to Molly, who was caught in the trap of his leash and his fingers. The faster she ate, the faster he fucked her, his fingers rewarding her pet play just as surely as she might have written them to, and within moments Molly was right on the brink of pleasure.

As though he sensed her imminent hedonism, Connor called out to her. "No coming until you're finished, little pet," he cautioned. "You won't like what happens if you disobey me on this point."

Gasping for breath and for control over her tightly furled senses, Molly heard his warning, willing her body to do the same. She pulled in a long breath, lifting her head to clear her mind, but her change in position was met with Connor's curt tone.

"Head down! "he snapped, and he used the hand nearest to her face to push down at the back of her neck.

The action caused his fingers to slide from her pussy, and she mewled, bereft at the loss as her mouth grazed the bottom of the bowl. There wasn't much chicken left now. Connor's ministrations had helped her to eat with surprising vigor, and she shifted her weight to grab the pieces lodged at the side of the bowl.

"Better," he told her. "Now splay those legs wider. I want to see this sweet pussy."

She reeled at that, or at least she wanted to, but the insistent impetus at the apex of her thighs simply would not allow it. Instead she obeyed, widening her stance as she devoured the remaining chicken, and all the while she waited, willing his digits to return.

Chapter Twenty-Seven

Connor transferred his weight, edging to the back of where Molly knelt. He ducked under the leash, which was stretched tight as she leaned over the bowl, and spent a long moment just watching her. Molly was utterly fucking mesmerizing, so much so that he couldn't even take another breath. He wasn't entirely sure what had changed in the last few minutes, but it was fairly clear that something had. Miss Clary had gone from fearful victim to wanton pet in less than half an hour, and this new version of his house-guest had made his already throbbing erection rock-solid.

He drew in a breath as he loosened his slacks, and within a moment, his thick cock sprung from its confines. Connor fisted his hardness urgently, watching Molly's wet, plump lips as she lowered herself back over the bowl.

"Don't forget what I told you," he growled, his voice thick with his own arousal. "No coming without permission."

He fully intended to allow her some pleasure, her recent obedience more than warranted it, but he wanted Molly to learn and learn fast – her pleasure would always come at a cost. And the price this time was her patience and endurance.

She muttered her agreement, and his view shifted to watch her chase another piece of meat around the bowl.

Fuck, what a sight.

He closed his eyes momentarily, willing himself self-composure. His own pleasure briefly abated for the time being, Connor edged towards Molly's bottom, catching the scent of her arousal as soon as he neared. Despite the painful pang of excitement which washed over him, Connor allowed his eyes to wander over her swollen sex. It was the first time he'd really seen her, so he took a moment to absorb every inch of her glorious sex. Molly was patently aroused. Connor could actually see the moisture dripping from her wet slit, evidence of her excitement dribbling down her inner thighs. Her lips were parted by her outstretched legs, and looked utterly delectable.

Connor lowered himself behind her body as best he could in the space he had. As soon as his mouth made contact with her body she shuddered, the pink flesh before him opening even further for his tongue. Balancing on his left arm he duly obliged, lapping at her pussy as he fisted his cock eagerly. The essence of Molly was divine, even better than he'd ever imagined. He crept closer, devouring her sex greedily. The groans which came from her mouth nearly pushed him over the precipice, but still he continued, offering his little captive the pleasure he thought she had earned.

Her body was so hot and so tasty that he wanted to consume it all. He lapped at her with such passion that it didn't take long for either of their orgasms to approach. He sensed the burgeoning power of Molly's, aware of the tension in her legs on either side of his face. Pulling away he knelt behind her, fighting the urge to just plunge his cock deep into her desperate pussy. Instead he replaced his mouth with his fingers again, fucking her into a relentless frenzy.

"Oooh, please!" she begged, raising her head from the bowl.

Connor used his left hand to smack her already reddened bottom. "How do you address me, pet?" he barked, irritated by her instinctive response.

"Sir!" she gasped, almost in tears. Clearly, the weight of her impending pleasure was becoming too much. "I'm sorry, Sir, but please. Please can I come?"

"Not yet," he growled as he pressed his hand against her sex so that one long digit made contact with her clit.

Molly squealed at that, the pressure apparently too intense as he massaged the throbbing bud gently.

"Beg me for it," he commanded, fisting his pulsing cock with his free-hand. "Get your head down over your food bowl, and beg me."

Molly mewled, the sound painfully arousing to Connor's ears, but he already knew she'd oblige him. She was way too deep into this debauched rabbit-hole to back away now, and anyway, he knew she wanted this orgasm.

"Please, Sir, please," she pleaded, still on the verge of tears. "Please let me come. I'm so close, please…"

He swallowed at the pitiful sound of her voice, the fingers of his right hand wedged deeply within her sex, while his other hand pumped away at his erection. "More," he ordered, on the verge of his own climax. "Beg harder!"

Molly continued to plead, her body demonstrating the desperation she felt, until Connor couldn't take any more, his own cock thicker and harder than he'd ever known. "Okay, little pet," he growled. "Come apart for me!"

Connor had barely concluded his sentence when the muscles around his fingers contracted, and Molly's body burst into a wave of hedonism. He watched as her head fell forward, her body slumped over the bowl as she offered him her arse. Connor stayed with her through round after round of climaxes until he eventually withdrew his fingers, slapping her spasming sex as he went. Molly jerked, raising her head in a gasp as he shifted his body around to her face.

Pulling at the leash which still held her to the wall, he forced Molly's body back to all fours, presenting her with his massively engorged erection.

"Open," he commanded, fisting his cock over her mouth as his left hand held her leash.

Molly gaped up at him, seemingly still dazed by the weight of her pleasure, and for one moment he thought she was going to resist him. Slowly though, her lips parted, presenting him with the perfect place to deposit his load, and within a second, his orgasm hit him like a wall, sending wave after wave of hot cum spiraling over her face.

There was silence as they both came down from their states of euphoria. Connor glanced down at Molly's cum-stained face, and a sense of satisfaction and pride filled his chest. Molly had enjoyed her orgasm, at her captor's hand no less. And now she owed him big time.

Chapter Twenty-Eight

It was some hours later when Molly roused, back once again on the bed in the same small room she'd awoken in the first time around. At least she thought it was some hours. Although she had no way of tracking time in this new state of capture, the light outside the window was brighter, and the air seemed distinctly warmer. Molly shifted on the bed, establishing that her wrists were once again bound, this time in front of her naked body. She noted that he'd left the chains on for good measure and sighed as they clinked with each of her small movements. Easing herself to a sitting position, she assessed her legs, finding that they were equally confined in smooth ropes which were wrapped around her ankles, over the top of the metal cuffs which held the chains in place.

Her attention turned to the room around her. It looked like Connor had been doing some tidying up since they left here. The duvet was now gone from the floor, and instead she found it bunched at her feet. She noticed that the small table she'd been forced to write at was now tucked away neatly next to the dreaded dresser where he kept his heinous toys and contraptions.

Blinking around at the pale, nondescript décor, the stark reality of the last day hit her all over again, concluding with the mind-blowing orgasm which Connor had given her over the dog bowl.

Connor had done that?

The man who had drugged and abducted her - he'd been the one who'd delivered the overwhelming pleasure, yet it had come at one hell of a price. Molly squirmed as she made herself recall all of the sorry, sordid details. He had fingered her alright, but only once she obeyed his dark commands, eating from a pet bowl, and then begging for her climax. She knew she was flushing at the memory alone. And then there was the conclusion. She remembered the taste of his hot salty fluid as it hit the back of her throat, and she wondered fleetingly what had happened to the rest that had covered her face. She raised her bound hands to her cheeks, running a finger across her skin, but found it smooth and clean. Connor had washed her then? She shuddered as she tried to remember what had happened after the orgasm. All she could recall was the pleasure and the shame which had flooded her system, and then was nothing but black sleep.

The memory of the indignity brought that sense of shame crashing back over her like a giant wave. What the fuck had she been thinking, playing along with his warped ideas like that? It was one thing to be the victim here, to be taken and used against her will, but what had transpired back in that kitchen was something else. She may not have wanted to eat from the bowl at first, a fact she'd be happy to insist upon, but deep down she'd desired the treatment for longer than she cared to admit. That's why Molly had written those scenes into her book, and that's why when push came to shove, she had conceded.

She shoved her back against the wall, pulling her bound wrists up to her hair as best she could. Why had she wanted to concede? What was this dark yearning that burned within her, and why could some crazy guy like Connor be the one to detonate an orgasm that could be in the running as the best of her whole damn life? She let out a long sigh as her mind ran through the riddle, allowing her head to fall backwards against the wall. It was then that she noticed the leather, still in place at her neck. Molly's fingers played with it uncertainly as the reality washed over her again. She was still bound, still naked and still collared. She was still his...

"Here's my sleeping beauty."

The sound of Connor's voice startled her, and she jumped as she caught sight of him in the doorway. He flashed her a brilliant smile, and she noticed that he'd changed from his earlier outfit into a pair of smart black slacks and a dark emerald shirt. The color really accentuated those dazzling green eyes, and for some bizarre reason she found herself gulping at the sight of him.

"How are you feeling now?" he asked, stepping forward into the room and closing the door behind him.

"Okay, thank you, Sir," she replied, squirming her sore behind against the thin mattress.

Molly felt awkward and embarrassed. The last time they had interacted, she had been on a leash swallowing his cum, and God only knows what transpired in the period she couldn't remember. All she knew was that he had cleaned her up, brought her into this room and re-bound her. And that knowledge alone was enough to humble her.

Connor's expression softened at her response, and he approached the bed slowly. "I figured you could use some rest," he explained as he reached the edge of the mattress where she huddled. "You're having one hell of a first day."

She glanced up to his face, seeing the satisfaction evident there. Clearly, he was very pleased with himself about the whole situation, and the fact riled her.

"I read the start of our story while you were sleeping," he went on, apparently not needing – or waiting for – a response.

Molly eyed him anxiously, wondering where this new line of conversation was going. "Did you like it, Sir?" she inquired, already feeling her heart pounding away in her chest as she awaited his verdict.

He offered her a small smile. "Of course, I liked it," he replied warmly, and as he spoke, he sat himself down on the bed next to her. "There were some errors, but I do appreciate you were writing under shall we say, unusual conditions?" His dark brow rose wryly as he concluded, and the look of him made her throat dry.

Unusual is right, she thought resentfully. *It's hard to create your best work when you're gagged, chained and fondled throughout the ordeal.* Molly met his gaze, acknowledging the amused look on his face, but she bit back her emotions, knowing some ill-timed remark now would only land her in even more hot water.

"I normally deal with errors when I edit," she offered him in a tiny voice which barely seemed to reach his ears, but he nodded to show he understood.

"Absolutely," he agreed, "but editing isn't the fun part of this process, Molly. The best part is the writing, the creative process, and everything we are going to do to inspire it."

He edged closer toward her on the bed, making her heart race as he neared.

"What are you going to do to me?" She squeaked at his approach, and the tremor in her voice made him stop and turn the weight of his powerful stare over her flushing body.

"Come on now," he cooed. "You don't still need to ask that silly question, do you?"

That made her halt, and she gasped at the way he'd asked it, as though she was his property and her resistance was utterly futile. Maybe it already was…

"I…" She began, but the words died in her throat as his brooding face neared.

"You're what?" he probed, inching ever closer to her wide-eyed face.

"Scared," she said, pushing the word out in one long exhalation.

The reply made the edges of his lips curl ever so slightly, but his body stilled. "Scared?" he repeated, sounding shocked at the notion. "Why are you scared?"

She balked at that, wanting to laugh in his face, but fear prevented the action. Instead she fought to find her voice, knowing that question would need an answer. "Of you, Sir," she responded. "Of all of this." She raised her bound arms into the air as she spoke, forcing the metal of the chains to clink together with the motion.

Connor smiled again, but the look was predatory. "Why should you be scared?" he asked her again. "Tell me, have I ever hurt you in any real way? Or in any way which you didn't ultimately enjoy and desire even?"

He paused, letting his questions hang between them as Molly reeled, aghast at his implication.

"You spanked me!" she cried, nearly spitting out the words.

"Yes," he agreed with a grin. "I did, and you, my little pet, you fucking loved it."

Molly squeezed her eyes closed at his response, not wanting to see those sparkling green orbs. He was right of course. She had loved it, despite the pain, but her response was based on more than that. He had called her his *pet* again, and all the ramifications and memories from the kitchen came flooding back in a split-second.

"You humiliated me," she began again, forcing her eyes open to find him only a few inches from her face. His sudden proximity was startling, and she pressed her thighs together out of instinct. The look on his face was completely devastating.

"Yes, I did," he concurred, eyeing her intently. "And I'll tell you something else, I will do again, little pet, as often as I like."

His gaze seared into her, those green eyes unblinking as he delivered the message, and every ounce of Molly's being heard it. Her nipples stiffened at his tone, and she actually felt the moisture pool between her legs. However much she protested, they both knew how good his threats sounded, and there was really no point denying it. An image of her splayed and convulsing body spasming to his touch flashed through her mind, and Molly felt her face blush at the embarrassment.

"It's okay, little pet," he murmured gently. As he spoke, he raised his right hand and stroked her hot flesh. "I know. This is all new and overwhelming. Perhaps you feel guilty about submitting to my authority, who knows. All I can tell you is this. This is how things are now. You are mine to torture and adore, and I will push you. Do you understand?"

There were tears in her eyes at his words, in spite of the softly-spoken delivery. Molly felt them collect, and she blinked them away angrily. Why was she so emotional about this, for fuck's sake? She drew in a breath, fighting for composure before she finally offered him a nod.

Connor laughed, the sound gentle, but the resonance connecting directly with her sex. It was the most fucked up thing, but something about his laughter made her really wet, and the genuine happiness on his face made him look all the more handsome. "That's not good enough, little pet," he told her, shifting his digits from her face. "You know how to address me, so I suggest you do so."

She gulped again, his authority taunting and tantalizing in equal measure. "Yes, Sir," she murmured, looking up into his gleeful green eyes. "Yes, I understand."

"Good." He grinned. "That wasn't so hard, was it?"

She shook her head as she mumbled a reply.

"Now, one last thing before I get to my plans for you."

Molly's body tensed at that, but she fought to contain the panic, listening intently to his words.

"I believe there's something you need to say to me?" he continued, his eyes dancing as he went on. "For the pleasure I gave you earlier? It seemed like quite an orgasm."

She felt the blood drain from her face at his question, her mind in free-fall. His words implied that he wanted her to thank him for fingering her while she was forced to eat from a fucking dog bowl. Thank him! What the actual fuck?

"Was it, little pet?" he asked, the question cutting short her feelings of disgust on the subject.

"Was what, Sir?" she replied, biting her lip anxiously.

Surely, he didn't want to hear the words out loud. She couldn't say them. It just wasn't possible.

"Was it a good orgasm?" he asked, pressing his advantage as he pushed his body against her bound legs.

A small shiver passed over her at the contact, and she knew her pussy was wet for him. "Y-yes, Sir," she conceded, flushing deeper at the admission.

He smiled, turning to keep his focus solely on his little bound captive. "So, thank me then," he commanded her gently. "Isn't it polite to thank people for gifts?"

Her head swirled with panic at his words. *Gifts*? Is that what that was? She certainly wanted to argue that point, but somehow there were no words to achieve the protest. There were only his smiling eyes, and the hand now ducking to her chin.

"Yes," she managed at last. "Thank you, Sir."

She didn't know how she forced the words out, but somehow, she did, swallowing back yet another rush of humiliation as it ran through her.

"Tell me what you're thanking me for," he demanded. "Be a good pet."

She shivered again at his words, emotion catching in her throat. She didn't know which sensation was more potent, the heavy one at the back of her eyes where fresh tears threatened to emerge, or the insistent one between her hot legs. "Thank you for pleasuring me, Sir," she answered him, and this time she made herself look into his dazzling eyes as she responded.

It was the damnedest thing. As their eyes connected, a sudden powerful surge of feeling passed over her, and it wasn't just terror or panic, or even arousal. It was something else. Something profound and unsettling.

"Good girl," he told her warmly, and the fingers at her face shifted again, stroking the side of her jaw. "Do you know how fucking beautiful you are?"

She shook her head, captured by the look in his eye and this intensity between them. "No, I…" she began, but Molly never finished that sentence. Connor's lips stole it from her as they swooped, pressing themselves against her open mouth as they claimed her.

She tried to gasp at the unexpected kiss, but his insistent mouth wouldn't allow it. There was a brief moment of fright, but then the sheer sensuality of the moment cascaded over her, and she realized she didn't want to fight him. For whatever reason his mouth felt wonderful against hers, and silently she willed him on, hoping that he'd possess her properly. As though Connor could read her mind, he did, probing his tongue into her mouth and fucking her with it, over and over. Her mind flitted back to the way that same tongue had attacked her

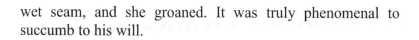

wet seam, and she groaned. It was truly phenomenal to succumb to his will.

Chapter Twenty-Nine

He hadn't intended to kiss her, not yet anyway. Listening to her actually thanking him for the finger fucking he'd bestowed on her earlier was almost hypnotic, and as he'd complimented her, the idea of claiming those lips had burst into his head. The thought had grown, overtaking him as he gazed into her flushed face and as the moment presented itself, Connor seized it.

Molly seemed stunned at first, as though she couldn't believe what was happening, but in a matter of seconds she surrendered. Connor had actually felt the moment she yielded, her body relaxing as she opened for his tongue. *Oh my God.* The kiss was exquisite, hardening his cock by the time he drew away.

She blinked at him, her breath coming out in short bursts. She was wide-eyed and utterly bloody gorgeous.

"Are you thirsty?" His tone was intentionally casual, disguising the intensity which coursed through his body.

She swallowed as she nodded. "Yes, Sir."

Connor shifted the hand at her face, using it to draw her forward toward him. "You never did drink from your water bowl," he scolded her in a quiet tone.

Molly bit her lip anxiously, although he noticed the way her nipples tightened into stiff peaks between them. She was clearly conflicted; just as aroused as she was horrified by his statement.

"I want to rectify that situation the next time you have a meal," he told her, watching her face carefully for her responses.

Molly's breath hitched, the flesh under his thumb growing warm to his touch. "Yes, Sir," she whispered.

He eyed her severely, wanting her to know that he meant what he said. She *was* going to drink from that bowl, and soon, but for the time being, she was dehydrated and that was Connor's problem.

"Wait here," he commanded, sliding from the bed and striding toward the door. It pained him to leave her, especially after such an unexpected intimacy had developed between them, but there was nothing else he could do. He had to get the little pet to drink.

Connor slipped from the doorway, leaving her bound on the bed and bolted the lock from the outside. Within a moment, he'd collected a fresh bottle of water from the kitchen fridge and returned to Molly's room. She hadn't moved an inch and the fact made him proud as he approached her again.

"Good girl for staying put," he complimented her. "Now, slide to the edge of the bed and open up for me."

Molly blinked at him before her body obeyed. Connor stood in the center of the room and watched as she wriggled her bound limbs to the edge as instructed. She looked absolutely fucking adorable. Once she was in place, she glanced up to him, before slowly parting her lips.

Connor cocked the lid of the sports bottle in his hand, and raised it to her lips, angling the water just above her mouth. "Drink," he instructed her. "I want it all finished."

Molly nodded as best she could as her mouth wrapped itself around the plastic, and he watched contentedly as she drained most of the bottle. Pausing for a breath, Molly panted in front of him.

"Finish up," he warned her, his tone lowering instinctively.

"Yes, Sir," she murmured, stirring his cock with her large eyes and compliance, and within a moment, she had done as he ordered, drinking the last of the water in the bottle.

"That's better," he cooed, removing the plastic from her mouth. "I need you well, and that means hydrated."

She nodded once more, flinching as he threw the bottle across the length of the room.

"Now it's time to get going again," Connor announced, glancing over his bound captive.

"S-Sir?" she stuttered, trembling ever so slightly as she glanced up at his looming frame.

Connor smiled, loving the power he had over her. "I want you on your belly," he commanded quietly.

She was shaking visibly as she moved to comply. He could see the questions on her lips as she turned, and a part of him fully expected them to be vocalized, but to her credit, none were forthcoming. That pleased him, more than he cared to admit.

"Arms out in front of you," he told her. "Stick your bottom out over the edge of the bed, and spread those legs." He produced a small blade from his pocket, swooping down in front of her, and cutting the ropes which held her ankles together.

He heard her gulp. "P-please, Sir," she whispered. "Why am I being punished?"

Connor snorted. "My sweet, little pet," he said as he chuckled. "This isn't punishment. Whatever would make you think that?"

Molly's body stilled, and she twisted her head to glance back at him. "I thought you were going to spank me again... Sir."

He stared down at her, a faint smile growing on his lips. "Not yet, sweet thing," he responded. "In fact, I have to say you've been a pretty good girl since I tamed you earlier. And while I appreciate your good behavior, it won't dissuade me from my endeavors. You're still writing our story and you still belong to me. Have you got it?"

Connor heard the emotion catch in Molly's throat, as she mumbled a suitable reply.

He grinned at her trembling backside. Whatever her real feelings on the subject, Molly was finally getting with the script. She was learning. He backed away from her body slowly, never taking his eyes from her until he reached the chest of drawers. Reaching behind him, he opened the first drawer slowly, before turning to quickly choose the item he wanted. He ran his fingers over the cold plastic as he selected a tube of lubrication. It was time to train that delectable arse.

Chapter Thirty

The wait over the bed felt endless, but in reality, he was back over Molly's body in a minute. She dared not shift or look back, but she had that ominous feeling again in the pit of her belly, and she reasoned she wouldn't care for whatever came next. The first thing she was aware of was the feeling of something cold and wet landing over her exposed ass cheeks.

Molly leaped from the bed reflexively. "Ooow!"

A hard smack fell upon her right cheek. "Get back into place," he ordered in a low and foreboding tone.

She whimpered lightly, but complied, panting as she repositioned herself. "S-Sir?"

"Silence," Connor ordered. "You will control that mouth, pet, or I will. I thought I already taught this lesson."

Molly nodded, trying to catch her breath as she felt the cold liquid dribble down between her ass cheeks. It was so undignifying, yet insanely erotic at the same time.

"The last time you wrote for me you had a lesson in gags, and this time, little pet, you get a lesson in plugs." Connor's voice trailed away, and as it did, one of his fingers followed the line of lubricant down into her cheeks. Molly tensed, mewling pitifully, and for one long moment Connor seemed to revel in the glory of that sound. "Relax, little pet," he purred. "This arse is mine, and this is going to help you remember it."

He pushed the top of his finger into her dark entrance, penetrating her gently.

"Oh," she gasped, softly.

In her peripheral vision, she saw Connor shake his head, apparently not impressed. Raising his free hand, he landed a hard swat against her rounded cheek, making her screech and sob lightly into the bedding. "Do you need that gag as well as my plug, pet?"

She shook her head furiously, although she did not reply.

"No?" he prompted, smacking her backside again. "No gag?"

"No, Sir," she whispered, her voice etched with raw emotions.

"Then no more noise," he growled, "unless I ask you a specific question."

Connor didn't wait for her response, instead he withdrew the digit from her bottom and scooped up more lubrication. "You are mine now," he told her. "That smart little mouth is mine, this hot little body is mine, that big writer's brain is mine, and this…" He paused, edging the finger back into her tight little hole. There was a small gasp from Molly, but nothing more. "This delicious arse is mine too, pet. Mine to plug, mine to punish, and when we're ready, mine to fuck."

Molly inhaled, the sound louder this time. Easing the finger in and out of her, he pressed his weight against her lower legs and began to fuck her with more vigour.

"Tell me, little pet," he continued. "Have you been fucked in this sweet arse before?"

Molly moaned, but he wasn't sure if it was agitation or arousal which inspired the response. He waited a moment, adding a second finger to her behind as she writhed.

"Only once, Sir," she admitted, her tone husky.

A spike of his own need shot through him, and Connor had to steady himself against the edge of the bed as his fingers continued their relentless rhythm inside her tight channel. "Only once?" he repeated, pressing deeper inside her.

A guttural grunt left her lips, and she struggled against the binds at her wrists. The act was futile though, and they both knew it.

"Yes, Sir," she groaned, dropping her head between her shoulders.

"Not a good experience for you, little pet?" he asked while his digits probed.

All at once Molly tensed, her body nearly pushing him out in the process. Connor waited for the pressure to rescind before he smacked the side of her left cheek again. "Do not push me out," he warned her. "I promise you that you'll regret it."

She whimpered, and he wondered fleetingly what it was about his question that had caused her such alarm.

"Tell me about your anal experience," he commanded, this time his wording giving her little choice but to respond.

There was silence for a long while, and all the time his fingers delved inside her. They pushed in and out, invading and claiming her near-virgin hole.

"There's not much to tell, Sir," she replied at last in a tone which sounded almost indignant. "I tried it, but it wasn't for me."

The reply surprised him. Firstly, he didn't like her tone. For a woman who'd been snatched from the street, drugged, stripped, bound and objectified, there was way too much sass in her voice for his liking. That would have to be dealt with... Secondly, her answer was startling. Molly wrote about anal sex in pretty much all of her books, and she did it with such depth and authenticity. Connor had always assumed that she'd be something of a connoisseur on the subject, but now, faced with the reality, he had found the opposite was true. She was practically an anal virgin.

"That's a shame, pet," he pondered aloud, shifting his rock-hard shaft in his pants as his fingers drove into her tight little bottom again. "Because you're going to be taking it in the arse from me whenever I demand it."

There was another gasp from his little pet and for one excruciating second, her muscles clamped down on his digits in panic.

"Relax!" he ordered her. "Breathe, pet."

It seemed to take all of her will power, but eventually Molly obeyed, pulling in a deep breath and forcing her muscles to release his fingers.

"Don't worry," he cooed, fingering her pussy idly with his free hand and drawing the additional lubrication north to her arse. "We'll start with small plugs, and build you up to my cock, but you will take it, pet."

There was no reply forthcoming, save for the moans and whimpers which escaped her mouth, so he glanced back to the butt plug which he'd deposited on the bed beside them.

No time like the present...

Connor withdrew his fingers, smacking her delicious arse for good measure as he reached for the lube again. He'd need a lot of it to ensure a smooth entry for Molly's newest toy.

"It's time, pet," he announced, watching the quiver in her arms at his edict. "I want you to relax and not try to resist me, have you got that?"

A small sob leaked from Molly's pretty little mouth. "Pl-please don't," she begged, the resonance sending his cock in an uncontrollable throb.

"Wrong answer," he replied, swatting her behind hard. "I asked if you understood?"

"Y-yes, Sir," she cried, pushing her face into the bedding to mute her apparent misery about his decision.

Connor smiled. He just couldn't help himself. This was going to be so much better than he could have ever hoped. An anal novice prepared to humiliate herself for him were assets he'd barely even dared to consider. He smothered the smooth head of the plug with lubrication before shifting in between her legs. "Let's start with what you already know," he mused as he guided it into her wet seam.

Molly gasped as it entered her pussy, but she didn't resist. Instead she moaned again, and the sound spoke directly to his hungry cock. He had no idea why he was being so kind to the woman. He should just have shoved the thing in her arse, and been done with it. This was it, her new reality. A world where he made the rules and she obeyed, and Molly would just have to get used to it, but there was just something about her that made his heart melt a little. And that part of him hadn't wanted to really hurt her or cause her any permanent harm, so he'd diverted to her sex at the last minute to warm her up. He inhaled, breathing in the exquisite scent of her arousal as he pulled the plug out, before sliding it back in again. What was it about this woman that pulled upon his heart strings? He shook his head at his own question, smiling harder at her animalistic responses to the plug. Whatever it was, it didn't matter. It wouldn't change her fate. All he was doing was stalling – playing for time – and as though he wanted to prove the point, he withdrew the plastic between his fingers altogether and slid it up to her waiting hole.

Connor nudged the plastic at the well-lubed hole and waited, hearing the panic in her voice as she moaned. "Spread those legs wider," he ordered her in a gravelly tone, "and push that arse high in the air."

She was sobbing outright now, but she did as he asked, moving her body to comply with his demands while she balanced on her elbows. He could sense there was still fight in his captive, but for the time being, all she demonstrated was resignation, as though she realized her arse was his now, and there was nothing she could do about it. He wondered fleetingly if the prospect made her as horny as it did him.

"I want deep breaths," he told her. "Nice long deep ones as the plug enters you. Show me."

Molly struggled, pulling in large shaky breaths as best she could in her current emotional state, and he patted her bottom approvingly.

"Good," he encouraged as he slid the first inch inside her. "Keep going."

There was tension in her hips and thighs as the plug invaded her body, but somehow his little pet managed to keep going, pulling in the air as best she could. As he reached the roundest part of the dildo though, she began to panic, and her breathing became shallow as her muscles clenched the foreign body. "It won't fit," she squealed, the desperation she felt evident in her tone. "Please Sir, it won't go any further."

Connor would have laughed at her pathetic little plea, had he not been so irritated with her. "Rubbish!" he barked, striking the vulnerable thigh nearest his palm. "It will fit just fine if you relax, now breathe."

The top half of Molly collapsed fully onto the bed, but Connor noticed her behind relax as instructed. He pressed forward with each new breath, watching as the five inches of plug disappeared snugly into the little pet's arse. In the end, there was only the base of the plug visible between her pert cheeks, a view which made him want to cram her wet pussy full of his cock without any further hesitation.

"All done," he said proudly, sitting back to admire the look of his butt-plugged little pet. One thing was for sure, he couldn't wait until she'd be ready to take one with a tail attached. Then she'd truly be his little leashed pet. "Now let me make this really clear, pet. That plug stays in until either I remove it, or I give you permission to do so. Have you got that?"

"Yes, Sir," she whimpered, her tone breathless and erratic.

If he didn't know better, Connor would have thought his little captive was quite enjoying this subjugation, although he felt sure she'd never admit as much.

"If you disobey me on this," he continued, "then you'll be meeting the end of my belt. Which I don't think you'll appreciate." He chuckled at the final sentiment and watched as her pale body shuddered.

"Now, what do you say, little one?" he asked, intentionally making his tone stern to startle the trembling woman before him.

It worked, and he watched as her body tensed all over again and she turned anxiously to meet his gaze. Her eyes were questioning, as if she had no clue what he expected.

He sighed, laughing to himself as he smacked her plugged bottom playfully. "I have just given you a gift, pet," he told her firmly. "So, what do you say?"

Molly's lips parted and he watched as her pupils dilated. "Thank you, Sir," she whispered, lowering her gaze at her obvious humiliation.

"Better," he responded. "Now tell me what you're thankful for."

Her face screwed into a tight ball at the question, and he gave her a moment to process the request, but only a moment.

"Molly," he warned in a low growl. "Answer me."

Her eyes snapped open and there were fresh tears as the words he longed to hear rolled from her lips. "Thank you for plugging my ass, Sir."

Chapter Thirty-One

S he was beaten. Or at least that's how she felt. She didn't even know how long it had been since he'd taken her, and in that time, she suffered the worst indignations of her life, all at this stranger's hands. The butt-plug was the final straw. She could feel the thing fully wedged into her bottom, and she clenched her pelvic floor tentatively, wondering if the thing would come out even if she willed it.

Okay, she wasn't really beaten. She knew that. Molly had reserves inside her that she'd never had to draw on, until now. But she sensed Connor was going to be the man who ripped right through her boundaries. Since he'd bestowed his most recent *gift* upon, or rather inside, her aching ass, Connor had left her bound on the bed while he busied himself in the room behind her. Molly peered back to watch him, seeing him setting up the small table and chair in the middle of the space.

"Up now," he ordered, turning to meet her gaze.

She shuddered at the instruction, her legs trembling as she wriggled back from the edge of the bed. Rising she twisted to meet Connor, who was already on her.

"Do you know what I need from you now, pet?" His voice was a lusty growl.

Something about the tone made her gulp, and she noticed how her nipples tightened at the resonance. "To write, Sir?" she whispered, too embarrassed to meet his eye.

The unyielding plug in her ass was a constant reminder of her latest denigration, and it stung. Her bottom felt stretched to its bursting point, but worse than that was the abject humiliation of the event. This man had forced the thing inside of her, and was going to make her wear it for as long as he wanted. It was utterly mortifying.

"That's right," he agreed, circling her body as he spoke. "You have a lot to catch up on, little pet, everything from your meal earlier to that nicely filled arse. I wouldn't want you to fall behind."

Molly stood anxiously before him as Connor's circle concluded. Her behind felt so full, it worried her. Were butts supposed to be treated this way? How long could she manage the damn thing? Letting out a small sigh, she felt her limbs tremble again. Even her own characters had never been subjected to such degrading treatment.

"On the chair," he commanded, pointing to the wooden seat which awaited her.

Molly's eyes fell over it, wondering how she could possibly sit still with this *thing* shoved inside her, and it was then that a new realization fell over her. She needed to use the bathroom, and soon. Gazing up at his stern face, her heart began to race again. Was Connor even going to let her use the facilities in this place?

"Sir?" she began, her voice quivering with trepidation.

Connor's eyes widened, as though he couldn't believe she had the temerity to query his command. "Sit on the chair, pet," he insisted, "before I make you write on the floor."

Molly pursed her lips, feeling her heart thunder inside of her chest. She didn't want to push him on what he'd think was such a trivial issue, but she was getting desperate. All of that water might have helped her head, but it had done nothing for her bladder. "Please, Sir," she tried again. "I need to use the bathroom." The words came out in one long rush, and she braced herself for his response.

"Is this some ill-conceived plan to escape?" he asked Molly, directly.

Molly shook her head in a panic. "No, Sir," she assured him. "I swear it. I just need to use the facilities. It's been hours, and I'm desperate."

Connor's eyes narrowed, and his right hand gestured toward the floor. "Get down at my feet," he ordered in a stern voice.

Molly was panting as she obeyed. Adrenaline flooded her body, but she couldn't tell if it was the danger she sensed at his intent, or arousal at the instruction which inspired it. Her heart was pounding so loudly she was sure Connor could hear its insistent rhythm as she obeyed. What else could she do? If she called out, he'd gag her. If she ran, he'd catch her. She was out of choices.

His gaze followed her as her knees hit the floor. For the longest moment there was a heavy silence, and Molly could still feel the weight of his stare, although she didn't dare to look up and meet it. She watched his feet move as they strode past her to the infamous dresser. Within a few seconds Connor had returned, and Molly eyed the metal leash in his hands.

"Okay, pet," he breathed in an exasperated sigh. "I believe you, and you may use the bathroom, but there are rules."

Molly pulled in a long breath, already dreading what maybe about to come from his lips.

"Rule one," he began. "If you're going anywhere, then you're doing it leashed on your hands and knees. You're my pet now, and that's how pets get around."

Her head was spinning, the weight of her bladder somehow combining with the plug inside of her to make her fuller and hornier than she'd maybe ever been.

"Look at me," he commanded, and something about the power in his tone made Molly comply. His green eyes burned into her, creating a new flame at her cheeks. "Rule two. I'll take you to the bathroom and leash you there." He paused, allowing the words to register in her head.

"Leash me, Sir?" Her reply was raspy and unsure.

He nodded. "Yeah, leash you," he replied with a smile. "I'll allow you to use the facilities, but I don't trust you to be alone. If you need the bathroom, then you'll use it in front of me."

That made Molly swallow, the act visible to her captor as she trembled below him. The thought was utterly demoralizing. After everything she had been through, the bondage, the spanking, the dog bed, he intended to humble her further in this most base way. She wanted to scream, she wanted to cry, but this was no time for either response. Instead, she squeezed her eyes closed briefly, accepting this new indignity as he attached the metal leash to the collar still at her neck. He reached for her wrists, releasing the ropes which bound her so tightly, leaving only the metal cuffs in place, linked by a second chain between her hands.

"Let's go," he huffed. "I want this second round of writing done before bed."

Connor tugged at the chain between them, forcing her onto all fours, and as he paced from the room she was forced to crawl after him.

"By my feet," he told her, and Molly could hear the glee in his voice. "A good pet will come to heel."

She sensed his words were designed to provoke, but Molly was caught in his trap, powerless to respond without repercussions. Ensnared between her fear and her terrible yearning, she was literally trapped in his house, so she did her best to obey, crawling as fast as she could until she was alongside Connor's shoes. They passed out of the bedroom, and Connor turned right, leading Molly down a corridor she'd never been to before. The worn carpet was hard and cold against her palms. Her knees screamed in agony, but she hurried on regardless, listening to the metal of her chains scrape across the floor as she moved.

Connor pushed the door ahead open and weak light flooded into the space around them. Molly crawled forward into the new room, eyeing the outline of a free-standing tub to her left and a sink ahead of her. He drew her right, pulling her toward a toilet. "Up you get," he ordered, tugging at her collar.

Molly swallowed hard as she rose shakily to her feet. She perched onto the edge of the seat, watching as he tightened his grip on the leash. The thought of him literally watching her made Molly angry and confused, and she turned away from him in disgust. Her head fell forward as much the chain would allow.

"Get on with it, pet," he grumbled from behind her. "Show me you deserve to be treated this way, or else I'll be forced to grab you a litter tray."

He laughed at the idea, but the thought made Molly's belly twist. Her mind raced at the concept, memories of the dog bowl flashing before her, and Molly knew in her heart that he absolutely meant it. He would degrade her further, and he'd probably enjoy it. She steadied herself, willing her body to calm down and give in, but it was to no avail. She was so tense and fearful, and at any rate, how could she go with him right there, beside her? Her ass was filled, and she was already under strict instructions about what would happen if that situation accidentally changed. Swallowing hard, Molly tried not to think about that scenario. "I-I can't," she stuttered, too full of alarm and shame to look up at him.

"Can't?" he repeated, tugging even harder at her neck, and practically yanking her from the seat completely. "What is it, pet? Performance anxiety?" His tone was sardonic, but also dark, and the sound of it did nothing to quell Molly's rising panic.

"Please," she begged, finally raising her head to catch his eye.

Molly hated the sound of weakness and desperation in her voice, but there it was. She was desperate. That's how he made her feel; she was completely out of control and desperate.

Connor's tone was hard and unrelenting. "Last chance, pet," he muttered, eyeing her severely. "Go now, or not at all."

The knot of anxiety twisted inside Molly's chest, rising into a low sob in her throat. "Okay," she sighed, exasperated at the latest humiliation, but knowing there was no choice.

Closing her eyes, she willed her body to relax, ignoring the whirring energy which was radiating from the towering man beside her. This was officially the most undignified, horrifying thing she'd ever had to do. It made the dog bowl incident feel almost decent. She inhaled, counting slowly in her head, before she blew the air out again. Something about the action helped to calm her, and finally Molly could relax.

She knew her face was flaming as she peered around after the event. "May I wash my hands, Sir?" she gasped, cringing at having to ask permission for such a basic occurrence.

Connor actually tutted at the question, rolling his eyes as she awaited his verdict. "Make it fast," he warned her, adjusting her leash so that she could shuffle over to the sink.

Once her hands were clean, she turned, eyeing him awkwardly. Connor stalked past her, evidently unimpressed with her performance.

"Back on your knees," he instructed, already pulling on the chain connected to her neck.

She sunk to the floor again, her heart sinking with her body. Whatever euphoria had affected Molly when Connor had made her come in the kitchen, or when he'd captured her mouth in the bedroom, had well and truly worn off. In its place, the reality smacked her hard in the face. This was not a work of fiction. There would be no happy ending unless she made one for herself, and so far, Connor had only sought to degrade and humiliate her. Even more worrying though, his commands and expectations were growing all the more debauched. Connor had been calling her his *pet* for hours, and now she really started to understand why. That's how he saw her – as nothing more than a pet who could write and obey him. She shuddered as the idea settled over her. Connor was actively dehumanizing her, and it was working. Now she just felt small and used, like a wilted flower straining for the sunshine. The question was, which way was the sun?

She was led down the narrow corridor without a word, and back into the room where the table and chair were waiting. One word ordered her onto the chair, and Molly obeyed, shifting awkwardly as her plugged bottom hit the hard wood. Connor unleashed her, throwing the metal to the bed behind her. She waited anxiously as he produced yet more chains, securing her ankles to the legs of the chair, before he rose to assess her.

"I'm going to get the laptop," he told her sternly. "Do not even think about moving from that chair."

Molly flexed her legs, now chained to the seat below her. How exactly was she supposed to move in this predicament? She watched as he paced from the room, apparently not waiting for her response. Drawing in a deep breath, she gazed out at the murky window ahead of her. Night was falling fast, and almost all of the natural light had faded. As though he wanted to reinforce the point, Connor flicked the small switch when he entered the room again, casting a dim, gray light over the middle of the space. He carried the device over to where she sat, and the screen flickered into life in front of her. Waiting was the document she had started earlier in the day. Her eyes scanned over the last few words, and she gulped as she recalled how utterly degraded and turned on she'd been with the hideous gag forced into her mouth. She fidgeted in her seat again as her mind compared it to the dildo now shoved into her bottom instead.

"Get writing, pet," he purred, shifting his body to lean over her right shoulder. "You have a lot of words to get down and neither of us is going to get any rest until you're done."

Chapter Thirty-Two

onnor watched her work from the corner of the room, the spearmint gum in his mouth doing nothing to cool his ardor. Her fingertips were almost hypnotic, the sound of their pressure on the keys mesmerizing as he eyed the woman chained in the center of the room. She barely looked up from the screen, her small frame hunched over it like it had some sort of protective qualities. He wondered idly how bad the position would be for her back, and then smiled to himself. How could he be concerned about the posture of a woman who he planned to leash and cage? It was ridiculous.

Molly worked on into the evening, fidgeting every now and then. Connor imagined how full her ass must be, stretched with the plug inside her, and his cock thickened at the idea. By the time he glanced out of the window to his right, darkness extended over the horizon. He rose from his chair to draw over the thin curtains, but his movement seemed to disconcert her, and for the first time in an age, Molly's digits stopped typing.

Their eyes locked for a moment. Her large blue ones were wide, her chest heaving as they appraised his intent. Connor had no idea what she saw in his, but he hoped she liked the view as much as he did from here.

He approached her slowly, rounding her body to read the screen over her shoulder. Molly was near the end of her butt plug scene, and reading it second-hand aroused him all over again, nearly as much as the real thing had done.

"Why have you stopped?" He whispered the question past her nape, watching as she shivered in response.

"I-I…" There was hesitation as she twisted to face him. He watched as heat collected in her face. The fact that she could find this embarrassing when she was chained naked to a chair made him smirk.

"What's wrong, pet?" he cooed from just behind her shoulder. "I've given the privilege of communication this time. I'd suggest you use it."

Molly swallowed at his tone, the implication in his words apparently obvious. If she didn't speak when requested, she'd find herself gagged again. He nodded at the panic in her eyes, wanting to reinforce the point.

"Nothing, Sir," she replied, her focus returning to the screen once more. "There's nothing wrong."

"Good," he answered. "Then hurry."

Her fingers began work again on command. Their *tap-tap-tapping* filling the room as she typed. Connor stayed in place for a moment, pretending to eye the lines as she created them, but in truth it was Molly he watched. The look of her was incredible, and he glanced up to ensure the tiny camera by the window would have a good shot. He was going to enjoy reliving these moments again and again at another time.

"What you need is some more decoration," he mused out loud.

The tap-tapping fingers paused, and he heard her draw in a fast breath.

"Keep working," he instructed as he turned and strode back to the place he kept all of his favorite toys.

In the bottom drawer of the dresser, Connor found just what he was looking for. Molly's tits were wonderful, but they needed something to make them even more perfect. Grabbing the implements from their place, he knew he had just the thing to help. By the time he was back by her, the typing had resumed, but he could feel the weight of her stare as he towered over the laptop.

"A little something for you," he said wryly, and without further comment, he leaned forward over the device and tweaked one, and then the next exposed nipple with his large right hand.

Molly yelped in response, her fingers faltering once again, and she watched on in dumbstruck horror as Connor's fingers resumed at her breasts. Producing two clothespins, which had been concealed in his left palm, Connor ran the smooth wooden edge of one down the length of her right breast, before taunting the left in the same way. Her nipples responded beautifully, puckering into hard bullets at his provocation.

He glanced down at her. Her face was a picture, a potent combination of shock and trepidation, as her gaze tried to follow the trail of the clothespins. He reckoned she knew what was coming next. She had certainly written the scene herself on enough occasions to see where this is going.

"Why aren't you writing?" His tone was intentionally stern.

Molly raised her gaze to meet his eye. "I'm sorry," she exhaled in a rush. "I didn't know what you were doing, Sir."

There was that word again. He loved how easily she had taken to addressing him the correct way, and every time it rolled from her delicious looking lips, he wanted to pull her face first over the bed and slam into her no-doubt sodden pussy.

"It doesn't matter what I'm doing," he told her, using this moment to tweak both of her nipples hard. She groaned, but interestingly there was no resistance. "Whatever I do, you're expected to complete this session of writing. Got it?"

Her breath was coming out in short, fast pants by this point "Yes, Sir," she gasped, forcing her eyes to the screen between his arms.

Connor allowed her a moment, waiting for the typing to resume, and then he pinched her buds again. There was nothing but a fast intake of breath this time, so he prepared the clothespin in his right hand. Opening the wooden arms, he grazed the edge of Molly's nipple with the wood. If it was possible, her bud tightened even further as if her body was silently begging him to continue. Smiling, he released the tension, forcing the wood to close around the expectant nipple. He watched her face carefully as he let go, seeing the flicker of pain etched into her features, but also that other emotion, the one she was fighting hard to keep in check – her arousal. Quickly, he switched his attention to the other breast, and in less than a minute, both of Molly's breasts were adorned with the wooden clothespins.

Connor stood up straight to appraise his work and was compelled to grin at the sight which met him. What a vision she was, naked and pegged for him to enjoy, while she wrote the story of their time together. His cock was rock hard inside his pants, and for a moment, he considered claiming her mouth while she was chained there, but he thought better of it. He needed to her write, and that would be impossible if his erection got its way.

Chapter Thirty-Three

Molly's head was clouded with the weight of all the sensations. The terror at what might be to come, the rage at being treated this way, and the stark horniness at how wet the treatment made her. They all combined to taunt her. The burgeoning pressure at her breasts was the worst, because it was the newest. She was more than aware of how her pussy had reacted to the clothespins. Damn, she could feel the moisture between her thighs, and she'd have gladly pressed them together if Connor hadn't chained her ankles into position. She'd always had a thing about nipple clamps. The feeling of pressure at her breasts was the surest way to get her hot and bothered, and of course, having poured her fantasies into her many books, Connor was well aware of this fact.

Somehow, she managed to keep the writing flowing, the momentum of her fingers at the keys the only thing to focus on while he tortured her. She didn't dare meet his eyes, but it was obvious from the tent appearing in his pants just how much Connor was enjoying the show. This fact also riled her, although maybe not as much as it should have done. As her digits sailed over the keyboard, she allowed her mind to wander to earlier, when he'd made her come in the kitchen. What had she been thinking, allowing him to pleasure her like that? God dammit, she hadn't just permitted it, she actually begged for it, while he made her eat from a dog bowl. She glanced away from the screen at the memory, her fingers stilling at the potency of the recollection. What had she done? She'd practically whored herself for this man. The same guy who'd taken her and degraded her at every opportunity.

"Are you finished?" His tone was husky, laced with the desire he was no-doubt trying to contain.

Molly swallowed, turning back to the screen. Her fingers were working again before her mouth responded. "Nearly, Sir," she murmured, wanting desperately to push the memory of her mortifying climax from her mind. "I'm just finishing now."

She had no idea how good any of this narrative would be. Christ knows her head had been in another place altogether since this ordeal began. She grimaced at her own choice of language. *Ordeal?* Could she really use that word? Did the term apply to a situation where the so-called victim actively sought their own denigration in return for a soul-shattering orgasm? Molly bit her lip as she considered the idea, wondering what the hell was wrong with her.

As she opened what she hoped would be the final paragraph for now, she swallowed back on her shame. *This is not your fault,* she reminded herself curtly. *You didn't ask for this, you didn't want this. He took you, he drugged you, he's the asshole here!* Her gaze fell upon him at the thought, and she quickly concluded the scene where he chained her here to write.

"I'm done, Sir," she mumbled, all too conscious of his gaze bearing down on her.

"Good girl," he replied, appearing over her right shoulder, his arms reaching down to save the document she'd been working from. "How do you like your new *additions*?"

Connor's body drew back, his hands cupping her breasts. She gasped at the contact, watching as he manipulated both her mounds in unison, causing the clothespins to jerk at the end of her nipples. Fresh sensation coursed through her, flooding the apex of her thighs with hot arousal.

"They're distracting, Sir," she conceded at length, although she regretted her choice of words immediately.

Distracting? Why say that? Why admit that anything about the experience was confusing? It alluded rather too well to her true feelings on the subject, and how turned on the wood at her breasts made her feel.

"Hmmm," came the reply, his voice vibrating over her skin. "I'm inclined to agree. The sight is very distracting."

His mouth skimmed her nape as he concluded, and instinctively Molly held her breath. What was he doing? Was he going to kiss her again, and did she even want him to? Connor's lips nipped at the sensitive skin between her neck and her shoulders, before exploring north, trailing a line of kisses at her jaw. Molly tensed, forcing her breath in and out of her mouth.

Oh God, she thought as the pressure at her jawline intensified. *Oh God, this can't be happening. I can't be enjoying this.*

But enjoying it she was, and by the time Connor's lips moved to the corner of her mouth, she was panting, reveling in the sensual contact between their bodies. His mouth felt amazing against her vulnerable skin, and the fact that she was chained and pretty powerless to prevent his exploration made the whole thing even hotter.

The hand at her left breast vanished, and in a second it collected the side of her face, drawing her gaze right to meet his eye. Molly's face flamed as new embarrassment assaulted her. She'd welcomed his advances yet again, and Connor was no fool, he'd be able to tell just how turned on the whole experience had made her. His green eyes seared her with an intensity she couldn't ever recall before.

"It's time for bed now," he purred, the minty scent of his breath wafting over her face.

Bed? She blinked at him wordlessly, unsure if the statement was a threat or a blessing.

"Yes," he said, as though he had read her mind. "Bed. You have a long day ahead of you tomorrow, and if you want to keep pleasing me, then you'll need some sleep."

Connor retreated, leaving her no-doubt vacant expression as he swept away the laptop from in front of her. She was so freaking horny at this point, her body whirring with unspent need. How could she ever rest in this state, let alone sleep?

"Where do I sleep, Sir?" she asked, cringing at how raspy her tone was.

Connor smiled. "Wherever I tell you, pet."

His answer came with a sardonic smile, and she squeezed her eyes shut, willing his smug, arrogant face to vanish from her mind. As she released the air, there was that low-lying crackle from her chest again. She guessed the food, pleasure and rest had temporarily relieved her symptoms, but it had still been hours, and she still needed her asthma medication. Molly had struggled with her breathing for years, and she knew the signs that she needed her inhalers. Christ knew how many hours it was since she'd taken the medication at the hotel, and by now her body badly needed another dose. Without her prescription drugs, her lungs were going to deteriorate pretty quickly.

She watched as Connor moved the small table to under the window, and then came to crouch down in front of her. "You're wheezing," he said, the words more of a statement than a question.

Molly blinked at him, surprised at his acknowledgement of her symptoms. "Er, yes," she answered. "I get puffed out at this time of the day if I don't take my—"

"Inhalers?" he offered, finishing her sentence for her.

She gaped at him, stunned at his ability to know what she was thinking. "Yes, Sir," she mumbled, awkwardly.

Connor eyed her in silence for a moment, forcing his gaze south. On route to her knees, his eyes cast over her naked form. The two clothespins stuck out from her chest humiliatingly, making her breasts ache gloriously, and goading the flames already rousing between her legs.

"You'll sleep in my room tonight," he concluded after a long silence.

Molly glanced up nervously, unsure if the latest edict was something she should be relieved or worried about. Connor offered no further words to reassure her, instead he reached forward and slowly released the chains which held her legs in place to the chair.

"I'm going to leash you again," he informed her, "and don't even try and think about running, pet. Remember, you're still chained, and I am faster than you. I will catch you, and then I will spend the rest of the night punishing you for your stupidity."

He paused, allowing that thought to sink in. "Is that what you want?"

She shook her head, although her mind was racing. There was a dark promise in the threat, and she knew from the sinful look in his eye that he would deliver, but there was a large part of her that wanted to run. Badly. She didn't want to be his, she didn't want to be chained, leashed and forced to live as a pet. These things were all very well on paper, but in real life, Molly was an independent woman with a smart mouth. This couldn't be her fate.

Connor reached forward, tugging hard on the end of the clothespins, still attached to her breasts. The sensation broke her train of thought in an instant and she yelped in response. "Is that what you want, pet?" he asked her again in a curt voice.

"No, Sir," she whispered, fidgeting against the plug wedged into her ass as the pain of the pins at her nipples radiated through her tightly wound body, straight to her clit.

He rose, sauntering to the bed and collecting the metal leash which he'd used to lead her to the bathroom earlier. "On your knees," he ordered, and Molly found herself complying, despite her patent desire to be free.

He connected the leash to the collar at her neck, moving in the direction of the door. "Come on," he commanded, without even looking back. "You know how to crawl by now."

Chapter Thirty-Four

He led her down the dark corridor, pausing at a door to the right before the bathroom. It hadn't been his original plan to keep her here tonight. He had thought to leave her tied to the bed in the spare room, where he could monitor her from his laptop, but hearing her struggle for breath had changed all that in a heartbeat. Of course, Connor had known she was asthmatic. He'd been studying her for too long to not be aware of her underlying health conditions, and anyway, he had people who dealt with that stuff. More than that though, he was ready for her condition. Using an alias provided by his old friends at The Syndicate, he'd been able to buy most of the drugs she'd need over the internet. He'd had them shipped to a proxy address, and had been stocking up for months now. Connor was certain he had what she needed to quell her symptoms. While he enjoyed watching the little pet suffer, he didn't want her to suffocate.

Twisting the handle, he pushed the door open. Soft green light flooded the area, the effect of his soft furnishings coupled with the spot lights around his room. He glanced down at the woman at his feet, watching her taking it all in.

"Inside," he commanded, his tone sensual and low as he watched her firm, little behind wiggle past his shins. The look of the butt plug sitting snugly in place inside her made him almost gleeful. He'd nearly forgotten she'd been forced to endure it the whole time she'd been writing.

Closing the door behind him, he slid the top bolt across for good measure and guided her into the space. She knelt on all fours on the emerald rug in the center of his room, and he allowed his gaze to take in the look of her there, nude in front of his large king-sized bed. There was a moment when the scene nearly overawed him. Molly Clary was here in his room, naked and leashed. It had been his aspiration for such a long time that it was almost unbelievable, and his cock pulsed greedily in his pants, reminding him of the fact.

"I wasn't going to keep you here tonight," he told her as he approached slowly.

She eyed him with a wary expression, but said nothing in reply. What could she say? He didn't even know why he had divulged the information to her. Moving past her, he secured the end of the leash to the nearest oversized wooden post at the end of his bed, before he shifted his focus back to Molly.

"You take the fluticasone inhaler at night. Is that right?"

Connor watched with some amusement as her gaze widened. Evidently, she had not expected her kidnapper to have done his homework. She was wrong.

"Y-yes, Sir," she replied in little more than a labored gasp.

Connor reached into the dresser behind him, pulling the desired inhaler from the drawer and presenting it to her.

"Like this?" His tone was sardonic.

Her body trembled as she appraised the asthma pump in his hand. "Yes, Sir," she said again, and he could hear the shock in her voice.

He ripped the inhaler from its protective packaging, shaking the pump as he approached his little pet. "Up onto your knees then," he ordered, ignoring his throbbing erection as she rose to obey.

"How many puffs do you need?" His voice sounded hoarse, and he wondered if she'd pick up on the fact.

She glanced up with large eyes. "Just one, please."

Connor nodded, dropping to one knee in front of her as he held the pump out. "Wrap your mouth around the end," he told her, trying not to overthink the analogy. "When you're in place I'll press the pump."

Their gazes locked for a brief second, but she parted her lips in response as he moved the inhaler toward her mouth. Connor watched, mesmerized as she took the pump between her lips, her eyes flitting north to await his command.

"Ready?" he asked, exulting in this bizarre act of intimacy.

She nodded as best she could around the end of the inhaler, and he smiled.

"Okay, after three. Three, two, one..." He pressed the pump, releasing a dose of medicine into the inhaler, and right on cue she inhaled deeply, taking the drug into her wheezy lungs.

He flinched at the sound of the breath, hoping the inhaler would now resolve the issue. Molly released the pump from her mouth, panting lightly as she drew back onto her haunches.

"Better, pet?" he inquired, watching her carefully.

"Yes, I hope so, Sir," she agreed, eyeing him as he assessed her.

"Do you need a blue inhaler too?" He had learnt from his research that asthmatics used this second drug to offer immediate relief from their symptoms.

"You have that one, as well?" she asked, sounding genuinely astonished.

The stunned look on her pretty face made him laugh out loud. "Yes, pet," he replied, rising to swap asthma pumps in his dresser. "You'll find I'm well prepared."

She nodded as her eyes clocked the latest asthma pump in his hand. Connor couldn't tell if it was panic, relief or gratitude which swam in those beautiful orbs. It was probably a potent combination of all of these and more.

"Open up," he instructed, lowering himself to her level again. "Same as before."

The little pet crept forward on her knees, the motion making her pegged breasts jiggle wonderfully as she moved to take the inhaler in her mouth. Connor watched as the leash attached to her neck tightened, but there was just enough room for her to take her medicine. Once she was in position, he counted down again, before squirting the drug into her throat. The act seemed to calm her almost at once, and she settled back on her haunches as he replaced the cap on the inhaler.

"Better?" he asked her, knowingly.

"Thank you, Sir," she replied, her gaze lowering to the floor.

Something about that gesture, her softly spoken tone or the humility, made his breath catch. He didn't know quite what it was exactly, but it was definitely *something*. The way his heart pounded in his chest was a testament to that fact. She was gorgeous. Of course, the collar and the clothespins helped, and the woman was fucking stunning in her own right, but it was more than even that.

"Bed now," he pronounced, forcing the words from his mouth.

The sound of his voice made her head rise and her gaze met his again.

"Where do I sleep?" she asked him again, her eyes darting around the space to try and find the answer herself.

He smiled as he strode toward the side of his bed. Putting the blue inhaler down on the small bedside cabinet, he fell to his knees, reaching underneath the mattress. Connor could feel the weight of her stare as he found what he was looking for, and slowly he pulled it out from under the bed to reveal the place his little pet would be sleeping.

"Here," he told her, turning to see her face as her eyes fell over the large dog bed in his hands. It was rather like the one he'd made her use in the kitchen, but this one was larger, and softer. In fact, he decided as he tucked it into place alongside the middle of his bed, he'd been rather generous when he'd made the purchase.

"In there?" she said, her voice disbelieving as she asked.

Connor had no idea why she'd struggle to believe he was going to make her sleep in the dog bed. Had he not made his feelings on this subject clear, after all? She was his pet now. What had she imagined would happen at this point?

"Yes," he replied curtly, pointing to the spot where the bed now lay. "In there."

She gulped as he approached, slipping between her kneeling frame and the bed to release the leash from his bed post.

"In you go," he ordered, gesturing for her to move. "Into your bed, pet."

Chapter Thirty-Five

Slowly she rose to all fours, crawling the short distance to the pet bed. The interior was cosy and surprisingly warm as she settled inside, but there was no getting away from the reality. She was in a dog bed – again – and that's where he expected her to stay.

Molly watched as Connor busied himself around the room. Producing a new length of chain, he worked at extending the leash attached to her collar so that now it ran from the post nearest his pillow to the dog bed. There was so much slack in the chain that it lay in a pile on the floor next to her, and she was eyeing it wistfully until Connor's movement drew her attention once more. He had begun to strip, and she crouched, huddled as best she could with the damn clothespins still attached, hypnotized by the look of him.

Connor unbuttoned his shirt slowly, almost as though he was putting on a show for her, and casually shrugged the fabric from his shoulders. Molly's gaze fell over his naked torso for the very first time. She had been naked and vulnerable for so long, that she hadn't really considered how he would look, but as the moment arrived, her eyes devoured the sight of him. His body was lean, yet strong and chiseled. He wasn't massive, but she could see the contours of his muscles, the defined pectorals, and the rippling abdominals and the vision made her breath catch. This man, the crazy lunatic who'd snatched her away from her life, was fine. He was the type of guy Molly wrote about. Not too young, not too old. Muscular, but not too big. He seemed intelligent, organized and determined. He should be damned perfect. Except he had taken her, without thought, without permission and without regard for her. Or had he? Connor could clearly be a sadist, but he was also thoughtful and kind. He had shown her compassion when he gave her pleasure, and what about her inhalers? How in the hell had he managed to get hold of those?

Molly's mind whirred with the internal conflict. She'd been captured by a thoughtful sadist, and now what? Now, she lived as his pet? Sleeping in dog beds and eating from the floor? She wanted to balk at the concept, and she would have done too, if it hadn't made her so damn horny.

"Face down. Show me your behind."

The command broke through her foggy musings, and her gaze darted straight back to the man who gave it. He was staring at her, his eyes loaded with some new, dark intensity.

"Sir?" she whispered, forcing the query from her mouth.

"You heard me," he replied, stonily. "Shift that body and stick your arse up in the air."

Her body was moving then, a new terror washing through her. Was he going to punish her again? Spank her, or maybe something worse? He'd threatened her with his belt earlier, and the thought made it difficult to breathe. Molly's head reeled as she tried to think what she'd done to piss him off this time, and all the while she was shifting, until she found herself back on her hands and knees. Pressing the side of her face down into the soft pet bed, Molly forced her ass up to meet his gaze. The clothespins were forced flat, sending a spike of pain through her body.

In her peripheral vision, she saw him approach her. Connor towered over her submissive frame, his eyes drilling into her exposed and vulnerable sex.

"Beautiful," he murmured, and a second later he crouched behind her, his long digits grazing the backs of her thighs.

Instinctively, Molly whimpered. Anxiety ricocheted around her body, dread resurfacing at the prospect of what was to come. Before she knew what was happening, she began to shake. She could feel her legs trembling under his touch as the fear inside her mounted.

"What's wrong, pet?" he asked, quizzically.

Molly caught her breath again, unsure if it was irony or concern she heard in his voice. "Are you angry with me, Sir?"

Connor's laughter filled the air around her, burgeoning the sense of apprehension in her belly. "Angry, pet? Why, *should* I be angry with you?"

She tried to shake her head as best she could against the fur of the bed. "No!" she implored him. "No, Sir." She caught the smile which reached his lips at her answer.

"Good," he cooed, his digits rising until they approached her sex.

Molly swallowed. Unbelievably, she knew she was still wet. She was horny, despite the fear which made her tremble. The power Connor had over her at this moment was terrifying and intoxicating in equal measure.

"It's time this came out," he mused as his fingers ran over her labia and rose to the plug still tucked inside her bottom.

Molly gulped, her heart racing inside her chest. The butt-plug? Is that what this was about? Relief flooded her system, but she steeled herself despite the response. Connor could still punish her. He could do anything he liked, and that fact made it impossible to relax.

"Do you want this toy out, pet?"

His voice was a seductive whir, and as he spoke Molly could feel his fingers at her bottom; one and then a second digit circling the base of the plug.

She hesitated, unsure how to respond. Was Connor just fucking with her? If she admitted how much she'd love the thing to be gone, would he insist she endure it even longer? It seemed just the sort of sick, head-fuck game he'd play.

"Pet?" he snapped, the timbre of his voice making her body jump. "Answer me!"

"Yes, Sir," she gasped, resolving in a matter of seconds that all she could do was be honest, whatever the consequences. "Yes, I would like it out... please."

A dark chuckle reverberated around Molly again, making her body tense. Connor slapped her right cheek playfully.

"It won't come out like that," he told her. "You need to relax. Remember how we got it in there?"

Molly nodded her head desperately, more than able to recall the degrading moment he had forced the cold plug into her bottom. "Yes, Sir," she squeaked.

"Excellent," came the reply. "Then you know what you need to do. Breathe deeply, pet. Let's do this."

Molly inhaled as instructed, her breath shaky as she pulled in the air through her mouth. Almost at once she was aware of a pressure on the plug, and Connor's fingers gripping the base.

"Breathe," he commanded, his tone firm.

She nodded, mewling as the pressure intensified.

"In," he ordered slowly, easing the force on her ass. "And out, slowly..."

With that he tugged hard at the plug, and as she pushed the air from her lips, Molly felt the thing ease out of her. The sensation was intense and uncomfortable, but she trusted him. What choice did she have? She wanted the thing out, and it seemed Connor was prepared to deliver it for her. As the last of the breath left her, the plug slipped away. A wave of emotion washed over Molly. It was absurd, but true. She was so utterly vulnerable and powerless at this moment, and she blinked away the tears which welled in her eyes.

"I can't wait to fuck that arse," he murmured from behind her. His voice sounded so warm, it was almost tender.

Molly's eyes flitted to his face, watching him gazing at her most intimate areas. His assertion terrified her, yet something about it also enthralled her. Connor was captivating as he knelt behind her, his authority making fresh moisture pool between her thighs.

"Get comfortable now," he told her, rising to his feet.

Molly twisted in the bed, curling up as best she could. Her ass felt more comfortable without the plug, and she was thankful for that small mercy at least.

Chapter Thirty-Six

He stepped back from the pet bed, watching Molly trying to acclimatize to her new environment. The clothespins were still clinging to her nipples, and he imagined how sore her breasts must be by now. Molly must really like the dull ache, because she hadn't complained about the pegs at all, but he noticed now her gaze was captured by them. A wry smile formed on his lips, and he felt his brow arch at the look of her.

"Do you like the pegs, pet?" he probed, as he unbuckled the belt at his waist.

Molly's eyes were on him at once, her gaze flaring at the look of his belt. "Erm, yes, Sir," she mumbled, coloring fast at the admission. "But they're making me sore now."

"Are they?" he inquired as he drew the trousers at his hips down in the direction of the floor.

Connor noticed her gulp as he stepped out of them, kicking them toward the corner of the room. He was still painfully aroused, and his cock strained overtly against his expensive boxers.

"Yes, Sir."

He paused, eyeing her severely. She seemed to shrivel under the weight of his stare, visibly becoming smaller as he began to inch back in her direction. "Perhaps they need to come off then? They have been on there a long time."

Molly was nodding, but she looked even more than apprehensive as he approached.

"Kneel up," he told her. "Let me take them."

She obeyed at once, the look of her kneeling nudity making his erection throb harder. Passing in front of her, he stilled, reaching down to take the ends of both clothespins in his fingers.

"Get ready," he purred from over Molly. "This may hurt a little." There was a sardonic edge to his tone, but he gave Molly no time to process it. The clothespins were whipped from her nipples the next moment, eliciting a large gasp from her mouth.

She raised her chained hands, as though acting on some reflex, and her hands cradled the weight of her breasts. Connor permitted the deed for a moment, before he tugged gently on the leash attached to Molly's collar.

"That's enough," he told her. "Hands down."

Molly raised her chin to acknowledge the command as she complied. He noticed her soulful eyes were full of tears, and he wondered fleetingly if it was the pain in her tits which had caused them, or the enormity of her situation. Not that it mattered of course, Connor was changing nothing about her predicament, but the pained look in her eyes troubled him. He wanted to own her, to control her and to belittle her. He enjoyed it, and he knew what a sick fuck that made him, but it was true. For all of that though, he didn't actually want to hurt her, not really. He just needed Molly to be afraid enough to do as she was told. It was a delicate balance to walk, but he was certain he could make it work. Connor would show her that any resistance would prove to be futile.

Gazing down at her, he reached forward to stroke her cheek. "You should rest," he said softly. "I have lots of things in store for you tomorrow."

Her eyes closed at his words, forcing one large tear to slip past her petite nose. "Please," she whimpered, trembling under his touch.

Connor grabbed the metal chain running past his mattress and stepped over it to sit down on the bed. "Look at me," he commanded, though his tone remained calm.

Molly shifted on her knees to face him, her eyes opening as he instructed.

"Are you afraid?" he asked, clutching the chain in his right hand to draw her body closer.

She swallowed, eyeing him intensely. "Yes, Sir," she breathed in a barely audible whisper. He could tell from the conflicted expression on her face just how much it pained her to concede the point, but he appreciated her honesty, even if it did arouse him.

He moved, painfully aware of the throbbing need at his groin. He knew Molly must have seen it too, and he realized that would be doing little to quell her rising anxiety.

"If you do as you're told, then you'll be fine, little pet," he told her. "I don't want to hurt you. I'm a keeper."

Connor watched as she transferred the weight between her knees, her lower lip catching between her teeth. "Keep me?" she murmured, her voice nervous.

"Yes," he asserted, assessing her responses carefully. It was critical that he moved with precision now. He wanted Molly to be pliant and aroused, that way she would learn to obey him without question, and ultimately, she would come to desire him herself. If she was too petrified, then there was a chance she'd become a flight-risk and liable to bolt at any moment. If that happened, then he'd be forced to keep her chained indefinitely. Alternatively, she could switch off altogether, becoming little more than a doll for him to play with. Connor didn't want either of those outcomes. He wanted a pliable little pet. A woman he could instruct and worship, and one who would love the power dynamic. Of course, it helped that Molly could also pen their story for him. After all the hot, dark romances he'd read, now he had the chance to live his own.

"Will you…" She hesitated. Evidently, whatever was about to come next was the crux of Molly's fear.

"Go on," he coaxed her.

Connor saw her physically brace herself as she complied. "Will you force yourself on me?"

Molly pushed the question out in one long breath, her gaze darting away from his muscular frame.

A long, deep sigh left his lips. "Pet," his tone was curt again. "Look. At. Me."

Slowly, she turned her head back to meet his gaze. There were tears in her eyes again, but she blinked them away hastily.

"I want you to listen to me," he ordered her, "and listen well."

She nodded, her expression anxious.

Connor's gaze captured her, and intentionally he used it to pinion her in place as he spoke. "I will never force myself on you," he told her. "I may be twisted, but I'm not into that."

Molly bit her lip again as he concluded. Clearly, she didn't share his optimistic view of her fate, and he supposed he could hardly blame her. "But, you said you wanted to fuck my ass," she countered him, her voice quivering as she tried to explain.

Connor chuckled lightly, stroking her hair back from her face. He noticed fleetingly how dank her locks were, making a mental note to shower her tomorrow.

"Oh, I am going to fuck that delicious arse, pet," he announced, glibly. "And that sweet pussy as well."

She gasped, but she said nothing by means of reply.

"But I won't need to force the acts upon you," he continued. "Do you know why?"

Molly shook her head. She looked absolutely stunned by his words.

"You'll be so desperate for me by then," he proclaimed. "So hot, so wild and so soaking wet, that they'll be no need for force. You'll beg me to fuck you, pet, just you wait and see."

She swallowed at that, but Connor noticed the satisfying blush which crept up from her neck. He had an idea that she liked the sound of what he described, and after her recent displays of arousal, she was really in no position to protest the point.

"Sleep now," he commanded as he rose. "Settle down in your bed."

Molly drew in another shaky breath at the order. She was no-doubt exhausted, and he watched as she curled her body into a ball. Opening his cupboard, he located the soft green blanket he'd chosen for her especially, and as he walked back toward the dog bed, he allowed it to unravel in front of her.

"This should keep you warm," he murmured as he spread the cover over her limbs and torso. "Now, stay in your bed and keep quiet. Unless you want to be gagged again?"

Molly was shaking her head violently before he had even finished his question, and the look of her made him laugh. She was adorable. Just too fucking adorable.

Chapter Thirty-Seven

The night was long and endless. To Molly, it seemed as though she now existed in some bizarre dream-like state, caught between the reality of her most explicit fantasies, and her very worst nightmares. Connor had complete control of her, that much was clear. He now got to decide when and how she ate, and even if she could use the bathroom. The thought made her shudder in the darkness, the motion causing her chains to jangle around her body.

She froze, praying inwardly that the sound wouldn't wake the sleeping giant in the bed next to her, but fortunately Connor didn't stir. Huddled in the darkness, she tried to recall the events which had led to this. Molly had always considered herself rather street-wise and savvy, yet in the same day she'd been attacked by a group of guys, and then taken by Connor. How had she become such an easy target? She sighed as she contemplated her fate, and then it occurred to her. He must have been watching her after the signing, following her and waiting for her. Once the group of other men had decided to attack, he'd pounced. She grimaced into the black space around her, trying to remember what had happened. She had a vague recollection of him taking down the whole group of men who'd attacked her, but, how was that possible? He must be some type of martial arts expert, but even then, could one man be so lethal on his own? Molly exhaled at the effort of trying to recall the event, but based on what she could remember, then the answer was yes. One man could be that efficient, and it seemed Connor was that man.

Her body flexed and shifted in the chains, but it was no use. Sleep was not coming. Molly had managed to doze for a few hours, her body overwrought with the effects of the drugs and the long, weary day she'd been forced to endure, but having woken, it now seemed impossible to get any more sleep. It was so ridiculously hard to get comfortable in this damn dog bed. These things were made for animals, not people, and Molly's body didn't bend in the right ways to make any position comfortable. She wanted to stretch out, but she didn't want to risk sleeping like that only to face Connor's wrath in the morning.

Twisting to the right again, she rolled her legs in the other direction, sending the chains at her ankles and wrists crashing down with her movement. Molly flinched at the sound, holding her breath in the darkness.

"Is my pet restless?" The sound of Connor's voice pierced the black air around her.

Molly gulped, her heart racing out of control. *Shit,* she thought wildly. The last thing she'd intended to do was wake her abductor.

"Pet?"

There was movement from the mattress above her, and all at once something tugged hard on the chain connecting her to his bed. Molly lurched forward abruptly, just managing to get her hands out in front of her face to break her fall.

"I'm sorry, Sir," she gasped, panic wafting over her in waves as she scrambled to her hands and knees in the pitch black.

A moment of silence followed, before a small clicking sound indicated his intention to light the area. All at once, the soft yellow light of his bedside lamp illuminated the area, and Molly peered up at him. She knew her eyes were wide and her breathing was frantic, but there was little she could do to calm herself. The fact this man could just yank her from her so-called bed was terrifying, reminding her more than efficiently just how vulnerable she really was.

"Why aren't you asleep?" he murmured, blinking at her from his bed. As he spoke he sat up, revealing his strong shoulders and honed abs to her startled eyes.

"I'm sorry," she mumbled again. "I couldn't sleep."

It sounded pathetic, and she hoped to God that he wouldn't be angry, but Molly didn't know what else to say. How were you supposed to sleep when you were chained up like an animal?

Connor's body tensed, his gaze narrowing as he assessed the woman by the side of his bed. "You'll find I'm rather irritable when I don't get my beauty sleep," he told her, his tone low as he gave the thinly-veiled warning.

Molly swallowed hard, her heartbeat now so loud to her ears, that it threatened to drown out practically every other sound. "I'll be quiet," she replied in a rush of fear and adrenaline. "I promise."

He tilted his head at her, apparently trying to decide if she was telling the truth or not. "Do you need something to make you sleep?" he asked, dryly.

She shook her head, furiously. "No, thank you, Sir," she answered him, retreating back into the relative sanctuary of her bed.

Connor watched the chain extend as she shifted back into the pet bed, and then his gaze returned to Molly. "Well, we're both awake now," he muttered, rising from his bed with a stretch. Stepping over the chain he rounded her small frame and stood, towering beside her.

"Hot milk?" he said, his tone softer. "Or maybe even hot chocolate if you swear to be a good girl and drink it all?"

Molly blinked up at him, her eyes devouring the look of his powerful thighs, and pausing over his semi-erect cock. Evidently Connor had fallen asleep without his boxers, and his manhood was now springing to life before her very eyes. The sight of him made her breathless for quite different reasons. Yes, he was still her abductor and he was dangerous, but Connor was much more than that. He was fit, strong and incredibly attractive, and now he was offering her hot chocolate? What the actual fuck?

"Pet?"

His voice brought her eyes up to where his amused face was waiting for her. *Shit*, she thought again, her face flaming. He'd clocked her staring at his cock like some sex-starved woman. What the hell would he think now? Her mind raced back to his words last night, and the smug way he'd assured her that she'd beg for his attention before he'd ever have to force himself on her. Molly has been astounded by the revelation, riled and sickened by his arrogant tone, and yet, look at her. Just a few hours later and she was eyeing his erection eagerly, like a little girl who wants a lollipop.

"Yes, Sir," she responded, flushed and embarrassed at the latest turn of events.

"Would you like a hot chocolate?"

She stared up at him, this time intentionally keeping her focus on his face. Was he serious? He was really going to make her a hot chocolate? It sounded absurd in the circumstance. The sound of her growling belly made up her mind for her though. She was hungry, and probably thirsty too, and the promise of something hot also sounded good.

"Yes, please," she replied, cringing at the desperation in her tone as she answered him.

He smiled. "Ask me nicely."

The order was softly delivered, but his tone was taunting.

Molly twisted in the pet bed again. Ask him nicely? What the hell did he expect? She'd already said please. She blinked up at his tall, strong body at his expectant, green eyes. Evidently whatever Connor expected, he wanted it now. Sighing deeply, she lowered her gaze as she replied. "Please may I have a hot chocolate, Sir?"

"Look at me," came the response, and his voice was so brusque that Molly jumped out of instinct.

"Better," Connor nodded. "Since you asked me so nicely, pet, then you may have a hot chocolate. Now stay put while I make it."

He patted her head as he gave the final instruction, and Molly couldn't help but think of a dog being trained to obey her master's commands. Heat rose between her legs at the shameful comparison, and she caught the smirk on his defined lips as he paced away from her toward the bedroom door.

Chapter Thirty-Eight

onnor prepared the drinks in record time, ensuring he bolted the outside of the bedroom as he left. Excited adrenaline coursed through his veins as he exited the kitchen with the small tray in his hands. Taking the weight in one large hand, he drew back the bolt, and entered his bedroom to find Molly chained and exactly where he'd left her.

"Good pet," he cooed as he placed the tray down on his dresser, reinstating the bolt on this side of the door. "You did as you were told."

He watched cheerfully as a fresh blush filled her face, and then watched her sweet expression shift into something resembling horror as he lifted the bowl and carried it toward her. "Here we are," he cooed, placing the metal bowl down on the carpet next to the soft dog bed. "Your hot chocolate."

Molly's face blanched immediately, her expressive eyes flitting from him to the bowl as she tried to make sense of it all. Apparently, she had forgotten how pets take their drinks, and Connor couldn't suppress his smile as he curled up into his warm bed with a steaming mug of chocolate.

"What do you say?" he prompted her gruffly, once he was comfortable against his pillows.

Her head turned in his direction slowly, the leash attached to her collar rattling as she eyed the white mug between his large palms. Her eyes were questioning, as though the answer was on the tip of her tongue, but she couldn't quite remember it.

"Pet," he said, pressing the point in an intentionally curt tone. "I asked you a question."

Molly shuddered a little, and he watched the bounce in her perfect tits. "I'm sorry, Sir," she gasped. "And thank you."

He smiled, or maybe it was more a sneer, he couldn't tell. "Better," he replied. "And you're welcome. Now, remember you swore to be a good girl, and drink it all up."

He was definitely smirking now, so he raised the mug to his lips to hide the expression from her. Molly nodded her head, before shifting her weight slightly to address the bowl of hot chocolate. Connor had placed it at the ideal angle for his viewing pleasure. She had to turn sideways to him on all fours to even approach the bowl, and he watched gleefully as her head lowered toward the steaming liquid.

Christ, she looked fucking amazing, her breasts full as they hung below her toned body, her face burning with embarrassment. And all the while she remained leashed to his bed – *his bed*! Connor closed his eyes at the sight, wanting to capture the memory in his mind for all time.

Molly's face neared the liquid chocolate, and he tilted his head to check her reactions. She looked predictably mortified at what she was about to do, yet he sensed her urge to consume the drink was driving her on, overriding her better judgment on the subject, and then, of course, there would be the throbbing between her legs. If he had learned anything from the last day with his pet, then it was how much she relished her own denigration, though, of course, she would never admit such a thing.

He sipped at his drink, watching her hesitation with interest. "Go on, pet," he urged. "Get your tongue in. Lap at it!"

She froze, seemingly paralyzed by his attention. Connor shifted on the bed, allowing a dark chuckle to escape his lips.

"I mean it," he warned her. "Don't make me get out of this bed again, or else you'll have a very sore bottom, and you'll still be finishing that bowl, only the chocolate will be cold."

A low gasp came from her cowering body, and she twisted her face to meet his gaze. "Sir," she whimpered. "Don't make me do this."

Connor's erection throbbed urgently at the sound of her plea, but he kept his eyes on his embarrassed little pet as he answered. "Oh, but I am going to," he told her with a wide smile. "Either you lap at your bowl now like a good girl, or I'll tan that gorgeous backside for you, and then you'll lap from it. But lap from it you will, my little pet, and you had better believe it."

She believed him alright, but Molly was frozen as wave upon wave of emotional responses crashed over her. Indignation rose from within her, followed by an unbearable, burning arousal, which radiated from between her legs. It was too much – all of it. She grimaced at the metal object as the scent of delicious chocolate wafted past her nose. It smelt so damn good, just the aroma made her stomach growl hungrily, but still she couldn't convince her mouth to lower into the warm liquid. Memories of how she'd eaten chicken from the same bowl only yesterday filled her mind, and she willed them away. She'd have to do this – she knew that now – but somehow the realization made the ordeal no easier to manage.

"Last chance," he growled from over her right shoulder. "Get in that bowl or I'm hauling you over my lap."

That made her move, and somehow, she forced herself down toward the liquid. She pushed her tongue out tentatively, testing the temperature of the liquid. It was no longer hot, but the chocolate warmed her tongue nicely, and it tasted wonderful. Emboldened by the sweet taste, and the knowledge of how much she knew she was going to enjoy it, Molly tried again. This time she pushed her tongue into the liquid, doing her best to ladle it into her mouth. She failed miserably of course, and most of the hot chocolate slipped from her mouth before she could swallow it. Molly sniffed sharply, frustration spiking as she tried again. As before, she plunged her tongue into the warm liquid, trying to scoop some of the contents of the bowl into her mouth. And as before, she lost the majority of the liquid before her tongue could retreat back into her mouth.

Her efforts were met by Connor's hearty laughter, and she stilled, beyond mortified at his response. Shooting a glare in his direction, she met his grinning gaze.

"Look at the state of you!" he chortled, assessing her face as she lifted it from the bowl. "You're covered in it. Get back over that bowl, I don't want chocolate all over my carpet."

Molly leaned forward as instructed. She could feel the chocolate dripping from her mouth and chin, and she forced her eyes closed as she imagined how utterly ridiculous she must look. Naked, chained and now covered in the liquid she was forced to drink from the dog bowl, it was simply too much to process.

"You'd better get on with it," he told her, taking another long swig from his mug. "It will be cold soon, and fun though this is, we both need more sleep."

She forced her eyes open again, wanting so badly to tell him to go and fuck himself, but knowing what sort of trouble that would land her in. Steeling what little dignity she had left, she began to lap at the liquid once more.

It was a long and messy affair, and her tongue was aching by the time she neared the bottom of the bowl. Molly tried not to stop, or to think. She only pressed on, cleaning the bowl as best she could, only she had a bad feeling that some of the contents may well have found their way over Connor's precious carpet, as well as in her loose strands of hair. All the while, she knew he was watching. She could actually feel the weight of his stare against her bare skin as she leaned over the bowl. At times she heard his chuckle again. The sick fuck was enjoying this, and she knew there was nothing she could do about it.

When she finally lifted her nose from the bowl, she realized something even worse. The shameful display had made her wet again, her need burgeoning more than ever. If Connor was sick for enjoying this, then what did that make her?

He placed the mug down on his bedside and twisted his body to look at her properly. "Head up," he ordered, and slowly she obeyed, lifting her neck and allowing him to see the state of her face.

Connor burst into laughter at the sight of her, and as if her humiliation wasn't great enough, he angled the head of his bedside lamp so that it shone in her direction. By now her nose and mouth were both smothered in the sweet liquid, and she could only imagine what she must look like.

"Just look at that," he chortled gleefully, and to her horror, Connor actually grabbed his cell phone and snapped a quick shot of her on her hands and knees on his floor.

Molly's head bowed in shame. She hated being messy, but worse than that, worse than all of this denigration, was how her own body responded to it. She was hot, and wet and hungry for attention. *His* attention.

"Let's get you cleaned up," he grinned as he put his phone away, and grabbed a handful of tissues from a box on the bedside table.

Crouching before Molly, he wiped the chocolate from her mouth and chin. It was incredibly objectifying, as though she had been reduced to this thing he could chain and clean. Her mind reeled, and as she knelt there, she couldn't even decide how she even felt anymore. The truth was Molly had always fantasized about being objectified; where she could be diminished to something less than herself and revel in the submission of the act. Connor however, probably did understand that much about her. He had already admitted to reading all of her books, so he'd have a better idea than most about what she fantasized about late in the evening. Their eyes met briefly, and he smiled knowingly.

Chapter Thirty-Nine

He threw her a devastating smile, and as their eyes locked, he could sense the hot, torrid arousal tightening in her. Connor sympathized. He had his own lust and desire to manage, and at this moment, nothing would have given him greater pleasure than to have scratched both of their itches. Nothing except what he already had in mind...

Connor's eyes glanced down at the bowl, taking in her effort, and then what remained of the chocolate stains dotted around the bowl. She'd done pretty well. The majority of the chocolate was gone from the bowl, and despite the mess, he knew she'd done her best. However, he was in the mood to play, and her best would not be good enough.

"How was that, pet?" he asked her. "Did you enjoy your hot chocolate?"

Molly's eyes widened, and she glared at him, indignation obviously rising in her.

"Pet," he warned her in a low tone. "Don't look at me that way. I asked you a question, which I would like answered."

She swallowed again, her face softening. "Thank you for the chocolate, Sir," she whispered, although Connor could tell there was no sincerity in her tone.

"Hmmm," he responded, intentionally holding her gaze before his eyes returned to the near-empty bowl. "You did a good job, pet, *but* there is some chocolate left in that bowl."

Molly's eyes immediately flew to the metal bowl, her breath becoming erratic as she clocked the small quantity of liquid still swilling in the bottom of it. "I..." She hesitated, eyeing him nervously. "I did my best, Sir."

Connor smiled. "I'm sure you did," he cooed, dropping to one knee before Molly. "But you still didn't drink it all up like I asked you to."

There was silence as his words resounded, but he could tell that she understood the implication from her body language. He watched as her nipples hardened, and her breath began to come out in small pants.

"I'm sorry," she whispered, apologizing yet again, but this time her tone was raspy, her lust evident as she spoke, or maybe it was her trepidation? Connor couldn't be sure.

He watched her, a small smile spreading across his face. "I know you are," he drawled, "but sorry isn't good enough. I asked you to drink all of the chocolate, and you failed in that challenge. That means, despite your very best efforts, you need to be punished." Connor didn't even try to hide the happiness in his voice as he cast his verdict, the look on her face making his cock throb with excitement.

"P-punished?" Her voice was low and sensual, but he could hear the anxiety in it.

"Nothing too dramatic," he reassured her. "It's the middle of the night for Christ's sake, and I'm shattered, but you need to learn obedience, pet. On this point, and on every point."

"I want to obey," she replied in a shaky tone. "Please don't hurt me."

That look in her eyes moved him. Yes, his cock was pulsating with undeniable need – a fact that Molly was no doubt aware of, given her close proximity – but it was more than that. It wasn't just the sadist in him that her doleful expression called to, it was the man as well. At that moment she needed looking after, and protecting, and he was the lucky bastard who'd get to fulfil both desires. He'd give her the spanking of her life, and then he'd be there to console her.

"Remember what I told you before?" he asked her. His voice had become a soft, sensual purr, and she raised her chin to meet his gaze. "I will hurt you, but I won't cause you permanent harm. You need to be punished, pet, but then, you already know that don't you?"

Molly was shaking her head, tears collecting in her eyes as she blinked at him. "But, I..." She hesitated, the urgency evident in her eyes. "I didn't do anything wrong."

Connor gave her an intentionally dark stare before he continued. "You don't get to decide when you're punished," he sneered. "Or whether your behavior is acceptable or not. You are my pet now. You exist to please me, write for me and do as you're told."

He saw her gulp at that, and he hoped the reality of his words settled over her. For a moment there was silence, apart from her ragged breathing.

"Do you understand?" he asked, his tone low.

Molly nodded. "Yes, Sir, I understand."

That was good enough for Connor for the time being, and he backed away, returning to his place on the bed. "Get up here then," he ordered, beckoning to her with the index finger of this right hand. "I need to spank you now."

She rose on shaky legs, her chains all rattling at the same time as she stood before him. Connor's eyes scanned over her gorgeous body, the metal at her wrists and the chain hanging between them. Fuck, she was fabulous, and she was all *his*.

"Over my lap," he commanded, patting his legs as though she wouldn't know where he meant.

Molly approached him with caution. Her gaze clocked his cock, and she gasped as she took in the extent of his arousal, instinctively coming to a halt.

"Remember what I told you," he said again, as calmly as he could muster. "I am not going to force myself on you. This is a punishment. Nothing more."

He hoped his words would reassure her, and was pleased when she inched closer to his naked body, though he could still sense the tension radiating from her. Connor could understand her trepidation of course. He'd taken her by force, and he knew that. She wasn't here by choice. But he meant what he said about not really harming her. He was no rapist. Naturally, he would love to fuck Molly, that went without saying, but he could wait and bide his time. He'd keep her, make her write their story, and train the pet, and then, when she was ready – when she was absolutely begging him for sex – that's when he'd claim her. The thought made his smile widen.

By now Molly had reached the edge of the bed, so he gestured for her to take her place over his thighs. Her body moved forward, but she hesitated again, so he took her left hand and hauled her into position. There was a small yelp as her body landed over him, but Molly offered no resistance. The warmth of her belly roused him, and his hands moved over her nudity at once. He may have no intention of taking her by force, but that didn't mean he wasn't going to enjoy this opportunity. The skin to skin contact was scintillating, and his left hand trailed up her naked body, exerting just enough force to keep her in place, while his right one came to rest over the orbs of her perfect arse.

"This spanking is designed to teach you an important lesson, pet," he told her, slapping both cheeks playfully. His voice was soft and tantalizing, much like the look of her body splayed over his lap, and he relished the soft gasp which escaped her mouth at the first swat. "Be a good girl and take what's coming to you."

Glancing left toward her face, he saw her pull in a shaky breath, but she didn't respond. She didn't fight either though, so Connor took that as her acquiescence to his demands, and concentrated on the task in hand. And what a task it was.

His new pet had the most stunning behind. It was pert, round and perfectly formed, without a doubt designed for his large palms to correct. That right palm rose from her flesh, before coming crashing back down against her. He relished the impact, watching as the strike reverberated over her flawless cheeks. There was no noise from her, not even a gasp, and the lack of response spurred him on. Delivering the second spank, he intentionally aimed for the same spot, this time observing her face as best he could as the impact vibrated around her body. Molly squeezed her eyes shut, but still there was no gasp, no yelp, nothing to suggest pain. Steeling himself, Connor delivered a further five swats in fast succession, and all the time he watched her even expression. His pet was stoic and strong, and a bizarre sense of pride filled him, but still, this was a punishment, and he wouldn't be happy until she was overwhelmed with the sting of his palm.

"Why are you being spanked, pet?" he growled, peppering her cheeks with hard smacks as he spoke.

She opened her eyes, his voice apparently bringing her back to the here and now. "I didn't finish my hot chocolate, Sir," she replied, breathlessly.

Connor nodded at her admission, but his palm did not relent. Instead, it continued to spank her, lowering its intensity toward the sensitive flesh at the top of her thighs. As his hand connected to this new target, a small whimper left her delicate lips. His cock throbbed furiously at the sound, his gaze assessing her face as he shifted to the next thigh.

"More specifically," he demanded, "tell me where your hot chocolate was when you failed to finish it as requested."

Molly gasped, her eyes flying back to meet his as his palm spanked her again, alternating between her pale thighs. Connor gazed at her coolly. Now he was really enjoying himself. Not only was he getting to discipline his gorgeous little pet, but even better, he had found a weak spot. Having her thighs spanked obviously hurt, and as his gaze flitted back to her upturned bottom, he could see the flesh there beginning to color wonderfully.

"I didn't finish the chocolate in my bowl, Sir" she answered him, her face flushing as she forced the words out.

Connor's palm stilled, pressing into the heat of her punished bottom. She'd said the words out loud, just as he'd wanted. "That's right," he told her, ensuring his gaze drilled into the exposed area of her pretty face. "You're going to have to get used to lapping from that bowl, pet, because that's the only way you'll be drinking from now on. Got it?" As he spoke his hand rose a few inches and swatted her upturned cheeks hard.

"Yes, Sir," Molly gasped, eyeing him wildly.

"Good," he replied, landing another three strikes against her now pink cheeks. "Bad pets who disobey me are punished, do you understand?"

"Yes, Sir," she whispered again. By now her voice sounded hoarse, and the timbre caught Connor's attention. He turned to see the exposed cheek of her face burning red, and he wondered if it was the pain or the embarrassment which caused her the greatest injury. The thought intrigued him.

Connor continued to spank her. Swat after swat landed against her reddening skin as his large palm connected over and over. All the while his gaze darted between her punished behind, and her face. She was exquisite, and all the more so as her previously calm exterior began to crumble. He watched excitedly as she grimaced, absorbing the blows, first in silence, and then as the pain built, with small, guttural whimpers.

Then came the begging; one of his favorite parts.

"Please, Sir," she mewled, her voice desperate. As she whimpered, her hips shifted over him as though her bottom was trying to dodge his palm. Connor chuckled at the sight, applying just a little more pressure to her back.

"Keep still," he ordered, though his tone was more amused than angry.

He glanced over at the expression of the squirming woman, watching her wince as each new spank landed.

"I can't," she breathed. "Please. I'm sorry, I'll drink everything from the bowl from now on, just please stop!"

Connor smiled. Now he was getting somewhere. "Yes, you will, pet," he agreed, sending his palm down to meet her exposed cheeks again. "But this spanking doesn't end until I say so."

Molly sniffed, blinking away fresh tears as she absorbed the hurt. She didn't press the point anymore, but he saw her small fists ball into his bedding as the onslaught continued, and he knew the pain was growing in intensity.

"Tell me what you are," he commanded, his voice loud and aggressive, all of a sudden.

Molly flinched, inhaling as Connor's palm rained down on her bottom. She blinked up at him, a single tear making tracks along her petite nose, and down to the bed. "I... I don't know what to say."

"Yes, you do," he growled, swatting her backside. As he lifted his palm again, he swept his hand between her thighs, making contact with her sex. Just the slightest touch made him hard. His pet was absolutely soaking wet, her seam dripping with her very obvious desire.

"What are you?" he demanded again. "Why are you kept leashed and why do you drink from a bowl?"

Molly gulped, her face blanching as his meaning became clearer. Connor's hand had stopped spanking her since its contact with her wet seam, and as he waited for her reply, his digits were tantalizingly close to her pussy. His gaze never left her though, and all the while, his stare penetrated her face as he pushed her to admit her new-found status.

"I'm your pet, Sir," she mumbled at length, and as she admitted the words out loud, her voice broke with her humiliation.

"Tell me again," he insisted, and this time he allowed just one finger to brush against her labia.

She gasped, but her body shuddered, and her hips began to move again, as though they were acting on some type of reflex. "I'm your pet, Sir," she conceded, her voice louder this time.

Connor rewarded her with one finger, which he slipped effortlessly into her tight channel. Molly moaned gratefully in response, her eyes still blinking away tears as she made eye contact with her captor.

"Do you understand who's in charge now?" he questioned her, pressing his advantage.

Her head nodded against the bedding beside him as a second digit joined his first inside her pussy. "Yes, yes, Sir," she gasped as he began to ease out, and then back inside her. Her cheeks had a blazing red hue by now, and he knew the spanking must have hurt, but unbelievably, his pet was wetter than ever. It seemed to Connor that she was caught somewhere between agony and ecstasy.

"Who?" he growled, fingering her slowly as he assessed her responses.

She panted as she replied, her legs splayed naturally to accommodate his intrusion. "You, Sir," she whispered. "You are in charge."

Chapter Forty

The admission was like a revelation to Molly, which was ridiculous given all of her recent experiences. It should have been obvious who was in charge; after all, Connor had never left her in any doubt. From the moment he'd taken her, she'd been controlled, commanded and coerced. Connor had been able to degrade her in ways she'd only imagined about before, or more precisely, *wrote* about before, but now it was a reality, and everything was different.

Being made to admit that this man, who had so clearly studied her, maybe even stalked her, and then snatched her, was actually now in charge of her, made her crazy. Molly's body was tormented with pent up energy. She was riled and mad with him for doing this to her when he had no right. The sense of injustice about her predicament was growing, creating a knot of emotion in her belly that never seemed to subside. At the same time, the way he denigrated her was doing the most amazing things to her body. It was like every deliciously debauched fantasy Molly had ever concocted for her stories, but better – and worse – because this was really happening, and she had no choice but to play Connor's games.

The air shifted perceptibly after she conceded the point to him, and she felt Connor tug at the leash attached to her collar gently. All the time his fingers continued to fuck her gently, slowly and relentlessly, driving her into an absolute frenzy.

"Good pet," he purred. "I know it won't have been easy to admit that out loud, but you did it, and you've pleased me."

She mewled, caught up in the pleasure his fingers were producing, but also reticent to concede anything further to him. What little dignity she had left, she was suddenly desperate to hang onto. A heartbeat later, his digits withdrew from her sex in a flash and he landed another firm swat to her now tender bottom.

"Oww!" she cried, twisting over his lap as she tried to wriggle free of the strong arm which held her in place.

"I just complimented you, pet," he told her sternly. "And I expect a response, unless, of course, you'd like me to take that pretty mouth out of action altogether?"

Molly squirmed, her mind flitting back to the odious plastic gag he'd made her wear before. "No, Sir," she gasped. "No, and thank you, I…"

She was cut short by his palm as it struck her again, but this time the swat caught her upturned sex, the impact resonating straight to her clit. Molly groaned, the pain now shifting into something else, something lighter, something sexier. She hung her head, despite the pressure at her collar, shamefully aroused and yet hopelessly yearning for more. If she had to endure all of this, the indignity, the painful punishments, then let there be some relief at the end of it. It was the least that Molly deserved.

As though he had read her mind, the hand at her sex paused, cupping her mound and caressing her throbbing little clit. Molly jerked at the stimulation, but her head flooded with fresh arousal, and she could feel the moisture pooling between her thighs. Connor had her right where he wanted her, and despite her irritation on the subject, she was too horny to care. She just wanted the pleasure, to chase her orgasm down if he'd allow it, whatever the cost to her self-respect.

"What's this?" he asked, wryly. "Is my naughty little pet horny after her punishment?"

Molly whimpered in response, her hips grinding over his naked thighs. He smacked her burning behind again, a swat which was no doubt designed to make her respond, but all the hurt did now was push her into a greater hedonism.

"You. Will. Answer. Me!" he snapped, accentuating each new word with a swat to her bottom.

She no longer jerked away from his hand. Now she was so turned on that she found herself splaying her legs, begging him silently for more of the same.

"Yes, Sir," she replied, her tone heavy with lust. She knew she should feel embarrassed at the admission, and perhaps on some level she did, but at this point, the humiliation of admitting such a thing only made her hotter and wetter.

Molly's words were rewarded with his fingers, which slid back past her swollen labia, and glided inside of her. She moaned appreciatively, rocking her hips as best she could as Connor began to finger-fuck her again.

"Look at you," he purred, practically cooing over her gyrating body. "So aroused at your punishment, and all mine."

Molly pulled at the chains which held her wrists in place, reveling in her utter degradation at his hands. Her eyelids fell closed as his fingers edged her toward ecstasy. She was close, so damn close, that just a couple of direct swats to her clit would be enough to send her spiraling out of control. As the realization hit her, Molly's lips parted of their own accord, her body braced for the impending pleasure.

"Yes, Sir," she gasped. It was all she could manage as she chased her orgasm, her body acting independently by now, as if she had no control over it whatsoever.

She heard his dark chuckle fill the air above her head, the ominous sound only fueling her desire.

"So wet and wanton," he murmured. "You're even better than I'd imagined!" As he spoke, his fingers began to slow, before they eased gently from her sodden pussy.

"No!" She groaned, the sense of frustration as her stimulation ceased was enormous, and she ground herself against his leg helplessly, desperate to find just enough friction to take her to the brink.

This time he laughed out loud. "Just look at you, pet," he chortled. "So fucking desperate!"

Molly screeched with irritation, annoyed beyond reason that he sought to deliberately build her up like this, just to disappoint her. Who does that? It was worse than being kept and chained, it was just freaking cruel.

"Enough!" he barked, smacking her writhing behind with three hard swats. "Unless you want me to turn this backside black and blue, you will hold your tongue and keep still."

She heard his words, and understood their gravity, so she willed her body to be calm, but all the while there was the unbearable, burning need that he'd inspired. There would be no relief, she knew that now, and as the reality washed over her, a low sob caught in her throat.

"Clearly, I have overindulged you," Connor mused as his hand explored the tender skin of her bottom. "This was a punishment, pet. I made that clear right from the start, and that does not mean you're entitled to pleasure afterwards."

Hot tears pricked her eyes as she listened to him, but still she couldn't make sense of what he said. Why play with her? Why stimulate her at all, if he had no intention of satisfying her? The guy really was a sadist if he thought this was fun. As she blinked the fresh tears away, she saw him gazing down at her, his expression lit with an ugly smirk.

"Up now," he commanded, shifting his hand to tug at the chain attached to her collar.

She drew her trembling body back across his lap, eyeing his erection as she passed it. For one crazy moment she considered taking the thing in her mouth, and she wondered what he'd do if she acted so boldly. Surely, he'd permit such an act, especially one designed to give him pleasure? Her gaze lingered on the veiny, swollen crown of his shaft as she considered the idea. It was clear just how aroused Connor was, and her eyes fell shut as she imagined how good it would feel inside her wet pussy.

"Get back into bed."

The sound of the order drew her eyes open again, and she caught the wry amusement which painted his face. *Shit.* He'd obviously seen her gawping at his cock, and had drawn his own conclusions about what she was thinking.

"Now, pet," he prompted her, pointing to the large dog bed behind her.

Swallowing hard, she turned and shuffled back in the direction of the fur-lined bed.

"Not like that," he snapped, the urgency in his voice making her jump. "How does a pet walk? Certainly not on its hind legs!"

Molly felt the color drain from her face as she dropped slowly to her hands and knees. It seemed there was to be no end to her ignominy, and she crawled the short distance back to the dog bed, painfully aware of how her punished ass and wet seam would be on display for her captor.

"Settle down, now," he warned her, as he reached over to switch off the bedside light. "There'll be plenty to keep you occupied in the coming days."

Molly snuggled down as best she could in the confines of the soft bed. She felt for her blanket, pulling it up over her body. She was trembling more from frustration than the cold, but somehow, the act comforted her. She had no idea how long she lay there for. Connor had turned on the mattress above her, and she'd long since heard the soft, rhythmic sound of his breathing. Reaching for the collar at her neck, she fumbled with the attachment, wondering if she could release it and be free of the wretched leash. Her fingers struggled in the dark for what felt like hours, but somehow Molly could never seem to release the damn thing. At some point, she collapsed against the fur-lined bed, exhausted and despondent.

Chapter Forty-One

He roused at seven, surprisingly refreshed considering his broken night of sleep. His little pet was curled into a tight ball in her bed, and he took a moment to enjoy the look of her sleeping. His gaze drank in the sight of her reddened bottom, which was left beautifully exposed by the green blanket she clutched to her chest.

Connor inhaled deeply, considering whether or not he had time to jerk off to the scene just beyond his bed. Certainly, it was tempting, and his cock came to life under the covers as if to remind him of the fact. Stroking the shaft adeptly, he shifted his position to get a better view. Molly was glorious, and the incident last night had been an unexpected bonus, but he must not allow himself to become side-tracked. There would be time for pleasure, but this was not it. With a long sigh, he slipped from his covers and began the day.

The house was quiet as he worked. Having left his pet sleeping and chained in his bedroom, with the door bolted from the outside, he knew she'd be safe for the time being. Time was of the essence though, so he finished setting up the basement with uncharacteristic haste. The next time she was naughty, or defied him, this is where he would bring her. His eyes surveyed the dark space. Each wall had been designed for its purpose, with racks and chains in place to hold and suspend her. There was a large, leather spanking bench to one side, a smaller bench nearby, plus a chair designed to hold her in place while he worked. In the far corner sat his personal favorite item, the large crate he'd had custom-made for holding her. It had a soft plastic floor, but all four sides were made of black metal bars, which matched the roof. To all intents and purposes, it was a cage. A cage intended to keep an unruly animal, and he smiled as the fitting analogy swept through his mind.

Deciding the basement was ready, he climbed the staircase back to the ground floor, switching off the light and locking up behind him. He imagined her alarmed face when it was time to take her down there, and yet again, his eager cock sprung to life. Shaking his head, he smiled as he made his way back to his bedroom. *That* thought would have to wait too, there was a list of things he needed to achieve this morning, and first thing was first, his pet needed a shower.

As he opened the door, he found her just where he'd left her. Clearly, the spanking last night had taken more out of her than he'd anticipated, or maybe it was just the whole ordeal taking its toll. Either way, it was nearly eight, and it was time for his sleeping beauty to rise. He approached her slowly, towering over her scrunched-up body. The contrast between them at this moment had never been starker. Connor held all of the power. He was dressed, fed and had a day of plans and schemes in mind. His pet, on the other hand, was so much more vulnerable. Naked, she was chained and leashed to his bed.

While he stood looking down at her, she stirred. Connor watched as her lids flickered open, and she took in her immediate surroundings. There was a moment of clarity when her eyes widened, and then she tilted her head to find him looming over her nudity. Molly jumped reflexively, and he struggled to contain the laughter which sprung from his lips.

"Good morning, pet," he told her chirpily. "I'm glad you're awake."

He surveyed the carpet around her bed, and his eyes fell over the chocolate stains again. His pet would have to get better at drinking from her bowl if she wanted the luxury of sleeping in his room. Striding to the end of his bed, he unwound the chain from its place at the post.

"Come on," he ordered, tugging the chain gently to coax her from the bed.

Molly's gaze followed his feet, but she obeyed nonetheless, crawling behind him sleepily as he unbolted the door. Once in the hall, he guided her right, and back into the bathroom she'd visited yesterday. She crawled to the center of the room, twisting to see Connor close the door behind them, before sliding another large bolt into place above her head. He hooked the end of her leash to the peg on the back of the bathroom door. That would hold her in place while he got things ready, and he turned to see her sitting back on her haunches in the morning light.

Fuck, he thought, watching the rays of light bounce of her dank hair. Even in this state of disarray, she looked amazing. "It's time for your shower," he crooned, breaking the silence.

"Shower?" she asked, her voice hoarse.

He smiled. "Yes, pet," he replied, turning on the tap at the end of the bath. Water poured into the small tub, and he moved his palm under the flow, adjusting the taps until the temperature was right. "You've been with me more than a day already," he explained, turning back to face her kneeling form. "It's time we cleaned you up."

"More than a day?" she queried, her face crumpling as she tried to make sense of his words.

It was clear to Connor that his pet had lost all track of time. He supposed it was hardly surprising, given everything she'd been through.

"Yes," he told her, flicking the taps off and grabbing the shower head from its place on the wall. "Now, get in here." Connor gestured to the tub, which now had a small puddle of water pooling at the bottom.

"In these, Sir?" she mumbled, raising her hands to display her chains.

He nodded. "Yes. I'll help you."

Connor reached his hand out to her, and she dropped back to the floor, crawling gingerly to where he was waiting. The sight of her compliance made him giddy, but he held his nerve, watching as she knelt before him. "Take my hand," he instructed her, and slowly she obeyed.

Time protracted as her tiny hand slipped over his own, and he curled his digits around her own to support her.

"Up and in now," he commanded, intentionally making the order as low and sensual as he could.

Molly's eyes flitted to his face for a moment, and then she rose to her feet, her right hand still swallowed up in his large palm. Lifting her left foot up to the top of the tub, the chains at her ankles strained tightly. "I don't know if I can manage it with these chains," she whispered.

Connor glanced at her face, watching the first flames of a new blush. He could tell she was mortified to have to admit it, but looking down at her struggle, he also knew it was true. "Fine," he replied, patting her knee away from the tub gently. "Foot down then. I'll lift you in."

He saw her fast intake of breath and the way her body tensed, but it didn't stop Connor. His hands were at her hips in a moment, and gently he lifted her over the edge of the bathtub. She weighed practically nothing, and although her limbs seemed strong and toned, he eased her into the tub with little effort. She eyed him warily as he shifted back toward the shower head, which he'd left running into the bath.

"Sit down," he commanded, offering her his left hand for support.

She gulped with obvious trepidation as she inched closer to it. He could understand why she didn't trust him, but that didn't matter. Trust could come, or maybe it wouldn't, but what she needed in the meantime was obedience.

"Pet," he prompted her in a much lower tone. "Take my hand, and sit."

The short, sharp collection of orders reminded him of the way he'd spoken to his dogs at The Syndicate in the past, and the thought made him smile. As he caught her eye, he wondered if Molly was drawing the same comparison.

Slowly, she descended, until she was stretched out in the tub as far as her long limbs would allow. Satisfied, he moved the shower over her body, directing the flow of water over her chest, and stomach. He stood, hypnotized for a moment as the torrent washed over her firm breasts, collecting at the hard buds which formed at its approach. *Christ, the woman was tantalizing,* he thought, and not for the first time, had to push his desire away as he managed the task at hand. Connor washed the warm water over her hair and shoulders, before he placed the shower head at the other end of the bath and reached for the waiting shampoo bottle.

"Are you going to keep me forever, Sir?"

The question startled him, and he spun to address her curious stare. She looked even better with her hair wet and flattened down her back, like some sort of Amazonian Goddess. Moving back toward her, he lathered the product into her hair, easing the strands away from her eyes. It was bizarrely satisfying to take care of her in this way, and it reminded him that he didn't want to only use and enjoy his pet, he wanted to nurture and protect her as well.

"Do you want the truth, pet?" he demanded, although his voice remained calm as he spoke. "Can you handle it?"

She drew in a breath, lifting her chains from the bath. "I don't know," she admitted, lowering her face in the direction of the growing pool of water around her thighs.

Connor reached for a near-by sponge, handing it to her. "Cover your eyes with this," he ordered, as he grabbed the shower head and rinsed away the soap suds from her hair.

"I know this isn't what you want to hear," he told her as he yanked the damp sponge from her face, "but it's taken many months of planning to get you here, and I have absolutely no intention of giving you up."

She eyed him wildly, her expression anxious as she listened to what he had to say. "But," she began, her voice thick with whatever conflicting emotions were battling inside her. "You can't have me," she argued. "I'm not *yours*. I not am not anybody's, I…"

He'd dropped the shower head in an instant, throwing it to the other side of the small tub, and a moment later his fist was at the chain still attached to her collar. Forcefully, he yanked her forward, pulling her upper body toward him at will. Molly gasped at his speed and strength, the rest of her sentence dying on her lips.

"You are mine, pet," he told her in an emphatic tone. "And if I haven't made this evident to you yet, then I swear, I'll spend the rest of today doing so."

Chapter Forty-Two

There was a heavy silence after the exchange. Molly sunk into a new low as his words echoed around her head. He didn't seem angry as such, more determined, and he maneuvered her with short commands which made her even more anxious.

As he lifted her from the tub and threw a green towel over her shoulders, the depth of her predicament really struck her. He caught her hand as it rose to dry her body.

"No," he instructed. "Leave it to me."

She nodded, biting her lip as she felt him move the towel around her body, shifting it under her arms and breasts, and down between her legs. She closed her eyes at the utter indignity of it. Somehow, this seemed worse than being made to drink from the damn dog bowl. However dehumanizing that had been, at least in some fucked up way she'd actually enjoyed it. There was nothing enjoyable about this at all, and as the towel slipped back between her thighs she saw the act for what it really was; a reinforcement of power between them. She would be passive and obey, and he would be active and in control. The thought made her want to cry again.

He skimmed the towel over the rest of her body, tucking it under the leather at her throat, before turning his attention to her hair.

"Kneel," he ordered, pointing to the floor by his feet, and seeing no viable alternative, she obeyed.

Her mind flittered from subject to subject as he worked on her hair with the damp towel. Where the fuck were they, and how long had she even been here? He had mentioned something about her being here more than a day, but could that be right? She could barely recall the last day, but then she knew he'd knocked her out cold, so maybe she had lost track of time? That idea made her even more fearful. As if this man didn't control everything else, now he even had control over time itself.

Next, her brain tried to think of a decent plan for her escape. As she knelt on the small rug, blinking into the gray light of morning, she knew one thing for certain. She *had* to get away. There may have been shameful parts of her confinement which had turned her on, but Molly was under no illusions. Connor was clearly a madman, a psychopath, or God knew what. He might say he wasn't going to force himself on her, but it was pretty damn obvious that he was enjoying himself. She'd clocked his hard-on on more than one occasion, and last night his erection had been fit to burst as he'd spanked her. She drew in a shaky breath at the memory, and a warm throb teased her at the apex of her thighs. The fact that she'd actually ended up reveling in her punishment was mortifying, and then when he'd refused to allow her any pleasure, it was even worse. How long would it be until his prophecy became truth? Connor had made it plain that he had the power to make her wetter than anyone before him. He could take her right to the brink, and then deny her. Somehow that was worse than the pain, and the confinement. It was soul-destroying, and she knew in her heart he was right. Much more of that treatment and she probably would beg him for release, and maybe even for his cock.

She lowered her head as the shameful realization settled over her. There was no doubt in her mind. She absolutely had to get away from his clutches, before she sunk any lower into the depths of whatever depravity he had planned... Before she started to *want* it.

Her internal monologue was interrupted by the towel which was flung over the edge of the tub. She turned to see him empty the water, and grab a large black hairbrush.

"Lean over this," he commanded, gesturing with the hairbrush that she should drape her torso over the towel.

Molly tensed. What was this? Did he mean to punish her with that thing? She could sense her body shaking at the prospect, and she had no control over it whatsoever.

"Now!" he ordered, and she gulped, shuffling over on her knees, and taking her place.

Relief emanated through her when she felt the brush tug through her wet locks, and despite the pain as he tried to force it between the strands, Molly knew it would be nothing compared to the sting of it against her bottom.

"Good," he concluded as he placed the brush back into a small drawer by the side of the tub. "Now ease yourself forward. I want your arms in the bath, and your arse up in the air."

She whimpered at that. She knew how vulnerable she'd be in this new position, but also that there was no choice. Shifting her weight over the damp towel, she pressed her face against the floor of the tub and wriggled her hips into place, splaying her legs as wide as the chains would allow to help her maintain the position.

"Perfect," he praised her, massaging the tender cheeks of her behind. "Good pet."

She inhaled at the intimate contact, tense with trepidation about what Connor would do next. Was he planning on punishing her, or would he go back on his promise not to take her without consent? Her breaths came out in short, sharp bursts as she pondered the awful possibilities.

It was with some shock then that she felt the cold liquid fall between her cheeks. Gasping, she squirmed, but her motion was met with one hard swat to her right cheek.

"Keep still," he told her gruffly. "I'm not going to harm you, pet. Just like before, remember. I'm going to fill your arse up, but this time you're going to wear a special tail for me."

He laughed darkly at his own explanation, and in her peripheral vision she caught sight of what he had in mind. It was a black, plastic dildo, probably around five inches in length. That looked bad enough. Her ass was still trying to recover from yesterday's intrusions, but worse than that was what was attached to the end of the dildo. Molly's gaze scanned it fearfully. It looked like a tail – an actual tail – small and dark and furry, like it belonged to a dog or some other furry animal.

He waved it in her line of sight for a moment longer, and she caught the gleeful smile on his lips as he swiped it back toward her ass. All of a sudden, she could feel the plastic rubbing between her lubricated cheeks. Molly panted, half terrified and half shamefully aroused at her fate. She knew once he had this awful thing in place, she really would look like a pet. Forced onto her hands and knees, kept leashed and made to eat from a dog bowl, she'd now have an actual fucking tail to go with it!

"Deep breaths," he instructed, reminding her of his expectation as she felt her cheeks part.

Instinctively she tensed, but Molly forced herself to breathe through the panic. Having this thing in her was going to be bad enough without trying to resist him. She had a feeling she knew what that would earn her. *More* punishment.

"Good," he told her, as he angled the dildo around her dark entrance. "On your next breath out, your tail arrives."

She could hear the excitement in his tone, and despite every logical reason why she shouldn't, at that moment she wanted to jump up and wallop him. She imagined herself doing it. In her mind, she pictured leaping to her feet and swinging for the guy. She may not have the black belt skills he'd demonstrated on the streets of London, but she had quite a right hook, and she knew she'd have the element of surprise in her arsenal. Connor was assuming her cooperation in all of this because she'd been reasonably compliant so far. She guessed he'd never expect her to lash out at this point.

Focusing on the image, she prepared to exhale, and as she did, he slid the head of the dildo inside her. A small groan escaped her lips as it eased deeper, and acting on some sort of reflex she began to panic.

"Please," she whimpered. "I don't want it."

The rational part of her brain hated the way she sounded. She was fucking begging, and worse still, she already knew he'd ignore her plea. As the dildo pushed in deeper, he swatted her aching right cheek. The impact resonated through her body, making her ass tense and temporarily halting her tail's progress.

"We've been through this," he warned her in a predatory tone. "You'll take what you're given, pet. What you think you want is no longer a concern."

Molly squeezed her eyes closed at that, willing herself to breathe and allow the thing in. Better to be complicit, then risk him coercing it into place. After another moment, he seemed satisfied, and she heard his body shift backwards from her upturned ass. She drew in a large, desperate breath, fighting the urge to cry at this latest indignity. This plug seemed bigger than yesterday's and she'd never been so full before in her life. Worse still, she could actually feel the soft fur of the tail dangling between her legs, and she envisioned how she must look with it now in place. A small shudder passed through her, yet she was also aware of the low thrumming arousal which stirred her clit. Molly had always imagined a scene like this. To be dehumanized this way was a massive turn on for her, and pet-play was something she'd written about for years.

Never in her wildest dreams though, had she dreamt that she'd be the recipient; that she'd be the pet.

A tug on her leash brought her back to the present.

"Get down now," he commanded in his usual matter-of-fact tone. "It's time for breakfast."

Chapter Forty-Three

The morning passed in a flurry of depraved acts of his choosing. Connor thoroughly enjoyed watching her chase the cereal loops around her bowl, particularly when her reddened bottom, and new tail were so gloriously on display for him every time she wriggled behind the metal dish.

He could see how much she despised the thing, both the tail and the humiliation of eating like an animal, and yet he was no fool. At the same time, he could see her increasing arousal. Damn, he could practically smell it, and the fact that she secretly relished his pet-play just made the whole thing even better.

By eleven o'clock Connor had her chained to the wooden chair in the spare room again, and he watched her writhe against the dildo stuck in her ass as he loaded up the laptop in front of her.

"Problem, pet?" he asked her with an intentional smile. He knew he was teasing her, but he just didn't care. Frankly, it was just too easy to avoid.

"I'm rather uncomfortable, Sir," she whispered, her face flaming at the admission.

"Oh dear," he answered in the least sincere voice he could muster. "Yes, I suppose it will be rather awkward sitting on your tail. It just goes to show, pets are not supposed to be on furniture." He paused, considering the conundrum. "I'll have to come up with another solution for you to write our story."

Connor heard her gasp, but wisely, the little pet didn't pass comment. He noticed how she forced herself to keep still after this reply as well. Taking his seat in the corner of the room, he set her to work, watching as her fingers flew over the keyboard without her even having to look. He checked his wristwatch after a while, and was surprised to learn that forty minutes had already flown past. Watching his little pet work really was a joy.

"How is it going?" he asked gruffly.

He didn't mean to be impatient, but he had a lot of plans for her today. Being a man of discipline, Connor knew the writing had to be happen first. There would be no fun without work first.

She tilted her head toward the sound of his voice, and her fingers fell silent for the first time since she'd begun. "I'm nearly done, Sir."

He smiled at the resonance in her voice. Her desire was pleasing. More than that actually, it was absolutely phenomenal. "Good," he told her, rising from his seat to stride in the direction of the window. "Because when you're done, I have a special treat for you."

That got her attention and he watched as her chest began to rise and fall in fast succession. "A treat, Sir?" she mumbled, clearly intrigued and yet terrified at the same time.

"Yes," he confirmed as her eyes rose to meet his. "Now hurry up, and finish."

It didn't take her long, and within twenty minutes he was saving her work, promising himself that he would get to read the updates later. So far Molly had proven to be far too distracting to get to the document, and that needed to change. It was then that the idea came to him. He could kill both birds with the same stone. Molly could have her treat while he read at the laptop. A broad grin spread over his face as the idea settled in his brain. It was going to be beautiful.

He released the chains at her ankles, before ordering her to the floor. "Are you ready for your treat?"

Molly lifted her head anxiously. Her expression told him that she knew she had no choice either way, but his sentiment had obviously intrigued her.

"Yes, Sir."

Connor nodded, tugging at her leash and guiding her out into dim hallway once again.

This time he led her past the kitchen to the top of the stairs, pausing to wait for her shuffling limbs to catch up with him.

"We're going down," he told her calmly. "Are you going to be able to manage on her hands and knees?"

She glanced up at him, and for a second, he saw a flicker of defiance spark in her eyes. "I don't know," she muttered, her attention turning to the carpeted stairwell.

Connor's gaze joined hers, and he made the decision for her. "I don't want you slipping," he told her matter-of-factly. "So, for the stairs you'll rise and walk in front of me."

Molly nodded, and wordlessly, she rose to her feet. It was strange to watch as she stood beside him. She seemed so small in comparison to his body. Somehow, he'd forgotten just how short she was.

"Go," he coaxed, gesturing with his head for her to move.

Her bare feet shuffled toward the edge of the top step, and gingerly she took the first one side-ways, clearly conscious of the chain which limited her range of mobility. Connor gave her some space. He wanted her to be careful, she was his after all, so he waited for Molly to reach the third stair down before he began to follow. Slowly, they made their way down the staircase. He gripped her leash as though his life depended on it. Somehow seeing her on her feet did nothing to quell his unease with the situation. Coupled with that was the fact that they were on the ground floor, and he knew she'd be taking in everything she saw. Still, he reassured himself, it would be worth it when he had her in place.

"Down now," he instructed as her feet made contact with the hard wood floor of the hall.

She blinked up at him, but didn't protest. He watched her eyes drinking in the light spilling in from the front door as she fell slowly to her hands and knees. He rounded her waiting body, allowing himself the pleasure of eyeing the furry tail which hung between her legs as he pushed open the first door in the hallway.

"In you come," he told her. "Crawl to the center of the room and wait for me."

Molly scuttled past his feet, not pausing as she crossed onto the carpeted floor of the lounge, heading in the direction he had instructed. He closed the door behind her, sliding the bolt into place before he headed toward his waiting pet. Connor permitted her a few moments to take in the look of the place. He figured she deserved that at least, and he wasn't sure what she'd make of the space until he explained things anyway. At first glance it looked like any other British lounge. There was a large teak dresser against the far wall, and a matching unit to the right which held all his electronics. A massive leather chair dominated the side nearest Connor. It was the sort with an incorporated footrest, which sprung out on demand, and he had spent many happy hours sitting there, planning Molly's fate. In the center of the room though, something was different.

In the middle of the oriental-style rug was a large wooden post. It looked a little like a scratching post you might buy a cat, but it was thinner, and harder, plus it was weighted securely to the floor. At the top were a number of wooden pegs, held in place expectantly. He stood mesmerized as Molly's gaze fell over the thing. Silently, she shuffled in its direction, turning to wait for his verdict. Connor strode over to the post, securing the end of her leash to the nearest peg, before securing the handle over the top of the thing.

"Here's how it's going to work," he informed her as he wrapped the length of chain over the wood. "Consider this your exercise post. Whenever you've warranted the privilege, you'll be chained here and allowed to burn off some calories, and when I say allowed, I mean of course, you'll be made to." He paused for a moment, wanting his words to sink in.

She lifted her head, her gaze flitting from him to the wooden post. "How do I... exercise?"

Connor chuckled. "I'm glad you asked," he chided. "You'll be crawling around the post in whichever direction I tell you. I want you to think about your form as you move. Think graceful, lithe motion, please. I also want you to consider your speed. You are to keep an even pace, and if I see you flagging, I'll be encouraging you with my favorite paddle."

She gasped at that, her eyes blinking wildly at him.

"Have you got it?"

She nodded, her features etched with anxiety. "Yes, Sir."

"Excellent," he declared, "and consider this. If you please me, I'll reward you with an orgasm." He hesitated, watching as she held her breath. "Would you like that, pet?"

"Y-yes," she mumbled, her face burning with embarrassment.

Connor couldn't tell if she was just answering with what she thought he needed to hear, or if she was genuinely interested in pleasure, but it didn't matter. The point was she had heard him and responded with obedience. And that made him happy.

"Good," he told her. "Then, let us begin."

Chapter Forty-Four

He'd secured her chains to the post in seconds flat. Molly looked on in horror as he worked, her head reeling at this latest humiliation.

"Begin counter-clockwise," came the order as he stood, and retreated toward the large chair.

Molly gulped, her eyes flitting to his face briefly before her hands and knees began to move. Dropping her head forward, she crawled in a circle around the wooden post, passing his bare feet and continuing onwards. The whole time she was held in place by her leash which kept her chained to the post, and the chain between her wrists, which rattled ominously with every movement. The sounds made the reality of her shame starker. Not only was she a prisoner – his prisoner – but she was being made to parade herself for his personal entertainment. *And your orgasm,* reminded the small voice in her head. If he followed through and even allowed her to climax that was.

Her circling continued, and all the while she fought to keep her form. She kept her belly tight and her ass pushed back, and she hoped the image was, what had he called it, *graceful?* Molly doubted it though. How graceful could crawling be at the end of the day?

"Marvelous," he praised, his tone approving. "You look great. Now, I want you to continue while I grab the laptop. And don't even think about stopping. I'll be watching the whole time, remember?" Connor tipped his head toward the corner of the room, and Molly's gaze darted to follow his eyes to the small camera there.

She swallowed as he left her there, her head falling forward again as she heard the bolt slide back into place from the outside. Mortified and disheartened by the reminder that she was being watched even when her captor wasn't there, Molly continued onwards. As she crawled, her brain began to race, considering the new space and whether being down here made escape any more likely. *At least I'm on the ground floor,* she thought frantically as she began her eighth circuit, or perhaps it was ninth pass? It was easy to forget when all you did was go around and around, like a freaking goldfish in a bowl. *A chained and naked goldfish,* the little voice reminded her, glibly.

Molly shook her head, making her eyes focus on the large window behind the chair as she passed the dresser once more. There were long, ugly, old-fashioned net curtains hanging at them, which obscured nearly all of her view, and frustratingly meant that no one would ever be able to see into the room. From her position on the rug it was impossible to see much more, but maybe if she could get up again, she'd be able to catch sight of a car or another house. Anything which would give her a clue about where the hell she was.

The noise of the bolt on the other side of the door made her heart pick up its pace, and her hand and knees redoubled their efforts as panic flooded her system. Somehow, she began to worry that he'd know what she'd been thinking, and would punish her for the thought alone, but that was ridiculous. Connor might be a thoroughly organized psycho, but he wasn't a telepath.

She didn't look up as the door opened, but she felt her body tense, her stomach drawing in as he entered the room.

"Good pet," he murmured, and she saw him turn to push the inside bolt back into position.

She noticed the silver laptop in his hands, and heard him move back toward the large leather chair by the corner of the window. As she began a new circuit he fell into the luxurious-looking seat.

"Start making a larger circuit," he instructed as he propped the device up on his lap.

Molly stilled for a second before she complied, widening her circles so she passed just in front of his legs this time. She didn't understand his reasoning, but she didn't counter it either.

"Don't lose that form," he warned her as she began to move in the direction of the fireplace. "Keep that derriere out, and those legs splayed. I want to see that tail. Show me what's mine."

Molly knew her face was burning at his instructions, but something about his words made moisture pool at the apex of her thighs. The way he talked about her was so matter-of-fact, and yet so dehumanizing. It should be freaking outrageous, and it was. But oddly, it made her insanely hot.

"Better," he muttered in response.

As she passed back toward his legs, she saw him begin to read at the laptop. She crawled on, moving past him, but by now it was becoming harder and harder to stay in the position he demanded. The pressure on her hands and knees was building, and her shoulders had begun to ache. Invariably her form began to slide again as her body tired. As she crawled away from his right foot, a small sound caught her attention. Molly couldn't make out what it was at first, but a fraction of a moment later everything became much clearer.

A firm wallop landed on her ass, catching the underside of her tail and most of her wet seam. The noise of the impact was so loud it made her physically jump, and she felt her hands leave the rug. Then the pain registered, spreading quickly throughout her lower body. Molly gasped, yelping loudly, and instinctively, she paused, turning to rub her sore behind.

"I told you to keep your form!" he barked from behind her. "What do you think you're doing?"

She glanced at him with stunned eyes as Connor rose from the chair in a flash. The sound of the laptop hit the leather behind him, filling the air like thunder as he came to tower over her. For the first time, she saw properly what he had stuck her with. As he'd threatened, there was a long, hard paddle in his right hand. No wonder the impact had been so forceful. He rounded her body quickly, coming to crouch down in front of her face. Once in position, his right hand rose to the chain at her neck and he pulled against it hard.

"Listen to me, pet." His voice was a near-growl.

Connor's sudden proximity, and the warning in his voice made her heart race inside her chest.

"This may be new to you," he began, "but you're a smart woman, so I'm going to need you to learn fast."

Molly bit her lip at the severity in his voice. His tone promised real threat, sending a shiver running down the length of her naked, vulnerable body. She nodded, unsure if he was going to expect a reply to that or not. "Yes, Sir," she mumbled, struggling to take the weight of her upper body as he yanked harder on her chain.

"You're my pet now, my animal to tease, and train. That means I can strike your bottom whenever it pleases me, and you pet, you have no recourse, do you understand me?" His voice was powerful, coming at her loud and clear, despite the fact they were only inches apart.

"Yes," she panted, trying not to resist the leather at her neck, but boy, she wanted to. She wanted to pull back from his grasp and get as far away from him as she could, yet at the same time she wanted that orgasm he'd promised her. She needed it.

"That means no pausing to examine your punished backside," he went on. "It means keeping your form, and doing as you've been told."

She flushed at his exasperated expression. For some reason, she actually felt remorseful to have disappointed him, and she recoiled at the ridiculous emotions as quickly as she could.

"You'll receive ten swats for your insubordination," he advised her, moving away ever so slightly. "And this time I want *good* form."

He was gone in a heartbeat, releasing the chain and allowing it to fall free into the space between Molly and the post she was leashed to. She heard him resume his place in the leather chair, and for a moment she hesitated. Should she keep going now, or wait for the ten swats he'd threatened her with?

As though Connor had read her mind, her question was answered a moment later. "Get going," he snapped, his tone irritated.

She drew in a quick breath before forcing her knees forward. Ignoring their pleas as they hit the rug in front of them, she crawled onward, trying to think about the position of her body as she headed back toward his legs and completed the circuit. She never saw him move. The noise of the paddle impacting with her exposed bottom registered before the hurt, and she felt her body leap from the floor at the force of it. Then came a flood of pain as the sting resonated, and her ass ached from the way the strike had clipped the dildo seated snugly inside her.

"One," Connor announced, his tone now evidently amused at her predicament.

Molly gasped, continuing onwards. Now she understood how her penance was going to be delivered, in single, unrelenting swats to her poor behind each and every time she passed by him. As she approached him this time, she knew what was coming. Instinctively, she tried to crawl faster past his feet, but Connor seemed wise to her game, and the strike came all the same. It seemed so damn powerful against her skin, that she imagined her bottom was already reddening around her Connor-imposed tail. The thought made her cringe.

"Two," he chuckled as she crawled on.

It continued this way. Connor punished her at every pass, spanking her thoroughly with the paddle and no-doubt intentionally ensuring it nudged her tail each time it connected with her. After every strike, he would declare the number, and Molly would continue crawling, her face falling lower with the shame and her behind aching more and more from the repeated onslaught. When he finally called ten, she wanted to cheer and collapse, but she didn't dare. Instead she carried on as she had been, waiting for some sign that her ordeal might be over.

"That's your ten delivered," he said, matter-of-factly, "but I won't hesitate to deliver more as required. Now, I have a lot of story to read, so the more you distract me with your bad behavior, the longer you'll be exercising. Do you understand?"

She passed him again, lowering her eyes so she didn't have to connect with his self-satisfied expression. "Yes, Sir," she mumbled.

"Crawl the other way now," he instructed. "I like a change every now and then."

She paused, sighing quietly as she turned her body in front of him and began her new clockwise circle. This was turning into the most humiliating deed of the whole time he'd had her. Being kept leashed was bad enough, but being made to perform like an animal was mortifying. She didn't have to feel between her legs to know how wet she was. However fucked up and wrong this all was, it was hitting her buttons with disturbing ease, and that reality made it all worse somehow.

Molly crawled on, completing circuit after circuit of the lounge rug. Time soon became a thing of the past, a privilege apparently not permitted for pets. She tried to keep her body in the correct position as he read, but after a while her lower back began to ache, and her hands and knees were in absolute agony. She wondered how far through the story he was, and how long this would go on for. Had she already blown her chance for pleasure? The throb between her thighs was growing stronger, taunting her with each movement. *You're his pet now*, it told her hauntingly. *His to tease, his to train and his to punish.*

She pulled in a deep breath at the thought, trying to push her desire away. It was wrong to be aroused at this treatment, and the rational part of her brain knew it, but the problem was, Connor was doing such a good job at dehumanizing her, that part of her brain was increasingly becoming silent. She forced herself to think about something else, anything other than how tantalizingly awful this situation was. Her mind returned to the prospect of her escape, and as she approached the window again, she tried to raise her head and get a glimpse of what laid outside.

She just caught sight of his arm moving, but it was too late. The movement of her head had thrown her form out completely, and his retribution was immediate. The paddle smacked her hard against both cheeks, connecting directly with her tail and forcing the dildo even deeper inside her ass. Molly gasped, wanting to cry out, but somehow, she bit the sound down.

"Do you need another ten swats, pet?" he asked her, wryly.

She shook her head desperately and mewled in response.

"I hadn't appreciated how bad you'd be at this," he mused as she neared him again. "Yet it seems my assumptions were incorrect. Apparently, you'll need lots of practise to perfect this task."

Molly's head fell at his words, her shoulders aching as she pressed forward. This time she expected the paddle as it landed against her bottom, but the knowledge did nothing to help her manage the pain.

"Another ten then," he announced with a sigh. "We begin on your next pass."

Chapter Forty-Five

The look of his little pet was absolutely delicious. He could tell she was tiring, yet she was young enough and fit enough to carry on, and continue she would, until he was happy with the effort. She passed by his feet and the paddle was already in the air, waiting for her. He took aim, landing the swat perfectly, and watching with pride as the impact reverberated around her little bottom.

"One," he told her, ogling the furry tail which jutted from her backside as she crawled on.

She was so fucking beautiful. So perfect for him, and he wanted her desperately. But of course, he was going to enjoy tormenting her first.

She neared him again, and his eyes fell over her face. As she moved, he imagined how good her pretty little mouth would look with a bridle gag forced inside, like the ones people used on horses. It wasn't quite in keeping with his pet theme, but it was close enough, and his already hard cock began to throb at the image. This time he spanked her harder, making her cry out as she passed him.

"Two," he announced, "and next time you will thank your master for the strike."

There was a moment of hesitation as he gave the directive, but her hands and knees continued onwards. It was the first time he'd used the word *master,* but it was accurate. He was her Master now, in every sense of the word, and master her he would.

"Yes, Sir," she whispered as she crawled on, her eyes lowering as she neared him again.

He placed the laptop on the ground to his left, wanting to give her his full attention. The reading would just have to wait, whatever his reservations on the subject. The third strike was firm and he made sure he whacked her pussy. The sound of moisture as the paddle connected with her wet seam made him smile broadly.

"Three, pet," he declared, waiting on the appropriate response from her.

"Th-thank you, Sir," she replied, breathlessly.

"Master," he corrected her as she wriggled past him. "From now on, you will refer to me as your Master."

He heard the gasp which escaped her lips, and the sound made him chuckle.

"Yes, M-Master," she sighed, her face turning an even deeper shade of crimson.

The game continued, his paddle making contact with his pet's reddening behind another six times as she crawled past him. Each time, he made sure he spanked the tail held beautifully in place by the dildo inside her, and each time he waited for the appropriate response. His cock grew harder every time she called him Master, and by the time she came around for the tenth swat, his desire burned almost as hot as her bottom.

Aiming for the final time, Connor landed the swat and sighed with satisfaction as he watched her shuffle away as quickly as her hands and knees would allow. Her bottom wriggled perfectly as she moved, sending the tail into a humiliating swing past the punished orbs of her behind. He hoped she appreciated those little touches as much as he did, but based on the visible evidence of her arousal, he reckoned Molly did.

"Thank you, Master," she conceded as she passed the fireplace, and he stood from the chair, rearranging the hardness in his pants as she crawled back to him.

"Stop," he ordered, and as she complied, his erection throbbed hungrily. "You made it, pet. Even if you did require a little instruction toward the end."

There was a small sniff from the woman at his feet, but she didn't raise her head or reply.

"Did you enjoy your exercise?" he asked, choosing to ignore the lack of response for the time being.

That made her face move, and she lifted her chin to look at him, her blue eyes burning with defiance. "No, Master," she replied, practically spitting out the final word. "I did not enjoy it."

He chuckled at her darkly, raising his right hand slowly to the side of her face. She shrunk away, trying to dodge the contact, but his palm insisted, following her flesh until there was nowhere else for her to hide. "That's a shame," he told her with a sigh. "Because I did enjoy it, very much, and you will certainly be back here for more exercise soon."

A small sob caught in her throat as his words resonated, but she didn't counter him. Evidently the sting in her backside was reminding her what the consequences of that action would be.

"And now to the pleasure," he murmured, intentionally shifting his tone to something more soft and sensual. Molly's eyes darted to him, burning with her apparent need, yet still she didn't speak. "Do you think you deserve your pleasure, pet?"

Her lips parted, and for a split second he imagined how it would feel to push his cock past them, into that wet, warm place inside. "I tried my best, Sir, I mean, Master," she replied, correcting herself quickly.

He smiled at her answer, enjoying the new blush which rose to her cheeks at the error. "Your best was not good enough," he told her firmly. "That is why you needed correction, and you will be punished more thoroughly for your mistakes later."

She trembled slightly at his verdict, and he used the hand at her face to hold her chin steady. "But, Master," she gasped. "You just punished me with the paddle!"

Her gaze darted to where the implement lay on the ground, but the hand at her face did not allow it to stay there. Instead, Connor shifted her face, forcing her eyes back to him.

"That was only for your instruction during exercise," he corrected her. "But don't worry, pet. You will be properly punished later."

Molly opened her mouth to speak again, but he cut her off before the words were out.

"If, however, you'd rather skip the pleasure part, and move straight to your penance, then that can be arranged?" He towered over her smugly, well aware of what little choice he gave her.

"No, Master." He could hear the utter desperation in her voice, and the conflict was etched across her pretty features. She didn't want to have to receive anything from him, but she couldn't deny how she was feeling either. And based on the hardening nipples and the short panting breaths he was witnessing; his pet was horny. Very horny indeed.

"No?" he repeated, holding her face in place as he spoke to her. "So, you do want pleasure?"

She sighed in defeat before she answered. A sound which spoke directly to his pulsating cock. "Yes, please, Master," she mumbled. "I want it."

Chapter Forty-Six

It was excruciating, absolutely excruciating to have to admit it, but it was true. As his large hand continued to keep her face where he wanted it, Molly was forced to concede the point. Despite her fear, her anxiety and her fury at being kept this way, right now her biggest and most potent driver was her own desire. Her arousal was out of control, burning like a life force between her legs, goading and taunting her with each new humiliation he offered. Much like her, it was desperate for liberation, but apparently, its need for release was even greater than her own.

She watched as he smiled down at her, his expression half lustful, and half predatory. She knew she'd have to trust both halves if she wanted the pleasure, at least for the time being.

"My beautiful little pet," he said, eyeing her with a new intensity. "Do you want to come?"

His gaze pinioned her to the spot every inch as much as his hand and the leash. "Yes, Master," she agreed with a shudder. "Yes, please."

A fresh wave of arousal shot through her at the concession. Somehow, humiliating herself for him just made her even wetter. However mortifying the act, it seemed to only fuel her fire.

"You may come," he told her. "If you do something for me first…"

Molly panted in frustration. Surely, she had already done something for him, by circling this freaking post for the last hour? What more could the man want? Again it was as if he knew what she was thinking as his smiled broadened, and the hand at her face shifted to stroke her hair.

"Come now," he teased her. "It's only fair. If you are to have pleasure, then so should I. What do you say?"

A small groan escaped her lips before she could control it. So, *this* was his game. He was going to make her engage in some utter debauchery, under the pretense of her agreement. Molly inhaled, her body shaking with need and tension. She must refuse him, she knew she must. She couldn't possibly consent to any act which offered him pleasure. After all, he was the one who had taken, stripped and ridiculed her for his enjoyment. *He* had enjoyed enough pleasure already.

"Pet?" His intonation had deepened, and something about it made direct contact with her throbbing clit. "Do you agree to this mutual exchange of pleasure?"

She glanced up at him again, struggling to contain the weight of her emotional conflict on the subject. This just wasn't fair. How could she withstand any more of this ordeal? She needed that release, she needed it badly; much more so than he did.

"Please don't make me?" she begged in a throaty tone, but to her utter exasperation he simply shook his head and smiled.

"I'm not making you," he replied softly. "I'm asking you. You have a choice in this one thing, pet, but your indecision is making me regret giving it to you. Now, do you agree, or not?" His brow arched at his own question, and she had the feeling that he was losing patience with her, despite his gentle tone.

Tears threatened to fill her eyes again as she replied, but Molly fought to contain them. "What do I have to do?"

Connor's mouth parted, and for a long moment their eyes connected before he spoke. In that time, she already knew the answer. Somehow, his gaze had told it to her, and it was nothing awful and nothing obscene. In fact, it was something which under different circumstances she would have done gladly to a guy as hot and authoritative as Connor.

"Just pleasure me," he told her as his free hand slipped to his trousers, releasing the clasp. "Nothing complex, and nothing you won't enjoy."

Molly's eyes followed the movement, and she felt her heart race as she waited. He wanted a blow-job, that much was obvious, and for better or worse the prospect did not appall her the way it should have done. She had already seen his cock in action, and she recalled the velvety crown and the veiny shaft. She'd wondered at the time how his cock might taste, and now it seems she would get to find out.

The hand at her face moved to join the other, and slowly she watched as his cock was released from its fabric prison. Molly drew in a gasp as she eyed it, totally unprepared for its size, despite her recollections from the kitchen. It was much wider than she'd remembered, and at least seven inches in length. Her heart began to thunder inside her chest as he inched it closer to where she knelt. She was giddy with excitement.

"Last chance to change your mind?" he offered, and she could hear the lust in his voice. "You pleasure me and in return, I'll make sure you get yours."

She opened her mouth, nodding to him as his erection neared. "Yes, Master," she murmured, enthralled by the look of his approaching organ.

It was the most curious sensation. She had no right to feel this way, and Molly knew another captive wouldn't. She should be scared to death, and at the start, she certainly had been, but Molly wasn't your average prisoner. Molly had form. She had a long-held desire to be treated this way, and Connor had spent time tracking and celebrating in her twisted fantasies. Faced with the reality, she'd found unmistakable arousal in her denigration, and this act was something of a completion of that journey. Or at least that's how it seemed to her as the tip of his cock slipped past her lips.

Time, which had already become her jailor as much as he had, began to stretch. As he slid his hard length into her waiting mouth, she swore time actually stood still around them. The air seemed weighted, and different than before. Something more than just this physical act was transpiring between them, and Molly could feel it. She bet they both could.

The taste of his cock flooded her senses with its salty sweetness, and she splayed her tired knees wider to gain her balance and accommodate him. As she shifted, her eyes connected once again with his hot gaze, and it held her in place as he slowly withdrew.

"Magnificent," he declared, his voice little more than a seductive whir.

She would have liked to agree, but his crown pressed at her mouth again before she could force the words out. There was no doubt he tasted divine, the essence of everything a man should be. He was clean and earthy, and the scent of his aftershave wafted over her as he pressed forward. Molly relaxed, allowing him access to her throat, and Connor took it, driving himself deeper and deeper inside her. There was a moment of panic when she had to remind herself to breathe through her nose, and then his hardness retreated, leaving a trail of her drool between them as he stroked his erection roughly.

"That is amazing, pet," he told her as he fisted his cock. "I want more of it. Much more."

Molly gazed up at him again as her saliva landed against her chin and slipped south. She could feel the very real bondage of the leash at her neck, which stretched right toward the post, keeping her in place. The chains at her wrists and ankles were another constant reminder of her place, but rather than degrade her, right now they just made her hotter. This was what she wanted, this was what she'd needed for fucking years, and it had taken some crazy fan like Connor to make it happen. She was panting as he reached down to ease back her hair from her face. She opened her mouth obediently, waiting like a good little pet as he repositioned his cock over her mouth.

"Kneel up higher," he commanded in a silky voice.

She shifted, straightening her back and lifting her chin to follow his erection as Connor held it aloft, just out of reach of her lips.

"Good, pet," he replied, approvingly. "You look glorious, but just one more thing. Put your hands behind your head and keep those elbows wide."

She blinked up at him, feeling the burning need at the apex of her thighs as she responded. She was aware of the ache in her arms as she laced her fingers behind her head, but she didn't care. Right now, the need to please him and receive her reward was the only thing on her mind, and she pushed her beading nipples out in his direction, as though she wanted to reinforce the point.

"Very good," he commended, swallowing hard at the sight of her. "You look so fucking amazing, I want to come all over your face right now, but I won't. I want to enjoy this. I intend to savor it."

Molly didn't reply. There was nothing to say. Instead she knelt at his feet, arms held back and mouth wide open as she waited for him. It seemed she had become nothing but a vessel for desire, whether it be his or her own, and all other thoughts were banished.

In a flash, he speared her with his massive cock again, burying himself as far down her throat as he could go. She gagged around him, startled by the sudden depth of his invasion, but she held still, using what strength remained in her thighs to keep her in place as he claimed her mouth. Slowly, he eased back, but he never left her lips again. Rather, he remained in place, enjoying short, insistent thrusts into her mouth based on the throaty groans that came from his lips. Apparently finding his rhythm, Connor widened his stance around her knees, and pushed one hand back into her hair to steady her head as he fucked her face.

She remained impassive, or as still as she could be in the circumstances. The whole time his cock possessed her mouth, all Molly could think about was her own lust. It was consuming, reminding her to keep her arms in position, and persuading her weary legs to hold on. *Just a few more minutes,* she told them. *Only a few more, and then we can have release.* By now his shaft felt enormous inside her mouth, and her jaw ached at the strain of being forced open to accommodate him. It didn't matter though. Connor didn't seem to care as he chased his orgasm, and unbelievably at this moment, all Molly could think about was how her mouth was now his to use, his to train, his to shoot cum all over. She felt the gush of arousal which rushed from her core at the prospect.

"Fuck," he cried, between gritted teeth. "I can't hold on much longer."

He sounded disappointed by the idea, and the hand in her hair tightened, forcing her head forwards, toward his body. Molly gagged again, straining for breath. As his pleasure loomed, she was pushed closer and closer to the coarse dark hair which grew at the base of his cock, and she eyed it wildly as he used her. Just when she thought she could take no more, Connor withdrew all at once, leaving her breathless and crumpled on the floor below him.

"Up," he ordered, curtly. "Now! As you were."

Molly heard the urgency in his voice, and knew he was close. She also knew what that meant. Once he'd been pleasured, it was her turn. She scrambled to obey, making it to her knees and parting her lips just in time. Hot shoots of cum landed over her lips, and she closed her eyes out of instinct as she swallowed the first load.

"Open them," he commanded in an urgent growl. "I want to see your eyes while I cum over you."

She could only pant in response, but she complied, watching as he deposited the rest of his climax over her nose and mouth. Like all of the other deeds, she knew this act should be humiliating, and maybe on some level it was. He was marking her as his property, after all. Yet still, the yearning between her legs kept her compliant, burning hotter than she'd ever known it before.

He let out a low, guttural groan as his orgasm shuddered to a conclusion. "Stay," he told her, waving the finger of his free hand in her face as he continued to stroke his recently satisfied length. "You are too perfect. I need to capture this moment."

She knelt on wobbly legs and watched as he reached into his pocket for his phone. There was the usual stirring arousal as he smiled down at her through the lens of the camera.

"Open wide like a good pet," he told her with a chuckle. "Let me see what I just fucked."

Duly, she obliged, parting her lips one last time and stretching them wide as he took his shot. By now her arms were trembling from their forced and unusual position, and she didn't know how much longer her thighs were going to be able to stay in place either.

"Fucking beautiful," he confirmed as he slid his phone back into place, and refastened the clasp of his trousers.

Chapter Forty-Seven

He glanced down at the trembling, panting mess at his feet. His pet was shaking, presumably with tension, and was still covered in the remnants of his orgasm. She was literally, a picture. Connor grinned as he re-seated himself, turning his attention back to the laptop by the side of the chair.

A small whimper escaped her mouth as his eyes flickered to the screen, and the sound made him gleeful. He knew what she wanted, what she needed so badly. Of course, he did. But, he was a cruel and sadistic fuck. He was going to make her work for it.

"What's that pet?" he asked, sardonically. He arched a brow at her desperate little face, supressing the urge to rise and fuck that sweet mouth all over again.

"Please, Master," she mewled.

Her voice sounded tiny to him. Tiny, just like the rest of her. She was so small and vulnerable, and naked and leashed, and... *all his.*

"What is it?" he probed, reaching forward to tweak first her right and then her left nipple.

She yelped, pushing her tits out to meet his hand. Fuck, she really was desperate. "Please may I come now, Master?"

He could tell how much it pained her to have to ask for permission. Perhaps it was as bad as being kept naked and leashed, or maybe it was worse. Connor had never given much thought to which ignominy would be her least favorite.

"Do you think you deserve to come?" he asked her, ensuring his tone took on a deeper timbre. His query was met with frantic, pleading eyes.

"Yes, please," she implored him, her arms quivering as she struggled to hold them behind her head.

"Hmmm," he mused out loud, intentionally taking his time as he perused her answer at a tantalizingly slow pace. "Perhaps you do, pet. You did do a very good job on your knees just now." He paused, offering her a smile, and he watched happily as a fresh blush rose to her cheeks.

"Th-thank you, Master," she replied as her gaze dropped to her thighs.

He nodded, relaxing back in his chair and stretching out his long legs beside her. "You may come," he began in a low, mocking tone, "but only if you do so as you are."

She tilted her head to one side, throwing him an inquisitive look. "But, I..." she started, "I don't understand what you mean."

Connor laughed at her, the sound dark, yet hearty. "It's simple," he explained with a smirk. "You'll get your orgasm, but only as the animal you now are. You can climb onto my legs, mount them and grind that hot little pussy onto your Master's shin."

Her eyes widened at his words, and his cock, so recently satiated, stirred at the image he'd painted.

Connor's grin widened. "Come now," he told her. "Don't be shy. We both know you're desperately horny and in need of release, and I'm offering you some. All you have to do is take it."

Molly eyed him wildly. She was practically panting again as she agonized over the decision. He chuckled gently at her apparent dilemma, shaking his head as new tears welled in her eyes.

"I can't," she protested in a small, throaty voice. She raised her head to meet his gaze briefly, but looked away quickly when she saw his beaming expression.

"Well if you can't then you can't," he agreed with a shrug. "I'm not going to make you, so I guess it means no relief for you, pet."

He sniggered at the way her face fell, waiting for the expected mewl. It came right on cue, her tiny hands fisting into balls as she contemplated her sorrowful predicament.

"But, please," she gasped again. "I can't, I just can't."

He eased back further into the comfy confines of the leather around his body. Molly was evidently keen to put on quite a show for him, and he intended to enjoy every moment of it. "You already said," he replied, curtly, cutting her protest short. "So, have you chosen not to come then. Is that what you want?"

A strangled noise left her throat and her eyes rose to him again, her obvious desperation deepening the blue of her irises. "No," she countered. "I need to come. I can't carry on like this... *Master*."

Connor swallowed. He needed a drink, and if his little pet carried on like this, he'd need another orgasm himself again – soon. "Then you know what to do," he told her. "You have my permission. Ask me nicely and I'll lift my legs for you. You can slide your wrist chain underneath me, and then climb on board." He offered her a sarcastic wink as he concluded, "So? Last chance, pet. Do you want to take it?"

She nodded slowly, her pupils dilating as her own needful lust apparently took command of her body. "Yes, Master," she replied in barely a whisper. "Please may I?"

Connor's cock swelled at her question, and he raised his ankles from the ground just enough to allow the chain connecting her wrists to slip underneath. As he lowered his bare feet to the floor, she was already mounting his legs, and he twisted to his side, freeing his phone from his pocket. This was going to be sweet. Too good to miss, and even though there was a camera in the left corner behind him, he'd need another version to enjoy for prosperity.

He watched as she tried to find a comfortable position. Connor had long, strong legs, so she had to splay her knees as wide as the ankle chains would allow to balance over them. Slowly she began to move. He glanced over her shoulder, down her slender back until his eyes fell over the tail lodged in her arse. It was gyrating backwards and forwards with every thrust of her hips. Her face was down against his thighs, and she stubbornly refused to look up and meet his eye. His smile widened even further. That would never do.

"Head up," he ordered softly. "Let me see my pet grind herself against my leg."

There was a small gasp from her mouth before her head rose, but when it did, she looked wonderful. Her usual glossy, dark hair was in chaos around her face, her blue eyes watering and the signs of his recent pleasure still drying all over her creamy skin.

"Does that feel good, pet?" he cooed mockingly. "Is that what your needy little clit wants?"

"Yes, Master," she replied, her breath catching as she spoke.

"Then tell me," he continued, reaching down to taunt her right nipple which was crushed just above his knee. "Tell me what you are, and tell me how you're going to come?"

Her lips parted, and he watched, mesmerized, as her hips began to pick up the pace, pushing her sex against his shin over and over again. Apparently, his words were helping to get her going. She appeared to be reveling in them.

"I'm your pet, Master," she panted. "I'm going to come over your leg."

"Yes," he agreed, squeezing the nipple between his thumb and forefinger hard. "Yes, you are, because that's how pets deserve to be pleasured, isn't it? By gyrating over their master's leg?"

Her face flinched, but she nodded in response. It seemed she was too close to her climax now to even register the humiliation of his words. Or perhaps he was wrong, perhaps it was his words which were pushing her closer? "Yes," she squealed, grinding over him with the regularity of a wind-up toy. "Yes, Master."

She sounded hoarse, and she looked desperate, on the verge of tears.

"Good little pet," he purred, reaching for his phone and flicking on the video camera with his right hand. "Show me. Show me what a good little pet you are. Show me how you grind over your master's leg. Tell me as you come."

Her eyes blinked up at him, catching sight of the camera and understanding his meaning. He expected her to pull away or retreat, but to his delight, she didn't. Evidently, she was close to release, and willing to bear any indignity in order to achieve it.

"I'm your good, little pet," she grunted. "I'll be coming over your legs, Master."

Connor grinned, watching her through the camera on his phone. He had an amazing view, catching her crimson face and those relentless hips as they edged her closer to her desire. The sight of the furry little tail swinging behind her completed Molly's utter denigration just perfectly.

Chapter Forty-Eight

The orgasm was hard and unyielding. It hit Molly like a tsunami, knocking her for a loop and threatening to drown her entirely. She called out, feeling her body tense and then shudder, before collapsing over his legs entirely. For the longest time she free-fell, spasming like an untamed animal over his body while he sat watching over her. She was vaguely aware of what had transpired; of her surroundings and the weight of the predicament she found herself in, but somehow it didn't matter. Not at this moment. Nothing mattered anymore, except the sweet liberation she found in the release, and the way her head seemed free, even if her body was not.

At some point she felt his digits in her hair. The sensation roused her, and she lifted her head to acknowledge him. There was no longer a smirk meeting her gaze, but his large, adoring eyes. He smiled down at her, his expression filled with what could best be described as pride, and she ceded the point, lowering her chin against his thigh as her body slumped back down against him.

"Is that better, pet?" he murmured, and she nodded slowly.

"Yes, Master," she agreed, and however absurd it may have seemed to someone looking in, she meant it. She did feel better. She was satiated physically of course, but more than that, Molly felt like she'd found a peculiar inner peace in her denigration. She had finally lived out a fantasy she'd kept locked away in her heart for decades, and the effect was cathartic. Her mind was still – quieted by the depths she had sunk to – and even though she knew she should despise the man who had forced her to sink so low, she found she couldn't.

Of course, some small part of her brain understood this wasn't real. It wasn't care or even pride she saw in Connor's eyes, but the look a collector of fine things might portray when they finally found the masterpiece they'd wanted to finish their collection. Connor was no hero. He had taken her and done the most awful things to debase her. She knew that, and she could rationalize it, but the problem was, she'd also loved practically every moment of that time. His fingers fell to her face, stroking away the strands of hair which covered her eyes. Molly found herself sighing as another spasm shuddered through her. Her climax had been one of the most powerful she'd ever experienced.

"I'm glad," he told her, his voice soothing. "You deserved your reward for pleasuring me so well." There was a pause as she rested over his legs, her body heavy as the pleasure finally subsided. "But now," he began again, his tone imperceptibly edgier. "Now, you deserve your punishment."

Molly's bubble of contentment shattered in an instant. *Punishment.* The word made her head ache, and her muscles tense simultaneously. She lifted her head from his leg, her mouth opening to protest, but his left hand shifted like lightning and Connor pressed two finger tips to her parted lips.

"Don't argue and make it worse," he advised with a wry smile. "You know what happens to naughty mouths that can't be quiet, don't you, pet?"

A new shudder passed down Molly's back, but this one had nothing to do with pleasure. "Yes, Master," she whispered, her eyes widening in response to his sudden change of tactic.

"Tell me," he commanded, softly. "What happens to those mouths? What will happen to yours if you cannot control it?"

She gulped, recalling the awful plastic he'd made her endure only yesterday. "It will be gagged," she replied miserably, although there was the throb between her legs again. Small perhaps, but insistent nonetheless, as she imagined the ignominy of being gagged once more.

"Exactly," he agreed. "You will be punished for not keeping your form during exercise, and for that I have a special place in mind to take you. Down from me now. We'll need to relocate."

The hand at her face brushed her from his lap dismissively, and within a moment she was untangled from his legs. She blushed furiously when she caught sight of the large, wet patch she'd created on his dark trousers, and he laughed as he rose, making his way to the post which had kept her in place for so long.

As he unwound the leash, he tugged at her collar. "This way," he instructed, leading her from the room altogether.

Molly followed behind him, on her hands and knees as was becoming her norm. Both her palms and legs ached from their earlier effort, but she didn't dare to complain. Instead, she did her best to keep up with his long paces, taking in as much as she could about the house as he strode from the hallway to a large reception room. She lifted her neck to gaze at the new surroundings. The room was surprisingly big for the size of the place, and was decorated almost entirely in white. There were high ceilings above her, and a large bay window on one side. As she took it all in, the sound of metal drew her attention back to Connor. He was standing at a door to her right, and she watched as he pulled a small set of keys from his pocket, slowly identifying the one he was looking for. He paused, probably aware she was watching his every move, and then slowly slipped the metal into the lock of the door.

Molly's belly tightened ominously. Something about this place didn't seem like good news. Whatever a man like Connor needed to keep behind a locked door would likely be terrible, and her mind began to consider all of the awful possibilities just as the door swung open. There was a threatening creak as the wood drew back toward them, and Connor stepped forward to flick a switch located just inside the new space. She gulped as her eyes took in the dark room which awaited her. It was a complete contrast to the light, airy space of the room she was currently in, and the reality seemed to make the prospect of what was to come even worse.

"Come on," he insisted, pulling her closer to his heel. "There's more steps I'm afraid, but since you're here for punishment, I don't really approve of you walking." Connor turned to face her, and she got the feeling he was musing out loud, rather than expecting a reply. She waited patiently on all fours, allowing her gaze to travel down the depths of the staircase which waited just over the precipice of the doorstep.

"Stand up, pet."

His order came out of the blue, especially considering his prior statement, but Molly did her best to comply. She rose, her thighs shaking as she stood for the first time in what seemed like hours. Connor watched her carefully, and as she found her feet, he closed the distance between them in one stride, reaching for her body. Within a moment he'd swooped, reaching for the roundest part of her thighs and lifting her straight over his left shoulder. She cried out as he swept her from her feet, the shock of the deed more disconcerting than the sound suggested. Her impertinence was met with one sharp swat to her bottom with his free hand, and she bit her lip to suppress the yelp which the sting produced.

"Quiet," he warned her, and she felt the arm at the base of her ass tighten to keep her in place.

Molly drew in a breath as she acclimatised to her new, upside down view of the world. She could feel the blood rushing to her head, and it was doing nothing to quell the rising sense of panic in her about what was now to come. A wave of dread passed over her as he moved, and slowly they began their descent.

Chapter Forty-Nine

onnor carried her over his shoulder with ease. She may be a fully-grown woman, but she was as light as a feather to him. Years of martial arts and training had made him fitter and stronger than nearly everyone he'd ever met, a fact which was easily demonstrated as he carefully negotiated the steps downwards.

There was only a small whimper from her now, and he patted her bottom gently as he entered the basement. The act was supposed to be reassuring, but the fact that her delectable pussy was so close to his face did absolutely nothing to quell his growing ardor. He strode to the center of the space before placing her gently back on her feet, and gesturing for her to resume her place on the floor. To Connor's delight she dropped to her knees without a single command from him, but he could see the fear and trepidation in her eyes as she took in the new, dark surroundings. Her gaze was fixed on the cage in the far corner.

"Yes," he told her, answering her unspoken question. "That is for you when you're a particularly naughty pet, but I don't have it in mind now."

She drew in a shaky breath at his words, lowering her head as though she needed to compose herself. He supposed he could understand the gesture. How many times in her life would she have been faced with a cage like that? But then, nothing about her life as his pet would resemble anything she had known before.

"If you're a good pet," he went on, "and take your punishment well, then I won't need to cage you."

He paused, crouching down in front of her as he twisted the end of her leash around his right hand. "Look at me," he instructed flatly.

Her head rose to reveal large, anxious eyes.

"Does the cage frighten you?" He already knew it did, but he wanted to hear the words from those delicious lips. His cock needed to hear them.

"Y-yes, Master," she conceded in a light, throaty tone.

Connor's cock sprung to attention at the admission, and he wondered if his face made it obvious. "But you have written about similar cages for naughty girls, haven't you?"

Again, his question was merely rhetorical. They both knew that she had written similar penances for her heroines, and he could guess how wet those scenes had made Molly's pretty pussy.

"Yes," she whispered, "but, I never thought I…"

His glare silenced her at once, her face flushing as she realized her mistake. "You have earned yourself another ten strokes for that outburst," he informed her dryly. "You will learn to only answer the questions I ask you. I don't want to hear anything else."

Her face fell, and she looked like she was fighting the urge to cry. Tears had never particularly set him on fire in the past, but Molly's were fascinating. He'd known other sadists who had been all about making their subs cry, and had pushed women harder and harder in pursuit of those tears. Connor had never really understood that until now, but as he watched Molly's expression falter, he longed to see that salty water leaking from her beautiful eyes. She seemed even more emotional than he had fantasized about her being, and it pleased him enormously. Although she didn't need to know that.

"That's enough," he told her firmly as he rose from his crouched position. "Let's begin your punishment. You'll have an unexpected new chapter to write about this afternoon, pet."

She mewled beautifully as he led her to the waiting spanking bench. Connor saw her gaze take in the perfectly rounded leather, and the straps which would hold her already chained limbs in place as he punished her. He allowed her those few seconds to absorb what was coming her way, and then he gave the order.

"Up onto the bench."

He would give her the chance to redeem herself, but if she failed to cooperate in her own punishment, then he wouldn't hesitate to remind her who was master. She climbed up gingerly, her long limbs trembling as she forced herself into position. He admired her toned, limber body, deciding that she seemed more feline than canine as she settled into place.

"Good," he said, pacing to the front of the bench to tuck her chain underneath the structure. He worked quickly to lock her cuffed left wrist into the large leather strap, before shifting to secure the right one.

There was a sniff of what he assumed was self-pity as he moved to the back of the bench, but he chose to ignore it. Instead, he focused on the amazing sight which greeted him as he rounded the end of the bench. The angle of the thing already had her reddened behind pushed high into the air for him. She was exposed and vulnerable, and looked absolutely bloody delicious, but as always, Connor wanted more.

"Spread your legs," he commanded, noticing the lust in his own voice as he gave the order.

His pet wriggled her bottom at him as she fought to obey, her upper body now entirely locked down over the front portion of the bench.

Fuck.

The sight of her struggle was exhilarating. Connor gazed hungrily at her wet pussy, which was now on display below her tail, a fact he hoped would humiliate and arouse her even more as he delivered her penance.

He caught her right ankle in his grasp, securing it into position at the edge of the bench. Connor didn't think she would be stupid enough to kick out at this juncture, but he couldn't be sure. She was after all, probably terrified of being in the basement, and of what he now had in store for her, so he decided not to take any chances. As he strapped her final limb into place, he stepped back to admire her.

Of course, he also had cameras set up in this room, too. It was going to be essential for when he did cage his pet and leave her here as punishment. He wanted her to feel alone and abandoned, but he would ensure that she never really was. Connor would have eyes on her at all times. All that said, however, sometimes there was no substitute for the real thing, and this was one of those times. The look of her bound limbs, pink bottom, and glistening pussy made him heady. He wanted to forget about the penance altogether, and mount her right there on the bench. He could already imagine how tight and warm that pussy was going to be. He'd already experienced his pet's mouth, and that had been wonderful, but he had a good enough imagination to envision how sweet her other orifices were going to be.

"You're going to receive a hard caning for your poor form," he told her, and as he spoke he strode to the basement wall, admiring the line of implements that hung there. "Have you been caned before, pet?"

He turned back to her as he asked the question, having already selected the long, thin cane he was going to use.

"No, Master," she replied, her voice hoarse, a symptom of her evident trepidation.

"Interesting," he went on as she resumed his place by her side. "Well, I can promise you, this is going to hurt. You'll receive fifteen for your form, and a further ten strikes for speaking out of line just then."

She mewled, a desperate sound which made his cock pulsate eagerly.

"Twenty-five swats," he reiterated as he loomed over her, and slowly, teasingly, he lowered the cane over the trembling cheeks of her behind. "Remember, I want you to be a good pet. If you make a fuss, then I will cage you."

There was a small murmur from her mouth, although he couldn't discern her words. It didn't matter anyway. Pets didn't need to articulate. They needed to obey.

Lifting the thin cane, Connor raised it high into the air. He paused, gazing down at his target and imagining how her bottom would look when he was done. He wanted to stripe it, and cause her pain, but he didn't want any lasting damage. His sadism extended predominantly to dehumanizing his little pet, not to inflicting serious harm, and he knew he'd have to go light on the early strikes to give her any chance of surviving the penance.

"Ready, pet?" he probed, glancing at her face which was half pushed against the sleek black leather.

Her eyes were squeezed shut, but she nodded in response. "Yes, Master," she squeaked, apparently resigned to her fate for the time being.

Connor's attention returned to the glorious, punished arse which awaited him. He had teased her for long enough, and now it was time for the waiting to end and the real torment to begin. The cane rose into the air again, but not so high this time. He judged the distance carefully, not wanting to go too hard, too fast. He brought the thin wood down, making contact with her flesh and watching as the impact resonated throughout her body. She cried out, forcing her face into the bench to muffle the sound, but he chose to overlook it. It was her first ever caning, and it *was* going to hurt. He'd expected some sort of response.

"That's one, pet," he informed her as he eyed the thin line which appeared on her backside. "I'd like to hear you thank me for each strike again."

A small snuffle came from her as Molly twisted her head back into its original position. Her eyes strained to see where he was, and as they found him, their gazes locked for a moment.

"Th-thank you, M-Master," she mumbled, her face flaming with the humiliation of having to thank the man who was willfully inflicting the ordeal on her.

Connor smiled, ignoring the urgent throb inside his pants. He lined up the next shot, bringing the cane down with a little more force. It swished through the air, creating a loud clap as it struck her prone bottom. Molly gasped for breath as the wood impacted, before once again forcing the required words from her mouth. As he gazed down, he saw the fresh stripe rise on her behind, the line appearing either side of her furry tail. Only strike two, and already this was by far the most satisfying experience he'd shared with his pet so far.

Chapter Fifty

The strokes were agonizing. Far worse than anything he'd made her endure so far. Each one felt like a line of fire had been branded against her forever, and at that moment, she was grateful that she couldn't actually see the damage he was inflicting upon her tender bottom.

"Thank you, Master," she said, forcing the seemingly mandatory reply from her quivering lips.

She was afraid of how far he would take this, but more than that she was angry that Connor was making her suffer the cane full-stop. There was no way she deserved a punishment like this, but then, she supposed nothing about the last couple of days could be considered fair, and this was just the latest ordeal to bear.

The cane struck her again, and she ground her teeth together as she absorbed the sting. Bound by her sides, she felt her hands ball into small fists at her treatment. Her fury seemed to be burgeoning with each flick of the dreaded implement, and she lifted her head from the leather, willing the punishment to be done.

"Pet?" His tone was ominous, and Molly realized with a sense of dread, that she'd forgotten the obligatory thank you he required after each stroke.

"Th-thank you," she stuttered, pulling futilely against the straps at her wrists, as though her will alone could make them disappear.

"Do not forget your manners," he growled from behind her, but before she could reply, the cane branded her bottom again.

For some reason this strike felt the hardest yet. Perhaps it had been? Maybe her delay had irritated him, causing him to hit her harder than before. She grimaced at the thought, wondering at the arrogance of the man. How dare he be mad at her! She was the one bound to the freaking bench and at his mercy, and yet he was upset with her? The thought made her dizzy with unspent rage, and she bit down hard against her lower lip until she tasted blood.

Connor struck her for a fifth time, creating a line of what felt like lightning across her backside. She gasped again as she took a lungful of air. The pain was becoming intolerable, and she could feel the bottled-up emotions in her rising to breaking point.

"Thank you, Master," she replied between gritted teeth, and she heard the dark chuckle which greeted her words.

"That was five, pet. Only twenty more to go."

Her heart sank at that, and as the sixth strike blazed a trail of fire over her flesh she felt the fresh tears leaking from her eyes. There was no way she was going to be able to manage another nineteen of those, and he must know it.

"Th-thank you," she sniffed, despising how pitiful she sounded, but knowing there was nothing she could do about it.

There was nothing she could do about any of it. Not the straps that held her limbs in place, nor the monster who was right now wielding the cane above her body. Right now, she had to endure, and get this over with, but oh fuck, she really didn't know if she could do it.

Molly's caning continued, each strike sending fresh agony coursing across her ass. She was in tears now, the leather at her face wet with the evidence of her misery. She'd have cared less about the shame of finding herself crying in front of him again, if the tears had gone some way toward relieving the pain, yet somehow, they never did. Each stroke was excruciating, sending them flowing hard and fast from her eyes, but the sting of the cane never lessened. Rather, it seemed to grow, becoming more intense as he went on. By the fifteenth swat, she found herself really sobbing into the padding of the bench, thanking Connor between shaky breaths.

"Ten more," he announced, and she heard him shift his weight, before beginning a circle of the bench.

He paused by the side of her head, and all of a sudden, she felt his digits in her mass of dark hair. He stroked the locks gently, drawing them back, away from Molly's face. "How do you like my cane, pet?"

Molly blinked the tears away at his question. Her will told her to be strong, and to offer him some wisecrack response, but the logical part of her brain overrode it. She was a strong woman, but she wasn't a fool. Connor could do absolutely anything he wanted to her. She was naked and bound over a bench for fuck's sake. He could really hurt her, or forcibly take whatever he wanted, and she'd be powerless to resist. However much she'd fantasized about the idea of being captured, she couldn't let her body's reaction deceive her. Connor was dangerous, and she was completely at his mercy.

"I don't like it, Master," she answered him finally, her voice shaking as she gave her response.

The fingers in her hair stilled, and all at once he shifted, crouching down in front of her, so that he was visible in her line of sight. "I'm sure," he replied, smugly. "My cane is not here to be liked. It's here to punish you, and to teach you a lesson." He paused, smirking at her as she eyed him fearfully. "What is it teaching you, pet?"

Molly gasped, realizing he wanted her to say the words out loud. "It's teaching me how to crawl," she sobbed. "To have better *form*."

Connor's face softened, and he nodded. "Exactly," he agreed. "You see, you *are* learning…"

"Please, Master," she begged, risking a chance to implore him now that they were face to face. "I have learned the lesson, and I swear, I'll try harder next time!"

He shook his head, answering her with a smile. "I know you will, pet," he told her softly, and as he spoke, those fingers roamed her face once more.

Molly closed her eyes, praying that Connor would relent and free her from the spanking bench.

"Open them," he commanded, his voice taking on a more masterful edge as he spoke to her again.

She complied, eyeing him warily as he rose to stand next to her.

"I believe you will try, but that doesn't mean you get out of your punishment. The strikes for your crawling are done, but now you have ten more strokes for the way you spoke to me."

Molly could feel the blood rushing from her face in horror. So, she'd have to tolerate another ten swats of the freaking cane, and it seemed there was nothing she could do about it. Fresh tears sprung from her eyes, though these were borne of frustration, rather than fear or pain.

"You are quite beautiful," he mused aloud, and she felt his fingers stroke her hair again. "Cry for me, pet. Your tears are most welcome."

Molly recoiled, squeezing the fingers of her hands into her palms to stop her from responding. *What sort of sick fuck was this guy? What sort of man wanted a woman to cry like this?* She shivered reflexively as he stalked away from her, and within a moment she felt the cool line of cane pressing gently into her bottom again. She flinched at the contact, wincing as he urged the cane down against her skin. Her ass was so sore, it was horrendous, and she wondered how long it would be before she could easily sit down again.

"Ten more," he told her. "Let's begin."

Chapter Fifty-One

onnor brought the cane down hard against her rump
again. Her flesh was already painted with numerous
pretty strikes, each crisscrossing the tail held fast in her
behind. He smiled as he rained down the next three in
fast succession. Molly was screaming now, crying openly and
writhing at each impact. It appeared she had lost all
composure, a fact he would need to address, but for now, he
concentrated his energy on concluding the caning. By the fifth
stroke, she was uncontrollable, pulling and straining against
the leather straps at her ankles and wrists. Of course, she had
no hope of escape, but the display made it obvious just how
desperate his pet had become.

"That's enough," he warned her, lowering his voice to
make the threat clear. "Settle down, pet, or I promise you, there
will be consequences."

Molly stilled at that, her breathing labored as she collapsed
against the leather. "Please stop!" she called into the bench. "I
can't... I just can't do this anymore."

A spark of irritation rose in Connor at the sound of her plea.
It was not only that once again she had spoken out without
permission, but she hadn't even addressed him correctly.
"You'll do whatever you're told, pet," he growled, lowering
his body over her back as he snarled. "And right now, you're
being told to settle down and take the remainder of your caning
in silence."

Connor stood upright, assessing her quivering body with a
curious smile. He would be the one to quiet that beautiful
mind. Once she'd been broken, he would rebuild her again,
and help her to find peace in her submission to him.

There were no more warnings. Instead, Connor flicked the cane over her bottom, landing it over her exposed cheeks. She sobbed quietly, but remained still, and based on the tension he could see in her shoulders, Connor could guess at the amount of effort that immobility took.

"Thank you, Master," she squeaked, and he paused at her words, pleasantly surprised at them. So, the little pet was contrite then, or so it would seem, but it wouldn't be enough to save her now. Her recent performance was already sufficient to condemn her to the cage once this penance was through.

Focusing on her behind once more, Connor delivered the final four swats. He landed them so fast that Molly had little time to respond, let alone thank him, and as the cane branded her flesh for the final time he threw the implement onto the black tiled floor for dramatic effect.

"Your caning is over," he concluded, assessing her as he spoke.

The release of tension was visible, and at the sound of his words, she broke down again, sobbing her heart out onto the bench. Connor sighed at the sight. Much as he appreciated her distress, she was going to make herself ill if she didn't stop.

He left her bound body, and wandered to the left of the room, to the small, black, integrated refrigerator he'd had installed. Opening the door, a bright light shone against the cold tiles as he reached inside for a bottle of water. Twisting the cap, he took a slug, and turned to assess his pet. She was clearly overwrought, and would need refreshment.

He opened the dark cupboard above his head, eyeing the collection of pet bowls and accessories which he'd prepared for this purpose. Choosing the one closest to him, he poured some of the cold water into the bowl, before striding back to where his pet was waiting.

"Time for a drink," he told her, as he placed the dish on the tile by the side of the bench.

She turned her head, revealing a tangle of dark hair over burning red eyes.

"Are you going to behave yourself?" he asked her, crouching and edging closer to her perturbed expression.

Molly sniffed, and nodded. "Yes, Master," she promised, the relief evident in her tone.

Poor little pet. She clearly assumed that this part of her ordeal was over, but that couldn't be further from the truth. "Good," he continued, reaching for her left wrist and slowly releasing her limb from the strap. "Stay where you are while I release you," he told her, shifting quickly to her left foot, before loosening the remaining straps.

He already had hold of her leash before he permitted her to move, and gingerly she shifted from the bench, her legs trembling as she lowered herself to the floor.

"Drink up, pet," he commanded, leading her straight to the place where the bowl of water waited.

She didn't query the order, and for the first time since he'd taken her and introduced the pet bowl, she crawled to it with some enthusiasm. Dipping her head, she lapped at the water, apparently glad for its cool refreshment. Connor seated himself on the edge of the bench, holding her leash tight as he watched her drink. She was such a delectable sight, particularly when he took into account the red stripes which now decorated her bottom. He exhaled deeply as he imagined removing the tail, and sliding his cock between those caned cheeks.

While he sat watching her, she paused, turning to glance up at him, her chin wet with water.

"Better?" he inquired, sardonically.

His pet nodded. "Yes, thank you, Master," she replied, lowering her head, although he couldn't be sure if it was her trepidation or embarrassment which triggered the gesture.

"Good, pet." He reached down, and began to stroke her head. "I'm pleased you're feeling better, because now we move to what comes next."

She startled at that, her head rising at once, and her frantic eyes assessing him. Evidently, she knew him well enough already to know what might come next, and Connor did nothing to reassure her.

"I asked you to take your punishment well," he began, gripping the leash in his fist even tighter as he spoke. "And at first you did so, yet when we moved to the last ten strokes, you were unable to obey."

Her face blanched as her crimes were laid out in front of her. She didn't try to counter him, but he noticed her limbs shaking as he continued.

"Rather, you kicked, screamed, sobbed, and as I recall, you called out for me to stop." He paused, waiting for his words to sink in. "Do you deny my claims, pet?"

Molly blinked up at him, "I didn't mean to be bad," she explained, meekly. "It was just so painful, I…" Her words trailed away as perhaps she realized how weak her defense really was.

"Do you deny them?" he asked again, his tone curt.

She shook her head, beginning to sob softly again.

Connor would have liked to hear the words, but there seemed little point in pressing the point. His pet clearly knew she was in yet more trouble, and he wanted to seize on that resignation to help him cage her. "Then you'll understand what I have to do next," he told her, rising from the bench and tugging her collar toward the corner of the room.

Chapter Fifty-Two

Blind panic seized her, and she knew without needing to be told what he had in mind. He was already leading her in the direction of the ominous-looking cage, and her belly tightened into a taut knot at the prospect.

Pressing her palms flat against the cold tile, Molly arched her back and resisted the pull which she knew would lead her to the metal prison. There was no way he was putting her in that thing. No. Fucking. Way! Molly had never been claustrophobic, but being confined into a pen no larger than a man was going too far, and she was not going to allow it. She'd tried to bide her time, to be a *good pet* and comply. She wanted to lull him into a false sense of security, assuming he might relent and release her that way, but things were only getting worse.

"Come on," he cajoled her. "You were warned, and now you're going inside. Don't make this worse by trying to fight."

Terror consumed her, rising up inside of her chest and threatening to seal up her throat completely. He may have had her confined in this house, but this was an actual fucking cage. "No!" she cried, trying to gain traction against the smooth tiles at her hands and knees as the leash at her collar pulled her onwards. "No, please!"

Molly's mind was in free-fall. She wanted to sob, but somehow, she couldn't take a breath, and there was no time anyway. There was no time for panic, no time to hyperventilate; this was happening and if she didn't fight harder, she knew she'd be forced inside the cage no matter what.

"You're making this difficult on yourself, pet," he cooed, his voice was an almost mocking tone. "You can't fight me, and you know it, so do yourself a favour and just obey."

"No!" She was screeching now, her eyes wide with alarm as he literally dragged her closer to the cage. The whole time she was trying to resist, her hands clawing at the floor, but it was useless. There was nothing to hold onto. Nothing to offer any friction. Nothing to stop Connor's progress. No hope at all.

By the time he had pulled her to the entrance of the cage, Molly was a mess of flailing limbs. He paused, holding her leash tight, but seemed to give her a moment to compose herself, and for the first time since her drink, Molly hesitated, glancing up to him.

"Don't make me go in there," she begged, her voice husky with the terror she felt on the subject.

Connor simply shook his head at her. "There is no discussion on this," he advised her. "You're going in the cage. Either you can go in yourself and get comfortable, or I can bind you and force you in. If you choose the latter, then I'm likely to gag you too, pet. It seems you have far too much to say for yourself today."

She blinked up at him, pulling the air into her lungs in short, fast breaths. The whole room seemed to be closing in around her, her every reality reduced to this one metal cage which was to be her fate. She eyed it with fear, certain that she wasn't getting enough oxygen into her body. Her head felt giddy, and the knot in her belly made her nauseous.

"I can't," she sobbed, breaking down at his feet. "I can't go in there, please…"

Molly's head crashed onto her palms, which were already flat against the floor, and she threw herself, quite literally, at his mercy. Even as her elbows landed against the cool tiles though, she knew it was futile. Connor was set on what he wanted. He wanted to cage her, and she knew he was going to have his way. He was enjoying it all too much.

"Time's up," he told her, ominously. "Will you go in on your own, or do you need me to *help* you?"

She was shaking as her head rose, her eyes red with tears as she answered him. "Don't gag me," she implored him. "I'll go in on my own."

There was a heavy silence as her words echoed around the dark basement. Time protracted somehow, and all Molly could hear were her own words, going around in her head like a nursery rhyme. *"I'll go in on my own... I'll go in on my own..."* What had she done? Why had she just given in to him and volunteered to go into the thing?

"I'm waiting."

His words stirred her, and she jumped a little in acknowledgement. She had made the declaration, and that was that. Now, she had to act upon it. Now, she had to crawl into the cage.

Pulling in a shaky breath, Molly shifted her weight and turned to face her nemesis. It was easily wide enough for her to climb into, but once inside, she wasn't sure if she'd have the space to turn around. Better then, that she edged in backwards, and then at least she could face the exit. A small mercy perhaps, but it seemed that was all she had. Slowly she began to move, maneuvering her body so that she could reverse her legs backwards into the cage. She inched herself into place, nausea rising as she moved. She was like a cornered animal, too afraid to resist her captor further, but utterly enraged at her confinement.

"Keep going, pet," he cooed, towering over her as she backed her punished ass into position.

She stilled at his words, glancing up at his shins and taking in the sheer size of him. Her palms were now in the entrance to the cage, and her head jutted out just beyond its doorway. She pulled in another deep breath, willing herself to be calm, yet all the while her heart hammered away inside her. *This was really happening*, she realized miserably. *He's going to lock me in the cage!*

Connor inched his foot forward, a small gesture which made her move again. His proximity was a warning, and she knew it. He didn't need to shout at her or make threats to intimidate her. Within a moment, she was in place inside the thing, her body now resting on the plastic base, as he crouched down in front of her.

"There you are." His voice droned jeeringly. "Finally, my pet has found her place."

Molly opened her mouth to speak, but there were no words for whatever she was feeling. She had already begged him to reconsider, but Connor had no interest in listening. *This is what he'd wanted right from the start. It must be, or why else would he have set up this cage in the first place?* Molly had always been destined to end up here, even before he'd snatched her from the street in London.

Her throat dried as she watched him shut the metal door in front of her face. It was surreal. She knew she was trapped, and there was nothing she could do. She wanted to scream, to cry, to shout, but there was no point. She had done those things already, and still, she found herself shut in like an animal. Connor's large fingers closed the two large clasps on the outside of the door, before reaching behind the side of the cage and producing a large metal padlock. He eyed her for a moment, simultaneously sliding the lock into place. She heard the ominous click as it sealed her inside, and her eyes flew south to take in the reality of it. *What if he lost the key? What if he never intended to let her out, and she was trapped in here forever?* She squeezed her eyes shut as the cold panic washed over, not wanting him to see the extent of the power he now had over her.

But Connor had the peculiar ability to be able to read her mind, and as he spoke, it was as though he had looked into her soul. "Your cage is for quiet contemplation, pet," he told her. "Emphasis on *quiet*. If you behave and please me, then you need not stay here long."

Molly opened her eyes and locked gazes with the man who had captured her. She nodded slowly, unsure if she should speak after his latest warning, and equally uncertain if she could do so without bursting into tears again.

"You may answer to show you understand me." His tone was softer now.

She bit her lip, fighting for composure. "Yes, Master."

Connor smiled, offering her a devilish look for a moment before he rose, and then he was gone. She watched his feet stride away from her, crossing the tiles to the bottom of the stairwell, and then, to her horror, she saw him climb the steps. She gulped as she twisted her head to try and see his ascent, but frustratingly he was already out of sight. And she was alone, locked inside a cage in his basement.

Chapter Fifty-Three

He sat in the leather recliner, watching his pet from the laptop resting on his thighs. The cameras he had put in place were working perfectly, and he could access images of her from the four corners of the basement, plus most importantly, from the one he'd positioned right next to the cage. This was his preferred view. It gave Connor a look right into the pen without him needing to be there, and of course, it also provided him with sound.

Dunking another chocolate biscuit into his hot tea, he eyed her trembling body crouched inside the metal cage. His gaze passed over her delectable form to the angst-ridden expression which was etched onto her face. He got an amazing view of her breasts which hung pertly at her chest, and he smiled idly as he watched her playing with the leash which slipped between them. Connor tilted his head to get a better look at her stunning blue eyes, and for a moment, even though she had no idea that he was watching her, she glanced straight into the camera, and their gazes locked. He couldn't be sure what he read in them. It could have been anger, or terror, or even paralyzing arousal at her predicament. Any of them were possible with his little pet. He smirked down at the image of her. Whichever emotion she was struggling to process, it didn't matter. This wasn't one of her famous paperbacks. There would be no happy ending for Molly, not unless she learned to find contentment in the life he now offered her.

Connor checked the time on his laptop, concluding that she had already been confined there for fifteen minutes. He wondered how she was coping, and how much longer he should leave her there. It was tantalizing to watch her confinement, but in reality, she'd be getting cold soon unless he activated the underfloor heating. Her bottom was no doubt also in a lot of pain. He could tell it was bothering her by the number of times she subconsciously reached behind to touch it, or at least, reached as far as her chains would allow. He couldn't get a decent shot of it from here, which was a shame because her derriere looked great with its furry tail in place, but he knew the caning he'd delivered would likely bruise. He made a mental note to attend to it later, whatever her feelings on the subject.

While he mused on the issue, he continued to observe Molly in her new environment. She did have enough space to wiggle round in the pen, but admittedly, it was a tight squeeze, and given the state of her behind, she seemed reticent to move too much. Instead, she huddled, pulling her knees to her chest for as long as she could presumably tolerate the pressure on her bottom, and then shifting back to her hands and knees. For a while she lurched forward, clutching the bars with her small fingers and peering out into the basement. Connor had set the lighting to a minimum, so there was enough light for her to see, but the main overhead fixtures were switched off, and he contemplated what she might be looking at. As her head tilted to the right, it suddenly hit him. She had no-doubt noticed the camera, and was now looking directly at him.

He supped at his tea as he smiled at her image. So, she knew he was watching her, and now she was watching him in return. A small snort left his throat at the idea, and he chuckled as he drained his mug. His little pet was smart, and while her sassy attitude would sometimes need correction, he didn't want her intelligence to falter. He wanted her obedient, but he needed her bright enough to write for him – for them – and to continue to create their stories for a long time to come. It was a contradiction he hoped he could overcome as they got to know one another better.

Placing his mug down, he decided she had suffered long enough. The last image he saw of his pet as he set the laptop back down onto the floor was of her resting her head against her palms in the cage. She now seemed calm and absolutely settled. It appeared confinement suited her after all.

Time it seemed, could be every inch as much a prison as the metal bars which surrounded her naked body. It felt like she had been here for a lifetime, but in reality, she had no way of knowing how long it had been. It could only have been ten minutes, but whatever the truth, she instantly despised being there, contained and kept like a prize.

After he'd left, Molly had wanted to cry again, and she'd expected the tears to come hard and fast. She was really more angry than scared now, but regardless, she'd wanted the release of the tears, to lessen some of the enormous frustration she felt at being locked up like an animal. She sighed as she considered the analogy. She was just like an animal now, complete with her own fucking collar and tail. She shook her head at the thought, the motion making her leash rattle between her breasts, and then remembering her sore behind, she shifted her weight onto her hip to try and reach around and quell her aching bottom. She wondered what sort of state her poor ass was in after both the paddle and the cane had delivered their punishments, but stuck in this place, it was impossible to know.

The next thing she became aware of was how ridiculously uncomfortable it was in the cage. It was barely long enough for her to stretch out fully, although her initial explorations had found she could just about relieve the tension in her legs. That said, she felt absurdly exposed and vulnerable being naked and caged this way, and it felt safer to curl into a ball as much as possible. Drawing her feet back to her torso, she tried to rest against the bars which were set against the wall behind her, but the weight on her punished bottom was so painful, she was soon forced to move again. This time she settled on all fours, a position she had become wearily used to after the last few days. In spite of the pain in her knees, she found the position bizarrely comforting. It was disconcerting, but as her stomach rested against her thighs, she felt warmer, and calmer, too.

Molly fell into something of a stupor. She was neither dazed, nor intoxicated, yet she was aware of a peculiar wave of tranquillity falling over her. She still hated the cage, and she despised what it represented, but it was the strangest thing, somehow being locked inside it made her mind quiet. She was physically still of course – she had no choice in that – but it was more than just the actual confinement, the experience transcended that. In this restricted space, her mind was bizarrely liberated, and rather than worry about what Connor would do next and whether she could endure it, she felt resigned instead, relaxed even.

She drew in a deep breath, shivering a little at the temperature in the room as her eyes moved around the place. It was all so dark and debauched. With its whips, chains and spanking benches, Connor's basement looked like the inside of one of the many scenes she had written over the years. She squirmed as she considered how long she'd thought about being dehumanized in the way he had treated her in the last day or so. The idea of being collared and leashed had seemed so kinky, and made her so hot, yet now, in this cage, the leather at her neck felt just like a second skin. She was so used to it being there, so wondered how she would reconcile the idea of being free of the thing when she escaped, and yet it had only been what? Two or three days here in this place with him? Christ, she didn't even know what day it was anymore. Just imagine what Connor could do to subjugate her given more time.

Molly shuddered at the thought, the motion shifting her dildo; the tail lodged deep inside her ass. If the leash had seemed kinky, then how did she rationalize that? Connor was well and truly making her his pet, and despite her every protest, and all the punishment, Molly couldn't deny the hot, simmering need it produced between her legs. She didn't need to slide a hand down there to know that even at this moment she was wet with need, her arousal spiking inside the cage, despite the humiliating orgasm she'd been permitted to achieve upstairs over his leg. Whatever this nightmare abduction was, and however it turned out, there was a part of Molly that was relishing the experience, and despite her logical abhorrence, she was tired of trying to deny it.

She sighed, blinking into the darkness. There was nothing to see, but still she stared. Molly shifted her weight to rest the side of her head against the backs of her hands. Ignoring the silent screams in her knees, she closed her eyes. Trying to make sense of her fate was giving her a headache, and the confines of the cage were doing nothing to help. Before Connor – before all of this – she used to take runs to alleviate the symptoms of her frequent bad headaches, but there was no hope of that here. With Connor as her Master, there was little hope of even being allowed to stand and walk, let alone go for a run, and somehow, she needed to make the best of it. At least until she could somehow devise her escape.

The realization hung over her like a cloud, and all at once, without any warning, the tears began to fall. Thick and fast they came, until Molly's eyes blinked open, and her vision blurred with the weight of them. It was then that sounds from the top of the staircase stirred her, and her heart raced as she heard footsteps. His footsteps. Connor was coming.

Chapter Fifty-Four

He towered over the end of her cage, watching her body tremble as she awaited his verdict.

"Has my little pet suffered enough?" He announced the question to the dark room around her.

Molly nodded her head slowly, craning her neck to make eye contact with him. "Yes, Master," she whispered, her tone imploring.

He crouched low, so that he was almost at her eye-level. "Have you learned your lesson?" His tone was calm. "Every time you refuse to take your punishment as I see fit, you will be locked in here, for more quiet contemplation."

She swallowed, as though she was pushing back the words she wanted to use as a retort, and the look of her made him smile.

"I understand," she mumbled, her face lowering to avoid his eye. "I will try to be good."

He raised his brow at her sardonically, wondering if Molly even had it in her to be good. Obedience, it seemed, was not her forte, however hard she may try. "And I shall reward you for your efforts," he told her, "and punish you for your failings."

She pulled her lower lip between her teeth at that, evidently uncertain how to respond. She had every right to be unsure, currently locked in a cage as she was.

"You may come out now," he went on, reaching into his shirt pocket for the small key which would release the padlock at the cage door.

Molly's eyes widened further as she watched him, as though she couldn't quite believe she would be free, but as the door swung open he heard her sigh of relief. She inched forward to the opening, glancing up at Connor for approval before she exited completely.

He rose before her, taking the end of her leash as he smiled. "Come on," he encouraged her, beckoning her forward with his index finger. "You need to rest, and then you will be fed and put to work. There's a lot to write since your last installment."

Tentatively, she crawled out of the cage, shivering as she made contact with the hard tiles again. Connor led her toward a large black box against the side of the basement wall, and lifting the lid, he produced a huge emerald blanket from within its confines.

"Here," he said, gently. "Wrap this around you, pet."

He offered her the cover, and watched as she opened it out, draping its length over her nudity as best she could in her chains. Once her body was sheltered, he swooped, catching her under the arms with one hand and under the knees with the other. He bundled her up in the blanket, and pulled her close against his body, his show of agility producing a shocked gasp from his pet.

"You've had a busy morning," he chuckled as he carried her up the stairs, past the unused lounge, and into the bright hallway. "It's time you had that rest."

She settled into the dog bed without a fuss. Connor was right, she was exhausted and despite the humiliation at being bundled from a cage to a basket, she had neither the will nor the energy to care. Her ass stung like hell as it nudged the outside of the fur lining, and she inhaled sharply. Hearing the sound, Connor turned to laugh at her once more.

"How's that bottom doing, pet?" he asked, evidently amused at her suffering.

"It stings, Master," she replied, feeling the heat at her face as she answered him. It was ridiculously humiliating to have to say so, but it was the truth, and based on how her ass felt, there could be no denying it.

He nodded. "I will tend to it while lunch is cooking," he mused. "I want you to be punished, but not to suffer for days afterwards."

Molly raised her head to look upon him, his kind gesture unexpected in light of recent events. She watched as he moved fluidly about the kitchen, marveling at how comfortable he seemed in the place. Molly had never been the best cook, and it was almost alluring to see Connor so competent as he busied himself. Soon the aroma of roasting chicken filled the room, and her belly grumbled in response. Apparently, she was not only tired, but hungry.

"Not long now," he told her, moving toward the place where she lay.

She glanced up to see a tube of cream in his hand, and she blinked at his towering form as it loomed over her.

"Let's attend to your poor, caned backside, shall we?" he asked with a wry smile, as he crouched before her.

She inhaled deeply. *What was this? First, he wanted to cane her, and now he wanted to play nurse-maid?*

"Come," he ordered, tugging at her collar with his end of the leash.

She left the dog bed, crawling slowly to where he stood. Pulling back a kitchen chair, he seated himself and waited on her arrival. As she approached his feet, she paused, once more staring up at him.

"Up you come," he instructed, patting his lap with his free hand. "Let's see the damage properly."

Chapter Fifty-Five

She was up and over his lap in a moment. One hard tug at her leash had got her moving, and she'd scrambled to obey as quickly as she could. Connor wound the end of 'her leash around his right hand, and then examined her delectable bottom for signs of cuts or significant damage. He was pleased to see there were none, and he credited his own, experienced hand with the cane for that achievement.

"You'll be fine," he told her, unscrewing the cap of the tube with his teeth after he had spoken. "Let me put this on now, and you'll be healed in a day or two, assuming you don't earn yet more punishment before then, of course."

She squirmed over him, her chained limbs hanging on either side of his body as he applied the cream around her furry tail. There was a loud hiss and a wince as he touched the punished areas, and he smiled to himself, pleased that her penance had been so effective. Connor wasn't sure if it was his cane, or his cage which had placated her, but she certainly seemed quieter since her visit to the basement.

Tamed…

The word sprung into his head as he massaged the toned orbs of her ass. But was she? Could you really tame a woman so quickly? After all, it had only been a matter of days, but there had certainly been an intense collection of experiences in that time.

"How's this doing, pet?" he asked her, tugging gently on the tail which sprang from her bottom.

Molly sniffed, miserably. "It feels huge, Master," she whined.

Connor bit his lip to suppress the chuckle which threatened to emerge. He loved how she moaned and begged. The sounds made him hard almost at once. "Are you sore?" He probed, running a digit around the outside of the dildo plugged into her behind.

She whimpered, nodding over him, but that wasn't going to be good enough. She had to know that about him by now.

"Tell me, pet," he snapped, wanting to demonstrate his disappointment at her response.

"Yes, Master," she replied, breathily. "Very sore."

He pursed his lips, turning from her toned shoulders to examine her gorgeous ass again. Connor wanted her plugged, as often as possible, but he didn't want to make it unbearable. His long-term objective was to fuck the sweet arse in front of him, and for that he needed her not only obedient, but relaxed and pliant. He had no desire to rip and damage her permanently. That kind of thing just didn't do it for him.

He had always been a man of many contradictions.

"Okay, let's get this out for now," he told her. "Like before, pet. Nice deep breaths for me."

She shuddered over him, but he felt the effort in her chest as she forced herself to calm.

"On your next breath out," he told her, gripping the end of the tail with his left hand.

As soon as she exhaled, he tugged, easing the black plastic from her bottom with a practised hand. She mewled softly as it slipped from her, panting for a moment until her breathing settled down. Connor eyed the dildo enviously. He couldn't wait to get his cock into the place it had vacated.

"Down now," he told her, using his right arm to guide her back to the floor. "Back into your bed until the food is ready."

She raised her eyes at him, but was smart enough not to speak. Instead, she turned and allowed Connor to lead her back to the dog bed, her eyes on him as he secured her leash to the D-ring on the floor.

Time was moving in random pockets. A few moments in his cage could seem like hours, and yet entire chunks of the day passed in what felt like no time at all. Connor fed her lunch as promised. It was roasted chicken and mashed potatoes, with some type of delicious, creamy sauce, and despite the usual humiliation of being served food in a dog bowl, she wolfed it down hungrily. It turned out she was starving, and Connor could really cook, so she suppressed her desire to throw the contents of the bowl over him, and just forced her mouth into it. Eating this way was more than just undignified, and she despised how she must look as she leaned into the metal, hearing the chain at her neck clink against it. But her growling belly drew her on, so she devoured what she could eagerly. All the time she was aware of Connor's hot gaze on her, and she knew the denigrating behavior was making her horny and wet again. She could feel the simmering need pulsing at her clit, and it riled her every inch as much as he did. It reminded her of the hard truth. He might be the bad guy here – the one who had taken her – but she was the sick one who'd actually started to enjoy it. *What the fuck was that about? Who relished being captured and dehumanized this way?* The urgency in her pussy gave her the answer. She did.

As she ate on the floor, Connor sat at the table to her left, eating the more conventional way. That annoyed her too. While she was made to lap potato from her bowl, he sat happily beside her, using his knife and fork. But Molly knew that was the point. This was all part of the game. The *let's dehumanize Molly, until she truly believes she's an animal* game. She was smart enough to understand what he was doing, and why, but she wasn't strong enough to stop him. She couldn't fend him off, and she knew she couldn't outrun him – even without the chains at her ankles. Worse though, she wasn't even sure if she wanted to.

After the meal, he rose, carrying his plate to the sink before he returned with a wet cloth in his hand. Crouching before Molly, he ordered her to look up at him, an instruction which took a few seconds to obey. She couldn't see herself, but she could feel the state of her face, so she had a pretty good idea of how messy she must be. He grinned at her gleefully as he wiped her clean, and all she could do was swallow down her pride, and take it.

"You did well with lunch," he praised her, cheerfully. "Now it's time to write, and after that you can rest for a while."

She met his gaze, uncertain how she was supposed to respond. The horrid tail was out of her at least, but she had no idea how she could sit on a chair with her ass as tender as it was right now. Apparently oblivious to her concerns, Connor took the bowl away, and strode to the door.

"Stay put," he warned her, as he unbolted the top lock, and slipped through the door. Molly heard the bolt slide into place from the outside, and let out a long sigh.

He was gone. For the time being at least. Her hand moved to the leash at her collar, tracing the metal down to the floor. How had it come to this? She didn't know if she wanted to laugh or cry anymore. She was exhausted and hurt, although the greatest wounds had undoubtedly been inflicted on her dignity. Connor had ripped that into shreds, and then made her lap up the pieces in front of him. She raised her head as best she could against the chain, taking in the look of the kitchen.

For the first time she thought of the life he had taken her from. She hadn't allowed herself to dwell on her home and her friends until that moment, but now the sense of loss hit her like a freight train. Gasping, she shifted in the bed, instinctively trying to sit with her legs crossed, but then remembered the shortness of her leash, and just how sore her bottom really was. She compromised by resting on her side, and then the tears came again. Would Hannah be worried about her? What would her friends think when she didn't make their appointments, and return their calls? Would they have called the police by now? Her mind wandered over every possible scenario, but at the end of every one was the bleak reality. Even when her absence was noticed, they'd never find her. She was in another country after all, her last known destination the author event in London. The only possible witnesses to her abduction were the gang of youths who'd also tried to attack her, and it was pretty unlikely that they'd have gone to the police themselves. They couldn't care less about Molly.

Whatever happened, she was on her own here – wherever *here* was – and if she ever wanted to see home again, she'd need to use her own wit and cunning. So far Connor hadn't really tried to hurt her, and that was good. Yes, he had punished her and right now her bottom felt like it was four times its usual size, but other than that, he hadn't been physically abusive. He hadn't beaten her, taken his belt to her, and he didn't seem inclined to do so. Of course, that was a pretty dangerous assumption to make with a man who had already shown an inclination to take what he wanted without thought or consent, but what choice did she have? Evidently, he was a sadist, but that didn't necessarily make him an actual psychopath. He had shown a level of compassion when he'd realized how sore the dildo had made her ass, so he was capable of empathy. That gave her hope, and right now hope was all she had.

The sound of the bolt jolted her from her thoughts, and she curled herself back up into a ball just as the kitchen door opened. Connor returned, closing the door behind him, and placing the laptop down on the table between them. He eyed her thoughtfully as he crouched down to release her from the D-ring which held her to the floor.

"You can have the privilege of sitting at the table for this," he told her with a small smile. "Although with that caned bottom, you might not be grateful for the opportunity."

He pulled the leash at her neck and guided her to the waiting chair, which she stared at warily. "Up you get," he commanded, his voice taking on that more authoritative edge again.

Molly moved slowly, using the chair to help her climb from the floor. It felt odd using her limbs again. She hadn't realized how much she'd become accustomed to being on the floor, behaving like an animal, until that moment. She forced her ass down against the smooth wooden seat gingerly. She already knew how much it would hurt, and as her flesh made impact with the hard surface, she wasn't disappointed. Flinching at the pain, she squeezed her eyes shut as she absorbed it.

"I bet that is sore, pet." The sound of his voice made her eyes fly open, her hackles rising at his tone. The bastard was practically laughing at her, and she knew she was scowling as she turned her attention to the screen.

In spite of the discomfort in this position, it was a relief to take the pressure from her knees, and she was looking forward to writing. Writing was one human trait she had that he desired badly, and she intended to exploit it. She needed a reason to be Molly again, instead of just his pet.

"May I begin, Master?" she asked, glancing in his direction.

His expression shifted into one of surprise at her conciliatory tone, but he nodded, gesturing for her to get started. Molly shifted forward carefully, wincing as each stroke of the cane smarted at her movement. Raising her chained wrists to the keys, she found her place in the document, and began to type.

Chapter Fifty-Six

S he wrote for hours, or maybe it wasn't that long, but it sure seemed like it. Even Connor lost track of time in the small kitchen as he watched her work. Her expression was lost to the melody of her fingers against the keys, and the words just seemed to flow from her. Molly's treatment at Connor's hands was apparently a good source of inspiration. When her hands finally ceased, he saved the work and led her back into his bedroom. He'd considered keeping her in the spare room. That had originally been his plan, but somehow, he couldn't tolerate being parted from her. If he must leave her somewhere, better it be there, in his personal space.

Connor tucked her into the large pet bed, noticing how she didn't try to counter him or protest at all. Such was her obvious weariness, that there was barely even a flicker of resentment in those blue eyes when she'd crawled into place, and he watched her snuggle down against the soft fur with pride. Molly *was* changing, he was sure of it. The self-contained woman he'd taken and spanked within a few hours of consciousness was barely recognizable to the one curled up in the pet bed beside him. She had almost seemed eager to reach its confines this time, as though she viewed it as a relative sanctuary, and as he glanced down at her, he noticed she'd already dozed into an exhausted slumber.

He watched her sleep for a long time, wondering what it was that filled her dreams. In her subconscious of course, she was still free. He could neither chain nor paddle her dreams, and the thought grated against him. He wanted to be part of those, too. He wanted to reach into them and claim them for himself, and as he sat there idly, he hoped he was punctuating them somehow.

The day passed, and he let her rest. She seemed to need it, and he took the opportunity to catch up with the story she'd been writing – *their* story. There was no doubt she was an amazing word-smith, her narrative style easy to follow, yet building pace beautifully as she went. More than that though, reliving their encounters through the tale made him hard all over again, and as he neared the end of what she had typed so far, his gaze fell to his sleeping pet, willing her to wake up. He needed her, and if she wasn't ready for his cock yet, then he'd use her to amuse himself until she was.

By the time she finally opened her eyes, he felt like cheering. Shifting from the bed above her, he plugged the laptop into the socket at his dresser and came to loom over the pet bed.

"Do you feel better now you've slept?" His tone was genuinely curious, and she blinked up at him, her eyes wide as though she'd somehow forgotten her predicament.

Molly swallowed before she answered, her voice wavering, although he couldn't be sure which emotion produced the quiver. "Yes, thank you... Master."

Connor smiled down at her. "Good," he replied with a nod of his head. "So, is my pet ready to play?"

"Pl-play, Master?" she repeated, straightening up in the pet bed.

As she moved, she obviously nudged the edge of her punished behind, and the motion elicited another loud wince from her lips.

"Yes, play," he told her, moving behind her to untie the leash from his bed post. "So far today you've been washed, exercised, fed and put to work, not forgetting punished for your earlier transgressions. Now I think it's time for something a little more *fun*." He paused at the word, shifting his position so he could gauge her response.

She eyed him wildly, and as his gaze drew south, he noticed how her nipples formed into stiff little peaks at the end of her gorgeous breasts.

"You like to play, don't you, Molly?"

It was a direct question, and it was also the first time he had used her name for a while. He did so now intentionally, ensuring all of her attention was on him.

"I…" She hesitated, evidently uncertain of his apparent new mood. "I don't know, Master."

He chuckled at that, crouching down beside her until they were eye to eye. "Come on now," he goaded her. "You can be honest with me, pet. There will be no secrets between us, and remember, I've read all of your books. I know the hot fantasies that fill your sordid little mind."

He watched as a blush formed at her neck and rose to spread over her flustered cheeks. He had her on that point, and there was nothing she could say to argue against him.

"What do you want to play?" she asked eventually, her voice barely a whisper, as though she had forced the words out.

Connor's smile grew. *Now*, she was talking his language. "I have a game for you, down in the basement."

Her eyes widened in alarm at his answer. Apparently, the thought of returning to his basement didn't tantalize her as much as it did him.

"Nothing nasty this time," he promised. "No punishment, at least not if you're a good little pet. This time I want to work on pleasure."

Molly's lips parted reflexively at his words. "Pleasure?"

"Yes," he replied, purposely making his tone as taunting as possible. "Pleasure."

She gulped, her gaze lowering over her body as though she'd forgotten how naked she was.

"Pet," he said, using just an ounce of authority in his voice. It was enough to get her attention, and she lifted her head to lock eyes with him again. "Do you want your Master to pleasure you?"

She was practically panting now, her blue gaze melting in front of him. It was so obvious to him that the answer was yes. She did want pleasure, and she wanted it badly. She wanted him to deal with the simmering arousal she'd so clearly been battling since he'd first stripped and spanked her. And he was more than ready to give it to her.

"I don't know what to say, Master," she replied, flushing harder. "This is all new to me."

Connor's fist found her leash and he drew her trembling body slightly toward his crouching frame. "New? Hardly, pet. Everything you have experienced with me; every single thing has come from one of your own plot lines. You're the genesis of the whole thing. Nothing here is new."

Molly drew in a shaky breath, her weight shifting back to her hands and knees to accommodate the reduced length of leash. "But those were just stories," she gasped. "I didn't mean..." There was a pause as she tried to make sense of her thoughts. "I've never actually done anything like this before."

The chuckle he gave in response sounded warm and he hoped, reassuring. "There always has to be a first time, pet," he whispered into her face. "And don't try and tell me this isn't driving you wild. I've felt how wet you've been, remember? Hell, I can practically smell how horny you are."

She was panting again now, her shame and arousal evident in her burning gaze. "It's not my fault," she whimpered, casting her eyes down to the carpet. "I don't want to like these things."

"Look at me," he commanded, edging ever closer to her. There were now only a few inches between their faces, and as her gaze rose to meet his, she seemed to be mesmerized by him. He wasn't certain if it was the order he'd given, the timbre of his voice, or just his proximity, but he knew he had every ounce of her focus now. "None of us know why we enjoy what we do. But we do, don't we?"

She exhaled slowly, gazing at him as she pulled her lower lip between her teeth. "Yes," she admitted, quietly. "Yes, we do."

A wave of triumph shot through him at the concession, as well as fresh shoots of arousal. *Fuck, he wanted this woman. He wanted to dominate her and train her into his pet, but it was much more than that. He wanted to possess her.*

"Yes, what?" he asked sternly, watching with glee as her eyes enlarged again.

"Y-yes, Master."

He nodded, but still he didn't release the pressure at her collar. "So, you admit that you like it, then? You enjoy being degraded and punished?"

He thought she was going to cry again at the question, but she somehow managed to compose herself. "Yes, Master," she mewled, her exasperation as evident as her arousal.

Clearly, Miss Clary was a very conflicted woman, unable to admit what she really wanted, and what turned her on. Writing stories was one thing, but saying them out loud was apparently quite another. Connor was glad he was the one who could help bring reconciliation to the matter. By the time he was through with her, there would be no doubt about what made his pet wet with excited need.

"Tell me then," he demanded, tilting his head as if he dared her to defy him. "Tell me what makes your hot little pussy wet."

If he'd thought she was blushing before, then he'd been wrong. The crimson hue which flamed at her cheeks was so intense he could nearly feel the heat coming from them from where he sat crouching.

"Please," she whispered, gazing at him with large, imploring eyes. "I can't say those things aloud."

He shook his head at her, intentionally making his face look severe. "Do you want to be reintroduced to my cane so soon, pet?" he snapped. "Because, I'm not sure your poor little bottom will survive it."

"No, please no!" she begged. "Don't cane me again. I'll say it."

He nodded, pausing to allow her a moment. "Go on then," he provoked. "Your Master is waiting."

She raised her eyes to look at him again, gauging how serious he was. Deciding that she had better comply, she took a deep breath. "I like being leashed," she admitted, "and spanked, and made to sleep here." Her words stopped abruptly, and Connor could tell just how mortifying she was finding the confession. The thought made his cock rigid. Something about objectifying her just drove him crazy.

"Tell me how it makes you feel," he said, pressing his advantage. "What does it do to your pussy?"

Molly blinked up at him, her eyes wide with embarrassment. "It makes my pussy wet, Master," she replied, her voice barely audible as she conceded the point. "It makes me want you."

Chapter Fifty-Seven

Molly couldn't believe she'd admitted it out loud, to Connor of all people! She'd had problems reconciling the way she'd been feeling to herself, let alone to him, but now it was done. The words were out there, and the smile which greeted them made her core ache with need. As she gazed up at the man who had taken her, the stark reality hit her right between the eyes. She *did* want him. She wanted him to make good on all the teasing and the punishment. The shameful orgasms she'd enjoyed since she'd been here were not enough. She needed his cock.

A moment of intense silence passed over them, and in that time his knowing gaze never left her. He was so close that she could feel the heat of his breath against her flaming face, and smell the sweet, minty aroma of his mouth. As his eyes seared her, she began to wonder whether he really could read her mind. She gazed at him, the knot of anticipation twisting inside her.

"I think my pet deserves her pleasure," he whispered at last, his soft, provocative words breaking the tension between them.

Molly gulped at the statement, nervous butterflies stretching their wings in her belly. God, she hoped he meant what he said. She wanted the pleasure right now almost as much as she desired her freedom, and as she watched him rising to his feet, she wondered how much it would take for that precarious balance to be shifted. How much of his attention would it take for her to want the pleasure *more* than freedom?

The tug at her leash drew her forward, and she crawled to join his feet which were already moving toward the door.

"First, I am going to shave you, pet and then you shall have your pleasure."

His voice echoed over her, and she lifted her head to try and catch his eye, but Connor was already out of the room, pulling on her leash. Her mind reeled as his words resonated. *Shave her?* Is that what he had said? But her thoughts were answered by Connor, who was already guiding her in the direction of the bathroom at the end of the hallway.

Once inside, he closed and bolted the door before securing the end of her leash to one of the many hooks in place around the house. She now had little leeway to wander, and watched anxiously as he collected a razor and a can of shaving foam from the nearby sink. Turning, he met her worried expression with a smile.

"Stand up now," he told her, his voice firm but gentle.

Surprised at the order, it took a moment for her limbs to respond, but slowly she climbed to her feet. Bizarrely, she found she felt even more exposed standing before him than she had kneeling on the floor. Somehow being on her hands and knees had become the norm, and Molly had found a perverse solace in it. On her feet, she was forced to meet his eye, and the reality was excruciating.

"Perch on the edge of the tub," he commanded softly. "There should be just enough leash."

She bit her lip, but complied, finding he was right as she placed her tender backside gingerly against the cold rim of the bath tub. She noticed his smile at her discomfort, but had no time to respond before he fell to his knees before her. Blinking down at him, she heard herself gasp. This was such a shift in dynamic, but rather than reassure her, the act made her even more nervous. He placed the shaving implements on the bath mat beside him, and moved toward her ankles. Fishing a small key from his pocket he released her left ankle from the metal, but his fingers remained in place as he glanced up to her.

"I'm trusting you not to disappoint me, pet," he told her. "I am going to shave that sweet pussy, and I need your legs wide. That means these chains need to come off for the time being." He paused, and Molly's breath caught as his hot gaze seared past her pebbling nipples to her face. "Don't let me down."

The last words were a warning, and she nodded at him, unable to articulate a reply.

"Shift forward and open for me," he instructed. His large hands were already moving between her knees and edging them apart even as he spoke.

Molly did her best to comply, wincing as the lines of fire the cane had inflicted made contact with the hard tub again. She balanced on the balls of her feet, her legs spread wide and her hands gripping either side of the tub beside her. The metal chain attached to her collar was stretched tight, securing her to the wall. She held her breath as Connor inspected her pussy. Sure, he had seen it before, he'd even had his fingers inside her before, but this was different. This was an intense and peculiarly intimate examination of her body, and all in the cold light of day. He edged closer, as though he was somehow being drawn in the direction of her sex. She swallowed as he raised his right hand, brushing his digits gently over the soft hair which had begun to grow over the last few days.

"Do you usually shave?" he asked her. His voice sounded raspy, and she wondered if he was as turned on as it suggested. Based on the large, dilated pupils which met her stare, she guessed he was. Worse yet, she couldn't decide how that made her feel. Molly was certain she shouldn't want him, yet she'd already admitted that she did.

"Yes, Master," she whispered in response. It felt strange calling him that now that he was the one kneeling in front of her, and yet she was still the only one naked and in chains.

"You're beautiful," he cooed as his digits explored her again. "But I want you bare."

Molly gasped as his fingers grazed over her needy little clit. She felt it throb under his touch, and squeezed her eyes shut tightly at the realization.

"Hold still," he warned her, "and keep those legs wide apart."

His touch disappeared, leaving her strangely bereft, and she opened her eyes to see him massaging foam onto his palms. Their gazes met momentarily, his full of authority even though Connor was the one on his knees this time. He shifted closer again, and as those hands made their second approach, Molly drew in a deep breath.

The foam was cold and foreign against her skin, and instinctively a small yelp escaped her lips. Connor's gaze darted higher, his eyes conveying an unspoken caution, and she pressed her lips together to ensure she obeyed. Satisfied, his attention refocussed on the foam between her legs, and he reached for the razor on the mat next to him. She could barely take a breath as he brought the blade down against her flesh. She'd never allowed anyone to shave her before, let alone down there, and she panted as she watched him work. Connor, it seemed, had an experienced hand at this sort of thing, and as she scrutinized each stroke of the razor, she realized he was not only doing a good job, but there wasn't a single cut to show for his work. He pressed against her thigh, gently pulling the skin back to accept his blade. The act forced her to tighten her grip on the bath on either side of her, yet bizarrely as she watched him, she could feel her arousal burgeoning once more.

The look of him there, between her legs, was mesmerizing. For his every cruel deed in the past few days, she had never anticipated that he was capable of this level of care. Even when he had tended to her caned bottom earlier, she would never have guessed this delicate workmanship lurked within Connor. Completing the left side of her pussy, he rose and cleaned the razor in the nearby sink. Molly stayed in place, leaning against the tub for support as she watched him.

His eyes met hers as he sunk back into position, and one of his dark brows rose over his green eyes. "Is there a problem, pet?" His tone was sardonic, and almost teasing.

She shook her head quickly, aware of how nipples beading painfully between them. "No, Master."

"Good," he purred, shifting to tend to the right side of her sex. "Now, keep still."

Molly did as she was told, and soon Connor had completed the job, kneeling higher on his knees to remove the hair which had grown above her clit. He wet a face cloth at the sink and returned, wiping the remaining foam from her body and dabbing it gently over her seam. The sensations made her come alive, and she bit down on the moan which threatened to rise from her mouth.

"There we are," he announced, proudly. "Even more gorgeous."

She shifted her position to examine his work as he applied foam to both of her legs. Connor slid the blade down the length of her thigh, and beyond her knee. Quickly, he rid first her left, and then her right leg of hair, before striding back to the sink to rinse out the flannel. Based on what she could see, she had to admit, Connor had done an amazing job, and it felt so much better being hairless again.

"Thank you," she murmured, her gaze meeting his as he stood before her.

He offered her a determined smile as he reached the end of her leash. Taking it in his right hand, he pressed against her naked body, his free arm snaking to pull her tight against his left hip. Molly reeled at the unexpected deed, but as her clit made contact with the fabric of his trousers, she couldn't think to care. She felt like a volcano, hot and simmering and needing to explode. If Connor was considering taking care of that need, then she didn't want to do anything to deter him.

"Are you ready for your pleasure, pet?"

She panted reflexively at the sound of his seductive tone. It was soft and haunting, and as she strained her neck to look up into his enthralling eyes, she wondered at the man. Connor was the sort of guy she could easily fall for, and she knew it. In fact, she recalled the realization had first come over her at the book signing, before he'd taken her, and before all of this. Gazing at him now, she was no less sure of their attraction, but since then he had mastered her in all sorts of debauched ways.

"Yes, Master," she replied, hearing the husky quality in her own voice.

She was ready. More than ready.

Those green eyes blistered her with intensity, and then the hand at her waist snaked south to grab her tender backside. Molly gasped sharply at the sudden hurt, yet almost instantaneously the sting shifted into something else. Something pulsing and pleasurable.

"Come on then," he replied in little more than a growl. "Let's get you downstairs."

She paused, expecting the order to drop to her hands and knees again, but it never came. Instead, Connor drew her forward with the leash, and as soon as there was enough space between her body and the tub he swooped, collecting her easily into his arms. Startled by his strength, she blinked up at the face now no more than a few inches beyond her own.

He turned to greet her shocked expression with a warmly reassuring smile. "Hold on tight," he told her. "Down we go."

Chapter Fifty-Eight

Connor descended the first flight of stairs with care, his long legs making short work of the hallway, and the steps to the basement. The chain and cuff at her ankle dangled low below her as he moved, and he mused on whether to release her from the bondage entirely. He would need her splayed wide for what he had in mind, but decided to leave them as they were for the time being. Connor had left the low lighting on in the basement from earlier and the place looked incredibly atmospheric as they arrived. His pet clung to him, her small arms holding onto his neck during the journey. He turned to gaze at her.

"Here we are," he whispered, hoping his tone was coming over as sensual, rather than impatient. Yet impatient was just how he was feeling. He couldn't wait to taste her, and then, if she was willing, to finally possess Molly.

He felt her body tense in his arms, and he turned to see her gaze fixed on the cage in the corner. Connor smiled at her instinctive response. It seemed the cage would prove to be useful in training his pet. "Don't worry," he told her, softly. "That's not where you're destined this time. Unless, of course, you'd rather I caged you?"

Molly's muscles felt rigid against him. "No, please!" she gasped, her head twisting to meet his eye.

He nodded, placing her down on the tiles. "On your knees now," he told her, and he watched in satisfaction as she complied without protest.

Once she was in place, he led her to the far wall, and adjusted the temperature of the under-floor heating. He'd had the system installed at great cost for exactly this moment.

Turning the dial right up, he looked around him for the other items he'd need. He chose the softest type of rope he had, and then led his pet back to the spanking bench.

"Up you get," he coaxed her gently. Molly hesitated, but moved toward the bench slowly as he instructed. "Lay on your back this time, keeping that pussy right near the end of the bench."

He watched as she complied, moving with caution as she contemplated the leather. She fell back against the bench quickly, squeezing her eyes closed as she absorbed the pain in her punished behind. Connor didn't waste any time. He drew her chained arms up, over her head and slid a piece of rope around the left cuff. Securing the other end to the underside of the structure, he moved quickly to the other wrist and replicated the same bondage. Now that her hands were held in place, he need only bind her legs wide, and then he could start enjoying himself.

Connor took the two remaining strands of rope and tied them around her ankles. She was passive the whole time, her chest rising and falling in short, frenetic breaths, and her nipples still formed into stiff peaks. Dragging his gaze away from her delectable body, he moved the nearby chair and another, smaller bench in the room. He placed one either side of his pet, securing the other end of the ropes to each separate piece of furniture. The ropes forced her legs wide, compelling her hips to roll forward and parting the lips of her glistening pussy. Connor settled on the floor between her outstretched thighs, breathing in the intoxicating scent of her sex. There was no doubt she was wet and excited, and the prospect of what was to come made his cock rigid.

"You are so fucking wonderful," he mused, shaking his head at the sight of her.

She whimpered meekly, her tone sounding desperate in more ways than one. For once, Connor agreed with her, and he resolved he could wait no longer to take what was now his. Starting at her right knee, he drew a finger lightly up the inside of her thigh. As he neared her cleanly shaved pussy, there were small gasps at the act of intimacy. The digit moved on, intentionally teasing her swollen lips before sliding higher to her waiting clit. Each mewl from her lips made his cock swell, and he noticed her hips beginning to rock forward, as though they were seeking his touch.

Naughty little pet. So desperate, so needy, and so fucking adorable.

Connor lunged at her lips, using his palms to press her legs apart even further as he brought his mouth to her sex. He flicked his tongue over her sensitive flesh, making her yelp from the other end of the bench. Smiling to himself, he continued, drawing his tongue up her wet seam, and tasting for the first time, just how delicious his little pet was. Spurred by her sweet nectar, he began to lap at her, pushing his tongue deeper and deeper into her pliant pussy. The moans which met his ears told him how much Molly was enjoying his attention, and the pulsating ache within his pants was inclined to agree. She was absolutely ravishing, especially now she was cleanly-shaven, and Connor devoured her hungrily.

With each lap, she seemed to blossom. Even though her knees were splayed wide, it seemed to Connor as though she opened further with each flick of his tongue, welcoming his intrusion. Her pussy rocked forward, searching for his mouth, and he wrapped an arm beneath her left leg and held her bottom in place. Molly cried out as he made contact with her caned behind, but his lips soon gave her a new distraction, and her cries turned to groans of pleasure as his mouth devoured her. He shifted his lips up her seam, lapping for the first time directly at her clit. The hooded nub was swollen, and she jerked violently as soon as he made contact with it.

"Settle down," he warned her playfully. "This little clit is mine now and if I want to kiss it, I will. You got that, pet?"

She seemed crazy with the sensations, her breaths coming out in short gasps between labored pants. "Y-yes, Master," she answered him, breathily. "I'm sorry."

Connor rose up between her legs, assessing her pretty face. The expression there was part torment, and part ecstasy, and he knew it wouldn't take much to push his pet over the precipice of her pleasure.

"Tell me," he commanded as he eased himself back into place between her legs. "Tell me who owns you. Who owns this clit."

His mouth was on her again then, not waiting for her to respond, although he had every expectation that she would. He lapped at her clit, holding her body down as it jerked beneath him.

"You, Master," she gasped, frantically. "You own me. You own my clit!"

If Connor could have grinned while nestled between her parted folds, he would have done so. As it was, he was content to suckle on her swollen flesh, listening as her calls turned from frenetic to lusty, and her thighs splayed wider of their own accord. Molly was close to her orgasm, that much was clear, but tasting her wasn't enough. He wanted to be inside her.

Balancing on his left elbow, he shifted his weight and slipped two fingers into her needy pussy. She writhed over his face at the intrusion, pushing her hips up as if she wanted to capture the digits and keep them there. Slowly, he eased out of her channel, before pushing back in again, fucking her into a new frenzy with his fingers. All the while, his mouth continued to work its magic, coaxing his pet closer and closer to the edge.

As it turned out, being pleasured by Connor was much like being punished by him. He set an objective, and then seemed hell-bent on achieving it, whatever the costs. As Molly lay, bound over the bench, the analogy flitted through her mind. She was his at this moment. His to pen, his to punish and his to pleasure, any time and every time he wanted.

His mouth was insatiable, alternating between lapping at her like his very soul depended on the act, and clamping down against her clit. The pressure, which was once an exquisite torture, now felt like heaven, and she gasped at the sweet intensity of it all. His fingers fucked her relentlessly, pushing her toward the edge. She was close, so close, and inwardly all she could do was pray that he wouldn't stop. That he'd never stop.

"Please, Master," she panted, vaguely aware of the raspy tone of her own voice. "Please, don't stop."

His digits picked up speed in reply, plunging in and out of her powerfully; pushing her into her climax. And when the pleasure hit her, it hit her hard, paralyzing her with breath-taking passion. There was a cry from Molly's lips as her muscles contracted around his fingers. Her body arched, suspended in ecstasy, as his mouth finally eased away from her pulsating clitoris.

"That was fucking amazing," Connor growled from down beneath her legs.

She wanted to reply, wanted to tell him how much it meant to receive the release, but somehow the words never came. She was still shuddering, clenching at his digits as he finally slipped them from her pussy.

Chapter Fifty-Nine

er murmuring whimpers were making him harder by the moment, and he shifted his place up the bench to straddle her nudity. Molly gasped at the change, her eyes flying open to find his face right there with hers. She gazed up at him with wide eyes, and he wondered fleetingly if she could smell the scent of her own arousal on his lips. Connor smiled at the thought, yet his own desperate desire pushed his amusement away.

"How was that, pet?"

She mewled in response, straining against the ropes holding her wrists. "Master," she cried, her voice frantic. "Please."

"What is it?" he whispered in reply.

Connor eyed her meaningfully, but he already knew. He knew how much she wanted him, but more than that, he could tell she needed him. Something in her expression was different, and it was perceptible. He'd spent so much time watching her, analyzing her every look and appearance, that he recognized the change at once.

"I…" She parted her lips in reply, but somehow the words did not come.

Resting his left elbow on the edge of the bench, Connor shifted his weight, and the fingers of his right hand moved slowly to her face. Molly whimpered at his touch, turning her face to the place his digits traced their invisible line over her flesh.

"It's okay," he told her softly. "It's okay to be honest with me."

Her lips parted once more and she drew in a shaky breath. "Connor," she replied, her tone husky with her own apparent need. "I want you."

It was singly the most ridiculous and dangerous thing she'd ever told him, or anyone for that matter, but it was the truth. She wanted him more than she could ever remember wanting anything. She ached for him with a yearning she would never have thought possible. It felt like a great part of her had been empty before she'd met Connor at the signing, and that he'd spent every hour since then filling that vacuum. He made her *feel* more, *want* more, than she even knew she'd been capable of wanting, and it had all been leading to this – this moment of connection between them.

Connor's eyes widened just a fraction at her words, and she was aware of his thighs nudging at her knees, splaying them even wider below them. "Tell me, pet," the timbre of his voice had shifted now into something of a seductive whirl. "What is it that you want?"

The glint in his eyes told her that he knew very well what she wanted, but still she knew him well enough already to know the truth, he was going to make her say it. He'd want to hear it, to make it real, and to make her suffer for the truth it represented.

"I want you, Master." In the end the words flew from her with relative ease. It was not so hard admitting something you needed with such ferocity. "I want you inside of me."

Connor's expression softened, before twisting into a smirk. "Which part of me do you want inside you?" he asked. "I mean, you've already had my tongue, and as I recall, now you've had my fingers twice? So, tell me specifically, which part of your Master do you need?"

Molly squirmed beneath his body, aware of her hips rocking forward to brush against his groin. Connor was still largely dressed, but she knew underneath those clothes there was an erection which would satisfy her. "I want your cock, Master," she breathed, her tone low and throaty as she finally said out loud the things that had been on her mind for so long.

A small growl escaped his mouth, and Molly stilled at the sound, unsure if danger or hedonism awaited her. But then, that was the way with Connor. She could never tell if his next move would be pleasure or pain.

"So," he began, his finger moving from her chin to trace a new line up the inside of her outstretched arm. "My little pet finally concedes the point, eh?"

She wriggled at his touch, giggling instinctively as his digits brushed past her sensitive, ticklish skin. "I concede it," she admitted in a rush.

There was no need for Connor to force himself on her when she wanted him this badly. She was his for the taking. His willingly, in spite of the chains and ropes which bound her. Connor's bondage may drive her insane, but it also drove her wild. His cage might pen her, but it also set her free. He may well be a monster, but he was also a marvel, particularly with his tongue, between her legs.

"Then you shall have my cock," he replied, offering her a wide grin as he gazed down at her squirming body. "But not here, and not like this."

Molly blinked up at him, breathlessly. She was surprised by his reply, becoming even more startled as she saw Connor retreat down her body. "Master?" she whispered, straining her body against the ropes to try and maintain eye contact.

Despite her unbearable need, there was still a part of her mind that despised her breathy, urgent display. She sounded so desperate, and she knew they could both hear it. Desperate, and chained and pathetic – so unlike the woman she once knew, the one who would spend hours at her writing desk, creating and shaping dark heroes. Now, it seemed, she had a dark hero of her very own, and this one was almost impossible to control.

"Settle down," he told her, rising to tower over her spread-eagled form. "You shall get what you want, but not in this dark place."

Molly complied, relaxing back against the leather bench as she watched him stoop to release the ropes at her ankles. He crawled forward toward her, his gaze locked onto hers as he moved.

"Behave yourself, little pet," he warned her as he shifted to look down over her face. "Do you promise to behave?"

Molly was nodding even before his sentence had concluded. She may well have thought of escape, but the idea didn't even enter her mind at this juncture. Right now, all she wanted was him. His dominance and his mastery of her, but shown in the sweetest possession of all as he finally lay claim to his prize.

"I'll behave," she agreed as she watched him work at the ropes from her wrists.

She lay there naked, and completely unshackled for the first time since she'd woken up in this house, and for the first time, she had no desire to flee. Connor swooped, capturing her in his arms and collecting her against his chest. Molly clutched at his neck as he swept her from the floor. Within a moment they were climbing the stairs, leaving the basement altogether, and the next thing she knew, the fading light of the hallway was also left behind. She found herself back in Connor's bedroom, his long stride cutting the distance between the doorway and the bed in a matter of seconds.

Connor kicked the soft bed which had been her most comfortable refuge, using his right foot to push it away as he flung her gently onto the mattress. The strength of his arms was such that Molly found she had no choice but to obey, and she fell backwards against the soft covers with a small yelp.

"Master?" she gasped, shocked at the dramatic change in events. One moment he had her tied in the basement, pleasuring her in the most scintillating way, and the next he had carried up here, leaving her on his bed no less! After everything that had happened to her recently, the coolness of the sheets against her skin felt like heaven.

Connor loomed over her, his face brooding with sensual intent. "I may be a sick fuck in so many ways, but I did not want our first time together to be in the darkness of the basement."

He pounced on the bed as he explained himself, kneeling over her splayed and pliant body. She watched as he shrugged out of his open shirt slowly, his gaze spearing her as each inch of his toned torso was revealed. She had rarely seen Connor in a state of undress, and she found herself riveted by his performance, her eyes devouring his toned pectorals and well-defined abdominals. With his shirt now entirely removed, Connor released the clasp on his trousers, easing them down his hips and freeing his enormous cock. He was stunning, his body formidable and strong, yet it was his lusty expression which really captured her. She found herself pinioned to the bed by the weight of his stare, despite the fact she was now free of any bondage at all.

Connor crawled over her until his face hovered only a few inches above her own, and his erection grazed the apex of her thighs. A small whimper escaped Molly's mouth at the sensation, and greedily, she rocked her hips toward his body.

He returned her fervor with his mouth, lowering his lips to her chin and trailing a feathery row of kisses to her neck. His mouth created a line of fire across her flesh, sending electricity straight to her core. She mewled gently as the caresses increased in intensity, desperate for his lips to reach her own. Her eyes flitted closed as his mouth retraced its journey to her jaw, until all of a sudden, the sensations stopped. Molly's eyes flew open at the loss, finding Connor's grinning face looming over hers.

"I see my pet enjoys my attention?" he asked, although she was sure her answer was more than clear already.

"Yes, Master," she swooned, gazing up at his strong jaw and dazzling green eyes.

She was astonished by his rugged beauty, and although she had noticed it before, at this proximity he seemed dizzying.

Connor shifted his weight, seizing her hands which had fallen idly by her face, and drawing them over her head. He held her wrists down gently, his fingers linking between her own digits as he pinioned her to his bed.

"So now, you are completely captured."

Molly merely nodded in response, for what else was there to say? She'd been captured right from the start, but this was different. Now she felt like she was *his*.

Chapter Sixty

Although he held her down with enough force to keep her in place, he had no desire to hurt her. Not now, not here and not like this. He understood, this moment was for something other than pain, and his sadistic streak would just have to wait. He wanted her, like he'd never wanted anyone, and now, after all of this time he would get to claim what was his. Without taking his eyes from her, his hand roamed left, searching the small bedside cabinet for the top drawer. Sliding it open, he felt inside for the shiny packaging he needed.

"Is this what you want, pet?" Connor asked her, spearing her with one of his most intense looks as he waved the condom in front of her eyes.

He wasn't sure why he inquired, having never sought her consent on any other matter, but at this moment, her agreement was crucial. He was a monster in so many ways, but he had always sworn he'd never take her by force. And then, once he'd abducted her, Connor had begun to see how pliant she was to his deviant whims. That was when he'd come to realize the truth, there would be no need for compulsion on his part. Molly would be the one to come to him, desire him, and as it turned out be wet and ready for him, and as he gazed down at her now, he knew he was right to have waited. This was going to be perfect.

Molly's lips parted in response, but her body was already giving its answer, betraying her propriety as usual. "Yes," she gasped, sounding unexpectedly emotional at her own verdict. "Yes, Master."

Connor didn't wait for her beg. Ripping the foil with his teeth, he rolled the sheath into place with his right hand. It took only a few seconds with his practised technique. Taking a moment to gaze down at her gorgeous face, he drove his cock inside her, parting her hot folds, and spearing her wetness with one, long thrust. Molly gasped at the intrusion, her mouth opening into a silent 'O' as though he had gagged her, and she arched her back as best she could beneath him. Staring down at her, he stilled, wanting to stop time and capture this moment in his mind forever. She was so beautiful, so fucking beautiful, and he wanted to possess her. He simply had to.

Easing from her body, he slipped inside her wet channel again, eliciting a guttural moan from Molly. *Fuck,* he thought, squeezing his eyes shut for a moment as he absorbed how wet she was for him. *Too fucking perfect.* He withdrew once more, and slammed hard into her, thrusting into her again, and again, and again. She felt divine, the closest a man like him was ever going to get to heaven. As he pinned her lush body down into his mattress, he allowed his mind to let go for once. He was so used to being in control, and in charge of the situation, but at this moment he knew he was close – too close – to losing control altogether.

Molly gazed up at him, this man who had become her Master. He had been so cruel to her, and sometimes an utter bastard, but this was somebody else, a side to him she had never known. And she liked this side, she liked it a lot. As he fucked her relentlessly, she melted into his sheets, relishing the sting of her ass against the cool covers. Molly loved his attention now, and she wanted all of it. She craved his mastery and wanted to be his, for this was sweeter than being paddled at a post, or penned like a pet. However hot those acts of debauchery had made her, this possession made her feel like a woman, and Christ, she'd missed that so much.

He slid up inside her again, pausing this time as he gazed down at her. She gasped at the delicious fullness, squeezing him tightly in the most intimate way.

"You naughty little, pet," he purred, "it is time that I claim you properly."

Connor lowered his face, capturing her lips in an instant. His kiss was demanding, but she relaxed into it, permitting his tongue to probe deeper into her mouth, as his cock began to dominate her pussy again. In this way he possessed her thoroughly, mastering both her mouth and her sex at the same time. As his lips drew away, his face hesitated over her own, his dark expression the very picture of sin itself.

"I want you on all fours," he told her, breathlessly. "You're going to get fucked like the animal we both know you are."

Molly gulped at him, watching as he withdrew from her body and shifted backwards, allowing her enough room to rise as he had ordered. She complied without a word, moving back to her hands and knees as she peered warily back at Connor behind her. Their gazes locked for a moment, his green eyes making her heart race with their lustful intensity.

"Are you ready, pet?" he growled, positioning himself at her smarting behind, and wrapping his body around her warm skin.

Molly arched her back, tilting her head back to meet his face. "Yes, Master," she panted, just before he speared her once more. "Oh, fuck yes."

That seemed to be all the incentive he needed, and with that, Connor began to move. He plundered her with long, powerful thrusts, which transitioned into shorter, firmer lunges into her hungry sex. For her part, Molly was lost to it. She had always loved sex this way, but with him it was so much better. He had already mastered her so entirely, dehumanizing her in the most wonderful, perverse ways, that when he took her from behind, she really relished it. She *was* his pet now. It was just as he had told her, and animals like her loved it this way, being filled and claimed over and over by his unyielding cock.

Connor slipped into a rhythm which seemed to please them both, and after a moment, his left hand rose, reaching for her breast on its route up to her neck. Finding her throat, Molly felt his large hand stretch wide and hold her in place there, his digits pressing deeper against her neck with each new thrust. She mewled, panicked by the pressure at her airway, and yet consumed by the hedonistic pleasure that Connor's cock had unleashed. He felt so fucking good there, commanding her body in this raw and primal way, that even when his hand tightened, she didn't try to resist.

"You're mine, pet," he snarled into her right ear. It was a low sound which made her pussy clench around his thrusting shaft.

"Y-yes," she gasped, her eyes fluttering closed at the sound of his voice.

"Tell me," he commanded.

"Yours," she panted, gasping for air around the hand at her throat. "I'm your pet, Master, yours."

He stilled at once, the shift so sudden that it caused her to groan against him. "Back on the covers," he instructed her, his tone a seductive whir. "I want to look into your eyes when I come inside you."

The hand at her neck vanished, freeing her to move, so she obeyed him. She slipped from his body and spun around, landing on her tender bottom as he waited patiently between her legs. Molly eyed him greedily as he crawled forward, and in a moment, he pounced on her. Connor's cock slipped back between her legs with ease, and she groaned at the exquisite sensation. He was so hard now, and felt absolutely massive inside her, but she wouldn't have had it any other way. As he settled down over her body, he cocooned her entirely, his strong arms landing on either side of her head.

"Look at me," he ordered, and at once her eyes flew to meet his.

His green stare was mesmerizing, and as he made short, insistent thrusts into her, she was unable to draw her eyes from him.

"Do you feel it, pet?" he probed, lowering his face to graze his mouth over hers. "Do you feel how much you're mine?"

Molly nodded beneath him, arching her back and splaying her legs wider to accommodate his length. Yes, she felt it, alright, and despite her every ignominious treatment, she was sure she'd never felt anything like it. Sex with Connor was incomparable.

There was a long shudder and a guttural groan as he reached his climax. All the while, Molly obeyed, her gaze unbreaking as she watched him splinter inside her, until at the edge of his pleasure, Connor collapsed over her body. The silence which surrounded them was punctuated only by their gasps, sighs and labored breathing as Connor composed himself, and for the first time Molly's right hand rose to his hair. She ran her fingers through the silky, dark locks, wondering at their beauty as he remained listless at her breast.

She glanced right, noticing for the first time that Connor's door was not only unlocked, but also ajar. Her mind wondered idly at the idea of fleeing. This was the only time she'd ever known him to be remiss about locking doors, and the first time she'd found herself free of his chains. But her mind was heavy with the scent and taste of Connor. It was as though he had intoxicated her, and clouded her better judgment, and she seemed unable to rouse, or consider escape in any serious way.

He lifted his head, his eyes darting to where her stare had wandered. "Not thinking of running are you, pet?"

Connor kissed the side of her chin as he asked the question. She smiled as she turned her head to meet his lips.

"No, Master," she reassured him, and for the very first time, she meant it.

Chapter Sixty-One

S he fell asleep quickly after his climax, and for a while Connor lay there, watching the rise and fall of her perfect tits. The day had gone even better than he'd hoped, and as he recalled how glorious his cock had felt inside her, he couldn't help but smile.

Still, he didn't want his little pet getting too comfortable, so after an hour, he slipped his arms beneath her body, and carried her carefully to the dog bed, which he had rescued from the other side of his room. She stirred a little at the change of environment, but he covered her naked body with the green blanket, watching as she snuggled down into the fur of the bed. Securing her leash in its usual place, he took another moment to enjoy the sight of her.

She was too fucking adorable.

Climbing back into bed, he made plans for their next day. Things were accelerating faster than he'd anticipated and he mused that it may be time to take his pet from the house already. He'd expected it to take days, or maybe weeks to train her to the point where he could safely go to the cabin, but to his amazement, Molly had been so compliant, now it seemed like a real possibility. His pulse quickened as the thought, excitement building at the prospect.

Before he fell asleep, he slipped from the room, bolting it behind him and made his way downstairs. There in the corner of the unused reception room, beneath the piles of paperwork which still needed filing, was the dog carrier he had bought for just this moment. He collected it, brushing it down and holding it up before him. In his mind, he imagined his little pet trapped inside, and his cock began to throb again.

She awoke in the darkness, aware all at once that she was back in the dog bed. A sense of panic rose in Molly. It began in the pit of her stomach and stretched upwards to her throat, as her fingers pressed into the soft fur around her. After everything, after all of that amazing sex and pleasure, he had still left her here? Her belly knotted in anxiety at the thought of it. What did that mean? He'd fuck her on his bed, but he wouldn't allow her to sleep in it? How fucked up was this guy?

She straightened up, aware of the leash trailing from her neck, even though she couldn't see it in the black of the room. Above her she could hear Connor sleeping, his breathing relaxed and melodic on the bed, and the sound stirred resentment in her. How come *he* got to rest up there, while she was left chained in the pet bed? Even though the idea made her pussy wetter than she wanted to admit, the realization taught her something else. This was what she meant to him, and this was all she would ever mean. He had taken her as a woman, but intended to keep her as his pet. *That's* what he wanted. A creature to keep and leash, and fuck when it pleased him. What had she been thinking consenting to sex with him, and what message had that conveyed to Connor? That all of *this* was okay, and she was content with it? Her mind raced as she considered everything that had happened between them: the abduction, the humiliation, the punishment. None of that was okay, however her messed up head had interpreted it, and now she'd planted the idea of her consent in his mind. What the fuck had she done?

The hours passed in miserable darkness as Molly mused on the conundrum. For a while she considered trying to make a run for it while he slept. It sounded like a good idea in theory, but when she actually thought about the practicalities, she realized how futile a plan it was. She was chained here in the dark, and she could feel the cuffs had been replaced at both her ankles. Even if she could untie herself from his bed somehow, she'd have to negotiate the bolt on his door in the pitch black, and all without waking him. And even if she supposed all that was manageable, what would she do next? Yes, she knew where the door was in this place, but what did that prove? A man like Connor would never have left it unlocked and accessible. The place would be secured like Fort Knox. The reality of it all depressed her, but she couldn't escape it. Connor had cameras everywhere, so even if she made a failed attempt, he would find out and then she'd be in trouble. Christ knows how long he'd keep her in that freaking cage for trying to flee. Maybe he'd never let her out again. A shudder passed through her at the thought, rattling the chains attached to her body.

At that moment she wanted to run. To get out and never look back. Not only was she physically exhausted, sore and tired, but she was now foolishly emotionally involved. The sex with him had been so good, she'd made the stupid assumption that she meant something to him. That *it* meant something, and he saw her as more than just an animal to chain and fuck, but evidently Molly had been dead wrong about that. The stab of that rejection stung more than the memory of his cane, and worse, she despised herself for allowing her mind to believe in the idea at all. Tears were burning in her eyes as she recalled the previous night. The way he had pleasured her, the way he had demanded her consent before he claimed her, and the way he had felt inside her. That hadn't all been in her head, surely? And yet, here she was, chained in a pet bed by the side of his mattress.

The light at his bedside flickered on all of a sudden, making her jump in shock.

"Pet?" His voice sounded husky with tiredness, and she glanced up to find him upright, that dark green stare penetrating her once again.

She blinked away from the light, shaking her head. What the fuck was she supposed to say? She was upset that he'd treated her like an animal after they'd fucked? That she'd secretly hoped for more? How was any of that even a logical train of thought? She shouldn't want any more of this. She should be thinking only of escape, of getting away from his clutches, and...

"Pet." He moved so fast she barely even registered the motion, but in a matter of seconds his hard, naked body was right there beside her, his hand at the leash connected to the front of her collar. "What's wrong? Why are you crying?"

She was crying? Somehow the hot tears making tracks down her face hadn't even registered. She'd known she was upset, but she'd conveniently ignored the inevitable consequence of her hurt.

"I..." she began, but then she hesitated, knowing there was no way to explain her thought processes. "It's nothing, Master."

Connor edged even closer, pushing his defined chest toward her. "You seemed happy enough when you dropped off."

Molly swallowed at that. He was right, she had been content then. She'd also been an idiot. "Yes," she replied, her tone breathy. "I was then."

"But not now?" He mused out loud. "What has changed, I wonder?" There was a pause as he considered the point dramatically. "Does my pet not like sleeping in her own bed?"

Molly's eyes widened perceptibly at his astute analysis, and she felt the tears fall harder. "No, Master," she sobbed, adding this new, pathetic display to her already substantial list of self-woe.

He smiled down at her, and for a moment she couldn't take a breath. He had such power over her now. Not just physically, but emotionally, too. Whatever he was about to say and do could either lift her up or crush her.

"My poor little one," he crooned, raising his free hand to stroke back the fly-away strands of her hair. "Has your Master neglected you?"

She could tell by his tone that he was mocking her, but she had no choice but to agree. Neglect was right. As ridiculous as it sounded, that was precisely how she felt after last night. She gulped, nodding her head in response.

"Words, pet," he growled at her. "You should enjoy the use of that pretty little mouth, while you still have it."

A shiver ran down her spine at his thinly veiled threat, and she hurried to reply. "Yes, Master. I missed you."

She'd missed him? Molly blinked at her own craziness. What the fuck had she said that for? Connor startled too, his self-assured expression faltering for just a second.

"Well, we can't have that, can we?" he whispered as his smile grew broader. "Does my pet want to join me in bed again?"

Molly knew she was nodding excitedly like some dumb puppy as she responded. "Yes, please."

He actually laughed at that. For one awful moment, Molly thought he was going to leave her there, the sound of his laughter her answer as he went back to bed and abandoned her to the darkness. It was absolute relief that flooded her as he rose and strode around her body to untie her leash from the bedpost. She watched his muscular thighs as they returned to his original place, but this time he tugged at her collar.

"Come on then," he commanded seductively. "I shouldn't really let pets on the furniture, but it seems I have a weakness for you. Up, into bed with you."

Chapter Sixty-Two

Connor had no idea why he permitted it, but he was smiling as she scurried between his covers. The notion of having her there with him was suddenly surprisingly compelling. He found himself shaking his head as he secured her leash to the post behind her head, before he turned out the light. Climbing in behind her, he drew Molly's body against him instinctively. They spooned in the darkness, his cock stirring immediately at her body heat.

"Is this better?" he murmured, exploring the length of her curves with his right hand.

She was so fucking hot, and as his fingers skimmed her hips he remembered how amazing she had felt last night.

"Yes, Master, thank you," she sniffed in response.

Her tone was breathless, but he couldn't tell if that was due to her being upset or being held against his body. He knew his erection was already nudging into her behind, and the reality did little to quell his fervor.

"No more tears then," he told her sternly. "Time to sleep. We have a busy day tomorrow."

Molly's body tensed beside him at his words, but she didn't say anything. Connor smiled into the darkness, the scent of her hair wafted past his nose as his cock throbbed impatiently at her bottom. Let her sleep in comfort for now. She had no clue what was in store for her when they finally woke.

The morning light spilling into his room roused Connor earlier than he would have liked. The presence of the body next to him made his cock spring to life immediately, and for a moment he considered fucking her again before they left. It was certainly tempting, but he knew there wasn't time. If he wanted this transition to be smooth, then he'd need the element of surprise, and that meant being ready when she woke up.

He shifted from the covers quietly, fisting his cock at the sight of her still tangled in his bed sheets. He still wasn't entirely sure why he'd given in to her emotional blackmail and let her share his bed, but somehow, he couldn't bring himself to regret it. It was great holding her, and anyway, just because she'd shared his bed didn't mean anything had changed. She was still his pet, and he was her Master, a fact he intended to spend the day reinforcing.

Slipping from the room, he made sure the door was bolted from the outside before he washed quickly, and headed downstairs to collect the pet carrier. His belly knotted with excitement at his plan. It was unlike Connor to be reckless or impulsive. There was only one other occasion he had fallen foul of his impulses, and the legacy of that still haunted his dreams today. Usually he planned things to perfection, and never, ever deviated from the blueprint regardless of what was happening around him. But this time was different. *She* made it different, and besides that vague acknowledgement, he couldn't quite put his finger on the reasons. He knew it was risky. Taking her out before she'd been trained properly was more than risky really, it was bloody stupid, but even so he found himself collecting the pet carrier, and laying it out by the front door, the little metal entrance sprung open and ready. Like the cage, Molly was going to have to put herself inside it, and that much he couldn't wait to see.

Connor darted up the stairs two at a time, before making a large batch of coffee. Pouring himself a cup, he placed the rest on a tray, along with some milk, sugar and of course, Molly's bowl. He balanced the drinks as he unbolted the door, entering his bedroom to find her awake. She was propped up on her elbows, watching him and her face burned crimson when she eyed what he was carrying.

"Good morning, pet," he purred as he carried the tray toward his bedside table. Putting it down carefully, he leaned forward over her pert breasts as he addressed her again. "Did you finally get some sleep?"

"Yes, thank you, Master."

The reply was barely a whisper, but it was good enough. For now.

He undid the leash from his bed, tugging gently. "Time for a drink before we get going."

Molly responded just as he'd hoped, climbing down from the bed and waiting on all fours, although he saw her bristle at his words. He was still holding her leash as he poured the coffee into her bowl, presenting it in front of her face.

"I hope you like it black?" he asked, sardonically. "Be careful though, it is hot."

She eyed him, her expression a curious combination of fury and desire, but as he backed away, Molly came forward, lowering her face into the hot liquid. *Fuck*, he thought, as he observed her submissive display. For all of her initial protests about being made to lap from the dog bowl, she really had taken to it like a duck to water. He smirked at the analogy, adjusting his cock as it strained beneath his pants.

Molly finished her coffee admirably, and he watched from the bed, taking sips from his cup as she finally lifted her face and glanced up to him. A blush engulfed her face, evident despite the black ring around her lips. Connor smiled as he grabbed a towel from the end of the bed, and wiped her clean.

"Good little pet," he told her, his tone deliberately taunting. "Are you wet for your Master?"

Her eyes lowered shamefully, telling him everything he needed to know, but still he goaded her, pressing his advantage. "Tell me, please," he said threateningly.

As she looked up again, he could actually see her swallow. "Yes, Master," she whispered. "I am wet for you."

Connor nodded as he led her from the room. It didn't really matter that she was aroused. He had no time to scratch the itch for either of them right now, but it made him feel amazing to know that she was. He loved the fact that spending the night with him while leashed to his bed, and being made to humble herself once more had left her so hot and needy.

Leading her into the bathroom, he set about cleaning her up. She knelt in the bath, still leashed to the wall as he washed and shaved her, before he finally allowed her out to rest on the mat while he dried her glorious body. Administering her inhalers, he then made her open wide as he cleaned her teeth. Connor suspected she'd never been so thoroughly cleaned before, but her shameful expression told him Molly had loved it almost as much as he had.

"We're going on a little trip today."

The words slipped from his mouth, making her head snap up to meet his gaze.

"A trip, Master?"

"Mmmm," he clarified as he began to brush her dark hair. "I have another place, which I designed especially for you, and today I want to take you there."

She was panting as the news resonated, her eyes wide with shock. "Please, don't hurt me," she begged, and as he loomed over her kneeling form, he could see her arousal shift into panic.

Connor squatted down beside her. "What makes you think I'm going to hurt you?"

Molly eyed him wildly. "I just…" she began, her tone full of fear. "I just thought if you were taking me somewhere, that meant…" She gulped as the words dried up, but her meaning was clear. His pet thought he was done with her already.

Connor shook his head. Her assumption couldn't be further from the truth. "Oh, no," he replied smoothly. "That's not what it means at all. On the contrary, I have a great many plans for you."

He rose and strode away before her response registered on that pretty face. Tugging her to follow, she scuttled behind him, her damp locks falling around her shoulders as she moved. At the top of the stairs he paused, waiting for her to catch up.

"Let me carry you," he told her, his tone making it clear that this was not a request.

He swooped before she could speak, catching her under the arms, and throwing her over his shoulder. There was squeal as she landed over his back, and he patted her bottom tenderly. The last thing he wanted as they descended was her to get a good view of her pet carrier. He didn't want that until the very last minute. As they hit the bottom step, he swung her around, preventing her view until she landed on the floor beside the carrier.

Chapter Sixty-Three

Molly's eyes landed on the contraption, terror rising in her chest even before the reality had hit her. It looked like some type of carrier, the sort you'd carry a large animal in, like a dog, but surely not... Surely, he doesn't intend this for her?

The question was answered by one of his large looming feet, which came crashing down by the side of her face. Connor's right leg now blocked her escape down the narrow hallway, and as she glanced right she saw his left side blocked the staircase. The door was immediately behind her, locked she presumed. She was trapped. Trapped with nowhere to run, and he was going to put *her* in the fucking animal carrier.

"Don't do this!" she gasped, imploring him with her eyes. "Don't make me go in there."

Connor tutted in response, his gaze darkening. "Do I need to gag you, pet?" he asked her, dryly, "because you know I will."

The panic in her chest rose to Molly's throat, threatening to cut off her air supply altogether. "No, please, Master," she panted.

He drew in a deep breath, as though he was considering her answer. "Get in," he growled as his index finger pointed at the open carrier. "And don't make me regret my decision to leave that mouth free. I won't hesitate to gag you if required."

Molly tried to pull in air, but it seemed it impossible. The edges of her mind seemed to be crumbling around her at the prospect. The carrier was significantly smaller than even the cage, and the idea of being stuck in there made her want to vomit. Yet Connor's voice had made it clear there was to be little choice. She knew if she acted up and disobeyed him, the consequences would be unbearable. She didn't know what he'd do. Cane her again, torture her, keep her locked in the cage? Who knew? Who could rationalize the thoughts of a man like Connor?

"Now!"

His voice made her jump and frantically she moved, limbs trembling as she considered what was expected.

"It will be better if you reverse in," Connor offered, his tone lighter, almost amused as her quandary.

She obeyed slowly, edging herself backwards into the opening, just as she had in the cage the day before. Her feet hit the back of the carrier faster than she'd anticipated and Molly was forced to curl into a tight ball to squeeze her head inside. She was more than panting now, practically hyperventilating as the small metal door swung closed at her nose. Watching closely, she saw his fingers close the lock, once again padlocking her into place, and all at once he was right there with her. His face glowered from the other side of the bars.

"Remember what I told you," he said in a low, menacing voice. "You'll stay quiet unless I tell you otherwise."

Molly nodded, too afraid and uncomfortable to say anything. She had no clue how long she'd be forced to stay in here, but she already doubted she could stand it. Connor's face disappeared out of her new range of vision, and all of a sudden, the carrier around her moved. She gasped as it lifted from the floor, her hands clutching for something to stabilize herself with, but there was nothing. Only the small space of smooth plastic around her digits. In a second her view changed as the pet crate was swung around, and Connor began carrying her down the hallway, past the entrance to the basement. They reached a door she'd never been to before, and he grabbed for the lock, twisting a long metal key inside it. As the door sprung open, she was plunged into the pitch black. Not a basement this time, so where? A garage, perhaps. One small click was all it took the reveal the truth, and as the lights overhead slowly flickered into life, Molly could see her guess had been correct.

Of course, it was a garage. He could never risk carrying her outside like this. She was a fully-grown woman after all, naked and packed into a pet carrier. Anyone passing might find that a rather odd sight. In a few moments she was packed into what looked like a large black car. She assumed it was the one she'd been taken in the night of the signing, but honestly, she couldn't recall. The crate was forced into the small space on the floor of the passenger seat, her nose practically against the gear stick as Connor took his place behind the wheel. She swallowed, musing at how odd British cars were for not having gear-changes on the steering column, the thought bizarrely calming in light of her current predicament.

He reached toward the seat, holding up a blanket as though he wanted her to see the thing. "This is how pets are transported," he told her, darkly. "I'm allowing you the privilege of seeing for now, but any misbehavior, and this will cover you up. Got it?"

"Y-yes, Master," Molly stammered in response.

"Good," he replied, throwing the blanket in her direction. The gentle thud as it landed on the plastic above her head reverberated through her, and then the engine started, the low thrum drowning out all other noise.

If Molly thought the cage had been arduous, then she was clearly deluded. This thing – this carrier – was actual hell. Molly could barely move, and even the act of drawing in a deep breath was impossible in her tight confinement. After a worryingly short time, she began to lose the feeling in her feet. The numbness began at her toes and spread north, already at her ankles by the time she tried to move them. It was quite unfeasible of course, there was literally nowhere for her to move to.

She had no idea how long they'd been traveling this way. It felt like hours, but logically she knew it couldn't be, or maybe it was. Who the hell knew? She could just make out the outline of his legs, and his hands gripping the steering wheel. Beyond that, her whole world was the leather interior of the car, and her trapped, aching limbs. Molly worked hard to avoid a new surge of panic taking control of her. She tried to remember how she'd quieted her mind in the cage, distracting herself from the misery of her new situation, but ultimately, her attempts were futile. She was imprisoned in a freaking pet carrier, and being taken God knows where. Only Connor knew what fate would await her once they finally arrived, and that thought made the dread inside her burgeon.

At some point, the car seemed to slow, and a wave of fresh anxiety washed over her. Wherever he was taking her, they were obviously nearly there. She kept her lips sealed tightly as he parked and got out of the driver's side. She wanted to speak, beg and yell at him, but what would be the point? Connor had made his position clear, and she knew she risked his wrath if she spoke out now. The crate was pulled roughly from the floor, and a burst of cool, summer air hit her exposed flesh as she was carried away from the car. Peering through the door, she tried to look about her and determine where the hell she was. The problem was, she didn't know where she'd been kept for the last few days. All she knew was the signing had been in London. But that was days ago, and this did not look like London.

She blinked, the light stinging her eyes after so long encased in the dark space. As they moved away from the car, all she could see was the thick roots and trunks of trees. Yes, trees. Actual trees, which looked absolutely freaking massive based on what she could see from her place in the carrier. He'd brought her to a forest? Molly didn't even know England still had forests, but the fact they were now in one made her shudder. It was dark, dank and foreboding, setting the tone for what she feared Connor now had in mind. Nothing good happened in woods like this, especially to women trapped in crates.

Chapter Sixty-Four

The trek through the forest was longer than he remembered, but the last time he'd made the journey, Connor hadn't been carrying his pet with him. They were deep into the forest at this point, but he knew Thetford like the back of his hand, and he'd spent many hours preparing for this moment. It took a good twenty minutes to reach the small hut he'd readied for the occasion, but there it was. The morning light filtered through the tall trees surrounding the cabin, highlighting it between the trees. He recalled the many hours of sweat he'd poured into making the place a reality. He'd needed somewhere isolated, but not too far away from his house. It was perfect, rather like his pet, and the sight made him stop dead in his tracks, until a small whimper from the carrier drew his attention.

She was mewling for him, and the thought made him smile. She'd been exceptionally well-behaved for a long time. He knew how squashed up she was in there, and a strange pride rose in his throat at what she'd had to endure.

"Not long now, pet," he mused aloud, knowing the sound would carry to the crate in his left hand.

Connor could understand her sentiment. The carrier was starting to weigh him down on one side, and the heavy bag of equipment he'd brought from the car was doing the same on the other. They would both be glad to arrive. It took about another ten minutes to get her inside. Placing the carrier down in the darkness on one side of the cabin, he spent time carefully unpacking the bag. He pulled the laptop from its confines, making sure it was safe as he went back to the large bag. There was no electricity out here, so he'd have to use it sparingly, but that wasn't an excuse for her not to write, particularly after everything they'd been through in the last twelve hours. He made her wait as he emptied the remaining contents. Connor knew she'd be in pain by now, her joints probably screaming, and the sadistic streak in him bloody loved the idea. He also knew she'd be able to make out most of what was going on from her position facing into the room. The fact she was trapped excited him, as it always did, but this different. Better. Hotter.

The expanse of darkness in the hut was never ending. The corners of the place made black look pale by comparison, and all she could really make out was Connor's preoccupation with the bag in the very center. The only light source was a weak trail coming from where the door was, illuminating his ominous frame as he unpacked. Everything hurt now, except the places which had lost the feeling in them altogether. Molly didn't know how long she'd been squeezed into this box, but that's what this was – a fucking box – and all she knew was humans weren't made for this shit.

When he finally approached her, removing the key to the padlock from his pocket, Molly couldn't say if it was relief or fury which rose in her. Whatever it was, the emotion caught in the back of her throat as the metal door was pulled open.

"Out you come," he told her, his voice irritatingly cordial, considering everything he had made her endure.

Her head moved first, her neck creating forward motion, and the shift in weight forcing the rest of her to join it. Her fingers uncurled, flattening against the smooth wood of the floor, and next her shoulders were freed. The relief at being able to stretch her back was bliss, but short-lived. Almost as soon as her legs were moving, pain flew from her knees, propelling her out of the carrier completely. Molly landed in a heap against the wood, her instincts telling her curl up into a ball, but of course, that's the last thing she wanted to do. What she wanted to do was stretch out all of her limbs, nursing her elbows, knees and ankles until the hurt went away, but she had the feeling pain like this might never really end. It felt deep and ingrained in her somehow, as though this moment would stay with her for the rest of her life.

Connor loomed over her the whole time, silent yet seemingly brooding at her performance. If she'd have had the energy, she'd have kicked him, cursed him or offered him some retort, but she had none. No energy, no inclination – no nothing. All she wanted at this moment was to be left the fuck alone to recover from the crate. If that was even possible.

It was like he read her mind again, or maybe he understood, but he didn't try to engage her. Instead he produced a blanket from the bag and opened it over her sprawled body, leaving her to rest. Molly's lids fell shut gratefully. The floor was hard and unforgiving against her soft curves, but the blanket was already warming her, and if nothing else, she could finally move. She could stretch, she could flex; she was free of the box. Possibly she was dozing when she felt the tug at her ankles. She considered opening an eye to assess what on earth he was doing, but the weight of exhaustion was so heavy, she chose not to. So long as she wasn't in the box, she felt sure she could survive anything else.

Molly had no idea how long she'd slept when she finally roused. All she knew was as her eyes took in the place around her, things were different. The hut was lit by a number of large candles flickering around the place. Fleetingly she considered how flagrantly unsafe it was to leave naked flames in a cabin made entirely of wood, but she pushed the thought away. Of all the dangers in this place, Connor was by far the greatest. What the fuck was he thinking keeping her in the dog carrier? The subjugation at the house had been one thing. It was totally fucked up, but there's no doubt she'd loved it. The orgasms she'd experienced with Connor had been sensational – literally the best in her life – but that couldn't compensate for this. He took objectification to a whole new level. A grim and perilous level, which left her as far away from arousal as she could imagine. Yes, he could be gentle and tender, but there was something else in him. Some sort of monster. Molly knew she had to get away from that monster if it was the last thing she ever did. She'd been crazy to think the sexual intimacy of last night could mean anything. Monsters don't have feelings, remember?

She wiggled her toes and ankles, before working the movement up her body slowly. Tentatively, she bent her knees, braced for the sharp pain of before, but now there was only a dull ache, the remnants of her ordeal. That's when the other change occurred to her. There was nothing at her wrists and ankles. Whilst the leather collar remained at her neck, the leash had been removed for the first time in days, and so had the metal cuffs which had connected her limbs. She was unchained! The thought produced a gasp from her lips as a rush of exhilarated panic rose to her throat. Her eyes darted about the place, searching for her captor. She knew he'd have to be here, he'd never have left her *unattended* like this, but wherever she looked she couldn't see him from her spot on the floor. Not wanting to draw attention to herself, she remained still, although her heart was now hammering in her chest.

This is it, she thought, her breath hitching as the reality hit her. He had finally left her unbound and unsupervised. *If you're going to run, then you have to run now.* She eyed the black corners of the hut hopefully. The door was to her right, a little more than a few feet away. She could reach it, there was no doubt about that, and she could reach it before him. But he could run faster. He was stronger and fitter, and he had the advantage of knowing where the fuck they were out in the middle of nowhere.

"Are you going to run, Molly?" His voice was calm, and almost amused as it questioned her.

She shifted her gaze to follow the sound of his voice, her face no doubt portraying her anxiety on the subject. "No," she lied, her tone breathless.

"No?" he repeated back to her as he stepped forward out of the black shadows of the furthest corner. His right brow arched in the tantalizing way it did when he knew he was onto a winner.

"No," she confirmed, shaking her head for good measure.

He moved toward her laughing. "You could run, you know," he went on, his gaze intense as his tall body loomed over her.

Molly blinked up at her captor. Free of her binds at last, she felt bolstered and no longer wanted to call him Master. She could never allow a monster like Connor to master her. "What?"

"You could run," he affirmed. "If you wanted to? Your stories have always had an element of *the cat and mouse* about them, haven't they, pet? I know you'd enjoy that, and if you didn't already know, I love the thrill of the chase."

Adrenaline spiked in her body as he spoke. Was he giving her permission to flee from him? Is that why he'd removed the chains? Was this just the latest game he wanted to play?

"Yes," he answered her, although she was certain she hadn't spoken the words out loud. "You can run, Molly, but you know if you run, I'm going to chase you, and you know I'm going to catch you."

Her heart was pounding in her chest as she sat up straight beside him, pinning her wide-eyed gaze onto his. "Why are you saying this?" she mumbled. And how do you *know* all of this?

His smile widened, and he pulled up a box from nearby, seating himself beside her. "After all this time, pet," he purred. "Don't you think I know you by now? I knew you before we'd even met. I know what you're thinking, Molly. You are quite literally an open book to me."

She flushed, her head falling forward as though the admission was shameful. She was ashamed, because he was right. He did seem to know her. He knew what she was going to be thinking, what she wanted, and just how to control her. It was freaking infuriating.

"Look at me." His voice was sterner, having taken on some of the quality which made the knot of anxious energy in her belly tighten. She complied, not wanting to rile the beast in him. Their eyes met, his mesmerizing green orbs utterly compelling. His hand came slowly to her face. Molly flinched out of instinct, but relaxed when he began to caress the side of her face with calm, gentle strokes. "This is your story, pet," he mused. "*Our* story. If you want to run, then I am not going to stop you."

"But you will chase me?" she whispered, her fear furling as simmering arousal at his touch began to flood her system. She knew she shouldn't crave him, but she found herself leaning into the warmth of his hand. It was like a reflex. Despite the fact this was the same hand that had captured, and tormented her, it was also the hand that had rescued and comforted her – and pleasured her.

Connor's chuckle resonated deeply inside of Molly's body. "Of course," he answered, his fingers tightening in her long dark hair. "I will chase you because you're mine, pet. You belong to me now, we both know that, don't we?" He hesitated as though he expected her to speak, but she merely blinked at him. Too terrified to respond. Too afraid of what her answer might be. "Molly?"

The sound of her name made her lips part. It was intimate, fanning the flames of her burgeoning need. "Yes, Master?" she said, her voice barely audible as she confessed the truth.

For a moment they just stared at one another, the admission lingering in the dank air around them.

"But that's not the only reason I'd chase you," he went on eventually. "I'd chase you because it's what you want, Molly, isn't it?"

She gaped at him, hating the way he did this. This man – this stranger – had taken the very fabric of her fantasies and made them real. He'd stitched each patch of hedonistic depravity together, and created *this*... whatever this was. "I don't know what I want anymore," she replied in a sigh.

The fingers at her face shifted, gripping her chin more tightly. "Now, now, that's not true," he said, admonishing her in a playful way. "Of all people, you need not lie to me, Molly. We both know what you are. We both know what you need."

Molly gulped at the severity in his expression. The look of it made her pussy ache for him, the dull sensation numbing all of her rational thought. "I'm afraid," she admitted, although she despised the sound of the concession the moment it left her lips.

Connor smirked at that. "Why would you be afraid now?" he asked, "I am giving you what you want. You are unbound and free to make an escape, if that's what you think you desire?"

She drew in a deep breath, her eyes darting momentarily to the door. She could run. She knew that now. He was even going to let her, but... How far could she get really with him on her tail? And what would he do to her when he caught up with her? She considered how he would make her pay for what he would no doubt see as her insubordination. He might be giving her the choice now, but somehow it would come back to bite her. And the price would be high. Maybe too high.

She glanced back to him. That brow was arched again, waiting for her verdict, daring her to defy him. "I don't want to run." The words flew out in one giant rush, expressed with feeling. She hoped they masked what she was really thinking.

"Are you sure, pet?" His tone was mocking, and she balled her fists beside her, trying to contain the anger it produced in her.

She shook her head, tears filling her eyes unexpectedly. She couldn't bear this, the way he played with her, the way he would always win. It was just too much. She had to get away, but it couldn't be now. It had to be when he wasn't expecting it. "What are you going to do to me here?" She whimpered, her eyes surveying the expanse of wood around her again.

He rose from the box in a heartbeat, the swift motion startling her. "Oh no," he told her, sauntering around the place she sat. Her eyes followed him, her instincts telling her that whatever was coming was not going to be good. "We're not playing this game."

"Wh-what game?" she stammered, twisting her body to watch him behind her.

He moved to the door, securing the bolt in place and then adding a padlock, which had been hiding in his pocket. Molly's heart fell. Her one chance to escape – the only one she'd had since that night he'd taken her – and she'd thrown it away. Connor turned, his gaze on her at once.

"You don't get to decide what happens next," he murmured, approaching her again. "And you don't get an agenda either. Now, get back on your knees, little one." His tone was low, and more predatory. "It's time to play."

Chapter Sixty-Five

The day was arduous. Even to Connor, the rounds of exercise, spanking and the almost ritual-style humiliation he inflicted on Molly was exhausting. Connor made his pet play for hours, and the small forest hut was the ideal location for his games. He didn't need gags anymore, Molly could make as much noise as she wanted, and no one would hear them. They were in the densest part of the woods, and he knew from experience no one came this way. He'd spent months tracking the movements around these parts. He knew where people camped, he knew where people played and trekked and took family holidays, and it wasn't here. This was as remote as southeast England got, and it was absolutely perfect for breaking in his new pet.

Hours after they'd arrived, he sat on the large box, watching as her thighs trembled, and her ass reddened under the weight of his paddle. All the while his cock was engorged and unsatisfied, wanting more than just her obedience, wanting *her*. Again. He wanted her the way he'd had her last night, only rougher and harder this time. He needed to satiate his desire, and soon.

"How are you enjoying my cabin, pet?" he asked, wryly as he paddled her bottom again.

Her gaze flew to his, her eyes wide with indignation at the sarcastic question. He'd been stripping away her defenses since she'd turned down his offer to run earlier. Slowly, peeling each one away, until there was nothing left except pain, obedience and he suspected, her own simmering arousal. Connor waited for her response, and while he did, he mused on her reaction earlier. He was certain she wanted to take his offer. He could tell how much she'd hated the pet carrier, and he'd meant every word he said. He would have let her go. He wanted her to run. He wanted to hunt her down.

"Please," she panted, "no more."

Connor smiled. Perhaps she needed relief, too? "No more of my paddle?" His voice was taunting.

"Please, no, Master," she choked.

His eyes darted back to her punished behind as she crawled past him again. They had been playing for a long time, and the flesh of her bottom was red and angry.

Poor little, pet…

There was no need for leashes and chains now. The door to the cabin was locked, and there was no other way out.

"What shall we play, instead?" he mused out loud as he stood. "Oh, I know. How about you polish your Master's cock for him?"

Speaking about himself in the third person amused him, and he chuckled as Molly gazed up at him. He guessed if she was that desperate for the paddling to end, then sucking his rod would seem like a relative reprieve.

She was nodding as she replied. "Yes, Master," she whispered.

"Yes, what?" he snarled, grabbing the leather at her neck roughly.

Molly's eyes widened in shock. "Yes, please, Master," she said, miserably. "Please use my mouth."

That was more like it, and he grinned as he undid his fly with his free hand. His cock sprung free immediately, bobbing in front of Molly's face. Her lips parted instinctively, and he drove into her, giving her no chance to change her mind. The cabin had no cameras. There was no option to record what was going on with no electricity, so Connor intended to make each moment count. He wanted each experience burned into his mind, so that he'd remember them without the help of film. Tears blinked in her eyes as he thrust deep inside her throat. He was anything but gentle now, fucking her face brutally as she knelt in front of him. Each lunge was exquisite, encircling his erection in her hot, satiny mouth, and he exulted in the intensity of it.

As his climax neared, he focused on the pretty little pet at his feet. She was completely his now, his in every way, and by the time he'd finished with her at the cabin, she'd never dare to disobey him again. This is where he'd break her, and they'd stay as long as it took. If Molly didn't want to be hunted, then she'd be haunted instead. By him.

He came over her open mouth, his semen mingling with her hot tears as they fell toward her lips. She looked spent again, and frankly, so was he, so he instructed her to crawl to the make-shift bed he'd erected at the end of the cabin. She obeyed him wearily, and he watched as her punished behind wriggled past him. She was just as hot without the chains, and he decided there and then to leave them off as they slept. After all, he'd be right beside her, and only he had the key to get out. There was no way she was escaping now.

Molly blinked into the blackness of the hut, counting her breaths as she lay beside him. She needed her inhaler, but she didn't even know if Connor had brought it with them, and she'd been too terrified to ask him. She had spent the entire afternoon playing his games, each as lurid and denigrating as the next. She gulped as she recalled how he'd made her lick his filthy boots clean, her ass receiving a hard paddling every time she'd failed to meet his expectations. She was ashamed to say she'd found the whole thing rather intoxicating, but she swore she could still taste the mud at the back of her throat. That was despite the water he'd made her take from her bowl after the event, and the hot, salty cum he'd deposited there before he'd slept.

She sighed, planning her next steps as he slept peacefully to her right. She might be messed up writing about this stuff, *liking* this stuff even, but there was no way she could endure much more of this. She had to get away, and she had to get away now. Rolling onto her right, she allowed her fingers to trace the outline of his hard torso. Her touch was feathery light as she traced a line north, searching for the pocket at his chest. The one she knew contained the key to the door.

Molly's heart began to race as the tension in her mounted. What if he stirred and woke up? How could she explain her hand on his body? Squeezing her eyes shut, she tried to calm her erratic breathing. She had to stay calm, and she had to concentrate. He'd been one step ahead of her since the signing. It was time she took control. If he woke now, she would feign an attempt at seduction, and fuck the guy. What difference did it make at this point? Despite her fear, she could still feel the slick lips of her sex between her thighs, and she knew she could use that if she needed to.

Finally, her fingers located the outline of his shirt pocket. She could feel the stitching under her fleshy tips, and she followed it slowly until her hand dipped inside. This was dangerous, and to reinforce the point, her heart pounded out of control inside her chest. If Connor woke now, there would be no explaining the situation, and no opportunity for seduction. She'd be fucked.

She inched her digits down the small pocket, barely daring to breathe as her fingers moved until they made contact with the metal. She grasped it lightly, easing her digits back up the length of the pocket. It was then that he stirred, his rhythmic breathing interrupted, leaving only black silence. Molly gulped, her body paralyzed with terror. Her hand was right at the edge of the pocket now, so close to comparative safety, and yet so far. There was a long moment of protracted stillness where she didn't dare to take a breath or move a muscle. Inwardly she prayed that he'd settle back into another deep sleep, but in the dark, there was no way of knowing. He could very well be awake right now, and plotting his next move. With terror clutching at her insides, all Molly could do was wait and see.

It was the longest period of her life, but at some point, she heard the sounds of his breathing settling back into a sleepy rhythm. She swallowed as she waited longer, her fingers still poised over his body, the small key between them. Her muscles were trembling, but still she refused to move, afraid that it was too soon. Molly had no idea how long she stayed that way, but after what felt like hours of blackness, she dared to finally move. She shifted away from him, rising slowly to an upright position. The key was caught tight in her fist as she slid from the blankets. She felt one wrapped at her ankles, so she snatched it up toward her breasts. Her ass screamed at every movement, but even the pain wasn't enough to stop her now. Adrenaline was flooding her system, and she felt defiant. Enough was enough. This was her time, and she *had* to seize it.

Molly edged in the direction of the place she knew the door to be, every moment filled with panic in case she nudged one of the large boxes around the place and woke Connor. In the darkness, the journey seemed to take forever. The cabin seemingly endless in the black of night. At last, she felt the abrasive wood of the other side of the wall, and her left hand rose to scan over the area. Her digits caught on metal, and to her relief she traced over what she believed to be a hinge. Her heart raced even more. A hinge meant a door, and the door meant freedom.

She inched left toward the door. Wrapping the blanket around her shoulders, she used her free palm to feel for the bolt she knew was overhead. The tension in her body was fraught. At any moment Connor could hear her, he could wake naturally and find her missing, and then what? She shuddered reflexively at the thought, trying to focus her effort on the bolt. She needed to find it, and the padlock, and then somehow, she needed to negotiate both in the darkness. Molly had no clue how long she was there searching, her fingers eventually locating the top bolt, and fumbling gently for the padlock. Time had very little meaning since Connor had taken her, but the hours had been punctuated by certain routines. In the blackness of the cabin, time had no meaning at all. Molly could have stood there for over an hour, or it could have only been minutes. All she knew was every second was perilous, and the next could mean the end.

When she finally negotiated the key into the lock, Molly was running on adrenaline alone. He'd stolen everything else, her time, her freedom, and her dignity, and this was the only thing she had left. On the one hand, she was relieved to hear the lock spring free, but on the other, she was petrified the sound would give her game away. When there was no sound from Connor, she pushed her fingers on, trembling as she unhooked the padlock and fumbled for the main bar. Her trepidation was so great that she felt barely able to take a breath as she pulled the latch back, praying that the bolt would be smooth and silent. It seemed someone answered her prayers that night, and as the bolt slid away, Molly knew all that was left to do was open the latch and slip away.

As she felt for it, her hands began to shake. Molly was close, so close now to the fresh air of the woods, and despite her nudity, she craved it like she'd never craved anything. Lifting the latch, she eased the door open slowly, sending a flood of fresh air rushing past her. She squeezed herself through the gap to the outside grass as quickly as she could.

She didn't want the cool air to wake him, not now – after all this effort. Swallowing hard, she closed the door as best she could from the outside and backed away, her eyes trying to make out the outline of its frame in the dark forest. Sharp, contorted branches and roots grasped at her calves, and she stumbled into the trunk of a large tree before she could finally tear her eyes from the way she'd come.

She'd done it! She was free of Connor's clutches, and as she pulled the blanket around her aching body, Molly was filled with a hope she hadn't realized she'd lost. Just yesterday the ordeal had seemed manageable, but his actions today had proven what a psychopath Connor Reilly was. There was no bargaining with that kind of man, and no reasoning with him. She was just an animal to him – a thing - and what does any animal with a reasonable sized brain want? *Freedom.*

Making her way through the forest, Molly's heart continued to bang inside her chest. She knotted the blanket as best she could in front of her body, and held her hands out, protecting her face from the punishing branches of the trees. She was blind, and had no idea where she was going, but Molly knew she had to keep moving. Connor could wake at any moment, and when he did, he would be out looking for her. He'd already told her as much. She began to run, breaking into a jog as his words rang through her mind.

"I will chase you because you're mine, pet. You belong to me now, we both know that, don't we?"

Paranoia ate away at her. Was he there, right behind her, hiding in the darkness? That was just the sort of mind fuck he'd play; letting her believe she was free before pouncing on her again. Her feet scuttled on in the black of the forest, catching on broken twigs on the ground, and tripping over exposed roots. Whenever she fell, she got back up again, thoughts of her friends and her family sparking her defiance, and her will to survive.

Somewhere out there was the main road, and with the road would come people, the police and a plane back home. This was England after all, the place was tiny. It wasn't anything like the expanse of Pennsylvania she knew and loved. Someone had to be out there, someone who would help her. Swallowing back her fear and exhaustion, she forced her feet forward. Molly had to keep on moving.

The End

The Dark Necessities Trilogy

Taken

Tamed

Entwined

ABOUT THE AUTHOR

Felicity Brandon is an Amazon Top 100 bestselling writer of BDSM spanking erotic romance.

You can find her on Facebook, Twitter, or on her website, felicitybrandonwrites.com

Join the reader group on Facebook: *Fierce AF*

<u>More sexy romance by Felicity Brandon</u>

The Viking Duet:

The Viking's Conquest & The Viking's Possession

Submission at The Tower

Goldie's Surrender

Taming Lady Lydia

Made in the USA
Monee, IL
11 June 2023

35630692R00203